"Lauren, there's something I want to tell you," Patrick said. "I didn't want to e-mail it to you or instant message it to you or say it to you over the phone or Skype it or text it to you. I wanted to hold you in my eyes when I said it so I could see your eyes." He pulled her close. "Lauren Short, I love you."

She rested her head on his chest. "And I love you." *Now kiss me to end this scene perfectly!* She closed her eyes and pursed her lips.

No kiss arrived.

She felt both of his hands leave hers.

She opened her eyes. *Where's my man?*

She looked down and focused on Patrick kneeling, a ring box in his hand.

Oh Lord! It's a ring!

"Lauren, I want you to wear this ring." He opened the box and removed a small ring, sliding it onto her left ring finger.

It fits! How did he know my size? Oh, it's so beautiful!

"It's a promise ring, Lauren," Patrick said, "and this is my promise to you. I don't have much, and I may never have much, and I may have to get another job so we can have something, but whatever I have is yours and yours alone for as long as you will have me . . ."

Books by J.J. Murray

RENEE AND JAY

SOMETHING REAL

ORIGINAL LOVE

I'M YOUR GIRL

CAN'T GET ENOUGH OF YOUR LOVE

TOO MUCH OF A GOOD THING

THE REAL THING

SHE'S THE ONE

I'LL BE YOUR EVERYTHING

A GOOD MAN

YOU GIVE GOOD LOVE

UNTIL I SAW YOUR SMILE

LET'S STAY TOGETHER

Published by Kensington Publishing Corporation

let's stay
together

J.J. Murray

KENSINGTON PUBLISHING CORP.
http://www.kensingtonbooks.com

KENSINGTON BOOKS are published by

Kensington Publishing Corp.
119 West 40th Street
New York, NY 10018

All Kensington Titles, Imprints, and Distributed Lines are available at special quantity discounts for bulk purchases for sales promotions, premiums, fund-raising, and educational or institutional use. Special book excerpts or customized printings can also be created to fit specific needs. For details, write or phone the office of the Kensington special sales manager: Kensington Publishing Corp., 119 West 40th Street, New York, NY 10018, attn: Special Sales Department, Phone: 1-800-221-2647.

Kensington and the K logo Reg. U.S. Pat & TM Off.

ISBN-13: 978-1- 61773-480-9
ISBN-10: 1-61773-480-2
First Kensington Mass Market Edition: May 2015

eISBN-13: 978-1-61773-481-6
eISBN-10: 1-61773-481-0
Kensington Electronic Edition: May 2015

10 9 8 7 6 5 4 3 2 1

Printed in the United States of America

For Amy, who has always been a star to me

But to see her was to love her,
Love but her, and love forever.

—Robert Burns ("Ae Fond Kiss"; 1759–96)

1

Dear Lauren:

I was sorry to hear about your breakup with Chazz Jackson, but when I thought about it, I wasn't sorry at all. You deserve a much better man than him. He always seemed fake to me, especially when he wasn't in a movie.

I know things are painful now, but they get better. I know because I've been there.

Please keep smiling.

A longtime fan,
Patrick

Former actress Lauren Short normally would have gone on to her next e-mail without replying, but something about the honesty and the heart of the message stopped her.

Chazz was *fake,* Lauren thought. *Both in the movies and in real life. Patrick nailed that one. If Patrick really knew how fake Chazz was. What's worse than calling someone fake? Calling Chazz "bogus," "phony," and "counterfeit" isn't enough. Chazz was more than that. He was the fakest person I have ever known.*

She sighed and sank deeper into her rented love seat, her feet propped up on a rented coffee table in her newly rented studio apartment in North Hollywood.

"I don't know what I deserve these days, Patrick, old friend," she whispered, "but I certainly didn't deserve to be two-, three-, and five-timed by a man who was with me *and* with a series of *men* behind my back."

She tried to shake the image of her fiancé, action movie icon Chazz Jackson, and those two men in Chazz's house overlooking the Pacific only seven nights ago.

She failed.

"In *our* house, Patrick!" she shouted. "In *my* house! Okay, he paid for it, but I lived there for seven years. And oh how I have paid."

I may have paid with my life.

But I'm not going to think about that right now. Think positive thoughts. Think positive thoughts. . . .

But I kept that place looking good! she thought. *I kept that place spotless! I made that place shine! But why does it matter so much to me* where *he messed with men? He was evidently messing with them in all sorts of places while I waited for three years, with a ridiculously huge engagement ring on my finger, to become "Mrs. Lauren Short-Jackson." And then I came home to see the man I gave up my acting career for acting the fool with two men on the Lorraine black leather sofa I bought for him for his birthday!*

"I'm surprised the three of them didn't collapse it, Patrick!" she shouted.

And now I'm talking to a man who isn't here, Lauren thought.

"I wish they had broken that sofa," she whispered. "Chazz should be feeling *some* kind of pain."

She had just finished watching Chazz play off their disengagement on *Entertainment Tonight* on the rented TV in front of her. "Telling them that *he* broke it off with *me*," she mumbled, "telling them that *we* didn't see eye to eye anymore, telling them that he would always have a *soft* spot in his heart for me, a woman who he *still* called 'his favorite leading lady.' " She looked again at her iPhone. "He even tweeted that he was 'single and looking for another future star,' Patrick! What kind of man does that only a week after a breakup?"

She shook her head. *Chazz's publicist is certainly earning his keep these days. I'll bet Chazz is messing with him, too.*

She shuddered.

She looked at the TV, the Rent-A-Center tag still attached to the base. *I've gone from a ninety-inch flat-screen TV to a twenty-seven-inch antique.*

That about sums up my life.

"You know, Patrick, maybe *I* should go on *Entertainment Tonight* and tell them how *I* broke the picture window looking out over the Pacific Ocean with my fists and a well-placed elbow. I shattered that huge window into a million pieces. Maybe I should tell them what *I* saw Chazz doing—and having done to him—with my own two eyes. Maybe I should tell them how fast those other two men were—both of them high-profile actors with wives and children, Patrick—about how they ran out of there with their pants on backward. I wish I had taken pictures. Those pictures could make me a millionaire overnight. Maybe I should tell *ET* that Hollywood's highest-paid he-man love interest has *really* been acting in those love scenes with women over the years."

She bowed her head. "But if I tell them all that, Patrick, they may give Chazz several retroactive Academy Awards for his excellent movie *deceptions*." She opened her eyes and laughed. "That's what the media does for fun in this town. They turn cowards into heroes and give the fakest people the most praise."

She sighed heavily. *But if I tell them all that, then I'd have to explain how I didn't know that the man I was engaged to for three years was gay or bisexual and heavy on the man love—whatever that confused man was.*

I have been the world's biggest fool, Patrick, I really have.

And I don't want anyone to know it.

Ever.

She looked at the e-mail, amazed she was still getting any fan mail at all. Before she started dating Chazz, fan mail used to flood into her in-box in droves, but except for the last seven days of people wishing her well, there had been only a trickle of fan mail ever since she became engaged to Chazz.

"It's painful now," she whispered. "You said it, Patrick. It physically hurts. My chest, back, and neck ache. My head and my eyes pound every time I think about what happened. Whenever I close my eyes, I see Chazz and those men. . . ."

She looked at her left ring finger, at the lighter band of brown skin. "I kind of miss the ring, Patrick. It was a rock and a half. I could have pawned it and bought a small country." *It cost more than, well, I'm evidently worth. I'm sure some golden seal is now swimming around it and admiring its beauty. I'm surprised I was able to throw it so far. I hope some surfer doesn't step on it. Maybe it will end up on some beach in Hawaii. I would so love to be there.*

Anywhere but here.

She glanced at the full name in the e-mail address. *Patrick Alan Esposito. Okay, Patrick Alan Esposito, I will do my best to try to keep smiling.*

That's about all I can do now.

"It isn't as if I'm going to get any movie or TV offers now, Patrick," she whispered. "I've been out of practice for seven years, and the biggest movie star on earth just dumped me. Therefore, I must be used up and burned out."

I must be old news.

I have been old news for seven years, and I'm only now realizing it.

I may even be an obituary. I'm sure some journalist has already written it.

She typed a quick reply:

Patrick:

Thank you for your uplifting letter. It came at a time when I was really down and I really needed it.

I will try to keep smiling. :)

You keep smiling, too.

Lauren Short

2

At eleven p.m. that evening in the Boerum Hill section of Brooklyn, New York, Patrick Alan Esposito blinked rapidly at his Acer laptop screen, duct tape holding its CD drive closed.

"I don't believe it," he whispered. "She wrote back. Lauren Short actually wrote back."

This is amazing.

He wiped dust from the screen with his sleeve. *Her e-mail is still there. I'm not seeing things. Lauren Short wrote back to me, and it isn't a form letter. She actually answered my e-mail, despite Chazz breaking off her engagement. She called me by name, and she included a smiley face!*

And she wants me to keep smiling, too!

I'm smiling!

I can't remember the last time I smiled.

It almost hurts my face to smile.

Though he was amazed at Lauren's response, Patrick

was more amazed that he had written to her in the first place. He had had a crush on Lauren Short ever since he saw her in *Crisp and Popp,* a TV show that debuted and then disappeared after only six episodes in the fall of 2001.

But that was fourteen years ago. How can I still have a crush on her?

He shot both his arms to the ceiling and shouted, "Yes!"

A Hollywood star, a TV actress, and a certified beauty wrote back to me. *I wish I had someone to tell.* He ran his hands through his floppy mass of thick black hair and scratched at his coarse beard. *But who would believe me if I did?*

I'm glad she can't see me now.

I can barely stand to see me now.

Patrick lived frugally, some would say "barely," in Boerum Hill, a thirty-six-block section south of downtown Brooklyn east of Cobble Hill and west of Prospect Heights. A handyman and jack-of-all-trades, Patrick was the go-to guy to fix problems at five Salthead rental properties in Boerum Hill. He imagined that most tenants had his cell phone number memorized by now.

Mrs. Moczydlowska probably chants my number in her sleep. It took me a month to say her name correctly: Mot-chid-LOVE-ska. I know I see her in my sleep, all four foot, seven inches and two hundred pounds of her. She's so chubby, I can barely see her eyes. "I call your boss," she says. "You do not fix, I call your boss. You not come, I call your boss. You are not here by eight sharp, I call your boss. . . ."

Even I don't call my boss.

Patrick wasn't even sure who his boss was.

For working up to sixteen-hour days, Patrick received a meager salary and half rent (eleven hundred dollars a month and all utilities) in one of the Salthead rentals on

State Street. He had seven hundred square feet of less-than-spacious living in a nineteenth-century house that had been carved into eight apartments. A lumpy brown cloth couch canted slightly on faux wood linoleum in the main room, in front of an antique coffee table holding a thirty-five-inch television. A queen bed swallowed most of the blue-walled bedroom, glass double doors to the only closet showcasing five pairs of coveralls, assorted stained jeans, hooded sweatshirts, and scuffed and discolored work boots. A light tan window shade on the bedroom window allowed the morning sun to streak across to the bathroom, the only "modern" room in the apartment with a double-bowl sink, postage-stamp green tile, and recessed lighting, all of which he had installed himself. Under the counter in the skinny kitchen were a dishwasher he never used and a washing machine he used once a week, thick red brick walls providing the only vibrant color.

Even Patrick's apartment was barely an apartment.

Patrick maintained, rebuilt, painted, and even over-hauled five-thousand-dollar-a-month apartments in build-ings on Atlantic, State, Dean, Bergen, and Baltic. He carried a heavy tool bag slung over his shoulder wherever he went, roaming daily past Boerum Hill's million-dollar "row houses" to unclog sink drains, replace chipped tile, seal drafty windows, remove former rodents from traps, set off bug bombs, rewire overworked electrical outlets, plunge toilets, swap out aging water heaters, clean shower traps, free blocked sewage drains, and anything else the tenants demanded that he do.

He had finished Mrs. Moczydlowska's daily "Do it today, or I call your boss!" list over on Bergen only half an hour before he had read Lauren's e-mail. *I'll bet Mrs. Moczydlowska is busy thinking up more for me to do to-morrow. There's always something wrong.* "What is this *bug, and what is it doing here? Why does the toilet take so long to flush? Why does the floor make so much noise?"*

Patrick had learned to save Mrs. Moczydlowska's apartment for last after she had once called him back six times in one day to "Fix the fridge!" or "Get me the hot water!" or "Make the sound go away!"

Patrick led an anonymous life in stained coveralls, but he wore his stains with pride, mainly because the stains held his coveralls together.

He hit the REPLY button, then warmed his massive hands and flexed his rough fingers. *How does a nobody like me write* back *to a movie star? Writing to her the first time was easy. I was only a fan then. Now I'm . . .*

I don't know what I am now.

A friend? A confidant? What should I say this time? Should I even write back? What if I do and she doesn't write back this time? Maybe she was just being nice. That's the kind of person I think she is. Yeah. She was being nice.

He sat back from the laptop. *But I don't want to leave this alone. It's not as if we're going to have a long "conversation." I just want her to know that someone cares about her, even if that someone is a nobody handyman who lives in Boerum Hill, Brooklyn. There's no harm in that. I care, and I want her to know that I care.*

I have to do this.

Lauren:
I'm so surprised you wrote me back.

Well, I am, he thought. *But I'm sure she knows that I would be surprised. She is a star, after all, and I am not a star.* He backspaced until he had a blank screen.

Miss Short:
I'm glad you wrote back.

I am glad, aren't I? Why tell her the obvious? And call-ing her "Miss" might remind her that she's still a "Miss" and isn't married after being engaged to that jerk for three years. He highlighted and deleted everything.

Lauren:
If you ever need someone to "talk" to, I'm here.

He sighed. *Am I being too bold? I am actually assuming that this wonderful person doesn't have anyone to talk to. Of course she has someone to talk to! I'm sure she has plenty of friends to see her through this mess with Chazz. She doesn't need me.* He sighed again. *And what if she thinks I'm some reporter trolling for information? I'm sure that's how some reporters operate. They get in nice and friendly with a seemingly innocent e-mail and then air the dirt they uncover on television or in magazines.*

He scratched his hair, a few dots of white paint floating to the coffee table. *What does it matter, anyway? She's not writing back.*

He signed it "Patrick" this time before adding a post-script:

Crisp And Popp is still the best TV show of all time. It
is the world's loss that they canceled it.

He hit SEND.

I am here if you need me, Lauren, he thought. He shook his head. *Maybe it's really me who needs someone to talk to. I am so tired of talking to myself.* He shut down his laptop.

As he was walking all of ten feet to his bedroom, his cell

phone buzzed. *Mrs. Moczydlowska. It figures. Doesn't she ever sleep?*

He flipped open his antiquated cell phone, one Salthead had provided for his use. "Yes, Mrs. Moczydlowska?"

"Oh, you are up," she said.

We handymen never really sleep. We only recharge our batteries. "What may I do for you?" Patrick asked.

"It is the refrigerator again," she said. "It does not keep the food cold again and it makes the noise again and I hear the rats in the walls again and what you painted today does not match anything after it is dry and . . ."

See you tomorrow, Mrs. Moczydlowska, Patrick thought as she droned on and on and listed something wrong in every room. *I wonder if she would care that I just received and answered an e-mail from Lauren Short, Hollywood actress. She probably doesn't even know who Lauren Short is.*

"Yes, Mrs. Moczydlowska," he said absently.

"You are writing this down, yes?" she asked.

"Yes, Mrs. Moczydlowska," he said, writing random letters in the air.

"There is much to be done!" she shouted. "When you come? You come first thing in the morning, yes? You must come here first thing."

He yawned and stretched his back. "I come first thing," he said, instantly regretting it.

"What time?" she asked.

The crack of dawn. "As soon as the sun rises."

"I will be waiting. Do not be late, or I call your boss." *Click.*

He edged into his bedroom and fell back onto the bed. *If I brought Mrs. Moczydlowska a new refrigerator or rid her walls of every rodent and bug, she would complain about how* quiet *it was. If everything was perfect, she'd worry that something was* about *to break.*

He pulled up the window shade, and the room filled with the amber light from Downtown Gourmet Deli across the street. *We're both open for business twenty-fours a day,* he thought. *And people expect us to be open and available no matter what.*

But it's a living.

"Just not much of one," he whispered.

3

At thirty-eight and now disengaged from the world's premier blockbuster movie star, Lauren Short couldn't afford to be choosy about getting work, especially since she had not been seen in movies or on television shows for seven years.

When her agent, Todd Mitchell, had sent her any script back in the good old days, she would begin reading it immediately, often finishing it before the envelope it came in hit the floor. The thicker scripts had excited her the most since they held the promise of extended projects and larger paychecks, and there were plenty of big paydays when she was in her twenties. She had starred or costarred in eight films over a four-year period, and while five were ensemble "sister" films, they had made her extremely visible to the moviegoing public. She had won half a dozen BET, Black Reel, and Image Awards for those movies, but once she'd started dating Chazz, the scripts stopped coming overnight.

Todd Mitchell, her agent, had tried to explain why.

"Lauren, baby, Chazz is white, and that's why, um, why you're not getting any more, um, *ethnic* scripts."

"But shouldn't I be getting more mainstream roles, then?" Lauren had asked. "Shouldn't I be 'crossing over' to multicultural movies? Sanaa Lathan has done it. So have Zoe Saldana and Kerry Washington."

"I'll look into it," Todd had said.

Todd had looked into it.

Nothing had come of it.

As a result, Lauren quit acting to become Chazz's arm candy at awards shows, premieres, and film festivals, spending stupid amounts of money on designer dresses she wore only once.

For seven years.

Today she held a script Todd had sent to her by express mail. She read Todd's brief cover letter:

Dear Lauren,
    Shantelle Crisp isn't quite dead yet!

In 2001 Lauren had starred in *Crisp and Popp,* a TV crime drama. She played the sexy, wisecracking detective Shantelle Crisp, and Hayden Billings played the no-nonsense white detective Richard Popp. They solved crimes when they weren't flirting, lusting, and sleeping together. The show received rave reviews, mainly for not being "overtly racial," but NBC canceled it because the stand-up comedian and lead writer of the show, Will Weaver, had upset the world during a live HBO special just after 9/11. . . .

"Why is everyone blaming George Bush for all this?" Weaver had asked a packed audience in Los Angeles. "Sure, our president is a little short on intelligence, foresight, and knowledge of the English language, but terrorists have been on the warpath since the seventies. Didn't *we* arm Saddam Hussein so he could fight the Iranians? And didn't *we* give weapons to the Taliban to fight the Russians? Didn't we know that this sort of thing was bound to happen eventually? If you give guns to pissed-off people, they tend to use them against whoever pisses them off at the time. Instead of pointing fingers, we should be pointing missiles . . . at Washington, D.C., and Langley, Virginia. . . ."

Lauren sighed. *I miss doing that show. Crisp and Popp was a smart, well-written, groundbreaking show that didn't deserve to die because Will Weaver told the truth. That show was funny in all the right places, sexy in even more right places, and looking back, just about everything Will Weaver said in his rant was the absolute truth. No one wanted to hear the truth back then, though. And no one's heard from Will Weaver since. They've barely heard from me or seen me, either—unless I was with Chazz.*

She nodded. "I need a job now," she said. *I need something that will show the world that I still have talent. I need something to show everyone that seven years with Chazz and our recent disengagement haven't ruined me forever.*

She returned her attention to the cover letter.

> *Please read over this first scene of* Gray Areas, *the pilot for an upcoming Tumbleweed Television sitcom. They want you to read for the part of Lauren Gray. You essentially get to play yourself!*
>
> *Call me back as soon as you can!*
>
> *Todd*
>
> *PS: The writing is a little stereotypical and over the top, but keep in mind that this is a comic starring role, Lauren. You need this. Chazz who? Knock 'em dead!*

True, Lauren thought. *Chazz who? I need this chance badly.*

She settled into her love seat, flipped the cover page, and began to read:

GRAY AREAS
By A. Smith
Episode 1

Scene 1

(A handsome, muscular white man in tight jeans, an unzipped hoodie, and unlaced Timberlands walks in slow motion past two black women who are drinking coffee at an outdoor café in Manhattan. They check out his butt longingly.)

LAUREN

He ain't bad looking . . . for a white man.

SHARON

Lookin' at a cracker don't cost nothin', Lauren.

Oh . . . no, Lauren thought. *I don't like the way this begins. Is this supposed to be comedy? The first two lines might alienate every white person in America!*

She forced herself to continue. *It can only get better, right?*
It didn't get better.

LAUREN

Sharon, he ain't got no booty. I'd have nothing to hold on to.

SHARON

Nope. Looks like a straight shovel back there. He probably has divots in his hairy cheeks.

LAUREN

You see the rest of him? His face was as hairy as a bear. Puh-lease. I bet he's all static clingy. He'd probably shock me every time he touched me.

SHARON

He had blue eyes, though. Gotta like them.

LAUREN

Yeah. (Sighs deeply.)

SHARON

You ain't thinkin' about getting a little cream in your coffee, are you, Lauren? What would your boo, Marcus, the lawyer, think?

This hoochie has a lawyer *for a boyfriend?* Lauren thought. *Why? What lawyer—or man—in his right mind would hook up with this coarse, uncouth creature? Only on TV.*

LAUREN

Marcus and I are through.

SHARON

Since when?

LAUREN

Since I caught him banging his secretary in our bed.

I knew that white hoochie was after him. (Smiles.)
*But she ain't gonna be able to smile right after what I
did to her.*

SHARON

You cut her, huh?

LAUREN

*No. I punched her out. Snapped one of her front teeth
in half.*

SHARON

She a snaggletoothed bee-otch now, huh?

Bee-otch? Lauren thought. *What in the world? What
century am I in? And does this Lauren have to be so violent? I don't have a violent bone in my body.*

LAUREN

Yeah. (Sighs.) *Nah, I am through with black men,
Sharon. They have never done me right. All of them
are dogs. I need to get me a white man and get me
some cream and some sugar.*

And now the script alienates black men, Lauren thought.
Who is left to watch this show? Do they want anyone *to
watch this show?*

SHARON

*I hate to burst your bubble, but white men ain't no
good in bed, Lauren. They ain't got no rhythm, and
they don't know how to work the booty. And the faces
they make? Puh-lease, girl. Trust me. It's a real horror show.* (Makes a horrific face.)

LAUREN

(Laughs.) *You're giving me nightmares. But how do you know all that? You been with a white man?*

SHARON

Just one. I forget his name. Chip or Joe Bob or Bubba or something redneck and Caucasian like that.

The script just lost most of the southern United States, Lauren thought. *This isn't comedy. This is an extended racist joke! They would have to use a laugh track for this show because a live audience would be booing or growling. I wonder if a live audience has ever walked out on a taping. If it hasn't happened yet, this show would guarantee it happening.*

She forced herself to continue.

LAUREN

Why you mess with him, girl?

SHARON

I was curious.

LAUREN

What was he like?

SHARON

Like a little puppy dog. Once he got a taste of my coffee, he kept coming back for more. I'm a regular Starbucks, girl. I'm better than caffeine for keeping a man up, and I kept him up all night. I bet he never went back to no milky-white heifer after me.

LAUREN
Once you've had black, you'll never go back.

SHARON
The blacker the berry, the sweeter the juice. (They
exchange some dap.)

Lauren shook her head so much, her neck hurt. *Todd
said this script is a little over the top. He's dead wrong. This
script is over the abyss and falling like a cartoon anvil.*

LAUREN
*Is it true that when their hair gets wet, it smells like a
wet puppy?*

SHARON
*Yes, girl. Joe Bob's hair smelled like mildew and
Grandma's draws. And white men's ashy skin smells
like onions sometimes, and not the good kind of onions,
either. And they have absolutely no table manners. They
eat food that hits the floor, just like the puppy dogs they
are. And the only thing they can cook is Hamburger
Helper. At least they can always get you a cab in this
city.* (Shared laughter.) *But they* love *to go down
there, girl.*

LAUREN
Why?

SHARON
*Evidently, it's the only way a white woman can have
an orgasm.*

And now we've lost the white women, Lauren thought. *This just* has *to be a joke now. Todd sent me this script to cheer me up in some twisted way. No one on earth would ever take this script seriously.* She stared at the ceiling. *No, Todd wouldn't send me anything unless it was real.* She looked back at the script and sighed. *I just wish he hadn't sent this piece of crap.*

> LAUREN
> *Oh.* (Smiles.) *Then Marcus's secretary ain't never gonna have an orgasm, cuz Marcus never did none of that.* (Slaps hands with Sharon.)

> SHARON
> *But a white man isn't that big or long, girl. Just warning you.*

> LAUREN
> *I hear they have girth, and that's enough for me.*

> SHARON
> *Yeah, the one I was with had some girth. He didn't know how to use it, though.*

Girth? Lauren thought. *Can they say* girth *on TV? This can't be for regular TV. This has to be for some late-night show only the truly desperate would ever watch.*

> LAUREN
> *How'd you meet him?*

> SHARON
> *I hung out where white guys hang out. Grocery stores,*

*in the meat section. Electronics stores. Bowling alleys.
Softball fields. Golf courses. Church.*

LAUREN

*Yeah, no brothers goin' to church these days. Where'd
you meet your white boy?*

And now we've lost any church folks, not that they'd ever
tune in to this filth, Lauren thought. If I were the writer, I'd
go into the witness protection program.

SHARON

At Stinky & Minky on Sullivan Street.

LAUREN

That old clothes store?

SHARON

*It's a vintage clothing store, Lauren. He was actually
buying an old Izod jacket, if you can believe that. I
said, "You want some of this?" and he said, "Cool."
(Laughs.) He actually said, "Cool." And he had no
trouble about wearing a condom, so I knew I wouldn't
get pregnant. And even if I did get pregnant, I knew I'd
have a little light-skinned chocolate baby with good
hair and a trust fund who could dance real good
about half the time.*

She didn't just say . . . Lauren closed her eyes. Oh, my
goodness. How many foolish, untrue stereotypes can we
squeeze into the first five minutes? This script is trying to
set a record! She opened her eyes.
The offensive lines were still there.

LAUREN
(Laughs. Gets up.)

SHARON
Where you goin'?

LAUREN
To the Hell's Kitchen Flea Market, girl. I'm gonna go get me a white man. . . .

Lauren squeezed the script so hard, it almost tore in half. "Wow," she said. She felt like gouging out her eyes.

Wow, she thought.

She felt like rinsing her eyes with hydrochloric acid.

No . . . way. A human being wrote this?

She looked for and found the writer listed under the title: A. Smith. *Only one human being wrote this and thought it was doable. I never want to meet this person. I do not hang out with ignorant people. But somehow a television studio executive passed this ignorant script up the chain, a producer put up the money for a pilot, and a director signed on to direct. Were any people thinking when they read this disaster of a script?*

I've read some bad scripts, but this script really sucks a rusty hubcap.

Badly.

Worse than badly.

What's worse than badly? "Abysmal" is close. "Appalling" is closer. This script is inexcusably abysmal and appalling.

She reread the script, and if anything, it got worse.

I believe the writer of this mess has never been in an interracial relationship because it contains every stereotype about white men ever created. And this is only the first scene!

She rolled the script up into a tight scroll. "If you stick into the ceiling, I'll read for the part."

She threw the script up at the ceiling. It bounced off and caromed into the kitchen.

She sighed deeply, falling back into the love seat. *How can I make a comeback with this mess? I know it's a paycheck, but do I really want to lower myself to this level for my first work in seven years? It's not funny. It's sad. I need something with some integrity here, not this . . . excretion.*

Oh, I know why they want me. I'd be playing the desperate single black woman in search of a white man. I have been there and done that. First, there was a white guitarist back in college who introduced me to his "other" girlfriend, who said she would be "cool" with me joining them in their mostly sexual relationship. I wasn't cool with either of them. I spent time with a premier athlete who worked out with performance-enhancing drugs more than he even spoke to me. And then I made the mistake of falling for Chazz, an actor who was, is, and shall always be more gay than straight. None of them were good to me or for me for very long, but at least I have some experience with interracial relationships. The writer of this script obviously doesn't.

But . . .

She sighed.

But I need to do something to keep from going insane. I have to stay busy.

I didn't leave D.C. for this.

Lauren had grown up near Martin Luther King, Jr. Avenue in Congress Heights, Southeast D.C.'s capital of car theft, robbery, and assault. While jets had screamed overhead to Bolling Air Force Base and Washington National Airport (since renamed Ronald Reagan Washington National), and cars had packed I-295, Lauren had tried valiantly to survive Ward 8. She missed going to Martin Luther King Elementary. She missed the barbecue chicken pizza from The Pizza Place. She missed the come-ons from the men at Fullers barbershop. She missed having her hair done at Styles Unlimited hair salon, where her first head shot still greeted customers as they entered the shop.

I can't go back there, Lauren thought. *That's what Congress Heights expects to happen to anyone who escapes. They expect me to crawl back with my tail between my legs. I'm sure they're all talking about me at Styles Unlimited. "Oh, that Lauren Short has the worst luck with men, doesn't she? That's what happens when you get uppity and mess with white men. . . ."*

I have to give them something better to talk about.

But not with this script.

She called Todd. "I read the script," she said as soon as he picked up.

"And . . . ?"

"It's a piece of rancid bat guano, Todd," Lauren said. "It's the cheesiest, most derivative, most clichéd, and ultimately most stereotypical and racist script I have ever read."

"Well," Todd said. "Say what you mean, Lauren."

"I can't see me doing this show," Lauren said. "I can't see any intelligent black woman doing this show. I can't see any woman living or dead doing this show. Even the most desperate actress would have to be either crazy or brain dead to do this show."

"Let's see," Todd said. "You haven't worked in . . ."

He has to remind me. "Look, I know my career took a seven-year hiatus," Lauren said, "but this show would end my career and tarnish my former career *completely* if I did it. Why did you think I would be interested?"

"You *are* desperate," Todd said.

"I'm not that desperate," Lauren said.

"Come on, Lauren," Todd said. "It's strictly for laughs. It's a comedy. You do remember comedy, don't you?"

"But it's not funny, Todd," Lauren said. "Comedy is supposed to be funny. It should at least be somewhat amusing, like *Seinfeld*. This show is demeaning and shameful and patronizing. It degrades just about every segment of American society."

"Geez, Lauren," Todd said, "don't take it so seriously. It's a job, and you need a job, right? Get back on your feet and all that, right? This is just the beginning of your comeback. All comebacks start small. We need to build you back up to the big time gradually. *Some* of the script was funny, wasn't it?"

"I tried to laugh, Todd," Lauren said, "but laughter shouldn't give you gas and make you want to remove your eyes with an ice cream scoop. I mean, the premise may have promise, and there's plenty of room for more interracial relationships on television, but the execution of the premise is horrific. Train wrecks have more class, dignity, and integrity. Horror films have more humor."

"You've only read the first scene, Lauren," Todd said. "I'm sure the rest of the script will improve."

"I doubt it," Lauren said. "My namesake is off to Hell's Kitchen to find herself a white man. The only way this script will improve is if they fire A. Smith, whoever that is, and hire someone who has some sense. I don't think the writer has ever even been in an interracial relationship. You know, I could write a better script than anyone else could." *I could base her love interest on Chazz. Yeah. That might actually be fun to write.* "Why don't I just *write* for the show? I have plenty of experience in interracial relationships."

"You, a writer?" Todd said. "Lauren, with your track record with men, you could only write something called *No Sex in the City*." Todd laughed. "Sorry. That was uncalled for."

"It certainly was," Lauren said.

I haven't had sex since we got engaged, since Chazz said, "I want to wait until our honeymoon." Why did I miss that obvious clue? I thought he was being sweet. And before that, it was all a performance. Chazz performed—but that's all he did. Every sexual encounter I had with that man was a performance. He never truly made love to me. Why didn't I notice?

"You knew Chazz was gay, didn't you, Todd?" Lauren asked.

"I think the word is *bisexual*," Todd said. "And you have to be the only woman in LA who *didn't* know. And anyway, I thought you knew all along and didn't care."

"I really didn't know, Todd," Lauren said.

"Come on," Todd said.

"Really."

"You were engaged to him and living with him for *three* years, Lauren," Todd said.

"I know, I know," Lauren said. "I have always been too trusting, and look at the mess I'm in because of it."

"Chazz doesn't seem worse for wear," Todd said. "In fact, his star may even be rising. I hear quite a few scripts went back into circulation the day he dumped you."

"*I* dumped *him*," Lauren said.

"That's not what *Entertainment Tonight* said," Todd said. "And without your rebuttal, his word is the truth now."

"But you told me yesterday to ignore all that!" Lauren shouted. "You told me to rise above the foolishness, keep a low profile, and say nothing!"

"And you listened to me?" Todd said. "We have some serious damage control to do, Lauren. I can set up an interview."

"I can't even remember my last interview," Lauren said. "It was at least eight years ago."

"And that magazine has since gone out of business," Todd said. "We can't go print media with this. We have to go live. I'll try to set up something with Fallon first, of course, and then *The Today Show.* NBC owes you for canceling *Crisp and Popp.* And then—"

"No, don't bother," Lauren interrupted. "I want it all to go away as soon as possible."

"Or we can keep it all going for a reality TV show," Todd said. "You know, that sounds doable."

"What?" *Is he kidding?*

"We could call it *Lauren: Short on Love,*" Todd said. "You get what I did there? *Lauren* and then a colon and then *Short*—"

"No!"

"Oh, come on," Todd said. "Doesn't that sound fabulous?"

"No!"

"I could have a deal done by noon today if you give me the green light," Todd said. "The groom dumped her for his best man—or men, as the case may be—and now Lauren is short on love but long on longing. See our angel rise to heavenly bliss again. What viewer could resist watching that?"

He's out of his mind, as usual. "No, Todd," Lauren said. "Never."

"Never say never in Hollywood, Lauren," Todd said. "Viewers will eat you up if you're on a reality show. They love to see the high and mighty in extreme pain. It's a *great* way to make a comeback. We could work on the script to-gether."

"What script?" Lauren asked.

"Don't be naive," Todd said. "Every reality show is scripted these days. It makes them more real."

"It's a stupid idea," Lauren said.

"You'll really cash in," Todd said. "You'd make six fig-ures easily."

"I don't want to cash in on my pain, Todd," Lauren said. "I want to cash in on my talent."

"There's no questioning your *former* talent," Todd said, "but your pain and suffering are worth millions right now, and we have to act fast. If you wait too long, no one will re-member you were even engaged to Chazz Jackson."

"I hope they forget by the end of this week," Lauren said. "Todd, I will not do a scripted reality show about how stupid I've been. I want to get on with my life and put all that mess behind me." *Check that. I just want to get on with life.*

"Why do that when you can make some money off that mess first?" Todd asked.

"The answer is still no, Todd," Lauren said.

Todd sighed. "You're missing a golden opportunity, Lauren. It's the American way. No one would fault you for making a few bucks off your mistakes."

"No. End of discussion," Lauren said.

"Okay, okay," Todd said. "Did you happen to see Chazz's pictures on TMZ? He was surrounded by gorgeous women."

"Who was he smiling at?" Lauren asked. "The photog-rapher or the women?"

"Why, the photographer, of course," Todd said.

"And the photographer was a man, no doubt," Lauren said.

"I think so," Todd said.

"Chazz has to keep up his rep on *both* counts now," Lauren said.

"And you have to build up your rep again," Todd said. "You only live once, Lauren, and a rep has to be maintained."

"No, Todd," Lauren said. "You only *die* once. You have to live every day." *No matter what little test hangs over your head.*

"You know what I mean," Todd said. "You need to get your name back out there again immediately. This show is an excellent way to do it. *Gray Areas* will be your ticket to future greatness."

"*Gray Areas* will be my ticket to anonymity," Lauren said. "Have you contacted the *Saturday Night Live* people?"

"Not this again," Todd said.

"Yes, *this* again," Lauren said. "I could rock that show, and you know it."

"Fifteen years ago maybe," Todd said, "but certainly not now."

"Why not?" Lauren said. "You know I would be perfect for that show. I was born for live television. When's the last time you talked to them?"

"It's been at least a decade," Todd said.

"Put my name in front of them again," Lauren said. "Tell them I'd even do a few guest appearances here and there to get my feet under me again."

"Lauren, you need to get *Saturday Night Live* out of your head," Todd said. "Chazz hosts that show once a year. You know that. It would be awkward if you were in the cast."

"For him or for me?" Lauren asked.

"For both of you," Todd said.

"People would tune in to watch to see if sparks flew, though, wouldn't they?" Lauren asked. *And fists.*

"Hmm, they would," Todd said. "That might be the angle I use. Big star live onstage with his ex. What might *she* say? What might they *argue* about? Yes, it has possibilities."

Todd is so dramatic. "Okay," Lauren said. "Use that angle."

"But NBC already has its black woman," Todd said. "Haven't you been watching? They have Erika James."

"Erika James?" *That mannequin? I can't call her an actress.* "That *sock puppet* made *one* appearance on *Meet the Browns* and appeared in less than ten minutes of *one* movie with Martin Lawrence and Eddie Murphy, and suddenly she's the next Angela Bassett. Erika wasn't even funny in that movie. She had a straight role and *read* her lines very well."

"Ah, but that movie made a *ton* of money," Todd said. "And Erika's gorgeous and young, and you're not exactly young. You're still gorgeous, of course."

"I am only thirty-eight, Todd."

"I know you *still* look young," Todd said, "but we live in an increasingly young world, and right now, Erika has the look."

Because Erika is so light-skinned, she could pass for white. "Erika James doesn't even look black."

"She's black enough for NBC," Todd said.

"And I'm too black, right?" Lauren said.

"That's not what I meant," Todd said.

"It's okay, Todd," Lauren said. "Whether you meant it or not, it is the way it is."

"So, will you do this reading for *Gray Areas* or what?" Todd asked.

Lauren started to pace. "I don't know."

"I have to tell them something soon, as in today," Todd said. "They actually asked for you by name, Lauren. Can you believe it? I mean, despite you and Chazz splitting up, they still want you, damaged goods and all—not that you're damaged in any way. How often does that happen these days?"

I'm old news and damaged goods. "I don't know, Todd. This script . . ."

"Lauren, they asked for you by *name,*" Todd said. "They created a character with *your* name. That means that they *expect* you to take the part. What's to think about?"

Plenty. Look at me. I am living in a claustrophobic apartment at Studio Village in North Hollywood, because I had the audacity to break up with the gay—bisexual, whatever!—movie star I was engaged to for three years. I have a college dorm refrigerator and a microwave only big enough to warm up one frozen entrée. My bathroom is a foot away from my kitchen sink so I can cook and take a shower at the same time. I can't even wash my hands in the bathroom because there's no sink in the bathroom. Who builds a bathroom without a sink? That can't be legal.

I have an in-wall air-conditioning unit that smells like pee and shakes as if there's a perpetual earthquake somewhere. I have a rented daybed/couch that gives me an unobstructed view of the polluted pool I refuse to use. I pay for a gym—one treadmill and some free weights—I will probably never use. If it weren't for the NoHo Arts District, where I plan to shop as soon as the paparazzi outside go away, I'd go crazy.

"Lauren?"

Lauren sighed. "I'm still here."

"Time is money," Todd said.

"I know that." *And I suddenly have plenty of time to*

make some money of my own now. "Could you just call the *SNL* people one more time?"

"It won't do any good," Todd said.

"Todd, please talk to them," Lauren said. "I'm not getting any younger, right?" *And if I were taller, "whiter," and leggier, and if I sported jade-green contacts and had processed hair and overblown breast implants, I could be a leading lady in anybody's movie again. Short, dark, curvy, natural, and brown-eyed just don't look good enough on American TV and movie screens these days. I blame high definition.*

"I don't want them to get tired of hearing from me," Todd said.

"It's been ten years since you talked to them," Lauren said. "How can they get tired?"

"I don't want to wear out my welcome," Todd said. "By the way, your star meter is down over six hundred points on the Internet Movie Database since your breakup, and you're losing friends at all your Facebook fan sites, so I'll be surprised if NBC even wants to hear your name."

"That star meter is a sham, and you know it," Lauren said. "And as for Facebook, I don't care. And you can't wear out your welcome, Todd, if no one is there to welcome you. You have never had the inside track in New York."

"Oh, try to flatter me so I'll help you," Todd said.

As much as I hate this man sometimes, I really need him now. "Just . . . make one more call," Lauren said. "For me. For old times' sake."

"For *ancient* times' sake."

"I'm still younger than you are," Lauren said.

Todd sighed. "All right, I'll make the call. But when *SNL* doesn't pan out, and it *won't,* you will do the reading for *Gray Areas,* right?"

"Oh, all right. I'll do the reading," Lauren said. *And ei-*

*ther I will fix that script as I read it or I will botch it up as
badly as I can so they don't want me anymore.*

"They'll be overjoyed to hear it," Todd said. "Bye."

Click.

"Wait!" Lauren yelled into the phone. *He'll forget to
call SNL. I just know it.*

Lauren trudged to her bed and booted up her laptop.
After reading and then deleting several screens of e-mails
suggesting new boyfriends and even a few girlfriends, she
came to the last page.

*A message from Patrick Alan Esposito. Nothing but a
"Re:" in the title space. I am intrigued.*

She opened Patrick's e-mail and smiled. *If I ever need
someone to talk to.*

"Patrick," she said, "I need someone to *vent* to. I suppose that's 'talking.'"

Patrick likes Crisp and Popp. *He's already wiser than
ninety-nine percent of the television network executives
who have ever lived.* She laughed. *Why am I laughing? Oh,
I guess it's because I'm about to vent to a stranger. I really
need to vent to someone. I have to get some of this mess out
of my head.*

She nodded at the screen. "Sorry, Patrick, but I have a
feeling that this is going to get pretty heavy."

She started typing. . . .

Patrick:

    I hope you don't mind if I vent for a bit. You see,
I've had a seriously bad week. I'm warning you,
though. It could get pretty ugly.

    No. It's about to get very ugly. . . .

4

After a long, cold late November day of unclogging sink traps, tinkering with water heater settings, and taking only four trips to Mrs. Moczydlowska's apartment to make "the sound go away," Patrick bypassed the deli and the lure of a delicious frozen burrito and a soda, climbed up the stairs to his apartment, 2B, and checked his e-mail.

She wrote back.

Again!

Wow.

She really *wrote back.*

She wrote an epic!

Okay, it's not that long, but compared to most e-mails I've ever gotten, this one is long. She says it's going to get ugly. Let's see how ugly this is going to get. . . .

> First of all, I was engaged for three years to a bisexual man. That's right. Don't let his action roles fool you. He's the modern Errol Flynn. He has sex appeal for everyone, but especially men.

So Chazz is fake, Patrick thought. *Lauren must be going out of her mind.*

> He (I refuse to even write his name) is much more gay than straight, despite the lies he's telling on TV. I didn't know it until I caught him with two other men in our house only eight days ago. The One Who Shall Remain Nameless Forevermore gave me no signs that he was messing with men, and I feel so stupid.
>
> Because of him, I went to get tested for HIV five days ago.

Oh, dear God, no, Patrick thought. *No!*

> How's that for an outstanding way to end an engagement? I should get my test results back anytime now, and I am scared . . . to . . . death. Angry, too. Scared and angry. It's hard to smile, you know? I'm trying, but I kind of have a possible extended death sentence hanging over my head, you know?
>
> Thank you for trying to help. At least YOU are. No one else is, especially my agent. He sent me a script today that isn't worth the paper wasted on it. If I had a dog, I'd use it to collect the poop. It might be the worst script ever written. They want me to play a character named Lauren in an interracial sitcom called Gray Areas. How "neat" is that? I get to play myself, but my real self would never say what's in this script. Let me give you a taste of what someone ignorant thinks is comedy. . . .

Patrick read the first scene of *Gray Areas* without laughing. He reread the scene and shook his head so much, he started to get dizzy. *This is . . . this is rotten! They're ac-*

tually serious about putting this on TV? They can't be! Ignorant is right. This script should be illegal.

> See what I mean? I'd have to be insane to take
> that role.
> And on top of all this, I have been trying for years
> to get on Saturday Night Live, but they already have
> Erika James, that skinny piece of driftwood, and I bet
> they give her the role of "the Loneliest Woman in the
> World." I *love* that character. She gets to verbally
> castrate the host at some point during every show,
> and it's completely ad-lib. I would love to do that,
> especially if The Nameless One is hosting. Erika
> James can't do ad-lib, and she can't do improv. She'd
> freeze up like the icicle she is. I would rock that role.
> Sorry I rambled. I haven't been having a good
> time. I should just turn that Gray Areas mess down
> and worry about my health. What do you think?
> Lauren

Despite his heartfelt concerns for Lauren's life and health, Patrick smiled.

Lauren Short, actress, wants my opinion. A talented, intelligent woman, the kind of woman every man dreams of simply meeting for a few seconds, wants my opinion. A woman waiting to find out if she's dying . . . He shook his head. *God, help her, please. Let that test be negative, okay?*

A woman with the weight of the world on her shoulders wants my advice.

He looked through the frosted window beside his bed at the deli across the street.

My burrito can wait.

I hope I can help her smile.

Lauren:

Yes, the script is ridiculous. I was offended. I don't smell like a wet puppy. I smell bad after a full day's work, but I do not smell like a wet puppy. More like an Irish wolfhound. And I don't think I have a "shovel" back there. I know how to use one, though. The shovel, I mean. :~)

I don't hang out at any of the places (except church) the script says I'm supposed to. Who goes to Hell's Kitchen to shop? The name alone should tell you something, right? That place is mostly industrial. She might go there to buy a car or pay too much for clothes in the Garment District.

If I ever saw this show, I'd turn it off quickly. Watching the Weather Channel would be more exciting. Watching my fingernails grow would be more entertaining. Watching water drip in a sink would be more hilarious. Rainy days are funnier.

And having Erika James play "the Loneliest Woman in the World" is an outrage. I've seen her, and she is terrible. Erika James wouldn't get a starring role in a kindergarten class play. If she played the tree, she'd have to be a birch tree, and she'd want to be front and center with a speaking role. "I am a tree. Hear me bark!" Erika James doesn't have the intelligence to know that a tree in a kindergarten class play doesn't speak. It just stands there, looking treelike, which is exactly how she acted in that Eddie Murphy movie. Wooden. Erika James is a skinny piece of light tan wood.

But you are . . . amazing.

Maybe you can make that Gray Areas show work. Let them know how false it is and turn it into something awesome.

I am not the person who should be giving you advice on anything to do with acting, but I do know that work is work when you can get it. Sometimes you have to make work, work for you. (Did that make sense?) Maybe this will all work out for you. I hope it does.

I am so sorry to hear about all your misfortunes, especially that test. I'll be praying for you. I'll light a candle at St. Agnes for you, too.

How are you now?

Patrick

5

He should be writing the script, Lauren thought as she read Patrick's e-mail. *The two of us could write a better script.*

She smiled. *Patrick knows how to use his shovel. I wonder if he meant it to mean the way I've taken it. I'll bet he did. What does an Irish wolfhound smell like? Those are some seriously big dogs. Maybe Patrick's a big guy. I have attracted yet another white man, though his last name isn't white. Esposito? Maybe he's mixed with something. He has to be mixed up to think I'm amazing. And he's praying for me and lighting a candle. That's so sweet. No man on earth has ever done that for me.*

She quickly replied:

Patrick:

    Erika James isn't skinny. She's an anorexic piece of balsa wood. She would splinter into a million pieces if she actually had to speak for more than five seconds at a time without cue cards written in big, bold letters. They may even have to spell out words phonetically for her. She has the acting range of a paraplegic snail and the stage presence of a dust bunny.

Thank you for asking how I am. You're the only one who has asked that. My agent just wants me to make him some money again. I made that man a bunch of money once, and now he wants me to make him some more money with Gray Areas. He isn't going to make much.

Thank you for caring, Patrick. And please don't stop. :)

How am I now? I'm okay. Not great. Just okay. I'm still worried to death about the results of that test, and I haven't been sleeping or eating much. Your encouraging words have helped me a great deal. And while I haven't had much to smile about lately, your e-mails have made me smile. :) <See?

Work is indeed work, and I should be thankful to get anything after taking a seven-year "vacation" and not knowing what my future holds. I'll probably do Gray Areas. I am getting older but not necessarily wiser, I guess. I wish you could fix this script. You're funny. And real.

At any rate, I will make numerous suggestions to the script, and if they don't want to make the changes, I'll just go off script whenever we're taping. ;)

Are you a writer by chance? You write very well.

Thanks for writing back. I look forward to your next e-mail.

Lauren

Lauren watched her in-box for several moments. *I wonder where he is.* She checked the times Patrick sent his previous e-mails. *He only writes late at night. What could that mean? Maybe that's the only time he has to write.*

After no e-mail from Patrick appeared, she called Todd. "I'll do the reading."

"I'm glad you came to your senses," Todd said.

"Work is work when you can get it," Lauren said. *Thank you for reminding me of that, Patrick.* "Have you talked to the *SNL* people yet?"

"No," Todd said. "It's only been one day. I have other clients, you know."

"Keep pestering them for me, though, okay?"

"I will," Todd said. "They'll expect you at Tumbleweed's main studio in Studio City at nine sharp tomorrow morning."

"Okay," Lauren said.

It's about time I left this apartment. The paparazzi will appreciate me leaving, too. They have to be bored out there in the parking lot. They've been taking numerous pictures of my car, which is splatted with bird poop.

"I've just sent you the next scene attached to an e-mail," Todd said, "and it is *much* better than the first."

"I doubt it," Lauren said.

"Trust me," Todd said. "You'll see. Bye."

Lauren didn't see.

If anything, the next scene made the first scene worse.

LAUREN

(Sees hot white guy. Voice-over: *He'll do. He has brown eyes, but at least he has an ass.*) *You like what you see?*

HOT GUY

What?

LAUREN

I said, do you like what you see?

HOT GUY

(Holds up a clay vase.) *It's not in very good condition. I wouldn't pay more than five dollars for it.*

LAUREN

(Voice-over: *This man is slow. Are all white men this slow? I guess I have to spell it out for him.*) *I meant,* (poses) *do you like what you see of me?*

HOT GUY

(Looks her over.) *Should I?*

LAUREN

(Voice-over: *Maybe I need to be blunt.*) *Are you interested?*

HOT GUY

In you?

LAUREN

(Voice-over: *No. In the vase, you idiot!*) *Yes. In me. Do you want to go out, maybe hook up, maybe go back to my place and get a little busy?*

HOT GUY

My husband might mind. . . .

LAUREN

(Voice-over: *Figures . . .*) *I'm sorry. I thought . . .
Yeah, I wouldn't pay a penny over four dollars for
that sorry vase. . . .*

Oh, this is tragically stereotypical! Lauren thought. *The
first white guy she tries to hook up with is gay. How often
does that happen in real life? Okay, it happened to me—with
my third try—but come on! I know art can imitate life, but
it's almost as if A. Smith wrote this part specifically for me!*

After nothing from Patrick appeared in her in-box, Lauren settled under her covers and fell asleep, and for some
reason, she dreamed she was shopping for vases. . . .

The next morning, Lauren showered, ate a light breakfast of toast and grape jelly, and stood in front of her
clothes closet.

*What I wear today has to show that I am capable, confi-
dent, and competent,* she thought. *I can't go slinking out
past the paparazzi looking defeated. I have to wear something that says, "Hey, Lauren Short looks great! Her
breakup hasn't hurt her one bit! That woman still has it
going on! She has come out of this mess with flying colors!"*

She laughed at herself.

*I have to stop taking myself so seriously. It's only a
reading, and no matter what I wear, someone in the media
out there will make something negative out of it. I'll probably end up on some worst-dressed list by the end of the
week.*

She put on comfortable jeans, a turquoise blouse, a
black blazer, and some black Dansko clogs. *This outfit says
I'm comfortable and I'm ready for anything.*

I hope I'm ready.

Lauren walked out to her emerald-green 2008 Jaguar XK convertible, a vestige from her more successful days, and past only three paparazzi camped out today near the pool. None of the photographers rushed her, instead lazily snapping pictures of her as she walked by.

"Where are you headed?" one of them asked.

Lauren opened her car door and got in. As soon as she started up the Jaguar, she put the convertible top down. "I am going to a reading."

The tallest of the three photographers approached. "You up for a movie?"

"TV," Lauren said. She adjusted her mirrors and put on some cheap sunglasses.

"So soon?" the tallest one said.

"I have to get back on the horse," Lauren said. *Though this show may be my hearse.*

"What show?" he asked.

"It's called *Gray Areas,*" Lauren said.

"Never heard of it," he said. He shrugged at the other photographers, and they shrugged back.

"It's in the pilot stage now," Lauren said. "You'll hear about it soon."

They took several more pictures and turned away.

I am definitely losing my appeal, Lauren thought. *Seven years ago a swarm of photographers would have been here, and they would be daring me to run them over. I wonder how much they can get for a picture of me now.*

"Hey!" Lauren yelled.

The tallest photographer strolled over. "Yeah?"

"What's the going rate for a picture of me these days?" Lauren asked.

He shrugged. "As much as I can get, I guess."

"Give me a ballpark," Lauren said. "A thousand?"

"Not the way you look," he said. "I'd be lucky to get two-fifty."

Ouch. "And how do I look?" Lauren asked.

He snapped one more picture. "Happy."

Lauren smiled. "I *am* happy."

The man sighed. "Happy doesn't sell."

"You mean if I came out here all sad and dressed horribly, you'd make more money?" Lauren asked.

"Yeah," the man said. "You're supposed to be . . . I don't know . . . broken up. You just got dumped by Chazz Jackson, right?"

"I'm not broken up," Lauren said. "And *I* dumped him."

"Yeah?" the man asked.

"Yeah. And I bet you can make more than a grand."

"I used to make that much for pictures of you and Chazz," the man said. "Without Chazz, I don't know."

"Well, sell it this way," Lauren said. "Here's a picture of Lauren Short on her way to jump-start her career, and unlike what you might expect, she's actually happy."

"I don't know," the man said. "It sounds too nice, and nice doesn't sell in this town."

"Should I frown, then?" Lauren asked.

"It would help," the man said.

Lauren laughed. "I'm too happy to frown, man. Have a good one."

After half an hour of fighting traffic on the 405 and the 101, Lauren arrived at Tumbleweed's low-slung studio.

It looks more like a strip mall than a studio, Lauren thought. *Oh, I have really come down in the world. I'm going to work in a strip mall.*

After finding a spot in the visitors' parking lot, she found a security guard, who escorted her to a low-ceilinged soundstage, where she met the director, Randy Ware, and

Barbie Perry, her character's buxom sidekick. They sat around a card table and highlighted scripts in front of them.

"I am *so* glad to be working with you, Miss Short," Randy said.

"It is *truly* an honor," Barbie said. "I saw *Feel the Love* twenty times when I was eight. I wanted to be Angel so badly."

Oh, thanks for making me feel old, Barbie. "Well, it's good to be here," Lauren said. "I might be a little rusty, so bear with me."

"It's like riding a bike," Randy said.

No, it isn't. Rosalind Russell once said, "Acting is standing up naked and turning around very slowly," and right now, I'm afraid to turn around at any speed.

"Randy, before we begin, I have to tell you something." Lauren glanced at Barbie. "This script needs work. This script needs an overhaul. This script is bad. I've read hundreds of scripts, and this might be the all-time worst script in world history."

Randy blinked rapidly. "Really? I think it's pretty good."

"I think it's funny," Barbie said.

My costar and director are idiots. "Many of these lines are beyond wrong. Don't be surprised if I go off script often today."

"For our purposes today," Randy said, "please read the script as written, Lauren."

"No half-intelligent woman would say these lines," Lauren said.

"This is only a reading, Lauren," Randy said. "We can smooth out the rough edges later."

They began the scene, and when Lauren read, "He'd probably shock me every time he touched me," she read it with absolutely no emotion.

"Come on, Lauren," Randy said. "Put some fire into it."

"Fire?" Lauren said. "The *writer* should be fired."

"Lauren, please," Randy said. "Put some emotion into it."

"Oh," Lauren said. "You want me to read it blacker."

"You know what I mean," Randy said. "Camp it up. This is comedy."

"This is a joke," Lauren said.

"Girl, don't you mess this up for me," Barbie whispered. "I *need* this. I got bills."

"What are you whispering for?" Lauren asked. "Randy can hear you. I need this, too, but *this* excretion won't get out of the pilot stage with writing like this."

"So it isn't going to win any Emmys," Barbie said. "But whether it's good or not, it's a paycheck, and I *need* a paycheck to pay back my college loans. *Please* read the line."

You want me to camp it up? I'll camp it up. Lauren stood, waved her hands, and threw out her hip. "*Girrrl,* did you see the *rest* of his *sorry* butt? His face was hairier than a Sasquatch on Rogaine. *Puh-lease.* Honey, I bet he's all frickin' static clingy from his frickin' toes to his frickin' nose. He'd probably frickin' shock me every time he frickin' touched me!"

Randy smiled. "Fantastic! Wow! I like your additions, too. *Very* real." He wrote down a few. "Perfect, Lauren. It sounds natural. Keep going off script like that."

Barbie held up her hand to give Lauren some dap.

Lauren left Barbie's hand hanging. "Randy, I was *mocking* the script."

"I know," Randy said, "and it was funny. I hope you keep doing it. Your overacting is going to make this show go! I am so happy to be working with you!"

Oh, God, Lauren thought. *I hate myself so much right now.*

Where's the exit?

6

Before Patrick lumbered home after another long day's work, he stopped by St. Agnes on Sackett Street to light a candle and say a prayer for Lauren.

"God, keep Lauren safe in Your hands," he prayed. "And if it's not too much trouble, let us . . . I don't know . . . help us get to know each other better. Amen."

After lighting another candle for his mother, Patrick went home to shower off the day.

He had spent the morning and most of the afternoon snaking the main sewer drain in the basement on Baltic until it cleared, because the Ouderkerks in 1A and the Schoonmakers in 2B, descendants of Dutch families who had lived in Brooklyn since 1675, had called him within seconds of each other, each complaining that their toilets were nearly overflowing. By the time he had arrived, he had received calls from the Vanderbeeks in 2A and the Gildersleeves in 1B, more Dutch families who did not appreciate pungent brown ponds in their toilets. Instead of checking out the four toilets, Patrick had gone straight to the basement and had found it already thick with backed-up sewage. He had deployed the snake he had left there for just such an emergency and had sat on an overturned plastic bucket for an hour as the snake chewed its way to the main line and the lake of goo sucked itself slowly back down the drain. While he had waited, he had heard from the other four tenants on Baltic, each loud and nagging.

"This happens every November. You know that?" Mr. Hyer in 3B had said. "Are you stupid? You must learn to do preventive maintenance in October!"

You could cut back on the fiber, too, Patrick had thought. "I will do that, Mr. Hyer."

"What do you expect me to do?" Mrs. Albertson in 3A had asked. "I have to *go,* Mr. Esposito. Where can I *go?*"

There's a McDonald's on Atlantic two blocks away, Patrick had thought. "It won't be long, Mrs. Albertson," Patrick had said. "I'll have everything fixed in a few minutes. It should be running smoothly any moment now."

"*I* will be running in a few *seconds!*" Mrs. Albertson had shouted.

When Patrick had mentioned the McDonald's, Mrs. Albertson had hung up.

After his shower and in clothing that did not smell like Dutch American poop, he settled under his covers and read Lauren's e-mail.

I'm not an entrepreneur, a writer, anything, he thought. *I have value, at least to people who expect their toilets to empty every time, but I'm nothing special. I'm just a guy from Brooklyn.*

Though he knew other people stretched the truth and even lied online, Patrick decided to give Lauren nothing but the truth.

Lauren:

Thank you for the compliments, but I am not a writer. I am a buildings maintenance supervisor, which is a glorified way of saying that I'm a handyman.

I have a staff of me, myself, and I, and "we" keep five apartment buildings in order in Boerum Hill, Brooklyn. Today I saved about two dozen people from having to use the restrooms at McDonald's. It's a long story involving a sewer line and a machine called a snake. I'll spare you the details. I lead such a glamorous life, don't I?

I did shower before I started writing this. :~) I use Safeguard.

For what it's worth, Boerum Hill can be pretty glamorous. We've had a few actors and actresses living here, like Heath Ledger, Michelle Williams, Sandra Oh, Keri Russell, Anne Hathaway, and Emily Mortimer. I never saw any of them, but allegedly, they used to live around here or still live around here.

They might have lived here for the restaurants on Smith Street. I can't afford to eat at any of them, not that I would. They have such pretentious names, like Saul, Café Luluc, Bar Tabac, Apartment 138, El Nuevo Cibao, Char No. 4, and Lunetta. Isn't Lunetta a drug for depression? Why can't they name their restaurants Eats or Good Food or We Cook for You or We'll Serve You? I know. Those names aren't trendy enough. I'd much rather eat at a place called Delicious and Cheap than at Café Luluc any day.

I look forward to seeing you on the little screen. I will have to buy a larger TV so I can see more of you. ;~)

Patrick

7

So he's a Brooklyn man, Lauren thought while munching on some microwave popcorn. *And a handyman, a workingman, a friendly, funny, "normal" man. I don't know many of those. Come to think of it, I don't know any of those. And despite what I've told him, he wants to see more of me.* She checked the clock on her computer screen. *It's eight o'clock here, so it's eleven there. He writes to me at the end of a long day of dealing with human sewage. He ends his day with me. That's kind of . . . nice.*

And here I am, ending my day with him.

Patrick:

    After the crap I've been through, no story you tell me can smell any worse. Thanks for taking a shower, though. :) You do smell nice. ;) I use Dove.

    I haven't been to New York in a long time. It's been almost 20 years, I think. I ended up in Brooklyn by mistake once. I took the wrong subway and almost made it to Coney Island before I realized my mistake. I met a lot of interesting people on the subway, though. Maybe I "met" you then, too?

I did a little summer stage work—a little stage work—in New York half a lifetime ago. I was one of the people who sat in the background and faked talking. I was good at it. It takes skill to make pantomime look realistic. It's kind of like being in Congress, huh?

I used to sit onstage, mouthing the lines I was practicing for auditions for other plays. If anyone could read lips, it would have made them trip. I had a few walkovers in crowd scenes, and I once got to yell, "Hey!" I was only 19. I had to start somewhere. Then someone "noticed" me in a little Off-Off-Off Broadway (practically in New Jersey) play the summer before I was to graduate from Howard U., called a producer, I did a screen test, and in a few short months, I was in Hollywood.

Thus ended my "career" on the New York stage, and thus began my movie career. And thus ended my college career, too. I suppose I could go back and get a degree now. It's something to think about now that I have so much time to think. Believe it or not, I was an English major. Really. I can quote Shakespeare and everything.

I did the reading for Gray Areas today, and I hated every second of it. My costar Barbie is young and eager, but the director is a certified idiot. He gave me scene 3 to read (which is as flushable as the first two) and introduced me to the actor playing my love interest. Ever hear of Gus Stanley? He's twelve. Just kidding. He's only twenty, and . . . (drumroll) he's gay.

I know because I also met his boyfriend today. I have since found out that the man playing the "gay guy" from scene 2 is straight.

The ironies of show business, huh? What you see is not always what you get. And that reminds me of you know who, and I don't want to go there tonight.

So in this show I have to somehow fall in love and have "chemistry" with a gay guy and make it believable. The One Who Shall Remain Nameless Forevermore could have played this role to perfection. (I know! I said I wasn't going to go there, and I did.)

Patrick, if this show ever makes it to TV (and I have some serious doubts that it ever will), watch my eyes and read my lips when I'm not talking. You will "hear" me cursing and see me looking for an exit in every scene. I've had trips to the dentist that were more pleasant.

I hope the sewers in Brooklyn give you a better day tomorrow.

Thank you for caring. Really.

Lauren

8

I got a wink, Patrick thought. *A smiley* and *a wink. And she's awake out in LA right now, waiting for my next e-mail.*

Patrick's hands perspired freely.

Well, maybe she's not exactly waiting for me to respond. But if I write to her and she writes back again, Lauren Short and I would be "talking." And in real time.

Sort of.

She left me so many openings. But should I wait and write to her tomorrow? That's been our schedule. I don't want to sound too eager, do I? I mean, I am eager. I got a wink! Yes! She thinks I smell nice. She thanked me for caring.

I have to write back.

"Talking" to her is becoming a physical need.

He clicked the REPLY button.

Lauren:

Don't feel bad about going the wrong way on a subway. A lot of people end up in Brooklyn by mistake, and most of them still live here.

What happened to you is not nearly as bad as what happened to the dolphin that got lost and swam up the Gowanus Canal a few years ago. I wonder what that dolphin was thinking. Maybe it wanted to see some of Brooklyn's fanciest houses before it died. Maybe it was looking for a good slice of pizza. Who knows?

I grew up a few blocks from here, in the Gowanus Houses. I obviously don't get out of Brooklyn much. I haven't been to Coney Island since I was a kid.

I've never seen a professional play or a musical. I'm sure you were an awesome mime. :~)

I can't afford to go to the theater on my pay. There are no cheap seats, and if you want to see the stage without binoculars, you have to pay up to $200. I tried to get work on a stage crew at the Brooklyn Academy of Music about seventeen years ago, but I didn't fit the "profile," I guess. I am a handyman, not a set designer or an artist.

I do have some acting experience. That's right. You're talking to a former actor. I played one of the Cratchit children in A Christmas Carol at Silas B. Dutcher, P.S. 124, when I was in the third grade. I put this acting credit on all my résumés. It has gotten me loads of work. My telephone never stops ringing. . . .

I didn't have a speaking part, mainly because I couldn't do a believable English accent. Once Brooklyn, always Brooklyn. I sang a few carols, though. Badly. I knew the words, but I couldn't carry a tune. Thus began (and ended) my acting (and singing) career.

I would have enjoyed trying to decipher your lips, though. Do you think any of those plays are on YouTube? I'd like to watch them so I could trip on your lips. That didn't come out right. I'd like to trip on what you were miming.

I think I know why they found such a young man to play your love interest in that TV show. You look young. You don't age. What is your secret? And please don't say mud baths. I've had too many of those to count.

You should be the writer. You made me laugh after a long, exasperating day. It sometimes seems like the whole world is falling apart, but some laughter and a smile put it all back together again.

You made me smile, too. Stopped-up sewage does not make me smile. It makes me want to rip out my teeth with pliers and sand my nose down with a belt sander.

Thank you for caring, too.

Patrick

PS: Thanks especially for the wink. No one has ever winked at me. I hope you don't mind if I wink back twice. . . . ;~) ;~) No, I don't have something in my eye.

Patrick waited an hour for Lauren's reply.
It didn't come.
Maybe I shouldn't have winked twice.
He shook his head as he turned out the light and dropped his head onto his pillow.
What was I thinking? I wrote too much. I shared too much about myself. I should have asked her more questions. She has no real reason to write back now.
Thus ends my conversation with Lauren Short.
It was nice while it lasted.

9

Lauren waved at only two photographers the following morning, and they took only one picture each and quickly left in separate cars.

I must be too happy again today, she thought. *This is such a strange town.*

She arrived late to the studio and was immediately rushed to wardrobe.

"What's going on?" she asked.

"We're filming promos today," a clipboard-carrying woman said.

"We haven't even read through all the scenes yet," Lauren said. "We haven't even had a full dress rehearsal."

"Don't worry about it," the woman said. "You're a pro."

Lauren had major difficulty getting into the size 7 jeans her character was supposed to wear. *If I had a shoehorn and some butter, this would be so much easier to do.* In addition to stiletto heels and a loud red top with a plunging neckline, she wore more bling than a rapper.

This is ridiculous! I'll ring like a bell whenever I turn my head!

Then Joanie, the makeup artist, painted her face in broad strokes.

She's trying to turn me into a white woman. "Stop," Lauren said.

"Almost done," Joanie said.

"I draw the line at three coats," Lauren said.

"Huh?" Joanie said.

Lauren left her chair and approached the mirror. "I'll do it. You're trying to turn me into a white prostitute."

"You've never done any HD work before, have you?" Joanie asked. "We'll be filming in HD, Miss Short. You don't want any of your pores to show."

"I want my skin to be able to *breathe,* Joanie, okay?" Lauren said. "You've added three inches to my face." *And hidden all my beautiful brown skin.* "Were you going to do my hands, too?"

Joanie nodded. "And your neck."

That isn't happening. "I prefer my own color, thank you."

"But they'll be lining up shots while you rehearse," Joanie said. "Today is promo day. They get on me if I don't do my job."

"They told you to whiten me up," Lauren said.

Joanie nodded.

Such foolishness. Lauren wiped off all the makeup before applying some eyeliner. "If they fuss at you, I'll take the blame, okay?" She squinted in the mirror. *Stupid crow's-feet. I wish you crows would stop landing on me and doing the Macarena in work boots.* "I'm ready."

"But, Miss Short," Joanie said. "They're expecting you to be . . ."

Lauren stared at Joanie. "Whiter?"

"Well, not so dark," Joanie said. "It's not my idea. I think you have a beautiful skin tone."

"Thank you," Lauren said. "I'll take the rap for this." Lauren picked some lint from her top and squared her shoulders. *This delicious piece of dark meat is ready to turn this turkey into a Thanksgiving meal.*

"That's all you're going to do?" Joanie asked. "Just some eyeliner?"

"That's all I need," Lauren said. "This face still has some mileage left in it."

Lauren walked onto the set, and it wasn't much of one. *We're filming an outdoor café scene indoors. Great. The budget for this show just shrank to half of what it should be to do this scene right. We should be outdoors! It's a beautiful day. The natural light out there would make me look even younger.*

"Lauren," Randy said, eyeing her closely, "you didn't get to makeup."

"I did, Randy," Lauren said, joining Barbie at a wrought-iron white table flanked by two white iron chairs. "But I didn't appreciate the paint job. I had to take most of the paint off before it dried."

"But why?" Randy asked.

"I looked ridiculous," Lauren said. "I didn't look a bit like myself." She nodded at Barbie. "She's not wearing much makeup."

"She isn't the star," Randy said.

"Star or not, you will *not* make me look like a white woman," Lauren said. "And, anyway, this is only rehearsal and something about promos, right?"

Randy sighed. "The execs want to see a full scene or two today, so we have to be sharp."

"What is the rush?" Lauren asked.

"Things move faster these days," Randy said.

"I haven't been gone from this business that long, Randy," Lauren said.

"Actually," Barbie said, "you have."

Lauren gawked at Barbie's cleavage, most of which spilled out of her electric blue blouse. *Those things will steal any scene I'm in. They look overinflated.* She turned back to Randy. "What happened to rehearsing a scene until it's perfect? We haven't even blocked these scenes, Randy."

"There really isn't much movement in the first scene," Randy said. "You're sitting and talking. What's to block?"

Lauren sighed. "There's plenty to block. Hand movements, gestures, what camera to look at, getting dap—all these need to be blocked. We don't even know how long we're supposed to laugh or how long I'm supposed to stare at the white boy's butt."

"Use your best judgment," Randy said. "Go with the flow."

This is so unprofessional, Lauren thought. *No wonder some TV shows these days aren't much better than a high school play.* "All right. I'm feeling sharp. Are you feeling sharp, Barbie?"

"I'm ready," Barbie said.

Lauren shrugged. "Let's do this." She looked up and saw several microphones. "How sensitive are those mikes?"

"They say they can pick up your stomach grumbling, girl," Barbie said. "And try not to fart."

Randy pointed at a girl holding cue cards. "We'll do a quick run-through with the cards."

"I don't need them," Lauren said. "Barbie?"

"I'm good," Barbie said.

"Okay," Randy said. "Let's . . . do this." He looked behind him. "Are we ready?"

An army of sound technicians and camera operators nodded.

"You're on," Randy said, and he moved behind the largest camera. "And . . . action!"

Lauren looked to her right as Mike, the heterosexual white man, walked by. She dipped her head slightly to look at his butt. As soon as he was safely out of range, she said, "Not bad. Not bad at all."

Barbie looked lost. "Um, lookin' at a cracker don't cost nothin', Lauren."

"Cut!" Randy yelled. He stepped forward. "The line reads—"

"I *know* what the line reads, Randy," Lauren interrupted. "I *can* read. I don't like the line, okay? My character doesn't like the line. Your viewers won't like the line. White people won't like the line. Republicans won't like the line."

Randy shook his head. "But, Lauren—"

"Look," Lauren interrupted. "He's a man. He's nice looking. A *real* woman wouldn't say, 'He's nice looking . . . for a *white* man.' She might not even say anything at all. She might only make a sound, like 'mmm-mm.'"

"Mmm-mm," Barbie said. "He was hot." She waved at Mike, who was putting on a pair of headphones. "You're hot."

"Thanks," Mike said.

He works here? "Is Mike a sound tech?" Lauren asked.

"He only has one part," Randy said.

How low budget is this show? Lauren thought. *They have sound techs doing walkovers.* "Ever?" Lauren asked.

"I'm sure we'll bring him back occasionally for crowd scenes," Randy said, "but you're missing the point. Mike *is* white, and he *is* handsome for a white man, right?"

"He's handsome no matter what his color is," Lauren said.

"Mmm-mm," Barbie said.

Randy sighed. "But the point of the show—"

"Let it go, Randy," Lauren interrupted. "I lowered myself to stare at his butt, but that's as low as I'm willing to go today, okay? Why don't you simply let the viewer *see* that he's white? Why *tell* the viewer what the viewer can obviously see? ABC didn't go out of its way to say that Olivia on *Scandal* was black, did they? They didn't overplay the fact that she was black and the president was white, did they?"

"Okay, we'll . . ." Randy sighed. "We'll go on. Pick up from where you left off." He stepped back. "And . . . action!"

I will not say, "He ain't got no booty." Lauren smiled at Barbie. "He had a nice ass, didn't he?"

"Cut!" Randy moved to the table, resting his palms on the back of Barbie's chair. "Lauren, it's a booty, not an ass."

"I use the word *ass*," Lauren said. "Women have booties. *Men* have asses."

Barbie nodded. "She's right, you know. And I should know. I have booty for days. What Mike has—*that* is an ass." She waved at Mike again.

Mike smiled.

Randy nodded. "Okay, okay. It's an ass, not a booty." He waved his hands in the air to the camera crew behind him. "Don't, um, don't do anything until I tell you to. We'll run the entire scene first." He turned to Lauren. "Go ahead."

Lauren repeated her line. "He had a nice ass, didn't he?"

"Nope," Barbie said. "Looks like a straight shovel back there. He probably has divots in his hairy cheeks."

"What's wrong with that?" Lauren said. "As long as he knows how to work his shovel, it doesn't matter what it looks like."

Barbie blinked.

Lauren smiled. "And I don't mind a hairy man at all. I wouldn't mind if we built up a little static cling. Wouldn't it be wonderful to have a man shock you every time he touched you?"

"He, um, he had blue eyes, though," Barbie said. "Gotta like them." She shot a glance at Randy, widening her eyes.

"Blue eyes are overrated," Lauren said. "I'll take any man who only has eyes for me."

"Cut!" Randy yelled.

That was actually pretty good! Lauren thought. *I could write this show.*

Randy's face began to sweat. "Lauren, please, I'm begging you—"

"But we're not even *filming*, Randy," Lauren interrupted. *Randy's so young for a director, and that tan looks sprayed on. Where do they get these guys? The Film School for the Overly Sensitive, Close-Minded, and Tan?*

"I know we're not filming, Lauren," Randy said. "Why can't you just say the line?"

"I'm getting into character," Lauren said. "My character wants to say better lines. I'm even beginning to like my character *because* I'm changing the lines to something better. Don't you want me to feel comfortable in my role?"

"Of course, but . . ." Randy knelt beside Lauren. "You're changing the entire vibe of the scene."

"Right," Lauren said. "I'm making the entire vibe of the scene realistic and interesting."

"It's a comedy," Randy said. "It doesn't have to be realistic or interesting."

What a ridiculous thing to say! "It *should* be," Lauren said. "And it *has* to be if I am to remain on this show. I will not play a caricature, and neither should Barbie. I have never played a stereotypical black woman, and I never will." She turned to Barbie. "Why don't you say something like, 'Would you look at that?' instead of calling him a cracker?"

"I can do that," Barbie said.

"No, you *can't*," Randy said, standing and shaking his head. "If you both go off script at the same time—"

"We'll have a watchable show," Lauren interrupted. "You know, we might even have a good show. Isn't that what everybody wants? Don't *you* want to direct a show that may actually last longer than a pilot? Let's keep going. Say your next line, Barbie."

Barbie read through the line on the cue card, closed her eyes, and puffed out her cheeks. "You ain't . . . I mean, *are you* thinking about getting a little cream in your coffee, Lauren? No. That's nasty. How about this? Are you thinking of hooking up with a guy like him? What would Marcus think?"

"Much better," Lauren said. She touched Barbie's hand. "Relax. This isn't rocket science. You are not a hoochie."

Barbie smiled. "Thank you."

Randy cleared his throat.

"Oh, right, my line," Lauren said. "Marcus and I are through."

"*Finally,*" Randy said. "You stayed on script."

"Because it's a line that doesn't demean black women or stereotype white men," Lauren said. "A lot of people say that." *I said it just last week in between the curses and the glass breaking and while two other men were putting their pants on backward. Now* that *was a dramatic scene.* "Let's keep going, Barbie, and maybe Randy will catch on. Marcus and I are through."

"Since when?" Barbie asked.

"Since I caught him doing two men on my couch," Lauren said.

"You did?" Barbie asked. "Oh, Lauren, that's terrible! That's . . . that's nasty! Who were they?"

"No, no, no!" Randy yelled. "Where did the two dudes come from?"

"You wouldn't believe me if I told you, Randy," Lauren said. "Known people. Men with wives and kids. Big names with beach houses and spotless reputations. Hallmark Hall of Fame people. I'll bet they were even closet Republicans."

"Really?" Barbie said. "That is so *sick!* What is up with men these days?"

"They say that *we* don't know what we want," Lauren said. "*They* don't know what they want, either."

"So you were Chazz's beard all these years?" Barbie asked.

What a nasty way to put it, but it's true. I was Chazz's cover. "I guess I was. He only needed me around so he could appear heterosexual."

"I always wondered why his eyebrows were so much nicer than yours," Barbie said. "Now I know. Did he use bronzer, too?"

"You know," Lauren said. "He did. He used it like I used blush."

"Time out!" Randy shouted, making a T with his hands.

I may have to buy Randy a whistle, Lauren thought. *He thinks he runs this show. The man is sadly mistaken.*

"This show isn't about you and Chazz Jackson, Lauren," Randy said.

Geez! Even Randy, a no-name director, knows about Chazz's other life. "I know that, Randy," Lauren said. "But you have to admit, two dudes is a lot more interesting than the old 'man banging his secretary' cliché. That is so played out."

"The network won't allow that," Randy said.

Lauren smiled. "They won't allow two dudes? They'll let *bee-otch, cracker, orgasm, girth,* and 'going down there' go, but they won't let a little realism go?"

"You said *doing,*" Randy said.

"The original line used the word *banging,*" Lauren said. "Should I have said, 'I caught him *banging* two dudes on my couch'?"

"No." Randy shook his head and sighed heavily. "Look. This is a heterosexual show."

"But the actor playing my love interest is gay in real life," Lauren said.

"In reality, yes," Randy said, gritting his teeth. "But not *on* this show. He promises to be heterosexual the entire time he's in front of the camera. He used to be bisexual, you know."

"The world knows he's gay *now,* Randy," Lauren said. "People will only watch this show to see how a gay white man and a heterosexual black woman fall in love and have a relationship. If that isn't sick and twisted, I don't know what is."

"You're telling me," Barbie said.

"Look," Randy said. "This is a sitcom, not high Broadway drama."

"I know that," Lauren said. "But it doesn't have to lower itself to the least common denominator, does it? Barbie and I are real folks talking, that's all. This is how real folks talk to each other. Let us finish the scene, okay? I guarantee you'll like it."

"I already don't," Randy said.

"Because you haven't heard the entire scene yet," Lauren said. "What's my next line?"

"Something about breaking teeth and cutting," Barbie said.

"We're cutting the parts about breaking and cutting," Lauren said. "I don't break teeth. Say your next line."

Barbie glanced at the cue cards. "I can't say that line. White men are good in bed, at least the ones I've been with. They *do* have rhythm, and they knew how to make my booty happy."

Lauren smiled. "You rearranged those lines well."

"Thank you," Barbie said.

"Stop! Just stop!" Randy shouted. "You two are missing the point of the show. Lauren's character is supposed to discover all this about white men *during* this show. That's what makes it funny. She *has* to be clueless about white men in the beginning. She learns more and more about white men as the show progresses."

"And while the show regresses race relations in America," Lauren said. "I will not play an idiot, Randy, and that's what this script makes me into. This script is pathetic. Barbie is 'a regular Starbucks'? My ex's secretary is a 'milky white heifer'? 'Joe Bob's hair smelled like mildew and Grandma's draws'? 'At least they can always get you a cab in this city'? 'Light-skinned chocolate baby with good hair and a trust fund'?"

" 'Who can dance real good about half the time,' " Barbie added.

"How are *any* of those lines funny, Randy?" Lauren asked.

"You're taking those lines out of context," Randy said. "In context, they are *all* funny."

"In context," Lauren said, "they are all offensive."

"Our test audience thought they were hilarious," Randy said. "They fell on the floor, laughing."

"Was there an earthquake at the time?" Lauren asked.

"No," Randy said. "They thought it was funny."

"You subjected a test audience to this?" Lauren asked. "Really? Are they currently in therapy?"

"No," Randy said. "I read all the parts to them, and they left laughing."

"Who was in your test audience?" Lauren asked. "Drunk and high people who will laugh at anything?"

"It doesn't matter," Randy said. "They *loved* this scene. They were dying laughing."

"Are you sure they weren't crying out in pain?" Lauren asked. "Sometimes people in severe pain *sound* as if they're laughing."

"There is *nothing* wrong with this script," Randy said. "Nothing."

"There is nothing *right* with this script," Lauren said. "Overall, it's racist, Randy, and saying that white men hang out in grocery stores, bowling alleys, and golf courses is simply wrong. Men of all races hang out everywhere, yet you want my character to go to a flea market in Hell's Kitchen to find a man. A friend of mine tells me Hell's Kitchen isn't a pleasant place to be, much less to shop." *I'm glad that Patrick is my friend.* "To be perfectly *black* about it, Randy, that scene ain't happenin.' Where's the writer? I know I could talk some sense into the writer."

"The writer wishes to remain anonymous," Randy said.

"I can see why," Barbie said.

"You beat me to it," Lauren said. *I am beginning to like Barbie very much.* "Well, who is she—or he?"

"*She* is from LA," Randy said, "and she has been in many interracial relationships."

"I can see why," Barbie said again.

"You beat me to it again," Lauren said.

"The script is based on her experiences right here in LA," Randy said.

"LA?" Lauren said. "But the show takes place in New York City."

"Her experiences are universal," Randy said.

"In which universe?" Lauren asked. "Her experiences are not the norm. I ought to know, right? I have dated interracially for half of my life."

"The writer is an expert," Randy said. "She knows what she's talking about. I've heard her speak."

"So she speaks in stereotypes, does she?" Lauren said. "I don't think I want to meet her now."

"What stereotypes?" Randy asked.

"Where *aren't* there stereotypes?" Lauren asked. "Let's examine this scene right here. Two sisters sitting at an outdoor café see a white man and immediately begin talking about his 'hairy shovel with no meat' ass. Plenty of white men have some serious back."

"Amen," Barbie whispered. She waved at Mike.

Mike waved back.

"Then this hoochie," Lauren said. "No offense, Barbie."

"None taken, Lauren," Barbie said. "I know I'm not a hoochie."

"Then this hoochie says that *all* white men have wet skin that smells like onions," Lauren said. "They *all* eat food that falls on the floor, they *all* wear condoms, they *all* like to go down on a woman, and they often like to hang out in the meat section of the grocery store. Stop me if you *don't* hear a stereotype."

"I'm not going to argue about this with you, all right?" Randy said. "Sometimes there are stereotypes in comedy. In fact, stereotypes form the basis of most comedy. So what if there are a few stereotypes in this scene?"

"The entire scene is *based* on two ridiculous stereotypes, Randy," Lauren said. "The first is, 'Once you've had black, you'll never go back.' It's as dumb as 'Once you've had white, you'll never be right.' These sayings are foolish rhymes made up by foolish people who think they can fool the world into believing their foolishness. These are false statements. Folks are folks, man. There are no gray areas about this. We're not airing this show in the fifties. The world has moved on, and the writer needs to move on with it. How old is she?"

"That's irrelevant," Randy said.

"She's old," Lauren said.

"Yep," Barbie said. "She probably marched with Dr. King."

"Or Marcus Garvey," Lauren said.

"Or Frederick Douglass," Barbie added with a giggle.

"I still don't see what's so stereotypical," Randy said. "Isn't there *some* truth to it?"

"No," Lauren said. "And there's nothing true about 'The blacker the berry, the sweeter the juice,' either."

"Well, in my case," Barbie said, "that *is* true. I am very sweet."

"I'm sure you are, Barbie, but that's only in *her* case, Randy," Lauren said. "I can name black women out there whose juices are not and may never have been sweet." *Including my mama.*

"If they're even juicy anymore," Barbie said.

"The writer is *black,* Lauren," Randy said.

"That doesn't absolve her from being a fool," Lauren said.

"Or from being ignorant," Barbie added.

"That, too," Lauren said.

"She's *not* a fool," Randy said. "This is a *good* script."

I'm tired of arguing with him. "May I make a suggestion?"

"That's all you're making today, Lauren," Randy said.

"Film us going through the first scene the way we've

been doing it," Lauren said, "and not only show the execs what we end up with, but show the writer as well. Maybe she'll wise up and start writing a show for the twenty-first century for a change."

Randy walked away, shaking his head and parting several sound technicians, until he disappeared from view.

"He's pissed," Barbie whispered.

"Yep," Lauren said. "But so what? He has to know he has a lame script on his hands, and no amount of camping it up is going to save it."

"What do we do?" Barbie asked.

"We wait," Lauren said. "We're still on the clock, right?"

"Right," Barbie said. She pulled out a cell phone and began playing a game. "This is so addictive."

Lauren took out her own phone to get online to check her e-mail. *No signal!* She tried to find a Wi-Fi hotspot and couldn't. *Tumbleweed is so cheap. This will, however, keep actors from doing exactly what I'm trying to do when they should be working.*

A few minutes later Randy returned with an elderly light-skinned black woman who wore a frumpy yellow fisherman's hat, blue rayon slacks, and a bright orange sweater.

What shipwreck did they pull her from? Lauren wondered. *She could have been on* Gilligan's Island! *Does she own a mirror? Did wardrobe do this to her?*

"This is Annie Smith," Randy said, "And she is the writer. Lauren, go ahead. Tell her what you told me."

Lauren shrugged, and for the next fifteen minutes, she raked the woman's script over the coals, reiterating the falseness of her stereotypes and giving examples of "rearranged" lines.

"If we tone down everything that's currently *way* over the top," Lauren concluded, "we can make this into a decent show we can all be proud of."

The woman turned to Randy. "You *told* me it was a good script."

"It *is* a good script," Randy said. "It only needs a few minor adjustments."

"But *she* just said it needed *major* adjustments," Miss Smith said. "I didn't think the truth needed to be adjusted."

"Miss Smith," Lauren said, "please don't tell me you based this script on actual events in your life."

Miss Smith straightened. "I did. It's all true."

"When?" Barbie asked.

She beat me to it again! Lauren thought. *I am getting old.*

"I was much younger then, of course," Miss Smith said, "but every bit of this script is true."

She seems sincere, Lauren thought. *Maybe it's all true— just not in this century.* "Well, I suppose I could dress up like Thelma from *Good Times* and we could have a funk soundtrack."

"I get to play Penny, then," Barbie said.

"This is *not* going to be another seventies show," Randy said.

"It might as well be," Lauren said. "Miss Smith, this is a dated script. It is not relevant to today's world. I keep hearing Martha and the Vandellas and Marvin Gaye in the background. Unless we all wear bell-bottoms and platform shoes, no one will take this show seriously. No one."

Miss Smith stared at Lauren. "You think you're the shit, don't you?"

Is she serious? Of course I still am! Lauren stood, the iron chair squealing behind her. "Yes."

"You ain't *done* shit in years," Miss Smith said.

"At least I can write about *this* century just fine," Lauren said.

"Lost your man, didn't you?" Miss Smith said. "Had to get a job because your sugar daddy's gone."

"I actually lost him *to* men a long time ago," Lauren said. "What's your point?"

Miss Smith blinked. "Chazz Jackson is gay?"

So everyone doesn't *know.* Lauren nodded. "He's heavily bisexual, yes. So what was your point?"

"Damn." Miss Smith shrugged. "I never would have thought that." She smiled at Lauren. "I didn't have a point. I was just pissed off, you know. I had to fuss at someone. You understand. It's what we ladies from *my* generation do when we're angry." She turned to Randy. "Is she going to rewrite everything I write?"

"No," Randy said. "She will not."

"Yes, she will," Miss Smith said, and she sighed. "Isn't that why you asked for her to play this role, Randy? To make my script better?"

"No," Randy said. "I didn't. She wasn't my first choice, anyway."

"That Erika James is a *mess,* Randy," Miss Smith said. "You should be glad she didn't take the part."

Lauren bristled briefly but regained her composure.

"Randy, I have told you a hundred times that my script was from the late sixties and early seventies, but did you listen?" Miss Smith asked. "You didn't. I told you it was a slice-of-life piece. That's the way we talked back then. That's the way we talked about white men back then. We weren't trying to be politically correct. We were just telling it like it was. I told you it wouldn't work for a modern audience, but you're as stubborn as your father was."

Lauren looked from Miss Smith to Randy. *Wow. There's*

a strong resemblance. I only thought he was extremely tan, like every other director in Hollywood. That's his mama? Well, no wonder he's fighting for her script!

"You're . . ." Barbie whistled. "You're Randy's mother."

Miss Smith nodded. "My son is trying to break me into show business." She smiled. "The entire first season is true, and it ends with me. That's your character, Lauren. It ends with me meeting Randy's daddy and having Randy."

"You met Randy's daddy at a flea market in Hell's Kitchen," Lauren said.

"No, at a Jimi Hendrix concert, actually," Miss Smith said. "The Hollywood Bowl, nineteen sixty-eight. I take a few liberties with the truth here and there."

What is going on? Lauren thought. *How does a Hendrix concert at the Hollywood Bowl turn into a hookup at a flea market in Hell's Kitchen, New York?* "So . . . you have a full-length movie script from the late *sixties* and early *seventies* that Tumbleweed is trying to pass off as a modern sitcom."

"Essentially, yes," Randy whispered. "I've helped Mama modernize it somewhat, but it obviously still needs some work."

"*You* helped modernize it?" Lauren said. "I thought that *she* was the expert."

"I made that part up," Randy whispered.

"Wow," Lauren said, and she started to pace. "Let me get this straight. You want me to play the part of *your* mama in a modern television show that actually takes place in nineteen sixty-eight."

"Right," Randy said.

I wasn't even born yet! "And I wasn't your first choice," Lauren said.

Randy shook his head. "I originally wanted Erika James."

"Why?" Lauren asked. "She can't act."

"I know," Randy said, "but she would have stuck to the script."

Which is true. Erika James can't think for herself. "Erika James couldn't *read* the script. So why was I your second choice?"

"Well, after all that's happened," Randy said, "I assumed you'd be desperate."

"What?" Lauren yelled. "I'm not desperate."

"You're not?" Randy said. "Your agent sure made you sound desperate."

I need to talk to Todd again. "What exactly did he say?"

"Just that . . . ," Randy said. "Well, that you might not be thinking straight, because of what happened with Chazz, and that maybe, you know, you—"

"Wouldn't care or notice if the script was straight pus, as a result," Lauren interrupted.

"Um, something like that, yeah," Randy said.

"Wow," Lauren said. She sat on the edge of the table. "Miss Smith, no offense, but your son and my agent must share the same brain cell."

"I tried to get him to sell my script to Sony," Miss Smith said, "but he was so sure it was a better fit for television."

It isn't even a better fit for fiction, Lauren thought. *It isn't a better fit anywhere.* She looked at Barbie. "What do you think?"

"What do *I* think?" Barbie said. "I don't feel qualified to judge any of this."

"But you're a pro," Lauren said.

"Thank you, Miss Short," Barbie said, "but I have only ever done toilet paper and J. C. Penney commercials until this, so I don't feel qualified to give my opinion."

Lauren laughed so hard, she nearly split the size 7s.

"Am I being punked?" She looked at the camera operators. "Are you all still filming?"

"No one's filming," Randy said.

"I must be out of my mind," Lauren said. *I should have quit after the first reading.* "I, uh, I have to go now."

"Yeah," Randy said. "It's been quite a day. We'll start fresh tomorrow. We'll postpone the promos until tomorrow."

"You misunderstand me," Lauren said. "I have to go, as in go *away* from this place forever. *That* kind of go."

"Why?" Randy asked.

"Well, for one, my agent actually thought I needed to do this show," Lauren said. "I don't. I don't need to do anything at this point in my 'career.' And I definitely don't need to do this . . . bad joke. This show is like backed-up sewage waiting to be sucked down a drain." *Even Patrick would agree with me there. He'd even appreciate the analogy.* "It has a literal stench about it. I also have to go before anyone can connect me in any way to this show. You aren't seriously still thinking of putting this disaster on the air, are you?"

"We've got a full green light," Randy said. "Or we did when you signed on. I'm not so sure now."

"What?" Barbie shouted. "I gave up a Windex commercial for this show!" She jumped to her feet. "Now I bet I can't even get a mouthwash commercial. Thanks a lot, Miss Short."

"I'm the only one leaving, Barbie," Lauren said. "You could inherit my part."

"You just heard him say that if you leave, the show's off," Barbie said.

"He says he's not so sure," Lauren said. "That means—"

"I *know* what it means," Barbie interrupted. "I have a master's degree, you know. I dropped over eighty grand on my MFA at USC, I got a few commercials, and now *this* is what happens when I finally break out. Thanks a lot."

I need to control some damage here. "Randy, I think Barbie should have my part. In fact, I think Barbie could carry the entire show. She certainly has talent. And I don't think she'll need a friend to advise her at all."

"I *told* you, Randy," Miss Smith said. "I *told* you that *I* didn't have any best friend like her in sixty-eight. I was one of the few sisters testing the waters on the other side, so to speak." She turned to Lauren. "And you know what my son tells me? 'Well,' he said, 'just talk to yourself while you're writing, then.' Is that crazy or what?"

Everything about this day has been crazy, Lauren thought. *From the three-layer white makeup to these tight-ass jeans to the surreal, time-warped absurd drama going on in this room.* "Before I go, may I make one last suggestion?"

"You're really leaving?" Randy asked.

"Yes," Lauren said.

"The first time I get to direct something big, I lose the leading lady," Randy said. "I'm doomed."

"Let me make my suggestion first, okay?" Lauren turned to Mike, who was the last remaining sound technician. "Have you been recording all this from the beginning?"

Mike nodded. "I've been testing all the mikes. I heard some stomachs rumbling."

Barbie smiled. "That was me. Wanna get lunch?"

"Sure," Mike said.

"Girl," Lauren said, "I'm trying to save the show. Flirt later."

"Sorry," Barbie said.

"Call me crazy, but . . ." Lauren shook her head. "Okay, I *am* crazy." She sighed. "I want you all to listen to the entire recording of everything we said here today, because *that* is your show—including this last little exchange between Mike and Barbie."

Lauren looked at several sets of blinking eyes. "I'm serious. I don't know where you go from there, but trust me, the show we put on in here today was insanely funny. It was even smart. The comedy was intelligent. Can you imagine what just happened as the pilot for a new show? The critics won't know what to do with it at first, and then one of these critics will write something like, 'It's so out there that it's cutting edge. They're breaking new ground. They're on the cusp of a new comedic art form.'" She laughed. "And I expect to get a writing credit for it, because I just 'wrote' at least half of the pilot."

"She's right," Randy said. "It is kind of funny."

"And edgy," Barbie said.

"Yeah." Randy turned to Miss Smith. "Mama, how would you like to be on television?"

"Will I get to meet your daddy again?" Miss Smith asked.

"Sure," Randy said. "You know, we could have you narrating the show, and we could even film your first meeting with Daddy at the Hollywood Bowl, too."

Oh, now *they get a budget.* "And whatever you do, Miss Smith," Lauren said, "do not, I repeat, do *not* wear any other hat than that one. That hat will be your trademark. You'll start a new fashion trend." *Or set fashion back fifty years.*

"So I can stay?" Barbie asked.

"Of course," Randy said, drifting over to Mike. "Start it from the beginning."

As the "real" show began, Lauren slipped away, put on her own clothes in her dressing room, kicked the size 7s into a corner, and left Tumbleweed Studios.

Patrick is never going to believe what just happened.

He can't.
Even I can't believe what just happened.

When she returned to her apartment, she raced to boot up her laptop, found Patrick's e-mails among the hundreds, and read his letter with amazement, talking back to the screen.

"Oh, Brooklyn can't be that bad, can it?" she said. "It's a shame about that dolphin, though. Maybe it wanted to see Brooklyn once before it died, and Brooklyn was on its bucket list." She laughed. "A dolphin with a bucket list. I am losing my mind." She smiled. "I *was* an awesome mime. Oh, and you left me a smiley." *He has me feeling like a teenager!* "The Brooklyn Academy of Music didn't hire you because you were too manly, Patrick. Oh, and you want to decipher my lips. You think I'm young! I don't have a se-cret, and I'd never do a mud bath. *Aha!* I *was* a writer today, and the world *did* fall apart. I felt like ripping out my teeth today, too. Why hasn't anyone ever winked at you? And here you are, winking at me!"

She immediately replied.

Patrick:

Of course I don't mind if you wink at me. I may turn shy on you, though.

What am I saying? I have never been shy. I am an actress. A shy actress wouldn't make any money, right? Not that I'm making any money now.

You see, well, today I sort of . . . quit. But I have a perfectly logical explanation. I didn't intend to quit, but you will not believe what happened at Tumbleweed today. . . .

10

Patrick didn't believe it at first, but because it involved Hollywood, he eventually accepted Lauren's story.

He didn't, however, believe Lauren would be interested in hearing about his day. "'How was *my* day?' she asks," he whispered. *When's the last time anyone ever asked me that?*

Patrick wished he had an exciting story to rival Lauren's, but there wasn't much to tell. It was another typically dysfunctional day in the life of an underpaid, overworked handyman.

Lauren:

I wish I had been there to witness that . . . show? That circus? That sham? That comedy of errors? I can't wait to see it on TV, though I'll be sad not to see you in the title role. At least I might get to see your name in the writing credits.

You asked about my day. I doubt this will be funny or interesting. But since you asked . . .

I found water pooling on the floor in the basement of my own apartment building. This has happened before, and there wasn't much water. I tend to keep my own building in better shape than the others. Don't tell anyone, okay?

I checked the first-, second-, third-, and fourth-floor apartments for leaks under sinks and around toilets, showers, and tubs and didn't find any. I am a pretty decent plumber. No plumber's crack jokes please—I wear coveralls.

I went up to the roof and crawled on my hands and knees, looking for holes in the tar. Yeah, the building is that old. I found numerous small holes, most likely made by pigeons looking for bugs. I pondered the possibilities. If I let the pigeons continue to peck, I wouldn't have to spray as much insecticide this spring. But if I didn't patch the hole, I'd have a bigger hole and more water in the basement.

I patched the hole.

The end. Roll the credits. Watch the blooper reel. See the previews you skipped at the beginning of the DVD. Write a one-star review at Amazon.com.

I told you it wouldn't be that interesting. I learned, however, that sometimes problems come from the top and trickle down, and if you don't fix the top, you lose your bottom.

Or something like that.

What will you do with your free time now?

Patrick

11

This man is a trip, Lauren thought. *I wonder how old he is. He sounds . . . older. Should I bust out and ask him? He has to know how old I am already. It's only fair.*

Patrick:

I'm sure you know that I'm 38. In Hollywood years, I'm around 64, and after what happened today, I'm feeling at least 98. I don't believe the hype that "40 is the new 20." 38 is old and pushing ancient in this town, especially if you don't believe in getting body work done. Every part of my body is my own from the day I was born. I contain no additives or preservatives.

How old are you?

I know that was kind of random, and I had originally planned to trick you into telling me, but the direct approach won out. I'm just curious. If you don't want to tell me, that's okay. I'm going to guess that you're . . . 45. I hope I'm wrong! :) And if you're, say, 30, I am really, really impressed at how wise you are.

I suppose you know a lot about me already. My bio is all over the Internet, so I won't bore you with any of that. I will tell you a few things that NO ONE KNOWS ABOUT ME. Don't you feel privileged? (Sorry I shouted. It was a tension breaker. I feel better now.)

1) I have a waiting problem. Not a weight problem (yet), though those size 7s were like anacondas on my booty. Can you get a blood clot from pants that are too tight? I don't like to wait. At all. I am the most impatient person I know. I have to know things up front, and I can't stand suspense, even in the movies I made. I have to know how things end before I get there. You don't EVER want to watch a suspenseful movie with me, especially if you've already seen it. I will question you to death until you tell me what I demand to know, and after you tell me, I still have to watch it to the end to see if you were telling me the truth.

2) My favorite color is brown. Don't ask why. It just is. I used to have an old brown Porsche. I like wearing brown, too. A fashion consultant once told me not to wear brown, because of my skin tone. She said it made me look bigger than I am. I still wear brown. Again, don't ask me why. Maybe I just like my clothing to blend in with my skin.

3) I am addicted to crime shows, and not because I was briefly in one. I know it makes no sense. Why would I, who am extremely impatient, watch shows full of suspense? Why would I watch shows that usually have surprise endings if I hate to wait for the ending? Maybe I'm trying to teach myself to be patient by watching these shows.

4) One more: I am a terrible judge of character. Obviously. Thank you for not asking how I could have been so clueless about . . . you know who. I haven't even begun trying to figure that one out myself. I may never figure it out. They say love is blind, and I'm beginning to believe it. I was blind. I saw in him what I wanted to see and only what I wanted to see. The media have been kind to me so far because he has even fooled them. But when they find out the truth, I don't know what I'll say. I can plead insanity, can't I?

What will I do with my free time? I have no idea. I haven't had much time to myself for many years. I'll probably veg for a few weeks. Or months. Maybe I need to do as much nothing as I can for a while.

Who am I kidding? I can't sit still for very long. The suspense would kill me. I'll do something eventually. After I get my results back . . . and I don't want to think about that right now, so I won't.

If you have time away from your dangerous, exciting life with the pigeons, I would like to know more about you.

Don't keep me in suspense. :)

Lauren

PS: This is the first PS I have ever written in my life. Really. I'm not sure what to put here. You have put nice things here. My turn: . . . . .nice . . . . .things. :)

12

She's writing to me more quickly now, Patrick thought.
We are actually having our first real conversation.

"I'm really talking to Lauren Short now," he whispered.
"I am actually talking to Miss Lauren Short." He took several deep breaths. "This is incredible."

What and how much do I tell?
Who am I kidding? There isn't much to tell.

Lauren:

   38 isn't old. You're two years younger than I am.
40 is old. I think my knees are aging faster than the
rest of me. The left one has to be pushing 60. That's
the one that complains the most. It mostly yells,
"Stop!"

   And you certainly don't look your age at all. I'm
sure you still get carded. I know I would card you, and
then I'd accuse you of using a fake ID.

Since you shared a few secrets, I will share a few, too.

1) If anything, I am too patient. I don't mind waiting in lines, on the phone, or at work. I really have nothing better to do. I have to be patient with my tenants, too. It's part of the job. They want everything done now, now, now. I try to tell them I can only be in one place at a time, but they don't want to hear it. If you were to question me, though, I'd probably tell you everything I knew, and I promise to do it very patiently.

2) I don't have a favorite color. I like them all. Is "rainbow" a color? If it is, I like that one. I've never owned a car, but if I did, it would be brown in your honor. I've never really needed a car. I haven't had anywhere to go, you know? I don't mind taking the bus or the subway. If I had a car, I'd probably get home at a more decent hour, but there wouldn't be anywhere to park it on State Street.

3) I was addicted to your show. It's actually the last show that I had to see, so you know how much I watch TV now. I sometimes rushed through a repair just so I'd get home in time to watch you. You changed my opinion of police detectives forever with that role. And you were certainly fun to watch. I don't watch much of anything on TV these days. I don't have the time, and you're not on the screen to watch.

4) I'm not a great judge of character, either, so I would never question another person's ability to judge anyone. You think you know people, and suddenly you don't. For years they were one way, and suddenly they're another way. What happened to the way you were? I liked the way you were! They've become someone else, and they've been someone else all

along, but you've been too wrapped up in your version of them that you've become blind to their true nature. The person you thought you knew becomes unknown.

I didn't mean to get deep. I must philosophize when I'm tired, and I am very tired. The tenants were especially needy today.

Since the pigeons are safely doing whatever pigeons do at midnight, I will tell you a few things about me. I could probably tell you everything about me in a few sentences. Here goes:

My first and middle names are Irish, and they both mean "noble" either in Latin or Gaelic. A nun pointed that out to me when I was little. "You're going to be a noble man," she told me. I don't know if I'm noble or not, but I try. My last name comes from an orphanage in Italy called Ospizio degli Esposti. That makes me a twice noble orphan. Father Giovanni told me about that orphanage. I sometimes feel like an orphan.

I grew up in public housing. The Gowanus Houses were and still are a dangerous place, and I was lucky to get out of there without a juvenile record. Many of my friends are dead or in jail. That makes me a success story. Why isn't someone putting my life story on TV?

Mama was Italian, and she told me that she thought my father was Irish. She wasn't sure. I never knew him. I could say I missed him growing up, but I didn't. When you only know one thing, you think it's normal. Mama raised me alone, and it was normal. Most of my friends were raised the same way.

I finished high school. That's about all I can say. Don't ask what my GPA was. I did like English class. Then I learned a few trades (HVAC, electrical) at

Lincoln Technical Institute over in New Jersey and went to work when I was 19. I'm one of the few people I know who were bused to school after high school. I rode a bus to and from Union, New Jersey, every day for two years. I'm sure I have "diesel lung" as a result.

Patrick read over his e-mail so far. *There's a lot more to me than even I thought there was. Now, how do I end this? I can't keep rambling much longer.*

I am currently single, and to be honest, I haven't been looking.

Do I mention Natalia? He shook his head. *Maybe another time. My sad love life isn't that important compared to what Lauren is going through.*

Enjoy your "vacation." You deserve a nice, long, quiet one full of peace.

Patrick

While Patrick waited for Lauren's reply, he surfed the TV for any of Lauren's old movies. Unsuccessful, he watched his in-box for several minutes before he fell asleep, dreaming of a wisecracking detective with the smile of an angel running through an alley and wearing some seriously tight jeans.

13

Lauren slept for twelve hours, waking just after ten. She brewed a cup of coffee and stayed in bed with her laptop.

The vacation begins. . . .

She read Patrick's latest e-mail several times. *He seems so sad,* she thought. *Well, maybe not sad. Accepting. He has accepted his life. He seems sadly content. He also seems to believe "It is what it is." I'm sure there's more to him than what he wrote. This e-mail tells me that he's a humble man. It is so rare to find a man who doesn't brag about himself in every other sentence. I wish I hadn't fallen asleep on him. I mean, I didn't fall asleep on him . . . though that might be nice, too.*

I wonder what he wears under those coveralls. . . .

Patrick:

Sorry I missed your age by five years, but I can explain. I thought you were older because you have so many wise things to say. You are wise, and you are patient. Maybe you can help me wise up and be more patient. So help me now, okay? I'm waiting! Hurry up! :)

Were you really addicted to my show? If you were, you had to quit me cold turkey. Trust me, I had a hard time accepting that show's cancellation. I actually cried for a few days. I thought my career was over. Luckily, it wasn't.

How exactly was I fun to watch? I was, of course, in much better condition back then than I am now. Were you staring at any particular part of my body? Inquiring minds want to know, because the owner of this inquiring mind needs to hear a few compliments. Please?

When you were talking about "someone else," was there a specific "someone else"? I told you I liked to ask questions. Feel free to ignore this one. You haven't pried, so I shouldn't, either, right? It's none of my business.

You know I'm going to ask about this "someone else" until you tell me, so you may as well come clean. I was a TV detective once, you know. Did I mention that I am impatient? I did? Okay, then you must tell me soon, as in *now*.

Unless you don't want to . . . (she wrote shyly) :)

You have an interesting name that means something. My first name comes from the laurel plant. I changed my last name from something else, and that information isn't online, and no, I will not tell you what it was. That makes me a plant that is short. I am kind of short. How tall are you?

I grew up in Congress Heights, in D.C. It wasn't a pleasant place when I lived there, and it's not that pleasant a place now. My mama still lives there, but

my mama is the toughest woman on planet earth. She
drives a D.C. Metrobus. Trust me on her toughness.
It's in her job description.

I, too, am currently single, and to be equally
honest, I'm not looking, either. I'm working on not
being so blind first, you know? I need to go through
life with my eyes open before I open my heart to
anyone.

I do like talking to you, though, and

Her doorbell rang.

"Just a second!" she called out. She threw on a robe and
went to the door, opening it to a FedEx man.

The test results . . . Oh, dear Jesus!

He handed her a thin envelope, turned, and left.

"Thank you," she said shakily as she shut the door.

She sat on her couch. She gripped the envelope.

This envelope is really thin. That's good, isn't it?

*If it were thick, it would have information on what to do
next if I had HIV, right? The doctor would have called me
in, too. I hope he would have.*

Okay. This is it.

I mean, I hope this isn't it.

She took several deep breaths.

Please . . . please be negative.

She tore open the envelope and read the cover letter
until she found a strangely comforting word: *negative.*

It's negative.

She took a deep breath, held it, and exhaled slowly.

I'm not dying.

It's negative, and I'm positively happy.

I don't have HIV.

I'm going to live.

She jumped up and down on the couch for several minutes, before flying back to her laptop and deleting the previous line.

> My HIV test results are negative!!!

She wiggled her fingers above the keyboard.
And I'm telling Patrick this because . . .
She sighed and shook her head.
That is so random. I tell him I'm not looking for anyone, and then I tell him, "Hey, Patrick, I'm not dying of HIV." I want him to know, don't I? This is cause for rejoicing, and he's the only one I can share it with. He took the trouble to light a candle for me. I have to tell him something.
She deleted the previous sentence.

> I have good news! My HIV test results are negative. I wanted you to know, and you're the only one I'll probably ever tell. I can truly enjoy my vacation now. Thank you for praying for me. I'm sure your prayers and lighting that candle did the trick.

Her cell phone buzzed.
Will you quit interrupting? I'm talking to my friend.
"Hello?"
"Lauren, I can't believe you quit the show already!"
"Hi, Todd," Lauren said.
"What am I going to do with you?" Todd asked.
"Dude, you put me on the new *Twilight Zone,*" Lauren said, "only this version had rayon pants and a yellow hat."
"What?"
He wouldn't understand even if I explained it in detail.
"I will not be part of that fiasco."

"Do you know how hard it will be for me to find you work now?" Todd asked. "If I can't get you onto a pilot, how can I get you onto an established show like *Saturday Night Live* or even a single episode of *Law and Order?*"

"I don't know, but stop trying so hard," Lauren said. "I am on vacation." *That sounds so good to my ears! Just the sound of that word fills me with elation and relaxation.*

"What do I say when people ask about you?" Todd asked. "What do I do when, miracle of miracles, someone wants you in their next project, maybe even a movie?"

"Tell them I'm on vacation," Lauren said. "People take vacations on occasion, right? I may even make it permanent. I don't know."

"I can't tell them that," Todd said. "After what you've been through, you need to get back to work, not go on vacation."

"After what I've been through," she said, eyeing the test results, "I *deserve* a vacation."

"Okay, okay," Todd said. "I'll tell them you're on hiatus. With all that's happened with Chazz, they'll understand."

"Whatever, Todd," Lauren said. *Now, go away. I'm talking to my handyman.*

"What do you expect me to do for you while you're on hiatus?" Todd asked.

"Just keep my name in front of *SNL*," Lauren said. "That's all." *And if* SNL *signs me, maybe I can meet this Patrick Alan Esposito in New York before or after the show and long into the night.* "Now, don't call me again unless you hear from *Saturday Night Live*. Bye." She hung up.

She reread Patrick's e-mail before continuing her reply.

Patrick, have you ever been in love?

I am being completely random today. I go from "No HIV" to "Have you ever been in love?" She shrugged. This is who I am going to be from now on! I have a new lease on life, and I intend to be as random as possible.

I mean, have you ever been truly, head-over-heels, my heart's on fire, I can't think straight, when I close my eyes, I see my lover in love? I'm only asking because I don't think I have and I want to know what it feels like. Your very first e-mail kind of hinted that maybe you've had this kind of love before. If it's something you can talk about, please do.

I know this is going to sound cliché, but I want to know what love is. The last "man" (I use that term very loosely) only loved himself and other men. He only kept me around for appearances. I want to know what real love is.

Help a sister out.

Lauren "The Short Plant" Short

PS: Thank you! :)

14

Mrs. Moczydlowska called Patrick at five a.m., claiming that she heard a skittering sound behind the sink in her kitchen.

"*Chuh-chuh-chuh-chuh* all night long," she said. "*Chuh-chuh-chuh-chuh* until I scream. It is rats!"

Patrick sat up. *Great. Mrs. Moczydlowska is being afflicted by the Norway rat "chuh-chuh," and they've been dancing the "chuh-chuh" all night behind her walls. It couldn't have happened to a nicer woman.*

"Have you seen any?" Patrick asked as he wiped crust from his eyes.

"I hear them all night," she said. "I do not have to see them to know they are there. *Chuh-chuh-chuh-chuh.* It is driving me crazy."

"It's that time of year," Patrick said. "The cold weather pushes them inside, and—"

"You *do* something," she interrupted. "No rats, or I call your boss."

When Patrick arrived half an hour later, he looked

around Mrs. Moczydlowska's kitchen at the scattering of crumbs on the counter, the kitchen table, and the floor. He knew Mrs. Moczydlowska couldn't reach her broom into every corner or reach every crumb on the counter with her stubby arms, but she had to have seen them.

If I didn't know better, he thought, *I'd think she was* leaving *crumbs so rats would come . . . so that I'd have to come visit her.*

He knew that Norway rats were indestructible, and once they had warmth and a food source, they were hard to evict. Norway rats were able to drop fifty feet to the ground without dying, jump four feet into the air to avoid capture, and squeeze through half-inch openings. They could also defeat any barrier he set up, be it wood, aluminum, bricks, cinder blocks, or lead sheeting.

"We have had this conversation before," Patrick said. "If you keep your kitchen spotless, no crumbs anywhere, that will keep them—"

"I do not want to *keep* them," Mrs. Moczydlowska interrupted. "I want to *kill* them."

"Yes, but if you don't give them a reason—"

"I keep a clean kitchen!" she interrupted.

"You do. You really do," Patrick said. "But it doesn't take much to attract a—"

"You say I do not keep a clean kitchen?" she interrupted.

"No," Patrick said. "You keep a clean kitchen, but rats don't know that. They're only looking for food and warmth, and your kitchen provides both."

"I cook all day," she said.

For whom? Patrick thought. *She lives alone.*

"There is no law against this," she said. "There is law against the rats."

"This is the warmest room in your apartment," Patrick said. "They are naturally going to be drawn—"

"Kill them all, or I call your boss," she interrupted.

I can't win. "I'll set out some traps," Patrick said.

"Use the poison," Mrs. Moczydlowska said.

"I don't want to poison them," Patrick said. "They could die within your walls and really stink up the place."

"I do not care," she said. "I do not want to hear the *chuh-chuh-chuh-chuh* anymore, okay?"

Patrick spent the next two hours under and around Mrs. Moczydlowska's kitchen sink, finding and filling the smaller gaps with caulk and wood putty and covering the larger holes with wire mesh.

"You are not killing them," she said.

"I first have to make sure they can't get in," Patrick said. "You don't want rats swarming around your legs, do you?"

"There is a swarm inside my walls?" she asked.

Wrong word choice. "There isn't a swarm, but there could be if I don't seal every possible entry point." He wiped sweat from his forehead and noticed the open oven. "Are you cooking anything now?"

"No," she said.

"But your oven's on," Patrick said.

"It stays on," she said. "The heater is no good. It does not work. It has never worked."

I just "fixed" it two days ago, and there was nothing wrong with it then. "I'll check your thermostat again."

He already knew what he would find. The thermostat was set for eighty degrees, and the sweat dripping down the back of his legs proved it. "The thermostat is working fine."

"Then why is it so cold?" she asked. "I feel drafts all the time."

Patrick checked her windows. "Your windows are

sealed tight, Mrs. Moczydlowska. Look, if you want the rats to go away, you have to turn off your oven and turn down your thermostat to something like sixty-eight at night."

"You want me to freeze to death," she said.

"I don't want that," Patrick said.

"You will find me one day all stiff and blue," she said.

He collected his tools. "Mrs. Moczydlowska, you will outlive us all." He started for the door.

"Where are you going?" she asked, shuffling rapidly behind him.

And now we get to dance. He turned and smiled. "I am going to set a few traps in the basement."

"You must . . . you must check my bathroom before you go," she said.

"What's wrong in there?" Patrick asked.

"There are water bubbles on the handles," she said.

No doubt from the condensation in this sauna of an apartment.

"And the lever gets stuck," she said.

There's nothing wrong with the lever.

"And the drain is slow, so slow," she said. "It takes two minutes to go down."

He nodded. "Could I come back and fix all that tomorrow?"

Mrs. Moczydlowska almost smiled. "Yes. You must come back tomorrow. You must fix. Or I call your boss."

"I will see you tomorrow, then." He opened the door. "Turn off your oven tonight, okay?"

"This *once* I will do," she said. "But if I freeze to death, it is on your head."

"Use lots of blankets instead," he said. "Good-bye."

"Good-bye," she said. "Good-bye, Patrick."

While he checked, emptied, and reset several traps in the

basement, he heard Mrs. Moczydlowska's creaking floor-
boards above him. *I wish she had someone else to check up
on her, and I wish she wouldn't feel she had to make up
things for me to do. I'd visit her if she asked me to. She's no
worse than any other tenant. She just doesn't want me to
know she's scared and lonely. In a way, this job only makes
sense to me because of the Mrs. Moczydlowskas of the
world. As much as she complains, in her own bitter way,
she is happy to see me.*

Before going home, he looked for *Feel the Love,* Lauren's first movie, at Video Free Brooklyn on Smith Street.
He had rented it a long time ago, and he was surprised to
find it wedged tightly between *Fast & Furious 6* and *Feel
the Noise.* At the counter, he showed the owner an ancient
rental card.

"You haven't been in here in a while," he said. "The previous owners used this card. Let me get you a new one. I'll
need to see a credit card."

"I, um, no longer have one," Patrick said. *I haven't had
a credit card since Natalia, and I only got one to impress
her. I didn't tell Natalia it only had a five-hundred-dollar
limit.*

"A debit card will do," the man said.

"I'm old school," Patrick said. "I write checks."

"I don't take checks," the man said.

"I'd actually like to buy this if I can." Patrick handed
him the DVD.

The owner looked at the case. "This is a classic. Surprised we still have it." He opened the case. "It's got a few
scratches. I'll let you have it for ten even."

"Done," Patrick said. He handed the man a ten.

"It's a shame about her and Chazz Jackson, huh?" the
owner said.

"Yeah." *No it isn't! I want so badly to tell this guy, this stranger, that I am talking to Lauren Short and that I'm about to go home to talk to her all night . . . sort of.*

"Funny how life sometimes happens," the owner said. "One second you have it all, and the next second you don't."

"Right." *And because Lauren lost it all, she found me. That doesn't sound right.*

"She'll land on her feet, though," the owner said. "She's an old pro. I can't wait to see her in what she does next. That woman is a true actress."

"You may have to wait a long time," Patrick said. "She just dropped out of a pilot for a sitcom."

"She did?" the owner said. "I didn't hear or read about that. How do you know?"

I'm "talking" to her. "I must have read it somewhere," Patrick said. *Which is true.* "Stuff happens, you know?" Patrick said. *And I've been waiting a long time for my life to happen, and it's all happening because I wrote an e-mail to an angel who wrote back.* "If you get a copy of *I Got This,* hold on to it for me, okay?"

"She was really sexy in that one," the owner said. "I may keep that one for myself."

After a quick shower and after watching a few minutes of Lauren performing in *Feel the Love* with the sound turned down, he read Lauren's most recent e-mail. After rejoicing over her test results, he tried to imagine her voice reading the e-mail to him.

I know she's relieved, but why am I so relieved? I mean, aside from knowing she doesn't have an incurable disease. It isn't as if she and I are ever going to—

He paused the DVD when the screen filled with a close-up of Lauren laughing. *I would love to see her laugh like that in person. My God, she is so beautiful. I may leave her like that all night. I don't care if the image gets burned into my TV screen.*

He started his reply.

Lauren:

   You said I sounded 45. I still don't know how I feel about that. I feel 65 some days. Today, though, I feel younger because of your great news. I've always believed that bad things happened to good people for a reason and that good things eventually happened to good people. You're the proof.

   I'm watching you right now in Feel the Love. You are really fun to watch. I have you paused on my TV while you're laughing in the second scene. You have a lot of teeth. I've counted at least 48 so far.

   I hope you're laughing now.

   I wish I had your grace. I know that sounds weird, but I'm not the smoothest person in the world. I bang into things. I don't mean to. I just do. I've gone through three tool bags from banging them around so much, and I find bruises on my legs and arms nearly every morning. You're fluid, smooth, and natural. There's something poetic in your every gesture. Even your hands speak. You may have a little Italian in you.

   I was engaged once, too. Her name was Natalia, an Italian girl from Carroll Gardens. Natalia was a nice girl, quiet, kind of shy. After she returned the ring (she didn't throw it into the East River or the Hudson, and it's probably still at the pawnshop), I had trouble speaking her name, too. At first. I can write her name now.

   I guess you could say that Natalia and I were high school sweethearts. She was my first real girlfriend.

She worked at Casa Rosa and then at Fragole, first as a waitress and then as a cook. Natalia could really cook. In fact, she cooked so well, she left this part of Brooklyn and me entirely.

She told me I wasn't part of her "plan," but she never told me her plan while we were together. Her plan was to marry a rich guy and start her own restaurant, and she did both, and in that order. She has a thriving restaurant in Bensonhurst, a rich husband, and two kids. She probably doesn't even have to work.

I run into her every now and then during mass at St. Agnes. We speak, but it's still awkward. There's more, but I don't want to depress you, and she broke it off nearly twenty years ago. Life must go on, right?

Guess what? We have something else in common. We're both not looking. If you're up to it, maybe we can "not look" together. I may be pushing 45, but my eyes are still young and strong. Maybe we can find what we're looking for together.

I think the love you described in your e-mail only exists in movies and romance novels, not that I have ever read any. I never felt that kind of love with Natalia. We weren't all that romantic, though I wanted to be. I didn't really know how to be romantic. I guess you could say we were kind of cool and calm. Maybe that's how I got to be so patient. Remember Talia Shire in the first Rocky? Make her taller and give her longer hair, and that's Natalia. I used to call her Adrian. She never called me Rocky.

You thanked me for some reason, and I don't know what for. I should be thanking you for giving me someone to come home to. You are definitely keeping me warm these cold November nights. Thank you.

I've now frozen Feel the Love at the face you made after your character's first kiss. You couldn't be acting. You have such an angelic look of wonder on your face. That had to be real.

Thank you for these "real" conversations.

Patrick

PS: Is freezing your face on my TV while I'm writing to you creepy? I hope not. If it is, please tell me.

15

Lauren read Patrick's e-mail and felt her cheeks warming.

Thinking she had an "angelic look of wonder" on her face, she took her laptop into the bathroom and looked at herself in the mirror. *There's something bright there,* she thought. *Whatever it is has faded my crow's-feet. Happiness does wonders for crow's-feet. I hereby resolve to be happy from now on. Crows, be gone!*

She swept into her bedroom, shot her legs under the covers, and started to type.

Patrick:

No, it's not creepy to "watch" me as you write to me. It's flattering. I admit I did laugh at the idea, though. And trust me on that kiss—it wasn't that great. We had to do five takes. The face you think is angelic is actually relieved that the scene is over. The boy couldn't kiss. Not . . . one . . . bit. I may have been his first kiss for real.

I was thanking you because you are keeping me sane. You're helping me make sense of things. You have an uncanny ability to wake me up and calm me down at the same time. That is a rare gift, and I like it. And it makes sense for you to watch Feel the Love. Thank you for choosing that one. You have good taste.

You think I have grace, but I really don't. At . . . all. I have to work at it. You need to watch some of my blooper reels. I managed to trip over wires and cords, even though they were all clearly marked and taped down. I even tripped over things that weren't there. I fell through doorways. I banged my shins on stairs. I walked into walls. I was a bruise by the time shooting was through. They used to joke that I needed a stunt double to walk across a room. Yeah, I was that clumsy. I'm not as clumsy now, because I'm getting older and move more slowly. And on my vacation, I intend to stay in bed, where I'm safe, warm, and cushioned.

I think I talk so much with my hands because if I do fall, they'll be ready to break my fall. I'm glad you like my hand gestures. Believe it or not, I learned to use my hands from watching TV newspeople, especially the ones who did the weather. There weren't any Italians in my neighborhood, so I had to improvise. Thank you for thinking I'm smooth and natural, though. It's nice to hear compliments, even if the creepy Brooklyn man making them is freezing my face on his TV in the middle of a laugh, smile, or kiss. (Just kidding . . .)

I have a few choice things to say about Natalia, but I better not. Like you said, that was a long time ago, and life must go on.

Oh, what the heck. She didn't deserve you. There, I've said my piece. And if I ever had to choose who to go not looking for a relationship with, it would be you.

That made no sense! Or did it?

Heart-to-heart time, and you must never reveal any of this to anyone, especially Entertainment Tonight.

I thought I was in love with Chazz. There, I wrote his stupid name. He was born Charles. He doesn't even look like a Charles. And his middle name is Ransome. Some screwy family name. Charles Ransome Jackson. He once told me he was going to name his first son Ransome. I guess his sexual preferences are holding Ransome for ransom, huh? (That was bad. Sorry.)

Chazz and I were good together (at first), and we had the same goals, ambitions, and plans (at first). We were supposed to star in a series of movies and become the "it" couple in Hollywood, but that didn't happen, mainly because he didn't want it to happen. He blew up and became "Action Jackson" after making *Killer Squad*. I swear, that script only had three pages of dialogue. What a farce! He told me once that he only actually appeared in one-third of the action scenes in that movie. His stunt double should have been paid a lot more than he was.

And then I became his "actress girlfriend" and eventually his "former actress girlfriend" and "longtime girlfriend" and eventually his "longtime fiancée." We weren't the "it" couple he promised we'd be. In every picture in magazines and online it was him featured front and center with me attached to his arm. Sometimes they cropped me out entirely. I had nice hands, though. They're still kind of sexy.

   Looking back, I realize that Chazz and I weren't
a couple. I know I will cringe the next time I see a
picture of us, because I will see me holding on to him
while he searches for another camera to take his
picture—or for another man to take off his pants.

   I didn't want to bring any of this up tonight, but I
did. I'm sorry if I'm depressing you. I have no right. It's
over. I need to let it die. I will write no more about
Chazz.

   And the thought of not writing about Chazz makes
me very happy. :)

   I don't know how to end this e-mail, so . . . bye.

Lauren

PS: Write back. Please. I'm all alone, with nothing to
do all night . . . and all day . . . and all night . . . and
all day . . . and . . . you get the picture. . . . ;)

16

"He was a fool," Patrick whispered after reading Lauren's postscript. "And you don't have to say please."
I couldn't stop writing to you even if I wanted to.

Lauren:

    "Chazz, the Spazz" was a fool. Any man who would even think of hurting you is a fool. Any man who takes you for granted is a fool. Any man who would even think of making you cry is a fool. Any man who jeopardized your life is a fool—and a coward.

    If I ever had the chance to speak to him, I'd say, "What the #!%! were you thinking, Chucky? You have to be the dumbest #!%! on earth! Lauren Short is an angel. Are you trying to send yourself straight to hell?"

    I would never hurt you, take you for granted, make you cry, or jeopardize your life. I am not a fool or a coward. I just wanted you to know that since we're "not looking" together and you have to trust your

traveling companion. I trust you completely, and I truly
enjoy your company.

I have just now decided to memorize Feel the
Love. Not your parts, of course. All the other parts.
That way we can "talk."

That is creepy, isn't it?

Patrick knew it was creepy, but he left it in the e-mail.
*Why aren't I talking to her on the phone? Why don't I ask
for her phone number? But if we're not looking for new relationships, we shouldn't be exchanging phone numbers,
right? Besides, if I say something creepy by mistake on the
phone, I can't take it back. There's no backspace button on
a phone.*

I just had a discussion with myself. I sometimes do
this. It is an occupational hazard of those who are 40,
work alone, and live alone. I won the argument. I
always do.

I was seriously considering removing all references
to memorizing Feel the Love. But then I told myself
that perhaps Lauren might think it was sweet.

Please think it is sweet.

I really like "talking" to you.

Patrick
PS: I, too, am all alone, with nothing to do all night
<frown>. . . . But I do have plenty to do all day. But
tomorrow night I'll have nothing to do <frown>. . . . But I'll
have plenty to do the day after tomorrow. . . . It's a
vicious cycle.

17

He is talking to my younger self by memorizing a movie, Lauren thought. *Hmm. Is that creepy, strange, or sweet? Let's just call it "sweetly strange." And what he said about Chucky . . . He's completely right. Chucky was and is a coward.*

But what does it say about me if I was about to marry that coward?

Patrick:

I talk to myself all the time, too. I usually ignore most of what I say to myself. It's better that way. I think I'd rather listen to you, if that's all right. You have so many good things to say. I even sometimes talk to you. Why won't you answer? Can't you hear me shouting? :)

I am so glad you're looking at Feel the Love and not at some of my other movies. I loved doing that one. That script was tight. That cast was stellar. They took me in when I was a rookie and helped me

shine. I wish I looked like that again. I had abs and a
flat stomach then. I had proportion, you know?

Lauren was relieved that Patrick hadn't picked *I Got
This,* the only movie in which she bared an intimate part of
her body. *It was only the* side *of* one *breast. You couldn't
even see the nipple, and yet fourteen years later my mama
still won't talk to me for more than a few seconds because
of it. "Oh, you've gone Hollywood now," she told me.
"What's next? Playboy? Penthouse?" That was fourteen
years ago! Get over it, Mama!*

Lauren relaxed her fingers.
Should I mention this problem to Patrick?

> Have you seen I Got This? If you haven't, there's
> this one scene where part of my breast is visible.
> Because of that one scene, my mama won't talk to
> me much anymore. She told me I had "gone
> Hollywood." What do you think?
>
> Lauren
>
> PS: About my mama, not about my breast. Unless
> you have an opinion . . . ;) Remember, I'm all alone,
> with nothing to do all night . . . and all day . . . and all
> night . . . and all day . . . and all night. . . . You still get
> the picture. . . .

Well, look at me fishing for another compliment, Lauren
thought.
She hit the SEND button. She bit her lip.
*I just asked a man I have never met for his opinion
about my problems with Mama and part of a breast I flashed*

*in a movie nearly fourteen years ago. I hope he focuses on
my problems with my mama. But what if he doesn't?*

She looked down at her breasts. *You two still look good.
The rest of me has sagged, but you two . . .*

She giggled.

I'm talking to my breasts. What is happening to me?

I do think I'm getting happy.

This man is making me happy to be alive again.

I am *happy to be alive again.*

18

Patrick could barely breathe. He remembered the scene. How could he ever forget it? How could any man with a pulse ever forget it? Fourteen years later even Google still had a screen shot of her partial breast a few rows down from the top on her first search page.

That is one sexy almost breast, he thought. *Should I give her my opinion on it? I shouldn't. That's the gentlemanly thing to do, but it's not the honest thing to do. She wouldn't have asked unless she wanted to know* exactly *what I thought.*

He made a decision. He would discuss Lauren's breast and ignore Lauren's mother. *Because if I talk about her breast, it will be extremely creepy to discuss her mother afterward.*

Lauren:

You have asked for my opinion on your almost breast, and I am happy to comply.

It is a flawless almost breast. I truly believe it is the

most flawless almost breast in cinematic history. I have watched a lot of movies in my life, and I have never seen such a flawless almost breast. Trust me, I have seen almost breasts in hundreds of movies, and none of them could compare to yours. If almost breasts could receive awards, your almost breast would win all of them. I am sure it would make the Almost Breast Hall of Fame. When God made it, He smiled.

It has been my honor to talk about your almost breast. I have tears in my eyes whenever I think about it. I am most certain that the other breast matches the almost breast flawlessly. Thank you for having them. Thank you for sharing that almost breast with the world.

Oh, God, I hope she laughs at that. He wiped his hands on the bedspread. *I had better continue with other parts of her body. Otherwise, she'll think I'm fixated.*

You also have sensational eyes. I don't know if they're flawless. I only have a 35-inch TV. :~) They look flawless. And the rest of you is equally flawless.

I need to make something flawlessly clear. I am *not* stalking you. I have long legs, but they aren't long enough to stalk you from 3,000 miles away.

I will, however, secure a copy of I Got This and watch the almost breast scene in slow motion. I hope it's on Blu-ray. The picture is so much clearer in Blu-ray. I want to see every square millimeter of your almost breast. I may even freeze your almost breast on my TV.

If I have embarrassed you, that was my intent . . . because you kind of embarrassed me when you

asked for my opinion about your breast. Lauren, I
think you're . . .

   So, do you want to make more movies like that
one? Please?

Patrick

19

He is such a flirt! Lauren thought. *I have missed a real man flirting with me.*

She wiped her hands on her thighs.

And look at me, getting all hot and bothered. I have to flirt back now. It's only fair.

Patrick:

You really know how to keep a girl hanging. And yes, I laughed my booty off. Well, not all of it. I'm afraid I'm stuck with most of this booty of mine for the rest of my life.

You think my almost breast is flawless! Thank you, thank you! Where will I put all the awards? I've been waiting a long time to do an encore performance with the other breast. She's jealous. She didn't make the final cut of that movie.

But *please* don't buy or rent I Got This. It doesn't come in Blu-ray, by the way. I checked (sigh). Your loss . . . :)

And seriously, what's flawless about the rest of me? I have plenty of flaws, so it will be a short list.

Now, Patrick Alan Esposito, you must finish the following phrase, or I will stalk you until the day you die, and no restraining order will keep me from harming you: "Lauren, I think you're . . ."

Go ahead. Finish the phrase. Now.

Lauren

PS: Since I have so much time on my hands right now, I might be persuaded to make a special movie, but only for you, provided your answers to the above are acceptable . . . and they embarrass me some more. ;)

20

The time between e-mails had been shrinking to mere minutes, and Patrick's eyes shrank to little dots.

A special movie . . . for me?
My answers had better be good, then.

Lauren:

   I think you're flawless.

   Really.

   Here's my list. I'll start at the top of your flawless body and work my way down. Forgive me if I get stuck in parts.

   Your hair is flawless because it's yours and it matches your eyebrows perfectly. I like natural hair, and yours seems especially soft.

   Your eyes are flawless because they have so much life in them. They also match mine. That doesn't make MY eyes flawless. I'm just saying that our eyes match.

Your nose is flawless because . . . it is. What do you say about a nose? It's cute, and as far as I can tell from all your pictures online, you've had your nose your entire life.

Your lips are flawless because they're kissable. If I go into any more detail here, I will offend you. I imagine that they are soft and tasty and smooth.

Your cheeks are flawless because they are so smooth and smiling. You have the rare ability to smile with your cheeks, even when you're frowning. You would definitely be hard to read. Is she happy or sad or both? Or neither? You are a woman of mystery.

Your neck is flawless because it holds up your flawless head. I know that was lame. I'm sure your neck is as soft as your cheeks.

I should probably stop there. For now. If I haven't earned a special movie, I will continue.

Patrick

PS: I hope I didn't offend you.

21

Patrick:

I was just getting interested, and then you kind of said, "Tune in next week. . . ." The suspense is killing me!

Not really. I know you'll tell me what I need to know. I am learning patience. I also know you will tell me because I will hound you to the ends of the earth if you don't.

You didn't offend me. You made my day, my week, my month, and my year. I'm 29+9 now and losing my looks. You made me feel beautiful again. Thank you. I really mean that.

You need to send me a picture of yourself. Or tell me what you look like at least. It's only fair, right? You aren't exactly Google-able. (It's a new word. Deal with it.) Yes, I Googled you, and no, you didn't show up. Some Boston Bruins hockey player named Phil Esposito appeared first, and that dude looked seriously like Rocky's brother. Do you look like that?

As much as I appreciate your compliments, however, I do think you need a reality check where my body is concerned. Yes, my hair is my own, but the only reason it matches my eyebrows is something called dye. I buy Dark and Lovely Eboné Brown in bulk.

You're right about my eyes, of course, and that does mean that your eyes are flawless, too.

My nose is my own. Sometimes I like it, and sometimes I tolerate it. I haven't been kissed in a long time. Therefore, my lips must not be that kissable, but thanks for the thought. I never looked that way at my cheeks before. Good looking out. Maybe my cheeks have been my claim to fame all this time. I do smile even when I frown. My neck is soft, but it's starting to grow little wrinkle rings. The rest of me used to be toned all the time, but I've kind of let myself go, especially this past week. I hope you understand why. I'm not going soft—I'm getting soft. There is a difference.

Alas, kind sir, you have not earned a special movie yet. <sigh> You must continue. You stopped at my neck. You have about 90% more of me to go. . . . :)

Lauren

PS: Please be kind. And if you can't be kind, be specific. ;)

22

Continue, be kind, and tell her exactly what she looks like. Piece of cake.

He Googled the latest batch of Lauren's pictures and compared them to the woman on the screen.

Lauren does not age. How is that possible? She could be twenty.

Lauren:

I will continue, but you must promise not to dispute what I write. I have excellent eyesight, and what I see is flawless. My eyes do not lie.

Your . . . torso . . . he wrote safely . . . is flawless because it is shapely in all the right places. Some places are shapelier than others. You have a nice silhouette. Your curves are especially curvy, especially in the hip, back, and thigh area. In short, you have a nice shape.

Your legs are flawless, shapely, smooth, and sexy. Overall, you are flawlessly flawless. I could look at you all day and all night and during sunrises and sunsets, too. I could look at you 24-7, and I wouldn't curse the clock, because time would stand still.

I am not handsome. At least I don't think I am. I am ordinary. I don't have a picture to scan or send to you. I don't think I look like anyone famous, or I'd tell you. I looked at Phil Esposito. There is a faint resemblance, but only in the scars on his hands.

I'm 6-2 if I stand up straight, and I weigh around 220. I have brown eyes, dark brown, almost black hair, and all my teeth, but I still have a couple dozen less than you do. I have 32. This is the first time I have ever counted my teeth.

I shave about once a week, usually before mass, if the tenants will leave me alone long enough for me to go. I'm in great shape from walking up and down stairs and crawling on roofs. My hands are calloused and dry and cut and scarred, and my nose is what you might expect from an Italian. I used to have some freckles, but not anymore.

How important is that picture? If I had a phone with a camera, I could send you any kind of picture you wanted. Salthead provided me with an old-school phone that only makes phone calls and sends and receives texts. My employer is cheap, and so am I, I guess.

I know there's a joke about being cheap but not easy. . . . I may actually be both where you're concerned. . . . ;~)

I hope I have earned at least a sneak preview of that movie. . . .

Patrick

PS: My mama once said I looked like Bruce Springsteen, but she was drunk most of the time.

23

L auren smiled broadly.
A mother wouldn't lie about what her son looked like, would she? Lauren thought.

She Googled "Bruce Springsteen at 40" and smiled some more. *Bruce Springsteen was kind of hot when he was forty. He's still kind of hot. So my handyman looks like the Boss, has big, strong hands, goes to church often, works sixteen-hour days, and is kind and humble. He says he's ordinary, and that makes him extraordinary. He's a noble orphan.*

I feel like an orphan sometimes. I should call Mama. The last time I did, she listened to my voice for five whole seconds before hanging up. One freaking side of one breast! She should have been proud! Instead, she said I shamed my daddy, who died when I was fifteen. He would have been proud of what he helped make.

And it was only an almost breast.

She looked at her torso. *He still thinks I have a nice body. He doesn't see what I see in the mirror. Things have fallen. Parts have slipped. Gravity is working. What was once tight now wobbles. Parts of me look like Jell-O. Hair grows where it shouldn't, and doesn't grow where it used to. And yet he's obviously interested in my body, with those honest eyes of his.*

And it excites me so much!

Patrick:

I need a picture of you so I can have a visual of you when I read your letters. You're looking at me on your TV, right? I need something to look at, too, okay? It's only fair. I need to see you so my imagination will calm down. So far you're Bruce Springsteen playing a guitar with Phil Esposito's scarred hands.

It's okay if you don't want to share a picture of yourself. You're my friend. It doesn't matter to me what you look like. Your words are beautiful. That makes you beautiful. You're a beautiful man, and it has been my privilege to get your e-mails.

And you make me feel beautiful. You said I have "the three s's"! I don't know if I'm shapely, smooth, and sexy or not, because I'm all alone . . . all day and all night. All this possible shapeliness, smoothness, and sexiness is going to waste. What should we do about that?

I, too, shave about once a week.

Just kidding.

But you haven't earned that movie yet. Sorry. You didn't go into enough detail. I asked you to be specific. The word torso is vague. I know you can do better than that. Shape is vague, too, and I know you can do better than *nice*.

Look at the time! It has to be after 2 AM in Brooklyn. I'm sure you're tired. I should let you go.

I don't want to, but one of us has to work in the morning, while the other one lounges around in bed all day . . . and all night . . . and all day. . . .

Sweet dreams.

Lauren

PS: You're 6-2 and 220. I'm 5-5 and 130ish. Don't ask for the specific number. My scale and I aren't on speaking terms. Because of our height difference, my forehead would come up to your chin. I'd be staring at your Adam's apple.

She turned out the lights but kept her laptop open after she sent her message. In moments, Patrick replied.

Lauren:

I am tired, but not of our conversation. You're easy to talk to. I promise to continue my description of your flawless body soon.

"See" you tomorrow.

Good night, Lauren.

Patrick

PS: Soon is *now*! Your breasts look firm and soft, your stomach looks caressable—is that a word?—and your booty looks like the finest sculpture, but my dreams would still be sweet and hot if I could only see your eyes.

"Aww," Lauren said. "That's so sweet."

I like him.

She wanted to write him back, but he had already said good night.

"Good night, Patrick," she whispered.

Caressable *isn't a word, but it should be. He says that I'm kissable and caressable. Someone over at* Webster's *needs to get on the job.*

And he looks at my booty as if it's fine art.

She went to the bathroom and posed.

He's right. My booty is fine art.

Patrick has excellent eyesight.

Oh, except for that spot there.

Mmm. It's kind of a divot.

I need to get some exercise.

But not now.

I'm on vacation. . . .

24

Before Patrick brushed his teeth in the morning, he checked his e-mail and found an empty in-box.

It was late. She was tired. It's cool.

He frowned.

Or I offended her with my description of her "torso." I hope I didn't. She asked for more specifics, and I gave them. Maybe I gave too many? Maybe I was too specific.

Although he had slept for only three hours, he felt more alive than he had in years because she had called him beautiful.

I have never been called beautiful before. She doesn't even know what I look like. I might have looked like Springsteen when he was young, but I don't look like him now. How can she say that I'm beautiful?

Wait a second.

She said my words *were beautiful and that I must be beautiful by extension.*

Or something like that.

He wrote her a quick message.

Lauren:

    Rise and shine! It's only 5 AM here in chilly (22 and cloudy) Brooklyn, so I imagine you'll be up in about . . . ten hours.

    You have my permission to be completely lazy today, not that you need my permission. Because you do everything well, I know you will do nothing well, as well. <There are too many wells in that sentence. Sorry.>

    Good morning or afternoon, as the case may be.

Patrick

PS: I hope I didn't offend you with my description of your torso. If I did, I'm sorry. I meant it as a compliment. If I didn't offend you, well . . . good.

He sent the message, brushed his teeth, ignored his beard, showered, and put on long johns under his coveralls. He smiled. Putting on his coveralls wasn't as much of a chore and a bore, and tying his boots wasn't as unfulfilling.

Because someone thinks I'm beautiful.

I mean, because someone thinks my words are beautiful.

He grabbed his tool bag and headed toward the door. He looked back at his laptop.

I could carry my laptop around with me today. Wi-Fi signals are everywhere these days, and many of my tenants have Wi-Fi, and that way I could check to see . . . He sighed. *Whether I offended Lauren or not. Do I want to wait until this evening? Can I wait that long?*

He took his laptop. Its case barely fit into his tool bag.

Because of the sudden cold snap, he started immediately for the apartment building on Baltic, hoping to get there before his phone rang.

The pipes in that building can't handle major drops in temperature, he thought. *They might even be frozen solid.*

His phone rang.

Like clockwork. "I'm on my way," he said immediately when he answered.

"I haven't told you what the problem is or where I am," the woman said.

That sounds like one of the Dutch women. "Mrs. Gildersleeve, right? You're in one of the apartments on Baltic, and I'm going to guess that you have standing water in your kitchen sink."

"I have water in my kitchen sink," she said. "How did you know?"

"Your pipes are an inch away from the west-facing brick," Patrick said as he started to jog, the tool bag banging against his hamstrings. "That's the cold side of the building. This always seems to happen when the temperature drops below twenty overnight."

"What can I do?" she asked.

"You can wait until the sun hits the bricks," Patrick said, "if the sun even comes out today, or you can try pouring boiling water into the sink."

"I'll try it."

"I'll be there in a few minutes."

When he arrived, he knocked on Mrs. Gildersleeve's door, and she let him in. A woman of about fifty, Mrs. Gildersleeve could have passed for a much younger woman, her golden hair still golden, her face still smooth. She reminded Patrick of the Nordic girl in a gum commercial, only Mrs. Gildersleeve was thinner and wore sweaters nearly every day of the year.

"It didn't work," she said.

"I'll have to torch it, then," Patrick said. He set his tool bag inside the door and found his trusty hand torch. His phone buzzed, and he answered it.

"My sink is stopped up," a woman said.

"Is this Mrs. Schoonmaker?" Patrick asked.

"Yes," she said. "How did you know?"

"Your drainpipe is frozen," Patrick said, "but it'll be thawed out in a moment. I'm already upstairs with Mrs. Gildersleeve. As soon as her sink drains, your sink should drain, too."

"Why?" Mrs. Schoonmaker asked.

"You two share the same drainpipe," Patrick said.

"Why?" Mrs. Schoonmaker asked.

Because this was once a one-family house, and whoever turned it into an apartment house combined lines to cut costs and cause me headaches. "Trust me, Mrs. Schoonmaker. It will be clear in a few minutes, but call me if it isn't, okay?"

"Okay."

Mrs. Gildersleeve blinked at him. "We share the same drain?"

"Everyone shares the same *main* drain," Patrick said, snapping his phone shut. "You and Mrs. Schoonmaker share the same sink drainpipe. It's not the greatest system, I know, but if I thaw yours out, hers should thaw out, too." *In theory.*

He went into the kitchen, opened the cabinet under the sink, stuck his head into the cabinet, lit the torch, and ran the flame back and forth above the coupling nut to the trap. In a few minutes, the water in the pipe was boiling, and a minute later, the water drained out in a rush. He pushed himself out and ran some water in the sink.

"That ought to do it for now," Patrick said. His phone buzzed, and he answered quickly. "Is it gone, Mrs. Schoonmaker?"

"No," Mrs. Schoonmaker said. "It has grown higher. It's threatening to overflow."

That's not good. "I'll be down in a moment," Patrick said. He closed his phone.

"Should I let it drip overnight so this doesn't happen again?" Mrs. Gildersleeve asked.

"The tap isn't the problem," he said. "It's where the water travels through the pipe near the brick. You might try pouring a pot of boiling water down your drain first thing in the morning to loosen up any ice."

"I shouldn't have to do that," she said.

"I know," Patrick said, "but none of the pipes in this building are insulated, and we'd have to rip apart the walls to do it right. That would take weeks." He showed her the torch. "You can always have one of these handy. They go for about fifty bucks."

"What if the bathtub ever backs up?" she asked.

"It shouldn't," Patrick said. "For some reason, the bathtub and shower drainpipes in this building are wider than normal." He noticed her cell phone on the kitchen table. *What a coincidence. She has a fancy cell phone, and I need a picture.* "Does your phone take pictures?"

"Yes," she said. "Why?"

"Could you take my picture and send it to me?" He smiled. *That has to be the strangest request I have ever made of a tenant—or of anyone, for that matter.*

"You want a picture . . . of yourself."

"I know that sounds strange, but I promised to send a picture to a friend of mine," Patrick said. "Salthead lets me use this cheap phone, and it doesn't have a camera."

"Just . . . take your picture." She picked up her phone.

"If it's not too much trouble," Patrick said.

"Dressed like that," she said.

Patrick shrugged. "She's a good friend. She'll understand."

"Okay." Mrs. Gildersleeve held up the camera. "Are you going to smile?"

"Oh, right." Patrick smiled.

She took the picture, looked at it, and turned the phone around. "That wasn't much of a smile."

Patrick looked at himself in his coveralls. *I thought I was smiling. I don't look anything like Bruce Springsteen, but Springsteen would probably never wear coveralls. I should have shaved. Geez, I'm a wrinkly clothes–wearing man.* "It'll work." He told her his e-mail address, and she sent it to him.

"Do you have Wi-Fi?" Patrick asked.

"Obviously."

"Oh yeah. Right." He dug his laptop out of the tool bag. "May I borrow your Wi-Fi for a moment? I'd like to send the picture to her as soon as I can. She's kind of been waiting for it."

"Mrs. Schoonmaker is waiting for you, too," she said.

Patrick nodded. "Her water isn't going anywhere, and I only need a minute."

Mrs. Gildersleeve sighed. "Go ahead."

"Thank you," Patrick said, and he smiled.

"Now, *that* was a smile," Mrs. Gildersleeve said.

"Is your Wi-Fi password protected?" Patrick asked.

"What?" Mrs. Gildersleeve said.

I'll take that as a no. "When you first get on the Internet, do you need to type in a code?"

"No," she said. "Um, is this friend your girlfriend?"

"She's a friend," Patrick said. *And she's hardly a girl. Lauren Short is a lady.*

"Have you known her long?" Mrs. Gildersleeve asked.

"No," Patrick said. "Not long."

Patrick booted up his laptop, connected immediately to

the Wi-Fi signal, and checked his e-mail. Lauren still hadn't replied. *Oh yeah. It's four a.m. there. She should still be asleep.* He opened the e-mail from Mrs. Gildersleeve and looked at his picture. *I've looked better, but this will have to do.* He saved the picture to his hard drive and attached it to a quick e-mail.

Lauren:
    Here I am in all my glory. Feast your eyes on a man in uniform.

Patrick

PS: I do clean up nicely. Really. You'll have to use your imagination.

After clicking SEND, he returned his laptop to the tool bag. "Thank you so much."

"What's your *friend's* name?" Mrs. Gildersleeve asked.

"Lauren," Patrick said. "Lauren Short."

"There's an actress by that name," she said. "It isn't the same one, is it?" Mrs. Gildersleeve laughed. "Oh, of course it isn't. What am I thinking?"

Patrick hoisted his tool bag. "It is."

Mrs. Gildersleeve blinked.

"My friend is Lauren Short, the actress," Patrick said.

"You're kidding," Mrs. Gildersleeve said.

"No," Patrick said.

Mrs. Gildersleeve squinted. "You mean I just took your picture with my phone, and that picture is on its way to Lauren Short, the Hollywood star?"

"I'm sure it's already there," Patrick said. "She probably

won't see it for a few hours, because she's sleeping in. She's on vacation."

"You're joking, aren't you?" she asked.

"No." He smiled. "She deserves a long vacation after what happened to her, don't you think?"

Mrs. Gildersleeve didn't answer.

"Have a good day," Patrick said. "It's supposed to be just as cold tomorrow. Call me if the boiling water trick doesn't work."

"I . . . will."

25

Lauren woke at the reasonable hour of eight and brushed her teeth over the kitchen sink. *All forty-eight of them,* she thought. *I don't have that many, Patrick.*

She returned to her bedroom, fluffed her pillows, and went back to bed.

All vacations should be this easy. I may even move my TV in here. Yes. That will be the extent of my labor today.

She checked her e-mail and deleted several hundred without reading them, until only Patrick's latest e-mail sat in her in-box.

Yes! He sent a picture!

She downloaded the picture.

He's . . . wow.

He's . . . tall.

Huge hands.

I am impressed.

Patrick is impressive.

She kicked off her covers to cool off from the heat rising from her legs.

He didn't say he was muscular. Look at those arms and shoulders! And those dark eyes. Wow. They're sexy and kind at the same time. Ooh, what a sexy beard.

This man is not ordinary at all.

He's hot.

Very.

But how do I to tell him he's extraordinary and hot without sounding as if I'm in heat?

I don't think I can.

And I really don't think I should.

She saved the picture to her computer and then replaced her lame California coastline background with his picture.

Yeah, I could look at him all day. He is tall. I wonder where he's standing, though. That can't be his kitchen. It's too girly. No man has blue ducks on his walls.

She popped up his e-mail and hit the REPLY button.

Patrick:

    You lied to me.

    You are hotter than the Boss.

    You are an extremely handsome man. I knew you were beautiful. And if you don't mind my saying so, if handymen ever did a calendar, you'd be the one I'd want for the months of December, January, February, and March. You're the kind of man who can make spring come early. You're the kind of man who can melt snow on the street. You're the kind of man the sun is jealous of. You're the kind of man who has seriously raised the temperature in my apartment. I had to turn on the A/C. I had to take a cold shower. I have an ice bag on my head right now.

    In other words . . . you fo-ine.

I like what I see very much.
Very.
Much.
Whose kitchen is that?

Lauren

PS: Very. Much. Please send more! I need a portfolio! ;)

26

Once he had Mrs. Schoonmaker's sink draining after a few minutes of torching her pipes, Patrick headed to the basement to make sure the main sewer drain was behaving.

It wasn't behaving.

At all.

A one-inch coating of brown, semi-frozen, glistening goo greeted him.

But I just snaked this drain a few days ago! Geez! Will these people stop eating so much roughage?

While the snake chewed and whined through the muck, Patrick found Mrs. Gildersleeve's unprotected Wi-Fi signal and checked his e-mail.

Lauren's awake! And I didn't disgust her with my picture. She even sounds . . . interested. If that's the right word. I've obviously warmed her up, but how would I know if a woman is truly interested? It's not as if I've had much practice. It's a good thing neither of us is looking for a new relationship.

Though she sounds as if she is. I think I shall test her.

Lauren:

I was in Mrs. Gildersleeve's kitchen. Her sink was stopped up because of a frozen pipe. I doubt you have frozen pipes in Los Angeles. She took my picture and said I didn't smile. I did. Really.

Right now I'm re-snaking (which isn't a word) a sewer drain in a cold basement and thinking of you.

See how unromantic I am? I guess I need practice.

Since I will be here awhile, and since I am borrowing a Wi-Fi signal while I wait, why don't you send me a recent picture of you? Send one that shows me what you look like without makeup or clothes.

I mean, send one that shows me what you look like without nice clothes on.

Oh, I'm sure you have nice clothes.

Send me what you look like at this moment.

Patrick

27

My handyman has gone from flirting to frisky, Lauren thought. *I like that.*

A lot.

I shall return the favor.

She looked at the thin light green T-shirt and thinner navy blue panties she was wearing.

This could get very interesting.

She picked up her phone, turned it on, and went into the bathroom. She looked at the towels on the floor, the mess in the sink, and the shower curtain crying out to be replaced. *A perfect background.*

She snapped several pictures of herself with her phone, each more daring than the last, her neckline plunging lower, her panties becoming a thong, her "torso" becoming more and more visible.

Now, which one do I send? I know I should only send him the head shot, but I'm feeling frisky, too. I should send all of them to warm up his day.

But what if . . .

No. I will show some restraint, because I am not a hoochie.

Yet.

She sent the first picture to herself and saved it to her computer before attaching it to a blank e-mail.

Patrick:

    This is me. No makeup, hair a mess and face dry, shirt wrinkled. It's what I look like when I get out of bed. Try not to gag, and ignore my messy bathroom.

Lauren

PS: I took several more pictures, but I'm afraid I got carried away. Use your imagination.

The second after she sent the message, Lauren closed her eyes.

And now I'm scared.

Why am I scared?

Millions of people have looked at me for years in movies and in magazines, but this . . . this one picture matters.

This picture matters more than any other because I need someone to like it.

I need Patrick to like it.

Please like it, Patrick.

Please like me.

She tried to slow her breathing.

I should have sent the last one. I still have a nice booty, and he called it sculpture.

Her breathing increased.

No, no, the head shot is the best shot. For now.

I hope.

28

Patrick watched the photograph as it downloaded line by excruciating line, and when he had Lauren in the flesh in front of him, his heart thudded.

She's . . .

My God.

There are no words.

If she looks this good when she wakes up and rolls out of bed . . .

He looked at the lake of goo receding sluggishly toward the drain as the snake churned on.

And this is what I look like sixteen hours a day . . .

An e-mail pinged into his in-box. He opened it.

Patrick:

You're keeping me in suspense, and you know I don't like to wait.

I'm sitting here thinking you lost the signal, or the picture froze during the download, or Microsoft decided to do an intrusive update and it slowed your computer to a crawl, or I should have sent one of the other more risqué pictures, or you don't like the one I sent you, or the one I sent you scrambled into something horrible.

If you haven't already figured it out, I'm slightly self-conscious, all right? Just slightly.

Oh, all right. I am very self-conscious, but I have every reason to be because I have just spent seven years with a bisexual man who told me I was beautiful almost daily when he didn't mean it at all. I just need confirmation, okay?

You have to have the picture by now. What do you think? And you don't have to sugarcoat it. I can take a bad review.

Lauren

PS: Why didn't you tell me you were muscular? I likes, I likes. ;)

She likes, she likes. I guess that's something. And I've never lifted weights in my life. I earned these muscles pipe by cinder block by wrench by hammer and by nail. He turned off the snake and cranked the hose back into its housing. *And especially by snake. I may not hate cranking this snake nearly as much from now on.*

Maybe there's hope, because my "job," such as it is, has given Lauren something to like.

She wouldn't like this aroma, though.

He turned his head away from the stench and searched for a clean gulp of air as his phone buzzed. He answered it. "This is Patrick."

"What in the *hell* is going on?" a man cried. "I sit down, I flush, and the toilet nearly overflows!"

Mr. Hyer. "I know, Mr. Hyer, and I'm working on it. I'm in the basement right now. It's slow going because of the cold."

"You should have fixed it right the first time!" he yelled. "Don't you know what you are doing?"

"I know what I'm doing, Mr. Hyer," Patrick said. "I'm doing the best I can."

"If you were doing your best, you would not be here again today!"

Patrick glanced at Lauren's picture. *She wouldn't take this abuse. Of course, she wouldn't be here in this basement to take this abuse.* "Mr. Hyer, try to understand. Instead of one family and two toilets, there are *eight* families and *eight* toilets all using one ancient drainpipe that—"

"I do not want to hear it," Mr. Hyer interrupted. "Fix it now!"

Click.

Patrick looked at edge of the pool of goo, which had suddenly moved two inches—in the *wrong* direction.

I am going to be here awhile.

I think I'll name this place Lake Holland.

He smiled at Lauren's picture.

At least the view is nice from the shore.

He again fed the snake through the muck and then restarted it.

Lake Holland sat unmoved.

While the snake sought out the main line again, Patrick turned and typed.

Lauren:
    You are too beautiful for words, although I have some thoughts going through my head that I'm afraid to share with you. I hope you understand.
    I'm in the basement of a building built during the

1890s, trying to unclog the same sewer line I unclogged the other day, and you want me to let you know what's going through my mind when I see a breathtaking picture of you. I'm afraid that if I tell you how utterly, painfully beautiful you are, you might be offended. So I won't tell you that my heart hurts to see your beauty. I won't tell you that you aren't stunning. You're astonishing. I won't tell you that I have never seen someone who has just rolled out of bed looking so beautiful. You can't make me tell you how much my hands are trembling as I type this because of your heart-stopping beauty. And I most definitely won't ever tell you that I will never be the same again from this moment until the day I die.

You can't make me talk, Copper.

Patrick

PS: You are the most beautiful woman I have ever seen.

29

Lauren Short cried for the first time since her father's funeral. She had often forced herself to cry in movie scenes, but this time her sobbing was real.

She had no Kleenex and had to use toilet paper. She realized she would need more toilet paper soon.

He thinks I'm beautiful.
He's beautiful.
Therefore, we're beautiful.
And we should be together.
Somehow.
And soon.
She wiped her eyes.
I'm still beautiful. Imagine that. And a real *man said so.*

Patrick:

Thank you for sharing by not sharing. You made me cry, but in a good way, a very good way. Your words . . . <sigh>! You have a devastating way with words. I'm not exactly sure what "painfully beautiful" means, but it touched me to the deepest part of my soul.

I know I said I wasn't looking, and I'm not. Really. Not anymore.

Why go looking when I've already found somebody in you? You've become more than a friend, Patrick. Much more. You're a lifeline, man. You've given me life. "Got to Get You into My Life" (the Earth, Wind & Fire version) is going through my head right now.

Okay, okay, you originally found me. I have to give you all the credit. And to think I might have skipped past your e-mail. You know how you got me to read your first one? You didn't put anything in the subject line. I'm a sucker for blanks, I guess. Now we have a long line of "Re:" up there. I wonder what the record is, but I don't want to set that record, okay?

It is obvious to me that we should meet face-to-face, and from what you've just told me, it is obvious to you, too. We are already in agreement, so what are we waiting for?

There's just one little thing I have to learn about you first. Really a technicality, hardly worth mentioning. (This is part of my "good cop" interrogating technique. You can't resist me, so don't even try.)

You see, since you sent me your picture, I have had numerous thoughts involving you in those coveralls. I feel you holding me in your strong hands and rubbing my back, and then you lift me into the air, and you gently whisper something into my ear. . . .

What do you whisper to me, Patrick?

Lauren

PS: Spill it, or the torture will continue. I'm good when I play the good cop, but I'm oh so bad when I play the bad cop. ;)

She sent the message and waited precisely one minute before Patrick's e-mail arrived.

Lauren:
    I whisper, "It's going to be all right, Lauren. I've got you. I won't let you go. You can hold on to me all night."

Patrick

Lauren began to tremble.
"That's . . . good," she whispered. "That's . . . the right answer. I need to hear that every day."
But I need to move this along a little faster. . . .

Patrick:
    I say breathlessly, as only an actress can be breathless (of course), "Take me somewhere, anywhere. Now!"
    Where do you take me, Patrick?

Lauren

30

The stench visibly rising into the warming basement air, the remnants of Lake Holland finally flowing into the drain, and the snake sullenly steaming in a corner, Patrick pondered his response while letting four service calls go to his voice mail.

This is a loaded question. Where do you take an angel? I could take her anywhere in an e-mail. In reality, I can take her to the deli across from my apartment for a burrito and a soda. I need to ask her for more directions.

Lauren:
Forgive me, but "take me somewhere" is somewhat vague. Take "take." (I hear an echo.) "Take" can mean to remove by force . . . and even to get busy with, right? And "somewhere" could be anywhere. There are a lot of somewheres to choose from. Too many, in fact.

Please be more specific. I only want to take you where you want to go.
Patrick

He sent his message and waited less than a minute.

Patrick:
    I like the second definition of "take" better . . .
though a combination of the two might work out, too. ;)
    Where do you want to take me?

Lauren

Anywhere but here, Patrick thought. *Especially here.*

Lauren:
    I take you to a couch in front of a fireplace. I make
a roaring fire and see flames dancing in your eyes.

Patrick

PS: I hate to interrupt this, I really, really do. I have at
least four service calls to make. I may not be able to
get online until I get home late tonight. I don't mean to
leave you hanging, but I have to. I hope you understand. :~

He sent the message. Thirty seconds later, he read:

Patrick:
    It's okay. You go on with your day. I'll wait here by
the fire. Write to me when you can.

Lauren

PS: You make a nice fire. It's so hot, I might melt. . . .
Ooh, it's getting hot in here. I may have to take off
some more clothes. . . . Oops. There goes my . . .

LET'S STAY TOGETHER 153

Patrick sighed. *I wish I could continue this! I want to know what she took off! She was only wearing two items, so if she took off her shirt . . .*

It is suddenly not nearly as cold as it was before.

Patrick wearily packed his laptop, hoisted his tool bag, and headed out into the cold while listening to Mrs. Moczydlowska's four messages about icy drafts, rats in the walls, a burned-out lightbulb, and one creaking floorboard.

I've got to "fix" Mrs. Moczydlowska's problems and hurry home, he thought. *I don't want Lauren to melt.*

And I certainly want to be there when her last *piece of clothing hits the floor.*

31

Lauren watched her in-box for several minutes, and when nothing but more junk mail appeared, she buried herself under her covers.

Patrick is a good, hardworking man who is sexy, kind, and romantic, even if he says he isn't romantic. Why isn't he married? He should be married. He should have ten kids and the happiest wife on earth by now. Okay, maybe not ten kids. She wouldn't be that happy with ten kids.

Two kids.

He must not have the time for a relationship. Either that or Natalia ruined him for life.

That could be it. Natalia was Patrick's Chazz.

And here I am, waiting patiently for my man to either "call" me from work or get home from work so we can "talk."

Her phone buzzed.

She looked at the caller ID. *Todd again, wasting his time.* She opened her phone and said, "I'm not interested, Todd."

"I haven't even told you what I have for you," Todd said.

"I'm not interested."

Now, go away so I can work on some handyman fantasies with my fingers under these warm covers.

"I have several projects you might be interested in," Todd said.

I can think of quite a few projects I need my handyman to work on. I need to have my plumbing worked on in a big way. I need him to make me feel like a woman again. I also need him to kiss me from my nose to my toes and work that snake of his.

"I'm not interested," Lauren said.

"Will you at least listen?" Todd asked. "I've been making calls like crazy on your behalf."

Lauren sighed. "All right. Go ahead."

"The first is a TNT sitcom called—"

"No," Lauren interrupted.

"Let me finish," Todd said. "It's an ensemble sitcom that takes place in Atlanta, and it's called—"

"No."

"Is it Atlanta or the fact that it's an ensemble cast?" Todd asked.

"Neither," Lauren said. "I'm not interested."

"Well, then there's a musical slated to open in Chicago this spring—"

"My stage days are over," Lauren interrupted, "and you know I don't sing."

"It's mainly a speaking part," Todd said.

"No," Lauren said. "Next."

"All right," Todd said. "I've just been on the phone with Pixar, and they need someone to do the voice of a rabbit."

"A rabbit," Lauren said.

"Right," Todd said. "I can tell you're interested."

I'm not. "What kind of rabbit?" Lauren asked.

"Well, it's not like Jessica Rabbit or Bugs Bunny, if that's what you're thinking," Todd said. "It's more of a scared rabbit kind of character."

"Gee, thanks," Lauren said. "The answer is no. I don't do voices." *I only want to hear Patrick's voice. We need to get on the phone soon.*

"But the money is huge!" Todd shouted. "And you'll be done in a week, so you can go back to feeling sorry for yourself."

Is that what I'm doing? "I'm recharging myself, Todd," Lauren said. "I'm not feeling sorry for myself." *Anymore. And I can thank Patrick for that.* "Have you heard back from *SNL*?"

"No, I haven't, but—"

"Good-bye, Todd."

She turned her phone off completely, then placed it on her nightstand. Safely in her cocoon of covers, she hugged her pillow and closed her eyes.

Please come home, Patrick. I need you. She hugged her pillow. *Patrick isn't this soft. I am already growing tired of this pillow, and I am suddenly tired of e-mails. They aren't immediate enough. If I had Patrick's phone number, I'd be talking his cute ears off all day.*

I have to get his number.

As soon as Patrick appears online tonight, I will instant message him until he gives it to me.

And then . . .

The suspense is killing me!

She smiled.

And then we will really talk for the first time.

I am beginning to like suspense. . . .

32

The daily drama with Mrs. Moczydlowska finished, Patrick trotted to his apartment, started a load of laundry, took a long hot shower, shaved, and put on clean clothes.

He immediately felt foolish.

As if she could smell me from LA.

He grimaced.

Earlier today she might have been able to.

He booted up his laptop, and as soon as he signed on, a series of instant messages flashed up on the screen a few seconds apart.

LS77: How was your day?

LS77: You there?

LS77: I'll bet you're in the shower. I hope you're in the shower. Oh, you missed a spot. Let me get it. . . . My, what big feet you have. ;)

LS77: I'll just talk to myself, then. Not much going on here. I rested today. Oh, I moved my TV into my bedroom. I must have slept for ten hours. I might actually eat something today, too. I've been forgetting to eat.

Patrick's fingertips began to sweat.

She's here.

I mean, she's there.

She's on the screen. Lauren Short is talking to me right now. Why can't I think of anything to say?

LS77: I haven't even put on any more clothes since I
took that picture for you. I'm feeling excessively lazy
for some reason. It must be because of this nice fire
you made for me. My skin is glowing. ;)

Patrick typed "No e-mail this time?" and quickly deleted
it. *Talk to her!*

LS77: I know you're there, Patrick. Surprise! I don't
know why we didn't do this before. This is fun. It's a
little one-sided right now, but . . . How was your day?
Did you do any more snaking today? I'll bet you're an
expert at using your snake. ;)

Patrick took a deep breath and started to type.

PAE1: My day is over and no more snaking. Yours?
LS77: Just beginning. I hope. How long have you
been watching me ramble?
PAE1: Not long. I didn't know what to say.
LS77: Say hi.
PAE1: Hi.
LS77: Hi back. Were you in the shower?
PAE1: Yes. Thanks for seeing that spot I missed.
LS77: You left it unwashed on purpose, didn't you?
PAE1: I did. It must be nice to be able to sleep all day.
LS77: It isn't. I was so lonely. An extremely muscular
man built me a nice fire, put me on a couch, and then

he abandoned me. Wasn't that mean of him? I've
been here all day alone, without him, while he's out
saving the world one drainpipe at a time.

PAE1: Funny.

LS77: I have my moments.

PAE1: How is the fire?

LS77: It's dying. ☹ I am getting so cold. My goose
bumps are having babies.

PAE1: I'll add more wood.

LS77: You devil. ;)

PAE1: More wood for the fire.

LS77: I know what you really meant. Don't be shy. . . .

PAE1: I'm adding a lot of wood.

LS77: You have a lot of wood?

PAE1: I guess.

LS77: You're so humble.

PAE1: Okay. It's blazing again.

LS77: Your wood is blazing hot?

PAE1: Ha-ha.

LS77: Ooh, it is. My hands are getting warmer
already. Get closer to me.

PAE1: Getting closer. Nervous.

LS77: Why?

PAE1: I'm sitting next to you.

LS77: Don't be. I don't bite on the first date. I only nib-
ble.

PAE1: But you have 48 teeth.

LS77: I may draw a little blood.

PAE1: Now I'm more nervous.

LS77: I'm nibbling on you. You taste good. Whoo, it
sure is hot.

PAE1: Not too hot, I hope.

LS77: It's very hot. Your body is so warm. Is that
sweat?

PAE1: No. I just took a shower.

LS77: So your hair is wet.

PAE1: A little.

LS77: I want to make you sweat.

PAE1: Too late.

LS77: I am too hot for this T-shirt. Will you take it off?

PAE1: You'll catch cold.

LS77: No I won't. The fire is blazing, and you're here to keep me warm. Take it off, Patrick.

PAE1: Taking it off.

LS77: Ooooooh, much better. Do you like what you see?

PAE1: Yes.

LS77: You didn't say YES! I am hurt.

PAE1: I am in awe. I don't shout when I am in awe.

LS77: You say the nicest things. You like them?

PAE1: Like what?

LS77: My breasts.

PAE1: Yes.

LS77: You're still in awe.

PAE1: Yes.

LS77: I want to see your chest.

PAE1: I'm not wearing a shirt.

LS77: Humor me.

PAE1: I'm taking off my shirt.

LS77: I want to take it off.

PAE1: Oh. Go ahead.

LS77: I'm taking off your shirt. Nice. Do you feel my hands on your chest?

PAE1: Yes. Your hands are soft.

LS77: I just lotioned them. I am jealous of your chest.

PAE1: Don't be. Your breasts are perfect.

LS77: Ooh, the things you say. Would you like to taste them?

LS77: Patrick? Are you still there?

PAE1: Lauren, can I call a timeout?

LS77: Why?

PAE1: While I would love to do anything you ask of me, I don't want you to get the wrong idea about me. I really like you.

LS77: I really like you, too.

PAE1: This is moving too fast for me, I guess. I don't want you to think that I only want your body. I must be old-fashioned.

LS77: I'm old-fashioned, too. I don't only want your body, too. Did that make sense?

PAE1: Yes.

LS77: Well. Hmm. It's obvious something is happening here.

PAE1: Yes. What do we do next?

33

Lauren sat on top of her covers, her laptop in front of her. *We're getting serious while sitting in front of computers three thousand miles apart! This is agony! This is torture!*

And I can't wait for it to continue.

LS77: Are you nervous?
PAE1: Yes. This is my first time for . . . whatever this is.
LS77: Mine, too. What do we call it? We can't call it our first time.
PAE1: Our first conversation?
LS77: It won't be our last.
PAE: No.
LS77: Where are you?
PAE1: On my bed. You?
LS77: On my bed.
PAE1: I'm more nervous now. Are you . . . cold?
LS77: Not really. I'm actually sweating. You?

PAE1: I'm sweating.

LS77: Were you getting . . . excited?

PAE1: I'm looking at your picture, the one you sent me today.

LS77: So you're not excited.

PAE1: I'm very excited.

LS77: Define "VERY."

PAE1: Extremely excited.

LS77: Be specific.

PAE1: It was getting difficult to sit comfortably.

LS77: You were . . . growing?

PAE1: Yes.

LS77: How much?

PAE1: Large.

LS77: Did you have girth? ☺

PAE1: !!! Yes.

LS77: I like girth. Are your curtains shut tight? I don't want anyone to see you . . . sitting uncomfortably.

PAE1: Only you can see me. I'm looking into your eyes.

LS77: I'm looking at your picture, too.

PAE1: No!

LS77: Your picture made me excited all day.

PAE1: Really?

LS77: Very.

PAE1: Define "very."

LS77: <panting>

PAE1: Really? I was wearing coveralls.

LS77: You look so sexy.

PAE1: I hope I look better now.

LS77: I'm sure you do. <groan> It's been a long while for me. I mean, it's been three years since my body has responded like this.

PAE1: It's been many years for me. Now I'm even

more nervous.

LS77: Me, too.

PAE1: Do you need a timeout, too?

LS77: Yes and no. I don't want you to think I'm a hoochie, but I don't want to slow down either. I'm feel-ing something, you know?

PAE1: You'll never be a hoochie, Lauren, and I'm feel-ing something, too.

LS77: We need to do something about these feelings, don't we?

34

Patrick wiggled his fingers over the keyboard. *Something is happening, something wonderful, and I can't think of anything to say.*

PAE1: I couldn't possibly sleep tonight.

LS77: Neither could I. You make me feel happy and wanted.

PAE1: I want you to feel happy and wanted. You deserve to be happy and wanted.

LS77: Believe me, I do feel that way because of you. But, Patrick, I am still on fire. I have a tingling in my neck and my nose, my whole body is hot, and my heart is trying to leave my chest.

PAE1: I'm feeling that, too.

LS77: If you hadn't called a timeout, I know I would be having convulsions right now.

PAE1: I had to call timeout. I can't type one-handed.

LS77: ROFL!!! HAHAHAHAHAHA!

PAE1: It's good to "hear" you laugh.

LS77: I'm laughing so hard, I'm crying. Are you right-handed or left-handed?

PAE1: Right.

LS77: So you were about to use your left hand to . . .

PAE1: Yes.

LS77: Me, too <she whispered shyly>. It seems as if someone else is doing it if I use my left hand.

PAE1: Really?

LS77: I've tried using my right index finger, and it wasn't as good. I guess my left index finger is more sensitive or something. Maybe it's more detached.

PAE1: I hope not!

LS77: ☺ I'd rather have you . . . touching me.

PAE1: Me, too.

LS77: I wish you were here with me.

PAE1: I wish I was there with you. It's too cold here.

LS77: I need to hear your voice right now. I want to call you.

PAE1: Let me charge up my cell battery.

Patrick raced to charge up his phone and returned to the laptop.

PAE1: Charging my phone.

LS77: I'll need the number.

PAE1: I'll call you.

LS77: I don't mind calling you.

PAE1: I mind.

LS77: Okay. (818) 555-2535. Hurry.

35

Lauren leaped out of bed and put on a slinky black silk robe.

I can't receive my gentleman caller without a sexy silk robe, can I?

She lounged in her bed, letting the robe part to reveal a lot of leg. *I feel so sexy right now. It is so good to feel like a real woman for a change.*

Although the sound of her phone made her jump, she let it ring twice before answering. "Hello," she said as huskily as she could. She ended up coughing.

"Are you all right, Lauren?"

Now, that's a real man's voice, she thought. *Strong. Virile. Deep. Definitely Brooklyn.* "I'm fine, Patrick. I was trying to do a little Bette Davis."

"I like Lauren Short much better," Patrick said.

"It's easier on my voice, too," she said.

"And my ears," Patrick said. "It's good to hear your voice."

"Yours, too," Lauren said. "What are you wearing?"

"Sweats and a T-shirt," he said. "You?"

"A black silk robe," she said.

"Oh," Patrick whispered.

"You don't have a black silk robe to lounge around in?" Lauren said.

"No, and even if I did, I wouldn't wear it in Brooklyn in late November," Patrick said. "Lauren, I want you to know that I have never done anything like this before."

"Talking on the phone?"

"You know what I mean," Patrick said. "Flirting like this."

"Patrick, we're not flirting with each other anymore," Lauren said. "I think this is lust."

"Yeah," Patrick said. "I didn't know I could be this lusty."

"I bring out the beast in you, huh?" Lauren whispered. She untied the robe and let it slide off her shoulders.

"I'm not much of a beast," Patrick said, "but you almost undressed me from three thousand miles away. How did you do that?"

"I have skills I didn't know I had," Lauren said.

"Yes," Patrick said. "You could probably get me to do just about anything."

"I couldn't get you to let me call you," Lauren said.

"No, and don't bother trying," Patrick said. "I'm old school like that. I should have already asked for your phone number."

"I respect old school," Lauren said. "It shows you had home training."

"I really trained myself," Patrick said. "So, um, how do we proceed?"

Lauren ran her free hand down her stomach. "How do we proceed? Isn't that what we're doing? Proceeding?"

"True," Patrick said. "But typing it is easier than saying it. At least for me."

She slid her hand over her thighs. "You're doing fine. We're only cuddling now, anyway, right?"

"Oh right." Patrick sighed. "How silky is that robe?"

Lauren pulled the robe back over her shoulders. "What robe?"

"So . . . you're naked," Patrick whispered.

No, my shoulders are cold. "Whisper to me again."

"You're . . . naked," he whispered.

That was sexy. "I wish you could touch me right now," she whispered.

"I wish I could, too, Lauren," Patrick said.

"Where would you touch me?" Lauren asked.

"I would start with your . . . left ear," Patrick whispered.

Lauren laughed. "Really? My ear?"

"I'd start at the top," Patrick whispered. "And then I'd work my way down."

"Okay, okay," Lauren said. She rubbed her left ear. "I'm rubbing my left ear."

"I didn't mean for you to do it now," Patrick said.

"It feels good," Lauren said. "Where would you touch me next?"

"Lauren, I'm not very good at this," Patrick said.

"Trust me, man," Lauren said, "you're doing fine."

"Okay, I, um, I kiss your neck while I rub your right thigh," Patrick whispered.

Lauren arched her neck, rubbing her right thigh with her free hand. "Your kiss is hot."

"Your skin is hot," Patrick whispered.

Lauren shivered. "Your kiss is making my skin hot." *And yet I'm shivering! What's going on?* She put on her robe, tying it tightly. "But I'm so cold."

"I wish I was there to keep you warm," Patrick said.

"So do I," Lauren said. "I want you to know that I'm really very shy when it comes to sex. I'm not shy about much, but I am shy about sex."

"You could have fooled me," Patrick said.

"It's the actress in me, I guess." She pushed herself back against her headboard, her body still shivering. "I love your imagination by the way, and I love your accent. It's more Italian than Irish."

"Because of my mama," Patrick said.

"Is she . . . still around?"

"No," Patrick said. "She died nine years ago. Cancer."

"I'm sorry to hear that," Lauren said.

"Thanks," Patrick said.

No father, no mother. He's really an orphan now. "No brothers or sisters?"

"No," Patrick said. "I feel the need to say something to you."

"Well, say it," Lauren said.

"Thank you," Patrick said.

Lauren stopped shivering. "For what?"

"For talking to me," Patrick said. "For listening to me."

"I should be thanking you," Lauren said.

"You don't need to thank me," Patrick said. "You're Lauren Short, the amazing actress, and I'm just a guy from Brooklyn."

"You're so much more than a guy from Brooklyn, Patrick," Lauren said. "And I can't for the life of me understand why such a handsome, strong, kind man like you isn't with someone."

"After Natalia, I gave up," Patrick said.

"There has to be more to it than that," Lauren said.

"I guess you could say that I put all my eggs in one basket," Patrick said. "And when she flew the coop, I guess I got chicken."

"Funny," Lauren said. "So you haven't even gone out with anyone in the last twenty years?"

"No," Patrick said.

"I'm having trouble believing that," Lauren said.

"It's true," Patrick whispered.

"You had to have had offers," Lauren said.

"A few," Patrick said.

"And you broke their hearts," Lauren said.

"I doubt that," Patrick said. "I wasn't interested."

Natalia broke him. "You're not giving up now, are you?"

"No, but please try to understand," Patrick said. "I'm not the kind of guy a movie star has on her arm. I'm more the kind of guy she gets to drive her places or to keep her safe."

Which is exactly what I need! "What if this *former* movie star wants someone to drive her places and keep her safe?"

"Well, that's different," Patrick said. "I can do that. Except that I don't have a car."

Lauren smiled. "There are other ways to drive someone."

"I would love to drive you all night long," Patrick said.

This man's timing is perfect! Oh, the movies we could make! "You would?"

"I meant," Patrick said, "I would love to drive you anywhere all night long."

"And I'd be right next to you all night long." She looked at her screen. *You know, we could make a movie right now. Sort of.* "Do you have Skype?"

"What?"

"Sorry," Lauren said. "Bad transition. Some people have random thoughts. I say random things. Does your computer have Skype?"

"Yes, but I've never used it," Patrick said. "Does it cost anything?"

"Not if we both have it," Lauren said. "Find the Skype button."

"Here it is."

"Did you click on it?" Lauren asked.

"Yes," Patrick said. "It says I have to download it first."

"Go ahead."

"That was a quick download," Patrick said. "Choose language. Ah, *Italiano*."

"English, please," Lauren said.

"Okay," Patrick said.

"Do you speak any Italian?" Lauren asked.

"Some," Patrick said. "But not enough to hold a conversation. Uh, it says to choose a Skype name."

"It's easiest to use your own name," Lauren said. "I'm Lauren-dot-Elizabeth-dot-Short."

"Elizabeth," Patrick said.

"Alan," Lauren said.

"Okay, I'm Patrick-dot-Alan-dot-Esposito. Oh, it's telling me my video works. That light has never come on before. Oh, there I am. The picture is so small."

"You can make it full screen," Lauren said. "Add me as a contact, click on my name, and let's . . . proceed."

"Okay, I'm clicking on your name. . . ."

"Do you see me?" Lauren asked.

Patrick didn't respond.

"Patrick?"

"I see you," Patrick whispered. "I can't believe it's you."

"Who else would it be?" Lauren asked.

"I meant . . ." He sighed. "I meant what I said. I can't believe it's you."

"I'm nothing special, Patrick," Lauren said. "I'm just an

ordinary woman. Well, tonight I'm an ordinary *horny* woman, but it's your fault."

"You're special to me," Patrick said. "I'm going full screen now. Wow."

Lauren expanded the dark box in front of her until it focused on a man's nice, hard chest. "Tilt up your screen. I'm staring at your chest."

The screen tilted up until Lauren could see Patrick's face. "Hi," he said.

"Hi," Lauren said. "You don't look like Bruce Springsteen."

"I told you my mama was drunk a lot," Patrick said.

"What do you see?" Lauren asked.

"I see a whole lot of delicious-looking brown skin," Patrick said. "Will this pick up sound?"

"I hear you," Lauren said. "You've noticed that our lips don't match our words."

"It's like a dubbed movie," Patrick said. "So I can hang up the phone?"

"Sure."

Lauren watched Patrick close his phone. "Patrick, I'm going to give you a tour of my body."

"This is the best movie I have ever watched," Patrick said. "I wish it was in HD."

"Hush," Lauren said. "Tell me what you see." She set her laptop on the edge of the bed and moved her foot close to the lens.

"I didn't know this would be in three-D," Patrick said. "Nice foot."

"I have two of them," Lauren said, "but my right foot is my best foot." She scooted closer and leaned forward.

"Um, are you cold?" Patrick asked.

Lauren looked down at her breasts. *Whoa. My nipples*

are trying to shred this robe. "A little." She tilted back the screen, set the laptop on the bed, stood, then turned around and shook her booty.

"Oh, Lauren," Patrick whispered. "That is *very* nice. If someone made a sculpture of you and put it in a museum, I would pull up a chair and look at you all day."

"Which part of me most?"

"Your booty," Patrick said.

She sat and brought the laptop to her chest. "Can you see the look on my face?"

"Yes," Patrick said.

"This is the face of a happy woman," Lauren said. "This is the face of a woman who feels like a woman again. You bring out the beast and the best in me. I am so happy, but I want to be happier. I have to be with you, Patrick. I need you beside me, and to be completely honest, I need you inside me, too. I want to come see you."

36

She wants . . . to come see me.
She wants me . . . inside her.

Wow.

"I want to see you, too," Patrick said. "I need to feel you. I need to hold you."

"Yes, you do," Lauren said. "I'm flying out tonight to New York."

Tonight? Tonight is too soon! Look at this place! "But I have to work tomorrow."

"You don't work all day, *every* day, do you?" Lauren asked.

"Just about."

"Could you make an exception for me?" Lauren asked.

She can't come here! Not here to this dump! "I probably could. I don't know." *How can I make her understand that? I'm forty years old, and this is all I have to show for it! Most of my furniture came from my mama's apartment after she died. The only thing I ever bought is the bed, and it's nearly fifteen years old!*

"Probably?" Lauren said. "You have to have some vacation time, right?"

"I've never taken a vacation," Patrick said. "I was supposed to be off last week, on Thanksgiving, but I ended up working. I'm on call twenty-four hours a day, and some people seem to wait for Thanksgiving Day and Christmas Day to call me. I have plunged far too many toilets on Thanksgiving Day and Christmas morning to count."

"I don't mind waiting for you," Lauren said. "I'll be warming up your bed."

"Lauren, that sounds wonderful," Patrick said. "Really. But I don't know if you'll want to wait that long." *How can I slow this down?*

"It's no trouble for me to fly out," Lauren said. "I *have* to be with you, Patrick. You have me aching, man, and I haven't ached in such a long time."

"I want you to be with me, but I'm . . . I don't feel . . ." He sighed. "Lauren, I live in a dump."

"So do I," Lauren said. "You should see where I live now. I live in a studio apartment, and there isn't even a sink in the bathroom. I brush my teeth and wash my face over the kitchen sink. Let me show you."

Patrick watched as she panned around a small apartment. "You're not in your mansion on the beach?"

"It was never my mansion," Lauren said, her face returning to the screen. "I was only the mansion's maid. Maybe that's all Chazz really needed me for, huh? To cook and clean for him. I was his housekeeper for seven years. I should sue him for back pay."

Her place isn't much bigger than mine, but . . . "But this place is a mess. I can afford only seven hundred square feet, and that's because I get half my rent paid as part of my salary. I don't have any carpeting, I sleep in a double bed, I have one window, the only things on the walls are dust and cobwebs—"

"I don't care about that, Patrick," Lauren interrupted.

"You might," Patrick said. "You're Lauren Short. You deserve better than this. Everyone in the world knows you."

"I doubt that," Lauren said.

"They do," Patrick said. *Even fifty-year-old Dutch women in Boerum Hill know who Lauren Short is.* "You deserve better than I probably could *ever* give you."

"But I don't care about that at all," Lauren said. "Trust me on that. I grew up in Congress Heights, in D.C. I grew up with very little."

"But you've gotten used to a lot more, right?" Patrick asked.

"While the money I've made is nice, I've never gone crazy with it," Lauren said. "I remember my roots. I don't care where you live, okay?"

"I do," Patrick said. "What kind of man would I be if I couldn't provide a nice place for you?"

"You *do* provide for me," Lauren said. "In only a few days, you have given me everything that has been missing in my life. You've just set my body on fire, and you didn't even touch me. You're magic, and I want to feel more magic. I might explode if you really touched me." She smiled.

"I don't want you to explode, Lauren," Patrick said.

"I think I need to, okay? I need to go buck wild or something. I have seven years of sexual frustration to unload, and I don't plan to be quiet about it." She laughed. "You even have me laughing, man. I have missed laughing so much. And if I have to explode, I can't think of a better way to go, can you?"

"No," Patrick said. "I can't. But seriously, Lauren, I don't have much. There's nothing I can give you."

"You've given me love, and that's everything," Lauren said. "Let me come to you."

I don't know if I've given her love. "I haven't given you anything you couldn't get somewhere else or from someone else."

"Yes, you have." Her face filled the screen. "I may even love you." She smiled. "I probably do love you, Patrick. I know that's a lousy way of saying it, but I've never been in love, so I don't know if I truly am. Yeah, we've only known each other a week, but in one week you have given me so much attention, you've given me so much of yourself, and I love that about you."

She may *even love me,* Patrick thought. *She* probably *does. I should be happy about that, but I'm not.* "But I really have nothing, Lauren," Patrick said. "I live month to month. I don't have much in savings. I don't have investments or a retirement plan or even a health insurance plan. When I get sick, I usually stay sick and keep working."

"You have so much more than you know, and I want it," Lauren said. "All of it. I want all of you. Please, Patrick. Let me come to you."

He minimized Lauren's picture, went to Google, and typed in "map of US."

"The screen is shaking," Lauren said. "What are you doing?"

"Hold on." He clicked on the first map that appeared. *What's halfway between Brooklyn and LA? Kansas? Nebraska? Oh. They're having a snowstorm out there now. Oh yeah, global warming is the real deal. Blizzards in November.* "Let's meet . . ." He focused on a city. *I guess this will do.* "Let's meet in St. Louis."

"What?"

"Let's meet in St. Louis," Patrick said.

"Why St. Louis?" Lauren asked. "I can be in New York and in your arms in less than twelve hours."

I haven't been west of New Jersey in my life, and I'm about to go about a thousand miles west to the banks of the Mississippi River. "I know you can, and I really appreciate the idea, but this is our first date and I want it to be special." *And anywhere but here.*

"In St. Louis?"

"Would you rather meet in Kansas City, Omaha, or Oklahoma City?" Patrick asked.

"No, St. Louis is okay," Lauren said. "But that's not the point, Patrick. It would be *so* much easier for me, who is currently unemployed by the way, to get on a plane and be with you in less than twelve hours."

"It's tempting, really, but let's meet in St. Louis first," Patrick said.

"I don't understand this plan at all," Lauren said. "Why do you want to meet me in St. Louis?"

Patrick sighed. "This is no place for a star."

"This star grew up in a much worse place," Lauren said, "and this star isn't a star anymore."

"You'll always be a star to me," Patrick said. "You'll always be a star to the rest of the world, too."

"I won't," Lauren said. "I will fade away in a matter of weeks. Trust me. The world has a very short attention span these days."

How can I convince her? "Lauren, my entire wardrobe probably cost less than a single pair of your shoes."

"You think I . . ." She laughed. "I don't spend a lot of money on my shoes or my clothes. I'm sensible. I still look for bargains."

"I have boots that are over ten years old," Patrick said. "Do you?"

"No," Lauren said.

"Do you have any clothes that old?" Patrick asked.

"No."

"I do," Patrick said. "Just let me do it this way, okay?"

Lauren sighed and shook her head. "But it makes no sense!"

"It does to me," Patrick said quietly. "And it's how I want it to be."

"Okay, okay," Lauren said. "But why St. Louis?"

"I want to meet you on neutral territory." *That sounded weird.*

"Neutral territory?" Lauren's eyes blinked.

It sounded weird to her, too. "Yes," Patrick said. "If you come to New York, what will most likely happen?"

"We'll get to know each other very well," Lauren said quickly, "and I won't let you leave the apartment for twenty-four hours."

"No, I mean, what will most likely happen when the *media* finds out that you're coming to New York? What will happen then?"

Lauren's lips wrinkled slightly. "I'm yesterday's news, Patrick. They won't care."

"Really?"

Lauren sighed. "Okay, so they'll make a little fuss, but we'll be together, and that's all that matters."

"Maybe I need a place to practice being with you before I bring you home," Patrick said. "Like normal people do when they date. I want a date before the hookup."

"A very nice hookup, but I understand what you're saying," Lauren said. "I don't want only a hookup either. But St. Louis, Missouri? Really?"

"I want to wine and dine you first, okay?" Patrick said. "I want to do this right. I can't do that if you come here. I can't afford to take you anyplace nice in New York."

"I *don't* mind paying, Patrick," Lauren said.

"I do," Patrick said. "A nice meal here costs what I spend on a month of groceries."

"So we'll eat in," Lauren said. "We don't have to go out. I'll even cook something for you."

"But I want to take you out," Patrick said. "I don't want our first date to be some microwaved burritos."

"I like microwaved burritos," Lauren said.

"Really?"

"Really," Lauren said. "I have normal eating habits, Patrick. I eat a little bit of everything, and I don't care what we eat as long as I'm your dessert."

"You will be," Patrick said, "but you'll definitely be my main course, not my dessert."

"You make me so hungry, man," Lauren said. "I'm starving out here. Let me come to New York!"

"No," Patrick said. "Not yet."

"How can I change your mind about all this?" Lauren asked.

"You can't."

"Please?" She poked out her bottom lip. "Pretty please?" She moved the screen closer to her lips. "Please?"

"You're not playing fair," Patrick said. "But I'm not changing my mind."

"All right," Lauren said, and her full face appeared again. "We'll meet in St. Louis first, but then I am coming straight to Brooklyn with you, okay?"

I hope so. "Maybe."

"Maybe?" Lauren frowned.

I shouldn't have said maybe. I don't like to see her frown. "Let's see what happens in St. Louis first."

"What do you expect to happen in St. Louis that would keep me from following you to Brooklyn?" Lauren asked.

"I don't know," Patrick said. "Nothing, probably, but

I'm hoping . . ." *What am I hoping?* "I'm hoping that we can be like any other couple, I guess. Just two people out on a date without . . . photographers."

"Is that what you think happens whenever I go out?" Lauren asked.

"Isn't it?"

Lauren winced. "Well, yeah, it does happen, and there might be a paparazzo or two hiding outside my apartment right now, but I doubt anyone will bother us in St. Louis."

Bingo. "You've made my point," Patrick said. "No one will bother us in St. Louis."

"Or *Brooklyn,*" Lauren said.

"You'd be bothered here," Patrick said.

"But it doesn't bother me," Lauren said. "I'm used to it."

Bingo. "I'm not used to it," Patrick said. "Look, I don't want anything to interrupt our first date anywhere. I don't want anything to distract me from you."

"Which is sweet," Lauren said, "but if I take a red-eye tonight from LA, and you pick me up . . . Oh yeah, you don't have a car. We can share a cab, then. It might still be dark, and we can sneak into your apartment and get to know each other in peace."

"We shouldn't have to sneak around," Patrick said. "Right?"

"Well, at first we might have to," Lauren said.

"I don't want to sneak around at *any* time, Lauren," Patrick said. "I don't want to have to hide. You understand?"

"I guess I'm so used to the attention, I didn't think how it might affect someone who's not. . . . Sorry. I don't know what I'm saying. Ignore me."

"I can't," Patrick said. "You said exactly what I'm feeling. I'm nobody. You're somebody. You're glamorous and gorgeous and sexy, and I'm not."

"That's not true," Lauren said.

"It is to me," Patrick said.

"You have no idea how important you are to me," Lauren said. "You're everything a woman wants and needs. And trust me, you are gorgeous and sexy, too."

"I don't know about that," Patrick said, "but I know I want this to last. I want to take my time and do this right, and I can't do it right if we have to sneak around or be harassed by photographers and reporters."

"Okay," Lauren said. "We'll meet in St. Louis, and we might have a quiet evening, or we might not. I hope we do."

Me, too, Patrick thought. *I'm going to be nervous as it is. I don't need an audience.*

"When?" Lauren asked.

"I'll have to get off work. . . ." *And make sure the buildings won't fall down without me there for a few days.* "How about two weeks from tonight?"

"Two weeks?" Lauren said. "Why not the day after tomorrow? Why not Thursday?"

"I don't know." Patrick quickly Googled "flight JFK to St. Louis" and found that the cheapest fare was $240 one way. *With fees and taxes, that's well over five hundred bucks round-trip!* He quickly went to Greyhound.com and checked bus schedules.

"What don't you know?" Lauren asked.

"I have to see about something first." *Bus fare is only one hundred fifty dollars one way, but it takes twenty-eight hours to get from Brooklyn to St. Louis! Twenty-eight hours on a bus! Is that even legal? If we meet somewhere at seven p.m. on Thursday, I'd have to leave at eleven p.m. on Tuesday night to get there in time.*

Tuesday is tomorrow.

This is happening too fast!

"Patrick?"

"Thursday might work," Patrick said slowly. *I'd have to work half a day Wednesday, get on a bus Wednesday afternoon, see her Thursday, leave Friday, and be back late Saturday. That's almost four full days off from a job that usually requires me to be somewhere every single day! This is impossible!*

"Where are we going to meet?" Lauren asked. "Some out-of-the-way hotel perhaps? I'll be the woman in the overcoat and high heels, and that is *all* I will be wearing."

Now, there's a sexy image. "Well, we'd meet at a restaurant first, of course," Patrick said. "I'll be hungry." *After twenty-eight hours on a bus, I'll be starving!*

"Okay. Which restaurant?" Lauren asked.

I have no idea. I can afford McDonald's, but I can't take Lauren Short to McDonald's. "It will be a surprise." *To me, too.*

"And then?" Lauren whispered.

I love that sexy whisper. "And then we'll go someplace private, where I can get to know that woman in the overcoat and high heels much better."

"That sounds good," Lauren said.

That sounds life-altering! "I'll set up reservations and give you the details as soon as I know them." *What am I thinking? She could come here and . . . see this dump. She'd see how much I have to show for my life, see how shabby I really am, how I live, what I do, how I smell at the end of the day. I can't have her come here! No. St. Louis is safer.*

"I'm checking flight schedules right now," Lauren said. "I can fly Alaska Airlines. . . . Isn't that funny? I can fly Alaska Airlines and arrive in St. Louis on Thursday at five. There. I've bought my ticket. Should we meet at the airport? When will your flight arrive?"

"I won't be flying," Patrick said. "I'm taking a bus."

"What?"

"I can't afford to fly, Lauren," Patrick said.

"I can wire you the money," Lauren said.

"I got this," Patrick said. "I'm buying my bus ticket now." *The Internet fare is nonrefundable, but it's the cheapest.*

"You wouldn't have to spend a dime if you'd just let me fly out to New York," Lauren said.

Patrick found himself on the payment page. *Greyhound lets you pay with cash? I can do that? Perfect. All I have to do is pay for my ticket when I get to the bus terminal.* "My bus arrives at five o'clock on Thursday."

"You're taking a *bus* from Brooklyn to St. Louis," Lauren said.

"Yes," Patrick said. "It's only a twenty-eight-hour ride." *Piece of cake.*

"Patrick, don't do that to yourself," Lauren said. "Let me fly you in."

Patrick then searched for St. Louis restaurants. Tony's four-star rating caught his attention, and he went to the Tony's website. He scrolled down to the chef's tasting menu. *Whoa. Over two hundred bucks for two people. If that's the worst that can happen, we'll be okay.* "We'll eat at Tony's on Market Street."

"Why won't you let me fly you in?" Lauren asked.

"Because I've already reserved my bus ticket," Patrick said. "Tony's is an Italian restaurant."

"I love Italian," Lauren said. "Can I at least pay for the meal?"

"No."

"Are you always this stubborn?" Lauren asked.

"Yes," Patrick said.

Lauren's eyes blinked several times. "I can be pretty stubborn, too."

"And I like that about you," Patrick said. "But I will pay, okay?"

"Okay," Lauren said. "Where will we be staying after dinner?"

Patrick found several hotels near Tony's. "Somewhere close to the restaurant."

"Such mystery," Lauren said.

These hotels are not expensive by New York standards, but they aren't cheap. "I'm also going to pay you back for your plane ticket."

"You don't have to do that," Lauren said.

"I'm asking you out on a date to St. Louis, Missouri, so I should pay," Patrick said. "How much was your ticket?"

"About two thousand," Lauren said.

She has to be kidding. "Really?" Patrick asked.

"I usually travel first class," Lauren said. "Let me change it from first class to coach first. Hold on."

"No, no," Patrick said. "It's okay." *Two thousand bucks!* "Is that one way or round-trip?"

"One way," Lauren said. "I do not intend to come back here."

Two thousand! "Will you take a check?" *There goes most of my savings.*

"You don't have to pay for everything," Lauren said.

"I do, okay?"

"Why?"

"I don't want you to look back at our first date and re-member how you had to pay for anything," Patrick said.

"But if I have the means," Lauren said, "I should con-tribute."

"I told you about Natalia and how I couldn't provide enough for her. I doubt I could ever provide enough for you either, but I will pay for this entire first date." *Even if it bankrupts me.*

"Okay," Lauren said. "You pay for this one, and I'll pay for the next date."

"No."

"Why not?" Lauren asked.

Patrick chose the Millennium Hotel and tried to make online reservations, but he needed a credit card. *I'll have to call the toll-free number later.*

"Patrick, why not?" Lauren asked again.

"We'll be staying at the Millennium Hotel, which is close to Tony's and has a great view of the Gateway Arch and the Mississippi River." *I hope we'll be staying there.*

"You didn't answer my question," Lauren said.

"I will pay for every date we go on," Patrick said. *Though I have no idea how.* "Tony's is only two blocks from the hotel."

"Patrick . . ."

"It's okay, Lauren," Patrick said. "It's something I have to do, okay? I want to impress you."

"You already do," Lauren said.

"Then I want to impress you more," Patrick said. "I want to impress you more than you've ever been impressed before."

"You already have," Lauren said.

"And I'll try to continue to do so," Patrick said.

"You know, we might not eat much at Tony's," Lauren said. "I know that I won't be that hungry, for food anyway." *And that would save me a nice chunk of change.* "I might not be that hungry, either." *After twenty-eight hours on a bus? Who am I kidding? I'll be hungry enough to eat the napkins!*

"And I doubt we'll be looking at that arch or the river," Lauren said.

"I'll only be looking at you," Patrick said.

"With the lights on or off?" Lauren whispered.

"With every light on," Patrick said. "I don't want to miss a thing."

"Good," Lauren said. "That's . . . that's very good."

"So, we're set," Patrick said. "Thursday at seven at Tony's on Market Street in St. Louis."

"Right," Lauren said. "But it's *not* right, Patrick. This is so crazy."

"I know it is," Patrick said. "But it will at least be different, something to remember, right?"

"I'll say," Lauren said. She smiled. "I can't wait to see you, Patrick." Lauren tilted the camera. "Are you looking at me now?"

He watched her hands moving up and down her body. "I can't take my eyes off you," he whispered. "You know that."

"I wish I could kiss you right now," Lauren whispered.

"I'd like that," Patrick whispered. "I like what you're doing with your hands, too."

"I want your hands on me," Lauren whispered. "I'd crawl into your lap and probably get very busy while I kissed your lips off. I better stop." The view shifted to her face. "I need to get packed."

"It's two days away," Patrick said. *And I have to leave in less than thirty hours. I need to pack, too.* He looked into his closet. *Why should I worry? It will only take me five minutes.*

"I have to do some laundry first," Lauren said. "I've been so lazy. How many days should I pack for?"

One. "Travel light, okay?"

"Right," Lauren said. "We won't need many clothes after dinner."

She's like a runaway train, and I don't want to stop her!

"Oh, this is already driving me crazy," Lauren said. "I *hate* to wait."

"I'm sorry I'm being so difficult about this."

"It's okay," Lauren said. "It's actually romantic. I've never been on a date like this before. We're going on a secret rendezvous to a place I've never been. Very mysterious and sexy. That's what you're trying for, right?"

"Right." He shook his head. "No, not really, but I'm glad it seems that way to you."

"You weren't going for mysterious and sexy," Lauren said.

"No," Patrick said. "I was going for ordinary and anywhere but here."

"You think riding on a bus for twenty-eight hours to have a date in St. Louis is ordinary?" Lauren said.

"That's the 'anywhere but here' part," Patrick said.

"And meeting someone for the very first time, and at an Italian restaurant two thousand miles from her home . . . You think this is ordinary?"

"When you put it that way . . . ." Patrick laughed. "It does sound extraordinary, but that's not what I had in mind. I just want to meet you someplace where no one knows either of us."

"I could wear a disguise," Lauren said. "I'm good at being incognito. I did it for seven years, remember."

"It won't matter what you wear," Patrick said. "Someone will recognize you, but maybe for a few moments in a dark restaurant, it will only be the two of us. That's what I'm hoping for."

"I hope so, Patrick," Lauren said. "What are you going to wear?"

"Most likely what I wear on the bus." *For twenty-eight hours!* "Jeans and my only button-down shirt."

"I'll try to dress incognito, too," Lauren said.

"I'm not trying to be incognito," Patrick said. "I'll be almost as dressed up as I get."

"Not for long," she whispered.

I have to do some laundry, too. "I don't want to say good night, but . . ."

"It's only . . . ten o'clock there," Lauren said. "The night is young."

"I'll have two really busy days in a row." *I have to inform all the tenants that I won't be around for a few days and that they'll just have to survive without me. Oh, and please, Mrs. Moczydlowska, don't call my boss.*

"Well, I suppose I can let you get some sleep," Lauren said. "I really love what you're doing for me."

"What am I doing?" *Besides complicating things!*

"You're trying to make our first date perfect," Lauren said. "So many men don't try to make *any* dates perfect, as if it's our privilege just to be seen with them. I have never had a man take care of me like this before. I don't want to let you, you know, so expect me to resist your efforts."

"And I'll resist back," Patrick said.

"And that's actually comforting to know," Lauren said. "You know what you want, and nothing is going to stop you."

Just my bank account. "I want you."

"You got me," Lauren said with a smile. "I won't be able to Skype you on the bus, so have your cell phone charged. I may send you a picture or two. Just keep the picture to yourself, okay?"

"I will." He looked into her eyes. "Thank you for . . . meeting me in St. Louis."

"I am certain it will be my pleasure," Lauren said. "Thank you for asking me. Good night, Patrick."

"Good night, Lauren."

He shut down Skype and immediately called the Millennium Hotel's toll-free number. "Hi. I'd like to make a reservation for Thursday in St. Louis, Missouri."

"Number of rooms?" a woman asked.

"One."

"How many adults?"

"Two."

"How many children?"

"None."

"Your name and address, sir?"

Patrick supplied the information.

"All the way from Brooklyn," she said. "How will you be paying?"

"With cash," Patrick said.

Silence on the other end.

"Hello?" Patrick said.

"Sir, we require a credit card to hold the room for you," she said.

"I don't have a credit card," Patrick said, "or I would have made my reservation through your website."

"Sir, we cannot reserve your room without a credit card."

"Why?"

"We just can't, sir," she said. "The system won't let us."

Patrick sighed. "Could you connect me directly to the hotel in St. Louis?"

"They'll tell you the same thing," she said.

"Hey, it's worth a shot," Patrick said.

"I'll connect you. Hold, please."

After some static, Patrick heard, "Millennium Hotel, St. Louis. This is Penny. How may I help you?"

"Penny, I'd like to make a reservation," Patrick said.

"Oh, we don't take reservations here, sir," Penny said. "Let me give you the toll-free number for reservations."

"I don't believe that," Patrick said.

"Excuse me?"

"I don't believe that you don't take reservations there," Patrick said.

"We don't," Penny said. "Reservations are made through our national reservations center."

"So if someone walks in off the street and asks for a room, what do you do?" Patrick asked.

"Oh, that's different," Penny said.

"How is it different?" Patrick asked.

"I don't understand you, sir," Penny said.

Isn't that obvious? "You don't make someone who walks in call a toll-free number while they're standing there in front of you, do you?"

"Oh, of course not," Penny said. "I first see if we have a room available, and if we do, I ask for a credit card."

"Why?" Patrick asked.

"So we are assured of payment, sir," Penny said.

"Isn't cash a form of payment?" Patrick asked.

"Well, of course it is," Penny said.

"So if I showed up and gave you a cash payment in full for one night," Patrick said, "wouldn't that be the same as handing you a credit card?"

"Oh, I see what you're saying. Sure."

"All right," Patrick said. "I am arriving in the afternoon this Thursday, and I will need a room for one night."

"A standard room?" Penny asked.

"Yes," Patrick said.

"Let me see if we have any vacancies," Penny said. "You're in luck. We have several. How about a king bed?"

"Fine," Patrick said.

"I'll need your name, address, and telephone number," Penny said.

He gave her the information.

"And now I'll need a credit card," Penny said.

Penny isn't quite playing with a full deck. "I will be paying in cash."

"Um, Mr. Esposito . . ."

This is ridiculous. "Yes?"

"The system won't let me complete your reservation without a credit card," Penny said.

"Can you hold a room without a credit card?" Patrick asked. "This is really important."

"Let me speak to a manager," Penny said. "Hold on."

While he waited, Patrick checked his bank balance online. He tried to make an extra zero appear before the decimal point, but no zero materialized. He mentally added up the cost of the date and arrived at $2,640: $300 for the bus ticket, $240 for the meal, $100 or so for the hotel, and $2,000 for Lauren's plane ticket. *She'll want to eat breakfast, so an even twenty-seven hundred dollars. I had better take out twenty-eight hundred dollars to be sure.*

He sighed.

And that only leaves me four hundred dollars for the ring—

"Mr. Esposito," a man said. "This is Frank Gill. Penny has explained your predicament to me, and I'm afraid we really can't help you."

"Mr. Gill, I believe that if you wanted to help me, you would," Patrick said. He looked down at Lauren's face on his screen. "What if a movie star or musician wants to stay with you? Do you have to have credit card information every time?"

"Yes," he said.

"Even in unusual circumstances?"

"I don't follow you," Mr. Gill said.

I can't believe I have to lie to this man to get a room! "Do you know actress Lauren Short?"

"Oh yes," Mr. Gill said. "I love her movies."

"Lauren Short is coming to your hotel this Thursday," Patrick said, "but she doesn't want to reserve the room in her name or use any kind of credit card information to keep the media from knowing where she is. The media is good at finding people who don't want to be found. Do you understand?"

"She's traveling incognito, is that it?" Mr. Gill asked.

"Something like that," Patrick said. "I need to reserve a room in my name and *without* a credit card so the media can't find her."

"Consider it done," Mr. Gill said.

Thank you!

"Your reservation will be under your name, Mr. Esposito," Mr. Gill said. "We look forward to having Miss Short as our guest."

"Thank you, Mr. Gill," Patrick said. "And please keep it quiet."

"We will, Mr. Esposito," Mr. Gill said. "We will be discreet."

I hope. "We will see you Thursday."

Patrick then called Tony's. "I'd like a reservation for two for Thursday at seven p.m."

"We are booked solid on Thursday," a man said.

"Really?" Patrick said. "On a Thursday?"

"We are a culinary institution," the man said. "The earliest I can get you a table is . . . December sixth."

What? "December sixth?"

"Correct," the man said. "Shall I book your reservation for that day, sir?"

Wow. We may be eating at McDonald's, after all. "I *must* have a reservation for Thursday at seven."

"It is impossible, sir," the man said.

Nothing is impossible. "Even if it's for Lauren Short, the actress?"

"Lauren Short . . . is coming here to eat on Thursday?" the man asked.

It must be so nice to be a celebrity. "Yes. At seven. She will be traveling incognito, so we'll need to put the reservation under a different name."

"I see," the man said. "One moment."

Patrick waited for longer than "one moment" was supposed to last.

"What name should I put the reservation under, sir?" the man asked suddenly.

"Esposito," Patrick said.

"Miss Short has a reservation for seven on Thursday," the man said. "Will she be dining alone?"

"No," Patrick said. "She will be dining with Patrick Esposito."

"Splendid," the man said.

"Can I trust you to keep this information confidential?" Patrick asked. "Miss Short wants a quiet evening with no fanfare."

"We pride ourselves on our discretion, sir," the man said.

"Thank you," Patrick said. "Miss Short and Mr. Esposito will see you at seven on Thursday. Good-bye."

Now where was I?

Oh yeah. The ring.

You can't have a perfect first date without a ring, right?

I wonder if they sell starter rings. . . .

37

I can't believe I told him I loved him, Lauren thought. *Wait. I only said that I may love him and that I probably love him, and I explained why . . . or tried to. The man tied up my tongue. It's his fault that I didn't make any sense.*

But how did he react when I told him that I probably love him? He didn't! He didn't even blink! I didn't expect him to return the favor, but I expected more than what I got. Maybe I'm expecting too much too soon. I wish I wasn't so impatient!

But why St. Louis? Of all the cities he could have chosen, he chose St. Louis. Why not Chicago or Pittsburgh or Atlanta? I really should just get on a plane and go see him anyway. What's he going to do? Turn me away? He couldn't refuse to see me, could he?

Her apartment phone rang. She threw on her robe and walked into the kitchen. "Hello?"

"Lauren, Todd. You have a minute?"

"Did *SNL* call?" Lauren asked.

"No, but you have to hear—"

Lauren hung up. She counted to ten. The phone rang again. She answered. "What?"

"Are you going to hang up on me?" Todd asked.

"It depends on what you tell me," Lauren said.

"Well, listen, I've just got off the phone with a screen-writer who wants to do your biopic," Todd said. "He wants to do your autobiography."

"My what? Is he crazy? I'm only thirty-eight!"

"Come on, Lauren. Listen to the angle he's dangling," Todd said. "Young black girl, wrong side of the tracks—"

"I didn't live near any railroad tracks, Todd," Lauren interrupted.

"It's a figure of speech," Todd said. "Young black girl from the *hood* rises out of the ashes of D.C., sets LA on fire, and then flames out because of her bisexual fiancé."

"You make me sound like a pyromaniac," Lauren said. "It sounds depressing and stupid."

"You'll get to play yourself, Lauren," Todd said. "From your early movie days to the present. You'll get to be twenty again."

"I don't want to be twenty again," Lauren said. *I just want to be in Brooklyn with Patrick!* "Tell the writer no."

"I just don't understand you!" Todd shouted. "I'm working my ass off, trying to get you back in the game."

"It's *SNL* or nothing," Lauren said. "I want to work in New York."

"But I've already told you that Erika James—"

Lauren hung up again. She poured a glass of water and drank it in two gulps. *Why am I so dehydrated? Oh yeah. Patrick set me on fire.* She drank another glass.

The phone rang.

I wish he'd give up. "You were saying, Todd?"

"What is your sudden fascination with New York?" Todd asked. "You told me that once you left New York, you never wanted to work in New York again. You said it wasn't laid-back enough, and like you said, I don't have the connections there that I have here."

"It's not a fascination," Lauren said. "It's a need. Make that need come true."

"How about this?" Todd asked. "We'll see if we can get *Saturday Night Live* interested in you guest hosting the show. Will that satisfy you?"

"Why would they want me to guest host?" Lauren asked. "I haven't done anything in years."

"Don't I know it," Todd said.

Lauren sighed. "Have you even talked to anyone at NBC?"

"I have," Todd said. "And they're flattered that you want to be a part of the show. They have great respect for you, but they're trying to appeal to a new generation of viewers, and Lauren, baby, you're from a different generation."

"You're right, Todd," Lauren said. "I'm from a generation of actresses who actually *learned* how to act, who didn't cut their teeth making rap videos, who didn't capitalize solely on their looks or their ability to sing to break into this business. I can perform my lines with more skill and conviction in my *sleep* than Miss Erika can in her *best* moments, if she ever has any. If *Saturday Night Live* doesn't want that, then I guess I'm through. Good-bye, Todd."

She hung up.

The phone rang.

Lauren let it ring.

When it stopped ringing, she dialed her mama.

"Mama, I'm thinking seriously about giving up acting and settling down with a good man," she said quickly. "In fact, I'm going on a date with a very—".

Click.

Lauren laid the phone in its cradle. "A very good man," she whispered. "A man you and Daddy would be proud of. He's a handyman, like Daddy, and we're meeting in St. Louis."

She sat on her bed.

That was longer than she usually lets me talk. We might be making progress.

She spent the rest of the evening doing laundry and packing three suitcases. One suitcase held all her important papers, including her tax returns and her birth certificate. *Because I am never coming back to this dump.* She had to sit on the last suitcase to get it to close. *I am bringing enough clothing for at least a week, because when St. Louis works out—and it will—I will be going to Brooklyn.*

She looked around her little apartment.

I will never be coming back here. There's no reason to come back here.

She fell back on her bed.

St. Louis—and Patrick—here I come.

Good-bye, Hollywood. It was somewhat fun while it lasted, but now you've become toxic.

I have to go to St. Louis now to find love.

She fanned her face.

I'm still hot and bothered and feeling goofy. True love must be intoxicating.

She laughed.

I will be drunk on love in St. Louis.

38

When he awoke at five a.m. on Wednesday, Patrick left a message for Salthead. "This is Patrick Esposito. I'm not sure who my supervisor is. I work the buildings on Atlantic, Dean, Bergen, Baltic, and State in Boerum Hill. I'm going to take some days off this week and need someone to cover for me. Please call me back as soon as you get this message."

A few minutes after eight a.m., after he had already cleaned the furnace flame sensors on Atlantic, Dean, and Baltic, Salthead called while Patrick trundled his tool bag toward Bergen and Mrs. Moczydlowska.

"Patrick, it's Jim Barber at Salthead."

"Hi, Jim," Patrick said. *Is this my supervisor?*

"It's going to be difficult to find anyone to cover for you," Mr. Barber said. "I'm looking at your file now. You have never taken a day off, so we don't have anyone who has ever subbed in your buildings."

They're just like any others. A building is a building. "Everything is in working order now, and I don't think there will be any trouble. The building on Baltic has some cold weather piping issues, but I think they'll be okay for a few days since it's supposed to stay above freezing. I have one more furnace to clean on Bergen, and then I'm knocking off for the day."

"How many days will you be gone?" Mr. Barber asked.

"Four," Patrick said.

"Four days? In a row?"

"Really three and a half," Patrick said. "I really only need a number my tenants can call in case of an emergency."

Mr. Barber gave him a number. "Hey, you're not quitting on us, are you?"

"No, Mr. Barber," Patrick said. "I'm not quitting."

"Because if you're thinking about quitting or finding work somewhere else . . ."

"I'm going on a little vacation," Patrick said. "That's all."

"Well, that's good," Mr. Barber said. "You've been with us what? Ten years?"

"Fifteen," Patrick said.

"Really?" Mr. Barber said. "That's a long time to work without a vacation. Yep, it says fifteen years here in your file. You know, you're due a bump in pay."

Good news? "I am?"

"You were actually due three years ago," Mr. Barber said. "I wonder why Campbell didn't put you in for it."

"Who's Campbell?" Patrick asked.

"Your old supervisor," Mr. Barber said. "He should have put you in for a raise."

I didn't even know the guy. "How much of a bump?" Patrick asked.

"At least ten percent," Mr. Barber said. "I'll get the paperwork started today, okay?"

"Sure," Patrick said.

"It might not show up on your check this month, but it will definitely show up next month in time for Christmas," Mr. Barber said. "You know, you have to have the cleanest file I've ever seen. There isn't a single complaint in here from anyone."

Not even from Mr. Hyer or Mrs. Albertson? "Really?"

"Many guys have a dozen complaints a month," Mr. Barber said, "and here you are with none for fifteen years. What's your secret?"

"I don't really have one," Patrick said. "I do what needs to be done when it needs to be done."

"I should have you train the rest of the guys," Mr. Barber said. "When will you be leaving?"

"I'll be off from now through about six p.m. Saturday," Patrick said.

"All right," Mr. Barber said. "You have a good vacation. You've earned it."

"Thank you, Mr. Barber."

As Patrick moved toward Bergen Street and Mrs. Moczydlowska, he called each of his other tenants, leaving messages for half of them. Only Mrs. Gildersleeve showed any interest in his absence.

"Three and a half days," she said. "What will you be doing?"

Mostly riding on a Greyhound bus. "I'm meeting a friend in St. Louis."

"Is this the same friend I sent a picture to?" she asked.

"Yes, ma'am," Patrick said.

"Is this friend named Lauren Short?" she asked.

"Yes, ma'am."

"You're meeting Lauren Short in St. Louis," she said.

"Yes," Patrick said. "It's our first date."

"Uh-huh," Mrs. Gildersleeve said.

She doesn't believe me. "Really."

"Why go to St. Louis when she can fly to New York?" Mrs. Gildersleeve asked. "I mean, if she's the *real* Lauren Short, the Hollywood star, she can fly just about anywhere she pleases, right?"

"Right," Patrick said. "But I've talked her into meeting me in St. Louis. If she flew here, photographers would most likely swarm us wherever we went. I want some quiet time alone with her."

Mrs. Gildersleeve laughed. "I don't believe you for a minute, Patrick, but you have fun, okay?"

"I will," Patrick said. "Call that number if you need anything while I'm gone."

"Oh, I will," she said. "Tell Lauren hi for me, okay?"

"I will." *I may even bring her by to meet you one day.*

As he had expected, Mrs. Moczydlowska took the news of his vacation the hardest.

"Why you go to this St. Louis?" she asked.

"I'm going on a date," Patrick said.

"This woman is in St. Louis?" she asked.

"Um, no, she's flying in from Los Angeles," Patrick said.

"Have her fly all the way to here," she said. "Tell her not to stop."

"We're meeting in St. Louis," Patrick said.

"Is it far?" she asked.

"About a thousand miles," Patrick said.

Mrs. Moczydlowska's eyes popped. "You cannot date her here in Brooklyn?"

I could, but I'm already committed to my crazy idea. "This is a special date," Patrick said.

"It is crazy," Mrs. Moczydlowska said. "To go so far for one date."

"It *is* kind of crazy," Patrick said.

"A good boy like you should not have to go so far for a woman," she said. "There are good women in Brooklyn, yes?"

"True," Patrick said.

"So you change the place," she said. "Tell her to meet you here. Tell her to fly here."

"But we already have our tickets," Patrick said.

"Get refund," she said.

"My ticket is nonrefundable," Patrick said.

She sighed and looked at the number Patrick had given her. "You did not think this through."

Patrick didn't dispute that.

Mrs. Moczydlowska sighed. "So if I have trouble, I call this number."

"Right," Patrick said. "Twenty-four hours a day."

"What if I call your number?" she asked. "By mistake. Will you answer?"

Patrick nodded. "I will always answer your call, Mrs. Moczydlowska. But only yours. I will ignore everyone else's."

Mrs. Moczydlowska seemed to smile. "I may call you by mistake while you are gone."

I would expect nothing less. "And I will answer every time for as long as my phone works. The battery doesn't last more than a day."

"You must get better phone, then," she said. She walked to the door. "You come back."

Patrick smiled. "I will."

"You do not come back, I call your boss."

"Yes, Mrs. Moczydlowska."

After cleaning the furnaces at Bergen and his own building, Patrick did something he had never done before.

He went to the IHOP on Livingston and ordered a western omelet.

For the first time in his working life, he ate a meal seated in a chair at a table. There was no machine whirring near him and no stench surrounding him. He was not hustling from one service call to another while wolfing down his food. He was not on the phone with an irate tenant. He enjoyed his omelet, rested his feet, and watched the world rushing by outside.

After his brunch, he went to the Chase Manhattan Bank on Flatbush and withdrew twelve hundred dollars in cash. That left $2,004.38 in his account to cover the cost of Lauren's ticket.

This will give me eight hundred dollars for the date and four hundred dollars for a ring.

He sighed.

Why did I offer to pay for her plane ticket? With twenty-four hundred dollars, I could get her a much nicer ring. Even that isn't what Lauren deserves by a long shot, but at least it would be nicer. I'll just have to get her a friendship ring this time. It doesn't have to be an engagement ring yet. I'm getting a ten percent raise. Maybe I should wait until that kicks in before looking for an engagement ring. With my raise, I might even be able to get store credit. Yeah. We could be engaged after Christmas and maybe married in January.

He sighed again. *But I can't afford to wait that long. I may only get one shot at this thing. Lauren Short is an impatient woman. Chucky kept her waiting for three years.*

I will not make Lauren Short wait.

Besides, the best first date in the world has to end with an engagement ring, doesn't it?

And where would I find such a ring?

He walked half a mile up Flatbush to Schermerhorn Street and Gem Pawnbrokers, which was sandwiched between two check cashing places and Swap & Shop. He banged through the door with his tool bag and went straight to the jewelry display case.

"May I help you?" a Hispanic woman asked.

Patrick looked through several dangling gold chains at her name tag. *Her name is Vicky. Is Vicky a Hispanic name?* "Do you have anything in . . . platinum?" *Lauren deserves platinum.*

Vicky squinted into the case. "I think so." She removed a small box with a thin sliver of a ring. "It's an Art Deco wedding band from the thirties," she said. She squinted at the tag. "Seven round diamonds, point-oh-four carat weight, size . . . six and a half." She handed the ring to Patrick. "Pretty light, isn't it?"

It doesn't weigh a thing, Patrick thought. *It's shinier than anything else in the case, though.* "Yeah. How much?"

Vicky turned over the tag. "Appraised for fifteen hundred, but . . . I'll let you have it for twelve hundred."

If I had twelve hundred, I'd get it. "That's a bit . . ." He sighed. "Much." He handed back the ring. "Pretty ring, though. Maybe one day." He scanned the case, which was mostly filled with gold rings, some exceptionally gaudy. "Anything, um . . ." *Lauren deserves much more than gold.* He shook his head. "Never mind. Thanks." He turned to go.

"What's her name?" Vicki asked.

Patrick stopped and turned. "Lauren."

"Nice girl?" Vicki asked.

Patrick nodded. "The best."

"Is she from around here?" Vicki asked.

"No," Patrick said. "She's from LA."

Vicky stared at him. "Los Angeles, California?"

"Yeah," Patrick said.

"How'd you meet her?" Vicky asked.

"We met online," Patrick said.

"Like on Match.com," Vicky said.

"No," Patrick said. "I wrote her a fan letter, and she wrote back. We've been writing to each other ever since."

"A fan letter, huh?" Vicky said. "Is she famous?"

"Yes," Patrick said. *She's so famous that I'm meeting her in St. Louis so her fame doesn't get in the way of our date.*

"What's her name?" Vicky asked.

"Lauren Short."

Vicky put the ring back in the case. "Like the actress?"

"No," Patrick said. "*The* actress."

Vicky blinked. "Really?"

"Yeah," Patrick said. "I'm meeting her in St. Louis on Thursday."

"Uh-huh," Vicky said, crossing her arms.

"Yeah, I wouldn't believe me, either," Patrick said. "I hardly believe it myself. Lauren Short and I are going on a date in St. Louis in two days. It doesn't seem real."

Vicky leaned against the case. "You're serious."

Patrick nodded. "I'm trying hard to impress her. I'm paying for everything—the meal, the hotel, and her plane ticket, first class, two grand one way."

Vicky whistled.

"And that doesn't leave me much to get her a ring," Patrick said. "What, with dinner at Tony's, a room at the Millennium Hotel, and my bus fare . . ." He sighed. "I don't know what to do, you know?"

"You're taking a *bus* to St. Louis," Vicky said.

"Yeah," Patrick said. "Twenty-eight hours on a Greyhound. I leave at one."

"Let me get this straight," Vicky said. "You're taking a bus to St. Louis in a couple of hours to have a date with Lauren Short, the world-famous actress."

"Right."

Vicky laughed. "And you came *here* to buy her a ring."

Patrick's face grew hot. "Right."

Vicky slapped the counter with both hands. "I have heard some tales in this store but *nothing* like the one you're spinning for me now. Tell you what. I'll knock that ring down to nine hundred for that crazy story."

More good news? "If you make it eight hundred, I could pay you half now and half when I get paid at the end of December," Patrick said.

"I don't know if I can go eight," Vicky said.

"How long has the ring been in the case?" Patrick asked.

"Good point," Vicky said. "All right. Eight hundred, but I'll need some collateral."

Patrick turned slightly, the tool bag swinging forward. "I only have my tools and the clothes on my back." *Why didn't I put the laptop in the tool bag today? That has to be worth at least . . . fifty bucks.* "I won't need my tools for a few days. They're all in good condition."

"Your . . . tools," Vicky said.

"I'm a handyman," Patrick said, putting the bag on the counter. "They're the most valuable things I own."

"You're a handyman going on a date with Lauren Short in St. Louis," Vicky said.

"Right."

Vicky shook her head. "Really?"

"Really."

"All right," Vicky said. "Let me take a look."

While Vicky pored over Patrick's tools, Patrick looked at the thousands of items people had parted with: guitars, trumpets, saxophones, amplifiers, jewelry, electronics, and even some expensive purses. *People even pawn what holds their money so they can get some money. There's something ironic about that.* He stared into the case at the diamond rings and gold wedding bands. *These used to be on peo-*

ple's fingers. I wonder where those people are now. He squinted at a particularly small diamond ring. *I wonder if that's the one I got for Natalia. It's about the same size.*

"You have a tool for just about everything in there," Vicky said.

"I do maintenance for Salthead Property," Patrick said. "Whatever can go wrong, I need the right tool to fix it."

"I really can't value these at more than three hundred," Vicky said, "and that's being generous."

"They're easily worth five times that," Patrick said.

"*New*," Vicky said. "These aren't new. And three hundred is their *loan* value. I'm giving you a loan, right?"

He nodded. "That leaves me a hundred short. What if I left them here with you?"

"You couldn't do your job," Vicky said.

"I'll be gone until Saturday night," Patrick said, "and then maybe I can come by to pay you the balance on the ring and pick up my tools." *How, I don't know! I'd hate to borrow money from Lauren to pay for* her *ring and the rescue of my tools!*

"We're closed Saturday night," Vicky said.

"How about Sunday?"

"We're closed on Sundays," Vicky said.

"It would have to be Monday, then," Patrick said. "I really want to take this ring with me to St. Louis."

"For Lauren Short," Vicky said. "Chazz Jackson's ex-fiancée."

"Right."

Vicky leaned closer. "Are you crazy or something?"

"No," Patrick said. "What I'm doing may seem crazy, but I'm not crazy."

Vicky shook her head, but she was smiling. "You sure you want to give up your tools, even for a 'date' with Lauren Short?"

"I know I shouldn't, but I want to get Lauren that ring," Patrick said. "If leaving my tools here means that I get to leave with the ring, I'll leave the tools." He dug out his roll of money and peeled off four hundreds. "I'd pay for the ring in full, but then I couldn't afford dinner at Tony's, and I might have trouble paying the entire hotel bill. I'd hate to ask Lauren to pay for any part of our date." He held out the money. "That would be embarrassing."

Vicky looked at the money. "You've really worked out this . . . date."

"I'm trying," Patrick said.

Vicky took the money. "All right. I know I'm going to regret this, but I'm letting you take the ring."

Patrick smiled. "Thank you."

"And though I don't feel right about taking your tools," Vicky said, "I kind of have to."

"I understand," Patrick said. "I will be back for them on Monday, so please don't sell them."

"I don't *sell* many tools," she said. "I 'buy' them, though. This economy, you know?" She handed him a form. "Fill this out while I get, um, *Lauren's* ring ready."

"Okay."

While he filled out the form, Vicky polished the ring with a cloth, seated it in a black fuzzy box, and handed him the box.

"I can carry the bag wherever you want me to," Patrick said. "It's kind of heavy."

"I'll manage," Vicky said. She handed him another form. "This is what you owe on the ring." She slid him a card. "And this is your claim ticket for your tools. Don't lose this."

"I won't. Thank you, Vicky."

Vicky looked at his form. "You're welcome, Mr. . . . . Esposito." She squinted at him.

"I'm Italian," Patrick said.

Vicky shook her head slightly. "Give my best to Lauren."

"I'll give her my best," Patrick said, "and then I'll give her this ring. Thank you for doing this, Vicky. See you Monday."

Before he left his apartment with a small duffel bag filled with toiletries and one change of clothes, Patrick sent an e-mail to Lauren:

> Lauren:
>   I had an extremely good morning. I'm on my way to the bus station. I'll leave my cell phone on, but the battery will probably die before I get to St. Louis. See you at Tony's, Market Street, St. Louis, tomorrow at seven sharp.
>
> Patrick
>
> PS: I know you hate suspense, but I have a secret, and you'll never get it out of me, no matter how many of your clothes you threaten to take off. But I really hope you try. ;)

He hoisted the duffel bag, locked his apartment behind him, and ran two blocks north to the Greyhound Brooklyn Bus Terminal on Livingston. After he paid for his ticket and settled into a seat in the back of a crowded bus next to an ancient Asian woman, his phone buzzed.

"Hey, Lauren," Patrick said.

"You have to leave now?" she said. "What is it? One o'clock?"

"Yeah," Patrick said. "It's a long ride, remember?"

"Oh yeah," Lauren said. "Tell me your secret."

"Nope," Patrick said.

"I'll send you some interesting pictures," Lauren whispered.

"One picture download will drain half my phone battery," Patrick said.

"It will? That's no fun. I'll send you the best one, then, but only if you tell me first. By the way, in the best one, I don't have *any* clothes on."

She doesn't play fair. "Well, I might give you some hints, but it depends on the picture."

"It is a *very* naughty picture," Lauren said.

"Hmm," Patrick said. "I don't know. One picture for an extremely important secret. That's not an even trade in my book."

"It is *very* revealing," Lauren said. "It will leave nothing to your imagination."

He smiled at the woman sitting next to him before turning slightly and whispering, "Tell you what. You send it, and I'll decide if it's worthy."

"Oh, it's worthy, all right," she said. "Sending it now. Let me know when it gets there."

The bus pulled out into heavy midday traffic.

"I'm on my way."

"Is the picture there yet?" Lauren asked.

Patrick watched a text message arrive, selected it, and watched the picture load. "Just arrived." He held the phone close to his chest, and in a few moments he saw Lauren's sexy . . . face.

"Well?"

"I could look at this naked face all night and all day," Patrick whispered. "Thank you."

"Now, what's the secret?" Lauren asked.

"I'll tell you when I get to St. Louis," Patrick said.

"Oh, come on," Lauren said. "Please?"

"You don't like surprises, do you?" Patrick asked.

"I do," Lauren said. "I just don't like to *wait* for them."

"It won't be long," Patrick whispered.

"You know, we could do a little sexting," Lauren whispered.

"Another first," Patrick said.

"Great," Lauren said. "Give me a few minutes, and then start."

"Why do you need a few minutes?" Patrick asked.

"I need to lose a few clothes, all right? Bye."

Patrick wasted no time.

U aren't naked r u?

Lauren wasted no time, either.

Yes. :)

Patrick shifted in his seat and tried to control his breathing.

Are you cold?
Yes. My nipples r like little Milk Duds.
I like Milk Duds. I once tried 2 eat an entire box all @ once.
How'd that wrk out 4 u?
Nearly choked. R u really naked?
Yes. R u?
No. I m on a bus.
Yr no fun. U really never sexted?
Never. What r the rules?

There aren't any. I m getting so hot. U hard?
I m on a bus! A woman is sitting beside me.
Answr the question!
I m not hard.
I wanna taste u.
Slow down!
Tasting . . . so good . . . hot . . . like butter.
U dont play fair.
I wanna do it w/ u.
On a bus?
Yes. Go 2 br.
Smells. Occupied. Bus crowded.
Go! I m waitin 4 u in the br.

Patrick stood, squeezed down the aisle, and moved to the tiny bathroom, stepping inside and shutting the door. *I can't believe I'm doing this. This woman has too much power over me.*

OK. In br. 2 small!
U cant escape me.
Dont want 2.
Make love 2 me.
How? Ppl w8tin outside.
Really?
Bangin on door.
Cool . . .
Not cool. It reeks in here.
Ok, ok. Go back 2 yr seat. I will ride u.
R u always this shameless?
I m so horny!!! :) :) :)
I m saving it all 4 u.
Good. I know it will b so good.

It will b better than good.
:) *Dream of me.*
Always.
Love u . . . really . . . totally. . . . My heart is yours.

Patrick hesitated as the banging on the door continued. *I don't want the first time I tell Lauren I love her to be in a text message sent from the nasty bathroom of a bus, but I don't want her to be hurt. This is the only way.*

I want 2 tell you face 2 face ok?
Ok. I want 2 tell you face 2 face 2.
Thank u 4 understanding. Get some sleep. Yr gonna need it.
Yessssssss!!!! :) :) :)
Sweet dreams.
Sweaty dreams.
Those 2.

39

Back in her early days of stardom, Lauren often sneaked past paparazzi by wearing a long black overcoat, a gray scarf, and a jet-black wig to make herself look like Whitney Houston did in a scene with Kevin Costner in *The Bodyguard*.

And the paparazzi never caught on, she thought. *I wonder why that was. Maybe it was because* Entertainment Weekly *said Houston and Costner looked like "two statues attempting to mate" and the* Washington Post *called* The Bodyguard *"a wondrously trashy belly flop."*

And I also look nothing like tall, thin Whitney Houston.

Yeah, that's probably the real reason.

However, today, a bright, sunny, and hot LA day, she didn't want to sneak by anyone.

I am going out in style today.

Just not my own style.

She looked outside and saw a lone photographer lurking near her car. *I'm down to one photographer. I hope I can make him some money today.*

She wore her bluest jeans, black suede Timberland boots, and a crisp white button-down blouse in an attempt to match Patrick. As an afterthought, she grabbed the overcoat.

In honor of Whitney. Besides, it might be cold in St. Louis.

She debated taking her car to the airport. *What will happen to my car if I don't come back? If I leave it here, the birds will turn it white. If I take it to the airport . . . the birds will still turn it white. In either case, someone will tow it if it sits too long. Do I really care what will happen to it? Patrick has lived his whole life without a car, and so can I.*

It guzzles gas anyway. It barely gets sixteen miles to the gallon.

She called a cab, and when it arrived, she rolled out her luggage. While the driver loaded her luggage into the trunk of the cab, the photographer snapped a long series of pictures.

"So, you're finally making your escape," the photographer said.

"No," Lauren said, posing idly beside the cab. *Well, take my picture! Don't you see me over here posing? Don't you see me showing you my best side?*

"Where are you off to, then?" he asked.

"I'm going on a little vacation," Lauren said. She draped the overcoat over her shoulder. *How's this, Mr. Photographer? Don't I look trendy?*

The photographer still didn't lift his camera.

Lauren gave up and tossed the overcoat inside the cab. *What a loser. He has pictures of me pulling some luggage.*

"Where are you going on this little vacation?" he asked.

"Will you make more money if you know my destination?" Lauren asked.

"I might." He lined up another picture. "I might not."

Click.

"What if I told you I was going to Australia?" Lauren asked.

"I wouldn't believe you," the photographer said.

"Really," Lauren said. "I'm going to visit the royal family in Australia. They spend their summers in Brisbane."

"You wouldn't go to see the royal family dressed like that," he said. "And you wouldn't be taking an overcoat. You must be going east. Back home to D.C. maybe?"

I'm not crawling back there just yet. "Queen Elizabeth is actually a down-home person," Lauren said. "I hear she wears Levi's in her drafty castle."

The photographer rolled his eyes. "So really, where are you headed?"

I cannot tell him I'm off to St. Louis, but I want the world to know something! "If you really must know, I am going on a date."

"You're taking three suitcases with you on a date," he said.

"Yes," Lauren said. "It's going to be an extended date."

The photographer took a few more pictures. "Really? Who with?"

"A real man," Lauren said.

"Does the real man have a name?" he asked.

This can't hurt. Patrick isn't on Google. "Patrick Alan Esposito."

"Never heard of him," he said. "Who is he?"

"A man of mystery," Lauren said, and she slipped into the back of the cab then shut the door behind her. "To LAX, please."

The photographer motioned for Lauren to roll down her window.

Lauren smiled as she rolled it down. "Yes?"

"No, really," he said. "Who is he?"

"Like I said," Lauren said, "a real man of mystery."

The photographer shrugged. "I'll bet. Bye."

As the photographer walked off, the cabdriver turned to her. "So I'm going to the international terminal?"

"No," Lauren said. "Alaska Airlines."

"So you're not going to Australia," the driver said.

"No," Lauren said. "I was just saying that to throw him off."

"I doubt you threw him off." The driver faced forward and pulled out of the parking lot. "I wouldn't go to Australia this time of year. It's summer in Australia now. Hot as shit. So where are you really headed?"

"You wouldn't believe me if I told you," Lauren said.

"Try me."

"I'm going to St. Louis," Lauren said.

"Why? They're about to have a major snowstorm."

Oh no!

"You'll be lucky if you get to land in St. Louis," the driver said. "Chicago's going to get slammed, too. Your flight might be diverted to Dallas."

What? "Really?"

"It's all over the news," the driver said. "Up to a foot all throughout the Midwest. Maybe more. They might even have a blizzard, like that Nemo storm a few years ago that hit Boston."

This can't happen! "Just . . . get me to the airport." She immediately called Alaska Airlines. "Hello. I'm flying to St. Louis in a couple hours. Is the flight leaving on time?"

"Yes," a woman said.

"I heard there is some bad weather on the way to St. Louis," Lauren said.

"All I know is that we're on time," the woman said.

"Thank you."

Lauren called Patrick. "Where are you?"

"Hi, Lauren. Thanks for calling," Patrick said. "It's so good to hear your voice."

"Oh, sorry," Lauren said. "Hi, Patrick. Where are you?"

"Ohio," Patrick said. "A little west of Columbus. We just finished a useless two-hour layover. Where are you?"

"I'm on my way to the airport," Lauren said. "How's your weather?"

"Cold, with some snow," Patrick said. "Nothing major. Mostly flurries. The roads are okay, and traffic isn't too bad."

Should I worry him? I have to. "St. Louis is about to be hit by a major snowstorm."

"That's what I heard," Patrick said. "But I'll be okay."

"My flight is leaving on time, but they're saying the Midwest could get a foot or more," Lauren said. "I might be diverted to another airport."

"I'm sure you'll be okay," Patrick said.

"I hope so," Lauren said. "But what about you?"

"This bus will get through," Patrick said. "We've certainly got enough weight. We have a full boat, and everyone just ate a ton of food at Dirty Frank's Hot Dog Palace."

"That's not a real place," Lauren said.

"It is," Patrick said. "I doubt we're going to run out of gas either."

Funny. "Are you on time?"

"After eight stops and four seemingly meaningless layovers, we're only about ten minutes behind schedule," Patrick said.

"That's good," Lauren said. "Um, I guess I'll see you soon."

"I can't wait," Patrick said. "Stay warm."

"I only brought one overcoat," Lauren said. "And you're supposed to keep me warm when I get there anyway. I'm going to wear you."

"I'm going to wear you *out,*" Patrick whispered.

"Ooh, I like that," Lauren whispered. "You're going to wear me outside?"

"Inside and outside," Patrick whispered.

"I like the sound of that," Lauren said. "You stay warm, too."

"I'll try," Patrick said. "See you soon."

"Bye."

When the cabdriver opened her door in front of the Alaska Airlines entrance, he asked, "Is everything okay?"

Lauren stepped out. "You know it is. You were eavesdropping."

"Yeah," the driver said. "Was that him you were talking to?"

"Yes," Lauren said.

"Where is he?" the driver asked.

Nosy! "A little west of Columbus, Ohio."

The driver opened the trunk. "What's he doing in Ohio?"

"He's on his way to St. Louis," Lauren said.

The driver set her luggage on the curb, and an old black skycap loaded it onto a cart.

"Good thing he's not in Cleveland," the skycap said. "They already shut down Hopkins."

Another eavesdropper. Lauren blinked at him. "Hopkins?"

"That's the airport in Cleveland," the skycap said. "It's already got two feet on the ground, and another foot is expected. It's mostly lake-effect snow."

"Oh." *I am so glad Patrick is on that bus now.* "How do you know that?"

The skycap showed Lauren his iPhone. "I watch the Weather Channel."

"Why?" Lauren asked.

The skycap pushed the cart toward the entrance. "We have no weather out here. I like weather. I'm originally from Detroit."

At the ticket counter, the ticket agent recognized Lauren immediately. "Oh, Miss Short, it is *such* a privilege and an honor."

Why do people have to gush? I'm just an ordinary girl from D.C. "Thanks."

The agent clicked through a series of keys. "What's in St. Louis?"

"Do you ask everyone that question?" Lauren asked.

"No," the woman said.

"Treat me no differently, then," Lauren said, collecting her boarding pass. "Say your next line."

"My next line?" the woman said.

"Aren't you supposed to say, 'Enjoy your flight'?"

The woman blushed. "Oh, yeah. Enjoy your flight, Miss Short."

"Thank you."

When she left the line, she tipped the skycap a twenty.

"Thank you, Miss Short," he said.

"Um, can you keep where I'm going under your hat for a while?" she asked.

The man stood up straight. "You don't think I'd rat you out to the media, do you?"

"You might," Lauren said. "It wouldn't take much for you to upload something with that iPhone of yours." She handed him another twenty.

"You know," he said with a smile, "I have no idea where Lauren Short was headed."

"Tell them Australia," she whispered, handing him another twenty.

The man laughed. "You can stop giving me money, Miss Short. Look around you."

Lauren looked around and saw phones and cameras raised in her direction. She also heard the whispers of "Is that . . . ?" and "Look, it's *her*."

"The media is going to know the second you get on your plane," he said. "It's a nonstop flight, right?"

"Right," Lauren said. "Oh, shoot. Is there anything you can do?"

He handed back two of the twenties and pocketed the other. "There isn't anything anyone can do, Miss Short," he said. "Folks know you."

But I don't want to be known anymore!

While she was slogging through the security screening and trying not to look at the camera phones aimed her way, her phone buzzed. "Hello?"

"Lauren, have I got a *golden* opportunity for you."

Todd. I need to block his number. "What is it?"

"They're doing a remake of *Mahogany*, and they want you to play the title role!"

"Why?" Lauren asked.

"Well, you're available, aren't you?" Todd asked.

Not at the moment, Lauren thought. *I've just had my boots inspected for bombs, and I'm putting them back on.* "I meant, why are they doing a remake of *Mahogany*? Can't Hollywood come up with something original? That movie is forty years old." *I wasn't even alive when that movie came out.*

"The producers think you're the next Diana Ross!"

"The producers are out of their minds," Lauren said. "And that movie is so creepy. Isn't Norman Bates in that one?"

"Yes, Tony Perkins plays a gay photographer who wants to woo Miss Ross," Todd said. "Remember that scene where he can't get it up?"

"And they want me . . ." *Will I ever live down what happened between me and Chazz?* "Tell them no."

"But, Lauren . . ."

"Tell them no!" Lauren shouted, and she turned off her phone. She smiled at the nearest security officer. "Sorry about that."

The security officer shook her head. "I would have said, 'Oh, *hell* no,' " she said. "I like Diana Ross and all, but that movie was seriously stupid. Of all the actors on this planet, they had to hook up a diva with Norman Bates."

Lauren arrived at her gate just in time for priority boarding. Once she was settled in first class, Wendy the flight attendant gushed over her.

"Miss Short," Wendy cooed, "this is *such* an honor."

"Please treat me like any other passenger," Lauren whispered.

"Oh, I will," Wendy cooed. "If there's *anything* you need, anything at all, you just ask me."

"I'd like some peace and quiet," Lauren said. *And I don't want you to coo at me ever again. I don't need a flighty flight attendant fluttering around me for five hours.*

"Oh, we'll keep it quiet," Wendy cooed. "*Anything* for you, Miss Short. And you'll be happy to know that the seat beside you will remain empty for the entire flight. Isn't that wonderful?"

She's still cooing. "How's the weather in St. Louis?"

"I have no idea," Wendy said.

"It's supposed to be snowing there," Lauren said.

"I'll check on it for you," Wendy said. She vanished and returned a moment later. "It is snowing, but it's not enough to keep us from landing."

"Now," Lauren said. "It's not enough snow *now*. What about later?"

"I'll check on it for you," Wendy said. She vanished again and returned several minutes later. "The captain says we'll be on time with no problems." Wendy touched Lauren's shoulder. "We'll be fine."

"Great," Lauren said. *And don't touch me.*

Wendy rubbed Lauren's shoulder. "Is there *anything* I can do for you before we depart?"

Leave me alone. "I'm good. Thanks."

"We'll be serving breakfast once we're in the air," Wendy said.

Remove your hand from my shoulder. Now. "I won't be eating breakfast," Lauren said.

"Oh, but you will be eating lunch, I hope," Wendy said. "We're having wild Alaskan salmon."

No way. "I won't be eating at all."

Wendy removed her hand. "Would like some champagne or some wine?"

At nine a.m.? "No thank you." *Now please go away. I need to rest up for tonight.*

Wendy crouched beside her. "Do you have an iffy tummy?"

"No, Wendy, I don't," Lauren said. "I rarely eat or drink while I travel, okay?"

"I have some Dramamine," Wendy said.

"I'll be fine." Lauren smiled. "Really. I have flown many times before, Wendy."

Wendy stood. "Well, if there's anything you need, anything at all, just let me know."

I still need you to go away. "I will." *Not.*

As the last of the passengers boarded, Lauren heard someone yell, "Miss Short!" She leaned her head out into the aisle to see a black teenager taking her picture with his phone.

Lauren squinted at the flash.

"Yes!" The boy looked at his phone. "Thank you, Miss Short!" He smiled.

This has got to stop! "Come here," she said.

The boy pointed at himself. "Me?"

"Yes, you," Lauren said. "Come here."

The boy took a hesitant step forward.

"Come on," Lauren said. "I won't bite."

The boy moved beside her.

"Sit," Lauren said.

"You want me to sit next to you?" he asked.

"Yes," Lauren said.

The boy sat, his feet rapidly tapping the floor.

"What's your name?" she asked.

"Terrance," the boy said.

"How old are you, Terrance?" she asked.

"Sixteen," Terrance said.

"Are you traveling alone?" Lauren asked.

"No," Terrance said. "My grandma's back there."

"Okay," Lauren said. "This is the deal. I don't mind that you took my picture, Terrance, but I don't want you to send it to anyone until *after* we land."

"I was just going to send it to my little brother, Jamie," Terrance said. "He'll be at the airport when we land. He's a huge fan of yours."

Lauren locked her eyes on Terrance's eyes. "I'm trying to just get away, you know? I don't want photographers there when I leave this plane. I'm trying to make a little escape here. I don't want to face a bunch of media. After what I've been through, I really need some anonymity. You understand?"

"Not really," Terrance said.

It does seem strange that a "star"—even a former one— doesn't want free advertising. "What would happen if you sent that picture to your brother?" Lauren asked.

"He'd be very happy," Terrance said.

"Would he forward the picture to everyone he knows?" Lauren asked.

"I seriously doubt it," Terrance said. "Jamie doesn't like to share."

"How old is your brother?" Lauren asked.

"He's ten," Terrance said. "He's a great kid."

Ten? And he's a huge fan of mine? He wasn't even alive when I made my first movie! "I'm sure he is, but wouldn't he brag to his friends about the picture?"

"He doesn't have many friends," Terrance said. "He has Down syndrome."

"Oh," Lauren said.

"He's seen all your movies," Terrance said. "He thinks you're his girlfriend. He wants to marry you."

That's so sweet. "If you hold on to that picture, I promise to have my picture taken with Jamie when we land."

"You'd do that?" Terrance asked.

"Of course," Lauren said. "I have to meet my biggest fan, don't I?"

"That'd be awesome," Terrance said. "Thank you."

This boy surely loves his brother. "I'll see you and Jamie when we land, okay?"

Terrance smiled. "Okay. Thank you, Miss Short."

"Call me Lauren," Lauren said.

"Okay," Terrance said. "Lauren." He moved out of the seat. "Thank you."

"See you when we land in St. Louis."

If we land in St. Louis.

As the plane backed away from the terminal, Lauren called Patrick, but the call went straight to voice mail.

"Patrick, I hope everything's okay," she said. "We're about to take off, and I've been assured that we're going to land on time in St. Louis. I'll be praying that you get there safely, too. Bye."

She closed her eyes.

God, You know I don't talk to You that often, and I'm sorry about that, but could You please keep the snow away from St. Louis, Ohio, Indiana, and Missouri for a few hours? I know it's a tall order, but You're God, so I know You can do it. Thanks.

"Miss Short," Wendy cooed, "is everything all right?"

Lauren opened her eyes. "Yes." *I only closed my eyes!*

"Okay," Wendy cooed. "If there's *anything* you need, anything at all, you ask for Wendy."

Lauren closed her eyes.

And, God, if You could . . . oh, I don't know . . . give Wendy someone else to harass, I'd really appreciate it.

She opened her eyes and glanced out the window.

Good-bye, California. I don't know when I'll see you again, if I ever see you again. We had a good run, but now it's time for me to go.

"Would you like me to close your window shade, Miss Short?" Wendy asked.

Stand down, Wendy! "I'm leaving it open for now."

"Okay," Wendy said. "You just let me know when you want it closed."

God, please get me to St. Louis quickly.

I don't want to harm Wendy.

But if she coos in my ear again, I just might.

40

"Yes, Mrs. Moczydlowska," Patrick said. "I'm still here."

I'm down to one battery bar, I missed Lauren's call because I didn't hear the beep, and I'm still here on the phone with the only tenant who truly cares about me.

"You are so quiet," she said. "It is like talking to no one."

"I'm sorry," Patrick said. *We need to wrap this up.* "So other than the *chuh-chuh-chuh-chuh*, everything is all right?"

"Yes," she said. "I did not expect you to answer when I called."

"I answered," Patrick said. "Are you sure everything is okay? If you need to, call that number I gave you."

"But you would not show up," she said.

"That's true, but someone would visit you."

"I need no visit," she said. "I need the *chuh-chuh-chuh-chuh* to go away."

"I'll work on it when I get back," Patrick said. "You take care."

"You come back," she said.

"Or you'll call my boss, right?"

"No," Mrs. Moczydlowska said. "You just come back. Good-bye."

Patrick quickly listened to Lauren's message as the battery bar began to flash. He shut off his phone to conserve the battery. He also pouted because he couldn't look at Lauren's picture anymore.

She's on her way to St. Louis, and there's no way I can tell her that we're now an hour behind schedule because of the snow.

Interstate 70 in Indiana was a mess. Traffic moved toward Indianapolis in a single file through heavy, blowing snow as the bus followed overmatched snowplows that were rearranging more than removing the snow. The bus crawled to a stop often, idling while emergency vehicles screamed out of the snow and disappeared into more snow to the west.

He rubbed the fuzzy ring box in his pocket with his thumb to calm himself, but every time he looked outside or looked at the clock he began to worry.

I shouldn't have taken the bus. I should have paid extra to fly. I'd probably be there by now. I'd be waiting at the airport for Lauren, and . . .

He closed his eyes. *And I'd be worrying the entire time about her flight. I'm sure she'll make it. I wish I knew for sure that I was going to make it.*

He gripped and released the ring box. *I don't even know for sure if she'll accept this ring, this little cheap ring. If this is my only shot, I have to make it count. But what do I say? When I asked Natalia to marry me, all I said was, "Will you marry me?" She said yes, we went out for ice cream at Baskin-Robbins, and . . .*

I have to do much better than that for Lauren Short.

To pass the time, he rehearsed in his mind what he would say.

Lauren, only a few days ago I was a lonely man who—

That is so depressing. I can't be depressing. A marriage proposal should never be depressing.

Lauren, you have brought light into my life, and—

That's still depressing, because it means I was living in darkness before I met her. Well, I was, but . . .

Lauren, there's been something I have wanted to say to you. I know we've only known each other for a short time—

Why introduce doubt? Why plant a seed like that? That's almost like saying, "You know, we really don't know each other well enough to make this lifetime commitment."

He sighed.

Lauren, I love you. I have loved you since the first time I saw you in a movie, and—

I'm sure plenty of men have thought that about a star! I can't make my love for her seem like a crush!

Maybe I can be blunt about it.

Lauren, look at me. I've just ridden twenty-eight hours on a bus, I'm grumpy, I'm smelly, I need to use a bathroom, and I'm hungry, but I love you. Marry me.

Patrick shook his head.

That was creepy. A marriage proposal should never be creepy.

Lauren, it's so good to finally see you.

That was weak. I don't talk that way.

Lauren, I'm so sorry I'm late. I know I should have flown in, but I'm cheap. I hope you haven't ordered anything yet because I can't really afford to eat here. Let's hit a McDonald's for some Chicken McNuggets with hot mustard sauce. . . .

While true, it has absolutely no romance in it. A marriage proposal should be romantic and should never involve fast food.

Lauren, I've been through hell to get to you, and I know you promise me heaven. Lauren Short, will you marry me?

That won't do, either. I have to build up to it somehow. I am terrible at small talk, though.

He opened his eyes as the bus slid to a stop behind a tractor trailer.

I'll think of something.

I have to think of something.

This is, after all, going to be my first public performance. . . .

41

"We're circling until a runway is clear, Miss Short," Wendy said.

I didn't ask you what we were doing, Wendy. I've been in a circling airplane before. Lauren looked out the window and saw only angry gray clouds. *Where's the ground? We should be getting close to the ground.*

"We've been circling for twenty minutes, but we made good time because of some fierce headwinds," Wendy said.

They're called tailwinds, *Windy Wendy. Headwinds slow down an airplane.*

"We'll still land on time," Wendy said.

I do not want to engage this person in conversation, but I have to know. "How much snow is down there?" Lauren asked.

"I don't know," Wendy said. "Would you like me to check?"

"No, it's all right," Lauren said.

"I can check," Wendy said.

Lauren sighed. "Go ahead."

The FASTEN YOUR SEAT BELT sign blinked on. Lauren fastened her seat belt tightly.

"Ladies and gentlemen, we're going to begin our descent into St. Louis," the captain said. "We may experience a little turbulence, but there's nothing to worry about."

Lauren worried.

She was right to worry.

The turbulence wasn't little. At times Lauren had to open her mouth wide to keep her teeth from banging together. Once the plane broke through the clouds, Lauren looked out to see a world covered in white.

That's a lot of snow, she thought. *I hope this plane has skis.*

Once the plane was safely on the ground and was crawling toward the terminal, Lauren released her seat belt and took several deep breaths. *That was horrible.* She called Patrick, and again it went to voice mail. She left him a message. "I'm here, and there is a lot of snow on the ground out there. The snowflakes are as big as my hands. I did wear my boots, though. Call me when you can. Bye."

"There are officially ten inches on the ground outside," Wendy said. "Are we meeting someone in St. Louis, Miss Short?"

If I feel her breath on my ear one more time, I will backhand this woman. "Yes. I'm meeting a little boy named Jamie."

Once she left the plane and entered the terminal, she walked directly toward a little boy and his family. "Hi," she said, kneeling in front of the boy. "Are you Jamie?"

Jamie's eyes widened. "Lauren!" he cried.

This boy has some powerful lungs. "That's me," Lauren said. "Your brother told me you were a fan of mine. Have you seen all my movies?"

Jamie nodded and grabbed her hand. "I love you, Lauren."

Lauren hugged him to her as flashes flew around them. *Man, they know I'm here now.* "I love you, too, Jamie." She kissed his cheek and turned to see Terrance embracing his mother and father, an elderly black woman following behind. "Do you go to school, Jamie?"

Jamie nodded.

"Do you get good grades?" Lauren asked.

Jamie nodded.

Such a sweet boy! "Good," Lauren said. She stood and smiled at Terrance's parents, Jamie still gripping her hand fiercely. "Hello."

"Thank you," Jamie's mother mouthed.

"Lauren," Terrance said, "could we take a family picture with you?"

She looked at Jamie. "I don't think Jamie's going to share me with anyone today. Why don't you take some with me and Jamie?"

Terrance—and half a dozen other people—took pictures of Lauren and Jamie.

Lauren squeezed Jamie's hand. "I have to go now, Jamie."

Jamie nodded.

"You be good and do well in school, you hear?" she said.

"I will," Jamie said. He hugged her fiercely. "Bye!"

Lauren moved with the throng toward the baggage claim, camera phones and some real cameras recording her every step. A man with a voice recorder detached himself from the crowd and approached her.

And this would be a real reporter, Lauren thought. *So much for anonymity. How much do I tell him, if anything?*

"Phil Thomas, *Post-Dispatch*," the man said, shoving

the voice recorder in her face. "Miss Short, what brings you to St. Louis?"

Lauren leaned away from the voice recorder. "Slow news day, Phil?" Lauren said. "I mean, there's a raging blizzard outside, right?"

"I do the entertainment news," Phil said.

"And a foot of snow in November isn't that entertaining, huh?" Lauren asked. She slowed to a stop, and most of the throng continued moving away from them. "I'm here in St. Louis, Phil, because I have a date."

"In St. Louis?" Phil asked.

No, in Reno, Nevada. "Yes."

"Who's the lucky guy?" Phil asked.

"I am the lucky *girl,* Phil," Lauren said. "His name is Patrick Alan Esposito."

"Is he here at the airport?" Phil asked.

I wish! "He's meeting me later."

"Where?" Phil asked.

Lauren noticed the crowd swelling around her again, cell phone cameras working overtime. *I have to get out of here before these flashes blind me.* "At a restaurant, Phil, but we're hoping for some privacy. I hope you understand."

"So it's a rendezvous?" Phil asked.

It's a date! Lauren shook her head and continued toward baggage claim.

While waiting for her luggage, Lauren signed several autographs and posed for a dozen pictures.

Phil sidled up to her. "Many restaurants are closing because of the weather, Miss Short."

Sneaky man. "And I suppose you'll call the restaurant for me to check, huh?"

"Something like that," Phil said.

"I'm not stupid, Phil," Lauren whispered. "If they're closed, they're closed." *In a way, I hope they're closed.*

That will give me more time with Patrick at the hotel. I wish my stomach would stop growling, though. We'll have to get room service.

"How long will you be in town?" Phil asked.

Lauren spied her first suitcase and maneuvered through the crowd to snag it. "I'm not sure, Phil."

"Why are you meeting here?" Phil asked.

"Truthfully, so we could get some alone time away from the media," Lauren said. She saw her other two bags and grabbed them. "So if you don't mind."

Phil stepped back. "Where are you staying?"

Lauren looked outside at a line of snow-covered cabs. "Are you going to follow me, Phil?"

Phil didn't answer.

"Don't follow me, please," Lauren said. She opened her biggest suitcase and pulled out her black overcoat. "Don't you already have enough for your story?" She closed her suitcase and put on her overcoat, buttoning it to the top.

"One more question," Phil said. "Did you know that kid back there?"

"Sure," Lauren said. "That was Jamie, and he is my biggest fan. Now I have a question for you. How did you know I'd be on that plane?"

"I can't reveal my sources, Miss Short," he said.

"How about if I guess, then?" *The cabdriver, the skycap, the ticket agent in LA, or Wendy?* "Was her name Wendy?"

Phil nodded slightly.

"Please don't quote me here, Phil," Lauren said, "but Wendy is an evil heifer. What do you owe her for the tip?"

Phil sighed. "Hockey tickets."

"Really? That's all?"

"Wendy is nuts about the St. Louis Blues," Phil said. "I have no idea why. They're not even that good this year."

"Well, that woman gave me the blues the entire flight,"

Lauren said. "She likes to hover. You don't have to go with her, do you?"

Phil nodded.

"Does she coo at you, too?" Lauren asked.

Phil grimaced. "All the damn time." He smiled. "Thank you for talking to me."

"I'd say anytime, Phil, but I have a date," Lauren said. "And it's a date, Phil, not a rendezvous."

"If you say so, Miss Short," Phil said.

While snowflakes as big as pancakes bludgeoned her hair, Lauren rolled her luggage out to the curb beside a cab. The cabdriver didn't move from his seat.

Lauren tapped on the passenger window, and the window descended. "I need some help here."

The driver rolled his eyes. "Where you headed?"

"The Millennium Hotel downtown," Lauren said, batting snow from her hair.

"Ah, lady, that's at least an hour ride in this weather," the driver said. "I-Seventy is closed, and they're about to close Sixty-Four."

"I'm sure there are other ways to get there," Lauren said.

He sighed. "Get in. I'll have to take Natural Bridge Road, but the whole world is taking Natural Bridge Road now. We'll get there in about ninety minutes."

Lauren opened the back door, threw in her soaked suitcases, and slid onto the seat. "As long as we get there." She handed him a fifty-dollar bill. "Fifty more if you get me there in less than an hour."

The driver peered back at her. "You famous or something?"

"Not anymore," Lauren said. She fastened her seat belt. "Let's roll, man."

"All right, all right," the driver said.

In just under an hour, after some nifty driving and a series of harrowing detours, Lauren arrived at the Millennium Hotel, a tall cylinder rising into the snowy sky with the Gateway Arch looming behind. She handed the driver another fifty.

"Thank you," she said. "You drive safely the rest of the night, okay?"

The driver got out, opened the back door, took out Lauren's suitcases, and carried them to the curb where a bellhop stacked them on a cart and rolled the cart inside.

Lauren stepped out and smiled, shielding her hair from the snow with her hands. "Thank you."

The driver shrugged. "I finally figured out who you are," he said. "You're that actress."

"Is that the only reason you took out my suitcases?" Lauren asked.

The driver didn't answer.

Lauren backed toward the hotel's entrance. "You need to work on your customer service skills, man. You should have done that for *anyone* in your cab, especially on a night like tonight."

As soon as she whisked the snow off her coat in the lobby, she headed straight to the reception desk.

"Lauren Short?" a woman cried. "Oh, my God! It's Lauren Short!"

Lauren read her name tag. *Calm down, Penny. I'm as human as you are, only I'm much calmer.* "Hi, Penny. I'm meeting someone who already has a reservation. Patrick Esposito. Has he checked in yet?" *And maybe we can skip dinner and go right to dessert.*

Penny fumbled with her hands. "What's his name again?"

"Patrick Esposito."

Penny's fingers banged some keys on her keyboard. "He hasn't checked in yet."

Lauren checked her phone. *It's a little past six, and he's left no messages.*

"Is he flying in?" Penny asked. "He might be delayed. They're canceling flights left and right."

You can't cancel a bus, Penny. "May I leave my suitcases here?"

Penny smiled broadly. "I can put them in the manager's office for you."

"That'd be great."

Penny squinted at the computer screen. "Oh, that's right. I talked to Mr. Esposito. I gave you one of our nicest rooms. It's a riverside room with excellent views of the Arch."

I'm not interested in that kind of view, Penny. I'm here to see a man. "Great." She looked through the lobby at the front doors. "How far is it to Tony's?"

Penny snapped up a phone receiver. "I can call you a cab."

That's not what I asked. "Isn't it close by?"

"Yes, but look at the snow, Miss Short," Penny said. "Think of your hair."

My hair will dry, Penny. Hair does dry. "I like snow."

"Do you want a hat or something?" Penny asked.

"I'll be fine, Penny," Lauren said.

Penny leaned across the counter and whispered, "But I thought you were supposed to be incognito."

They knew I was coming. How? "I'll be fine," Lauren said. "The snow will keep me hidden. Now, do I turn right or left out of here?"

"I'll draw you a map," Penny said. She wrote a single line on a Post-it. "Turn right when you leave us and walk to

Market Street. It's only a little ways. Tony's is on the corner." She handed Lauren the map. "You won't get lost."

Not with an excellent "map" like this. "Thank you."

Lauren shot her hands deeply into her pockets and left the Millennium, turned right, and walked through a wall of falling snow on what she hoped was the sidewalk. *This coat isn't nearly warm enough, and this snow is entirely too wet. I used to like snow. I guess I'll have to get used to eastern weather all over again.*

She crossed Fourth Street when she got to Market Street, walked up some steps, and entered Tony's, shaking off her coat just inside the door.

"May I help you?"

Is that Joe Pesci's father? He looks just like him! Nice dark jacket, white oxford shirt, no tie, and even Joe Pesci's squint from—what was that movie?—Casino.

Lauren smiled broadly. "Hello. I'm a little early. Reservation for Esposito."

The man smiled. "We've been expecting you, Miss Short."

"Yes," Lauren said. "But Patrick Esposito made the reservation."

"Oh, yes, he did," the man said. "I talked to him the other night. A fine gentleman. I am Vincent Bommarito. Please call me Vincent."

"Hello, Vincent."

"Are we going incognito tonight, Miss Short?" Vincent asked.

Lauren took off her coat and folded it over her arm. "No."

"But you're wearing . . ." His eyes danced. "I mean, most women who eat here wear . . ."

"Clothes?" Lauren said.

Vincent nodded and smiled. "That they do. And it is a snowy night, isn't it?"

"If I didn't keep moving out there, I would have been buried," Lauren said. "I take it there's a dress code here." *Patrick didn't tell me that.*

"There is," Vincent said, "but we always make exceptions, especially for you, Miss Short."

You had better, Lauren thought. *I just flew two thousand miles with a flight attendant's sour breath in my ear.* "Thank you, Vincent."

"We have our best table ready for you," he said.

The best table is usually the most visible table, and I want to be invisible. "I prefer something out of the way," Lauren said. "We'd like our privacy."

"Oh, but of course," he said. "We're short on staff tonight. You understand. This unexpected snowstorm. Please follow me."

Lauren followed Vincent to a table in a far corner that was shielded from view somewhat by a frosted-glass partition. As she moved past other diners, she smiled and tried not to make eye contact.

I am seriously underdressed! There's more bling in here than in some bistros in LA. And here I am, wearing boots, real boots, while these other women are wearing insensible high heels. Don't they know it's snowing outside?

After Vincent pulled out her chair and Lauren sat, he asked, "Will your date be joining you soon?"

"I'm really early," Lauren said. "If the snow lets him, he should be here by seven."

"I will bring him here to you as soon as he arrives." Vincent smiled. "I have to tell you, Miss Short, that I have followed your career. I would love to have your picture join Sammy Davis and Frank Sinatra on our wall."

Little old Lauren from D.C. on the wall with those icons? "I'd be honored."

Vincent whisked a single crumb on the table into his hand. "Enjoy your evening." He returned to the front.

Now that's service with some style, Lauren thought. *Patrick chose this restaurant well. I already feel like royalty.*

A young man wearing all black rushed by. "I'll be with you in a—" He stopped.

"Hi," Lauren said.

The man blinked.

"What's your name?" Lauren asked.

"Donnie," the man whispered.

He doesn't sound too sure. "Take your time, Donnie. My date isn't here yet. Take care of your other guests first. I know you're understaffed tonight because of the snow."

"Okay." Donnie swallowed. "What may I get you to drink?"

"Water will be fine," Lauren said. "But there's no rush."

"Okay." Donnie sped away.

It's nice to know I still have that effect on people, but it's really creepy to have strangers look at you like deer frozen in headlights.

"Miss Short, hi," a smiling man said as he approached.

I know what he's after, Lauren thought. *They say my name first and then throw in a "hi" or a "hello." How nice. The man still has his napkin tucked into his shirt.*

"Could I trouble you for an autograph and maybe a picture?" He pointed behind him. "My wife is a big fan."

For the next half hour, nearly *every* diner at Tony's made his or her well-dressed way to Lauren's table for an autograph, a picture, or both, and Lauren obliged them because she had nothing better to do.

After Vincent took her picture for the "wall of fame," Donnie brought her a glass of ice water. "Is your date running late?" he asked.

244244244244 244244244244244244244244244244244244244244244244244244244244244244244244244244244244

"The snow must be holding him up," Lauren said.

"They just closed Lambert," Donnie said. "When was his flight?"

"He'll be here," Lauren said.

"But it's a little after seven," Donnie said.

Do they need this table? This place isn't at full capacity. What's the rush? "I would be more surprised if he were on time in this weather. Don't worry, Donnie."

"I'm not worried," Donnie said. "I'm just . . ." He shook his head. "It's just that with all that's happened to you recently, I'd hate to see you get stood up."

Why are perfect strangers so interested in my dysfunctional love life? They should be working on their own dysfunctional love lives! "Patrick is not going to stand me up," Lauren said. "But thank you for your concern."

She took out her cell phone and called him. Once again, her call went straight to voice mail. "I'm here at the restaurant, Patrick, and it is *very* nice. Please hurry." She closed her phone. "I'm sure he's on his way."

"I hope so, Miss Short," Donnie said. "Are you sure you don't want to order something? Some bread, an antipasto, or osetra caviar perhaps?"

I'm starving, and it smells so good in here! "I'm fine, Donnie," Lauren said.

But I'm not fine.

It's ten after seven.

My man won't answer his phone.

These Timberlands aren't as waterproof as I thought they'd be. My toes will not thaw out.

Donnie is about to have a fit.

Some of the people around me seem to be getting ready for another round of pictures.

Come on, man.

Let's get this date started.

42

At 7:25 p.m. a weary bus full of cranky people arrived over two hours late at the Greyhound bus terminal in St. Louis. After getting directions to Tony's from the man behind the ticket counter, Patrick snatched his duffel bag as soon as the driver opened the luggage hatches and took off running through Triangle Park to Clark Avenue. The thick snow confused him momentarily until he saw the colossal outline of Busch Stadium.

North to Market . . . and Lauren, he thought as he panted, his boots throwing clusters of heavy, wet snow behind him. He turned on his phone and grimaced at the flashing battery sign. After listening to Lauren's messages, he turned it off. *She's there safely,* he thought. *That's a blessing. I'm only a half hour late for dinner. I hope she's not too angry.*

Once he hit Market Street, he slowed to a fast walk to catch his breath, and once inside Tony's, he assessed his condition.

I have some serious body odor, a mixture of funk and diesel fumes. My jeans are soaked up to my knees, my boots have changed from light brown to dark brown, and it looks as if I've just gotten out of the shower.

I am officially a mess.

Let the date begin.

Patrick looked into the dining room. He saw flashes around a crowd of people in the corner. *Unless there's a birthday party going on, Lauren Short is definitely here.*

An elderly gentleman wearing a dark dinner jacket appeared in front of him. "I am Vincent Bommarito. May I help you, sir?"

He looks just like a taller, older Joe Pesci. He's even wearing a pinkie ring. "I am really late," Patrick said. "Reservation for Esposito."

Vincent raised his eyebrows. "Esposito?"

"Right, Patrick Esposito," Patrick said. "I was supposed to be here at seven. I'm sure Lauren Short is already here. She's my date." Patrick noticed that every man inside was wearing a dinner jacket or a suit. *Oops. I suppose I could wear my belt as a tie.*

"Miss Lauren Short is your date," Vincent said.

"Yes."

"The *actress* Lauren Short," Vincent said.

Patrick stared down at Vincent's bushy gray eyebrows. "Yes, Lauren Short, the actress."

"Forgive me, but I am going to need to see some identification," Vincent said. "I hope you understand. Miss Short is an important guest."

Patrick pulled out his wallet and removed a Salthead ID badge, one he rarely wore. He handed it to Vincent. "I don't drive, so I don't have a license."

Vincent stared at the ID. "I knew an Esposito who came over here from Salerno, in Campania." He looked into Patrick's eyes. "You could be his twin." He handed back the ID. "You have kept Miss Short waiting, Mr. Esposito."

Patrick straightened to his full height. "I know. I've just spent over thirty hours on a bus from Brooklyn, I'm soaking wet, and this is our first date."

Vincent smiled. "I am sorry I doubted who you were, Mr. Esposito. It would be my honor for you to wear one of my dinner jackets."

Patrick sighed. "I'm soaking wet."

Vincent nodded. "The jacket will warm you up."

"I'm now forty minutes late," Patrick said. "Why can't I just go in?"

"We have a dress code, Mr. Esposito," Vincent said. "Business casual on weekdays."

Patrick sighed again. "My business is buildings maintenance. If I had worn my coveralls, would you have let me go in?"

Vincent laughed. "I think I would have, especially on a night like this." He nodded. "Forgive me for hindering you. Allow me to escort you to your table, Mr. Esposito."

"I can manage," Patrick said.

Vincent shook his head. "I may have to block for you. Follow me."

Patrick followed Vincent carefully around several tables toward the crowd around Lauren. *They're all so well dressed, and I am not. They all smell nice. I do not. I am at least forty-five minutes late now, and I'm carrying a soaked duffel bag full of soaked clothes. I need to shave, my hair will dry in all directions, and I am not wearing a tie or a dinner jacket.*

So far, so good.

Patrick waited beside Vincent while the last few groups of people took pictures with Lauren.

She's so beautiful.

I can't believe I'm here.

He watched a woman tug on a man's arm until the man

turned and said, "Huh?" She then pointed at Patrick. "Oh," the man said, and he and the woman stepped aside.

Like the parting of the well-dressed sea.

Vincent motioned to a chair.

Patrick looked into Lauren's eyes. "Sorry I'm late."

Tony's quieted completely. No fork scratched a plate, and no glass dinged. Servers paused in mid-serve. Even the delicious garlic aroma seemed to dissipate for a moment.

Lauren smiled. "I wasn't worried, Patrick. I knew you'd get here eventually."

Patrick set his duffel bag on the floor, took two long steps, leaned down, and kissed Lauren's cheek as flashes lit up the corner. "Hi, Lauren."

Lauren laughed slightly. "Hi, Patrick. How was your trip?" She smiled. "No, don't tell me. I can already tell. It was pretty horrible, huh?"

That's the smile and the laugh I've been longing for, Patrick thought. *I'm not worried about a thing now.* "It was worth it. You look exquisite."

"No I don't, but thank you," Lauren said.

Patrick looked under the table. "I like your boots."

"I like yours, too," Lauren said. "Please sit."

Patrick smiled at the diners around them. "I've been sitting for a long time."

Vincent held out his chair, and Patrick sat.

"I haven't been sitting in anything this comfortable, though," Patrick said. "Thank you."

Several more flashes bathed them in light.

"Nothing this bright, either," Patrick said. "I'm seeing spots."

Lauren laughed and motioned to Vincent. "Vincent, could you please do something about the picture taking? Patrick is here now, and we'd like to eat in peace." Lauren looked at Patrick. "I'm sure that kiss is already on its way to the Internet."

Patrick took Lauren's hand. "It's okay, Lauren. I only see you. Sort of. In between all the spots."

Lauren looked up at Vincent. "Is there anything you can do?"

"I am sure they will go back to their meals," Vincent said, and he sauntered away, pausing at tables here and there to chat.

Lauren turned to Patrick. "It is so rude for them to take pictures of two people eating," Lauren whispered.

Patrick squeezed Lauren's hand. "It's okay. I think I would be more amazed if people *didn't* take your picture or ask for your autograph."

Lauren squeezed his hand. "Your hands are cold. But I am so glad I can finally touch you."

Another flash caused Patrick to see more spots than Lauren.

"I *really* hate that," Lauren said. "Are they going to take a picture of our every bite?"

"They do that?" Patrick asked.

"Sometimes," Lauren said.

Patrick nodded. "I don't always chew with my mouth closed."

"Neither do I," Lauren said.

Patrick shrugged. "We could make faces."

Lauren bit her lip. "We could."

Patrick smiled. "Let's."

"On the count of three," Lauren whispered. "One, two, three . . ."

Lauren and Patrick turned to the diners around them and made ridiculous faces while even more flashes went off.

"I have had *enough* of this," Lauren said, and she stood.

Tony's quieted to a dull murmur.

"You all should have plenty of pictures already," Lauren said. "Do you mind not taking any more? This is our first date. Do you remember your first date? Did anyone film your first date from start to finish?"

Another flash went off.

"Come on, have a heart," Lauren said.

This is the moment, Patrick thought. *This has to be the moment. Chaos has its uses.*

Patrick stood and took both of Lauren's hands in his. "It's okay. I don't mind having my picture taken with the most beautiful woman in the world. I've been dying to kiss you all day, and I don't care if I go blind."

Lauren looked up into Patrick's eyes. "Then . . . kiss me."

Patrick placed his lips squarely on hers, and for a few moments, he couldn't see her at all because of all the flashes. As he removed his lips, he whispered, "I will never forget this kiss."

"Neither will I," Lauren whispered. "I hope some of their pictures turn out so I can see the kiss, too. Man, I'm seeing spots now, too."

Patrick squinted. "You're slowly becoming brown again."

"Doesn't all this bother you?" Lauren asked.

"It's a new thing for me," Patrick said. "If it bothers you, I can stop it."

Lauren laughed. "I'd like to see you try."

Patrick moved behind Lauren and put his arms around her waist. *Oh, she feels so good. Soft, solid, and sensuous.* "Ladies and gentlemen, may I have your attention, please?"

Tony's quieted down.

"Lauren Short and I are indeed on our first date," Patrick said. "We have both traveled a long way to get here. Lauren flew in from LA, and I took a bus for over thirty hours through the snowstorm all the way from Brooklyn."

Patrick heard several whistles.

"This is the first time we have ever been face-to-face," Patrick said. "We have been corresponding by e-mail, instant message, text, and phone, and we finally decided to meet in St. Louis, right here at Tony's. We didn't plan on a snowstorm, and I didn't know about the dress code, but whatchagonnado?"

Lauren laughed and held his arms tighter around her waist.

She likes the accent. Very cool. "Now, I want you all to do something for me. I want you to record the next few minutes with your cameras and camera phones, and the second we leave, I want you to upload everything to the Internet, okay?"

"What?" Lauren whispered.

"Trust me," Patrick whispered. "But I don't want you to do anything with your pictures or videos until we leave," he said to the crowd. "That's important. Don't forward or upload anything until we leave the restaurant, okay?"

"Patrick, what are you doing?" Lauren whispered.

He turned her slightly, pulling her hips closer to him. "I'm trying to make this the single greatest first date in world history, Lauren, and they are going to help us."

43

Lauren's heart skipped several beats before banging into her breastbone. "What do you mean?"

Patrick maneuvered her away from him slightly and clasped her hands. He turned to several men who were standing and holding up cell phones. "Start filming now." He looked back at Lauren. "Lauren, I practiced all the things I would say to you when I finally saw you face-to-face, and now I've completely forgotten what to say because of your beauty."

Lauren heard a collective "ahh" from the crowd. *Well, it was sweet,* she thought. *But he must still be blinded from those pictures. I am looking anything but beautiful.*

"Did you forget *everything* you were going to say?" Lauren asked.

"Not everything," Patrick said. "I know we haven't known each other long, but we're both getting old."

Lauren laughed. "Speak for yourself."

The crowd laughed.

Hey, Lauren thought. *We're the floor show.*

"We're both getting *older,*" Patrick said. "Is that better?"

"Yes," Lauren said. "Proceed."

Patrick's eyes softened. "We're both at a time in our lives when we know what we want and we're too stubborn to settle for anything less. I believe in my heart that I have waited twenty years for you."

Oh, my heart. "But I've only waited seven years for you." The crowd laughed again.

"Well, I have," Lauren said.

"I also believe something happened twenty years ago that made this moment possible," Patrick said. "I didn't get the *wrong* girl back then so I could get the *right* girl now. You understand?"

"I do," Lauren said. *And here come some tears. Wow. Right on cue.*

"Lauren, there's something I want to tell you," Patrick said. "I didn't want to e-mail it to you, or instant message it to you, or say it to you over the phone, or Skype it, or text it to you. I wanted to hold you in my eyes when I said it so I could see your eyes. I know you love me." He pulled her close. "Lauren Short, I love you."

She rested her head on his chest. "And I love you." *Now, kiss me to end this scene perfectly!* She closed her eyes and pursed her lips.

No kiss arrived.

She felt both of his hands leave hers.

She opened her eyes. *Where's my man?*

She looked down and focused on Patrick kneeling, a ring box in his hand.

Oh, Lord! It's a ring!

"Lauren, I want you to wear this ring." He opened the box, removed a small ring, and slid it onto her left ring finger.

It fits! How did he know my size? Oh, it's so beautiful!

"It's a promise ring, Lauren," Patrick said, "and this is my promise to you. I don't have much, and I may never have much, and I may have to get another job so we can have something, but whatever I have is yours, and yours alone, for as long as you will have me."

"I'll have you forever, Patrick." *He said he wasn't romantic, and he has me crying.*

He stood and lifted her chin. "And I also promise that I will never hurt you in any way or betray you in any way or leave you lonely in any way. Ever. That is my promise to you."

Lauren stood on tiptoes and kissed his chin. "Are you asking me to marry you?" she whispered.

Patrick moved his head away from their audience, his lips hot on her ear. "I can't afford to marry you yet."

Lauren shook her head. "Patrick, you're the richest man I have ever met. Ask me."

Patrick dropped again to one knee, and Lauren distinctly heard someone crying. She looked into the crowd but saw only a sea of smiles.

A tear slid off her nose.

It's me. I'm the one who's crying.

"Lauren Short, will you marry me?" Patrick asked.

"Yes, Patrick," she said as more tears streamed down her face. "I will. But I can't possibly survive another long engagement, okay? I am through with long engagements."

Several diners laughed.

Lauren turned to the nearest table. "Three years is entirely too long, don't you think?"

Patrick stood and lifted Lauren high into the air. "We'll have a short engagement. I promise."

Lauren's lips found his, and for the next minute, her tongue counted all his teeth.

Tony's had never seen so many flashes.

Lauren pulled back to catch her breath. "I can't believe that you're real."

"So you know exactly how I feel about you," Patrick said.

Lauren looked down at the floor. "You're still holding me in the air."

"I know," Patrick said. "I don't want to put you down."

"Then don't." *I feel weightless in this man's arms!*

"Are you really hungry?" Patrick whispered.

Lauren shook her head.

"Do you want to go somewhere else?" Patrick asked.

Lauren nodded rapidly. *I want this entire man inside me now, and I want to get loud.*

Patrick gently returned Lauren to the floor. "Did you order anything?"

"No. I've only had water."

Patrick put a ten on the table and took Lauren's hand. "Ladies and gentlemen, before we leave—and we're leaving right now—I want to make sure you know exactly what has happened. I am engaged to be married to the . . ." He smiled at Lauren. "To the only woman I've ever truly loved."

"And he's the first and last man I will ever truly love," Lauren said.

Patrick picked up his duffel bag. "Let's go."

Lauren let Patrick drag her through the tables until they reached the center of the dining room. She tugged on his hand, and he stopped. "I think we've earned a little applause, don't you?"

Patrick nodded.

"Come on now," Lauren said. "Put your hands together." *This might be my last public performance, so I have to milk it for all it's worth.*

On a snowy night in early December at Tony's on Market Street in downtown St. Louis, the diners, servers, and even Vincent gave Lauren Short and Patrick Esposito a standing ovation.

44

Lauren and Patrick raced through heavy snow toward the hotel, laughing and smiling, not a soul on the street staring at them, nothing flashing but red traffic signals overhead. They were finally alone, and Patrick didn't want to leave this solitude. He let Lauren pull him along, and for a moment he felt as if they were the only two people in the world.

He held the door for her, and she burst inside the Millennium, clumps of snow in her hair, her jeans soaked up to her knees, her face dotted with water, and he decided at that moment that she was the most beautiful woman who had ever lived.

"Is this him?" a woman cried from the reception desk.

Lauren approached her. "Yes, Penny, this is him. Penny, meet Patrick. Patrick, meet Penny."

Patrick pulled out his roll of bills. "How much do I owe you?"

Penny clicked through a series of screens. "One hundred ten ninety-seven."

Taxes must be ridiculous in Missouri, Patrick thought. He handed her one hundred and twenty dollars and received his change.

"Could you get my suitcases, Penny?" Lauren asked. "Not that I'll need any clothes," she whispered to Patrick.

I like how she thinks, Patrick thought. *I just wish she wouldn't think these things so quickly! I haven't been with a woman in twenty years!*

Penny disappeared into the office and returned with one of Lauren's suitcases, an older man carrying the other two.

"Hello, Miss Short," he said. "Welcome to the Millennium. I am Tony Gill, and I am the manager. I do hope you'll enjoy your stay. If there's anything we can do to make your stay more memorable, just give me a call."

Patrick collected Lauren's luggage.

Penny handed Lauren two key cards. "You're in twenty-five-oh-seven," she said. "Enjoy your stay."

In the elevator Patrick set down her luggage and his duffel bag and enveloped her in his arms. "I hope you don't mind lots of hugs."

Lauren slid her hands into his back pockets. "I hope you don't mind me doing this."

Patrick didn't mind. He kissed her tenderly. "I just want you to know that I'm really nervous."

"Good," Lauren said.

The elevator opened on the twenty-fifth floor. Patrick collected Lauren's suitcases and his duffel bag. "What's good about it?"

"It means you'll be a gentle lover," Lauren said. "At first."

Patrick followed her to their room, smiling at Lauren's beautiful booty. "And if I get over my nervousness?"

She slid in the key card and opened the door. "Then you are going to tear my booty up."

Patrick entered the room then slid her luggage into the closet.

Lauren put out the DO NOT DISTURB sign and closed the door, locking it behind her. "You're all mine now," she said.

Patrick looked at the king-size bed, which took up most of the room beside floor-to-ceiling windows that gave him an excellent view of the Gateway Arch and the river.

"I didn't reserve a room like this," Patrick said. "I shouldn't have a view." He looked out the window at the snow blowing in waves through an amber glow.

Lauren came up behind him, her hands busily working on his belt buckle. "They must have upgraded you because of me."

No wonder it cost so much downstairs. Patrick turned as she pulled out the belt and tossed it onto the bed. "You asked them to?"

"No," Lauren said, bending down and taking off her boots. "Penny said they had some cancellations because of the weather, and they sometimes upgrade me without me asking. It's one of the perks of being me." She slid off her socks. "These are soaked." She tossed them toward the television. "I'll pay the difference."

Patrick pulled her to him. "I can afford it. We didn't eat." *And that saved me about two hundred bucks.* "You have to be hungry. Do you want some room service?"

Lauren's hands again found Patrick's back pockets. "I'm not that kind of hungry, man."

Patrick rubbed Lauren's shoulders. "I don't want you to pass out."

Lauren smiled. "Are you going to try to make me pass out?"

"I hope not," Patrick said. "But I might make you pass out if I don't shower off thirty hours of bus."

"I like that idea," Lauren said. "Then I can see what I'm getting."

Patrick kissed her forehead. "But first I need to dry out my clothes, or I'll have nothing to wear tomorrow."

"Oh, don't," Lauren said. "I don't want you to wear clothes tomorrow . . . or the next day . . . or the next."

I can't tell her that I have to get back on a bus tomorrow morning, Patrick thought. *Not now. I am not going to spoil this.*

"It won't take long," Patrick said. "I didn't bring much."

Lauren slid her hands around his waist and grabbed the front of his pockets. "I suppose I can unpack the clothes that I *won't* be wearing."

While Lauren unpacked, Patrick emptied his duffel bag and hung up the sopping wet pants, T-shirt, shirt, underwear, and socks he would wear tomorrow. He glanced at her as she took out pants, shirts, socks, underwear, and some sexy lingerie and placed them neatly in the drawers of a dresser.

She's expecting to stay here for days, he thought. *I have to make this night last as long as I can.*

Patrick stepped into the bathroom, turned on all the lights, and started running hot water into the tub. In moments, the room filled with steam.

Lauren came into the bathroom wearing only blue panties and a thin green T-shirt. "Do I look familiar to you?" She turned slightly and posed, lifting the bottom of her shirt to expose soft brown skin.

"I was seriously underdressed at Tony's," Patrick said, "but I am seriously overdressed now."

"I can fix that," Lauren whispered. "You just stand there being sexy."

Patrick watched as Lauren unbuttoned his jeans, unzipped his fly, and pulled his pants to the floor.

She hung his pants on a hook and unbuttoned his shirt. "Feel free to narrate."

"Narrate?" Patrick said.

"Tell me what is going on in this scene," Lauren said.

"I'm standing here, nervously hoping I remember what to do," Patrick said.

"You'll remember," Lauren said. "Keep narrating. Like a voice-over."

Patrick smiled. "I can do that. As Lauren took off his clothes, Patrick began to get very nervous."

Lauren smiled.

"And hard," Patrick added.

Lauren laughed. "I can see that."

"His penis was about to shred his underwear into a million pieces," Patrick said.

Lauren drifted one hand to the front of his underwear. "You need bigger underwear." She removed his shirt and threw it behind her. "Is that T-shirt important to you?"

"The T-shirt he wore wasn't important," Patrick said. "Patrick was extremely grateful that Lauren had removed it."

"You're a good narrator," Lauren said.

"He thanked her and wanted to rip her T-shirt off," Patrick said.

Lauren raised her arms. "Rip away." She closed her eyes.

Patrick began ripping her T-shirt in front until two delicious breasts spilled out, their nipples ripe and hard. He tore off the T-shirt and tossed what was left of it into the sink. "He wanted to rip off her panties, too."

Lauren moaned.

That was the sexiest groan I have ever heard. He knelt in front of her and made a small tear in the fabric with his fingers. "He decided to use his teeth."

"He had better," Lauren whispered.

He bit down on the sheer fabric and pulled it to the side until it tore past smooth, brown, hairless skin to her clitoris, her panties dropping to the floor. He took off his underwear and stood, his penis erect against her stomach.

"Patrick was about to come already," he whispered.

Lauren opened her eyes. "So am I." She pushed his penis down, rubbing it rapidly against her clitoris. "Oh, man," she panted. "Kiss me."

While Lauren sucked on his tongue as she came, Patrick tried to hold back.

"Lauren, I—"

"It's okay," she whispered. "I want you to come."

Patrick could hold back no longer, ejaculating onto Lauren's thighs, legs, and stomach as he tried to retrieve his tongue from Lauren's mouth.

They looked wide-eyed at each other for several long moments as their spasms decreased.

"We have to take a quick shower," Lauren said.

"Patrick agreed that it was a good idea to take a quick shower," Patrick said.

"You can stop narrating now," she said.

"Patrick didn't want to stop narrating," he said. "He felt he could say things as a narrator that he wouldn't normally say."

"Keep narrating, then," Lauren said. "I want to hear what you wouldn't normally say."

Lauren turned a lever, and the shower came on. As she stepped in, Patrick cupped her booty and stepped in behind her, pressing his penis against her back. While she stood under the spray, he massaged her shoulders.

"He truly enjoyed the view of Lauren's booty, so shapely and sexy," he said, "but he realized they had no soap."

Lauren turned to him, the water soaking her hair. "I don't ever use the hotel soap. I brought some of my own. It's in the smallest suitcase."

"He didn't want to leave her, especially since her hairless, um . . ."

"Come on, Narrator," Lauren said.

"Her hairless*ness* excited him very much," Patrick said.

"Go get us some soap," Lauren said.

Patrick left the bathroom, found a container of Dove Go Fresh Body Wash, and returned to the tub. He turned off the water, and Lauren held her arms in front of her breasts.

"It's cold, man," she said.

"Patrick wanted to see Lauren's nipples pop," Patrick whispered. "He also wanted to soap her from head to toe."

"Lauren agreed to be soaped," Lauren whispered.

After putting far too much soap onto two washcloths, Patrick started at her neck and worked his way down, working the front with one hand and the back with another. He crouched and soaped her hips, thighs, booty, and legs until Lauren shivered.

"Patrick saw that Lauren was turning into an icicle, so he turned on the water."

Lauren smiled. "I'm more of a Fudgsicle."

Patrick turned on the shower. "Patrick liked to lick Fudgsicles, so he did."

Lauren spread her legs slightly. "Lauren liked to be licked like a Fudgsicle."

Patrick put the tip of his tongue on Lauren's clitoris, which was already engorged. He licked her in slow, lazy circles.

"Lauren is about to come again," she whispered. "Hold it right . . . oh, damn, *geez!*"

Patrick stood. "Patrick was wondering if Lauren cursed whenever she had an orgasm."

She threw her arms around him and ground her hips into his. "It's the only time I curse, and I only say 'Damn.'"

"Patrick hoped to make Lauren curse often," Patrick said.

Lauren nodded. "Would you like me to soap you now?"

"Patrick agreed that having Lauren Short soap him was about the best way a man could get clean," he said. "Patrick was really dirty after riding over thirty hours on a bus."

Lauren squirted gobs of soap onto one washcloth. "Then I will have to be thorough."

Patrick watched as Lauren soaped his face, neck, and chest. "Patrick closed his eyes because it felt so good."

Lauren scrubbed his back, his stomach, his arms, his shoulders, and his ass.

"Patrick's penis became erect again," Patrick whispered.

Lauren stroked his penis with the washcloth. "Lauren wondered how Patrick's penis could get so large so quickly."

Patrick opened his eyes and looked down. "Patrick knew that she was the reason." *That and twenty years of nonuse.*

"Close your eyes," Lauren said. "Tell me what I'm doing."

In moments Patrick felt Lauren's lips on him, felt her tongue running up and down the length of his shaft, felt her fingers massaging his balls.

"Ahem," Lauren said. "Where's the narration?"

"The narrator is trying not to come," Patrick said.

"Tell me what you're feeling," Lauren whispered. "I want to know."

"Patrick felt her tongue sliding mercilessly around the tip of his penis while her soft fingers stroked him," he whispered. "Now she's trying to swallow his penis whole."

Patrick tried to pull away, but Lauren held on, stroking

and sucking until he finished. *That was a first. Oh, that was unbelievable.*

She stood up and nibbled on his nipples. "Keep narrating," she whispered.

"Patrick was amazed that Lauren, um, swallowed," he whispered.

"Did it feel good?" she asked.

Patrick opened his eyes and looked into hers. "Yes, but I was afraid I would hurt you."

"You didn't," Lauren said. She moved him into the spray. "Was that a first for you?"

Patrick nodded. "Am I allowed to say that I liked it very much?"

Lauren laughed. "Yes."

"I liked it very much," Patrick said.

Lauren rested her head on his chest. "Are you nervous anymore?"

"No," Patrick said. "I'm intimidated."

Lauren turned off the water. "By me?"

Patrick nodded. "We haven't even done it yet."

"I know," Lauren said. "But we're about to, right?"

Patrick stepped out of the tub, took her hand, and led her to the bed. He threw back the bedspread until it spilled onto the floor. He ripped off the sheet until it, too, ended up on the floor. He propped up the pillows against the headboard and pointed.

"Is this a silent movie?" Lauren asked as she slid onto the bed and rested her head on the pillows.

"I doubt it will be silent for long," Patrick said. "I know I won't be silent. Let me know when you're ready."

She grabbed his hand and forced it between her legs. "Feel me."

She's already wet. "You're very wet."

"And getting wetter," she whispered. "I'm ready when you are."

Patrick looked down at his penis. "I'm ready."

"Don't be afraid to let go," Lauren said. "I won't break."

He parted her legs and raised them to his shoulders, kissing her calves and squeezing her feet. She reached down and guided him inside her, and while she squeezed her breasts and panted, Patrick began a slow grind.

"Tell me what you're thinking," Lauren said. "I want to know how it feels for you."

"It feels . . . like silk," Patrick said. "Wet silk. It's like there's a hand inside you pulling me deeper."

She smiled. "I haven't done Kegel exercises all these years for nothing. What else do you feel?"

"I feel your thighs against my hips," Patrick whispered.

"You got a nice rhythm going, man," Lauren whispered.

"I want you to come again," Patrick said. "What can I do?"

Lauren's left hand shot from her breast to her clitoris. "You just keep doing that, I'll do this, and I'll be coming in no time."

"What are *you* feeling?" Patrick asked. He kissed the bottoms of her feet.

"I feel something huge pushing me through this bed," Lauren said. "I feel your lips on my feet, and trust me, that is *so* erotic. I feel your hands on my legs, and my nipples are trying to touch the ceiling, and . . . oh, *damn!*"

As Lauren began bucking, she grabbed Patrick's ass and pulled him completely into her. In moments, Patrick came so hard he banged the back of Lauren's head into the headboard.

"Oh, I'm sorry!" Patrick cried. He slid her back to him.

"It's okay," Lauren said. "I was seeing stars when I came, and now I'm really seeing stars. I think I see the entire universe. There's the Milky Way, and, oh, is that a comet?"

"Are you okay?"

Lauren nodded. "Oh yes." She wiped beads of sweat from her chest and his. "I have never felt better."

45

That's what I'm talking about! Lauren thought. *Yes! Yes! Yes!*

That's the way a man is supposed to make love to his woman. If he had put me through the wall, I wouldn't have felt a thing! I would have smiled at our neighbors and shouted, "Patrick, don't you dare stop!"

She watched as Patrick backed out of her. *He comes, and he's still hard for me.* "You're still hard."

Patrick nodded. "I know."

"Is that normal?"

"I don't know," Patrick said.

"You don't know?"

Patrick shrugged. "You're only my second lover, Lauren. This has never happened to me before."

Only his second. Wow. "Well, I have an idea about what we can do with that thing," Lauren said. "I have many, many years of pent-up sexual frustration."

"Me, too."

"If you don't mind, Patrick, I'd like to go a little buck wild right now," Lauren said. "I don't want you to treat me like a fragile lady. I want you to . . ." She smiled. "I want you to give me all you've got."

"Are you sure?"

From the size and girth of that thing, no. "I'm sure. And if we break anything, I'll pay for it." She swiveled off the bed and stood. "I want you in every way possible in every place possible in this hotel room."

Patrick spun her around. "Please put your hands on the bed."

Lauren nearly fell to the bed, bracing herself with her hands. "You don't have to say please."

"I am a gentleman," Patrick said.

"I don't want you to be a gentleman now," Lauren said.

She felt Patrick's hands roughly widening her stance, and in a moment, he was deep inside her.

Lauren began to pant. "Hit it *hard*. . . ."

After pounding into her on the bed, he turned her over and lifted her into the air. "This gentleman wants to see you hit the ceiling." His feet left the floor as he jumped into her.

They then fell into a swivel chair, and while Lauren rode him and held on to a desk for dear life, the table lamp clattered to the floor.

He turned her around and slid off the chair, grinding her into the carpet in front of the bed.

"Harder!" she cried.

He stood her up and pinned her to the wall beside the bed, her elbows making the pictures and light fixtures dance.

I have never felt such reckless abandon! I am losing myself in him. I'm not sure where he begins or I end. We are one person, one flesh, one mass of sweat and skin and sighs. This is the way a man is supposed to satisfy a woman!

I am never letting this man go!

Ever!

I hope we don't break this wall!

46

After they came together, Patrick carried her to the bed, nestled her head among the pillows, and picked up the sheet and bedspread, settling them over her. He slid in beside her and hugged her from behind.

"Hi," he whispered.

"Hi."

"Are you warm enough?" he asked.

"Yes," Lauren said. "Are you?"

"I am now," Patrick said. "Are you okay?"

"Yes, very," Lauren said. "Wow. It's still snowing."

"Yeah." Patrick sucked on an earlobe. "I like your ears."

"They like you," Lauren said. "You like my booty, too, don't you?"

"Very much," Patrick said. "I'm thinking about it right now. And wondering."

Lauren turned to face him. "What are you wondering about?"

"Didn't you say that you were shy about sex?" Patrick asked.

"I am," Lauren said.

"After what just happened," Patrick said, "that can't be true."

"Well, tonight I wasn't shy," Lauren said. "I don't think I could ever be shy around you because you're so open. I can say what I want to say to you. I can do what I want to do with you. You'll tell me anything I want to know. When I asked you what you were feeling while you were inside me, you told me."

"I am an open book," Patrick said. "You can ask me anything."

"Was that the best sex you ever had?" Lauren asked.

"Yes," Patrick said.

"Do you want to have some more?" Lauren asked.

"Yes."

Lauren sighed. "Don't you ever get tired?"

"I have too much of you running through my veins to sleep now," Patrick said.

"We could talk a little first," Lauren said.

"We can do that," Patrick said. "I may kiss you while we talk."

"I may kiss you back," Lauren said. "It's so strange talking to you without typing."

"I may type on your body," Patrick said, kissing her neck.

Lauren smiled. "I have a whole bunch of exclamation marks on my body right now. You hit my booty hard."

"I wasn't moving, I swear," Patrick said. "You were doing most of the work."

"I was, wasn't I?" Lauren said. "I can give as good as I take, huh?"

"Yes," Patrick said. "Did you get enough?"

"Oh yes," Lauren said.

"Are you content?" Patrick asked.

"With what just happened? Oh yes."

"I meant, are you content with me?" Patrick whispered.

"Of course." She buried her nose in his chest. "I've been worrying whether you'd be content with me."

Patrick stared into her eyes. "I'm not content, Lauren. I'm amazed. I am astonished. All this is still a dream for me."

Lauren pinched his arm. "It's not a dream."

"And that's what still amazes me. You're here. With me."

"Get used to it," Lauren said, kissing his chest.

"I don't know if I want to get used to it," Patrick said.

Lauren pushed him over and straddled him. "What?"

Patrick rubbed her back. "If you amaze me every time we're together, I will never get tired of you."

"You think you can get tired of me?" Lauren asked. "I wouldn't let that happen."

He stroked her hair. "I know you wouldn't, and I know I will never get tired of looking into your eyes. Your eyes drew me to you from the second I saw *Feel the Love*. When I saw your eyes and the rest of you, I said to myself, 'She's perfect.' "

"I'm not, you know," Lauren said.

"You're perfect to me," Patrick said. "I even thought about writing to you after I saw that movie, but I didn't."

"Why didn't you?" Lauren asked.

"You were a star," Patrick said. "Boys from the Gowanus Houses don't write to stars. They only dream about them." He pulled the bedspread over her back and pulled her close. "But now that the dream is real, I'm kind of sad."

Lauren rested her head on his shoulder. "Why?"

"If this dream is real, what will my nightly dreams be like from now on?" Patrick asked. "What will I dream about when my dream is lying beside me?"

Lauren kissed his cheek. "You're going to make me cry."

"I never want to make you cry," Patrick said. "And I'm surprised neither of us passed out. Do you want to get some room service now?"

"Not yet," Lauren whispered. "I want you deep inside me again."

"I like being deep inside you," Patrick whispered.

"I'm glad you do," Lauren said. A few tears fell. "Sorry, but I'm living a dream, too, Patrick."

"I don't believe that," Patrick said.

"Really. I feel like a woman again. You have no idea how long I've waited to feel so alive."

"I'm not exactly dream material," Patrick said.

"Yes, you are," Lauren said. "Everything about you is a dream. I lived in a mansion, drove an expensive car, had fame, glory, awards—but I have never had love before. I wish you had written to me back then so I would have had love like this for the past fifteen years. We could have had ten children by now."

"That's a lot of mouths to feed," Patrick said. "Would tonight have happened if I had written to you back then? And be honest."

Lauren sighed. "I might have written back to you, but I probably wouldn't have. I got a lot of mail back then, and I couldn't keep up with it."

Patrick smiled. "So this is perfect timing for a perfect lady."

"I'm not so perfect," Lauren said. "I'm still too impatient, right?"

"That's why I proposed to you on the first date," Patrick said. "And you don't seem impatient now. You seem calm, hot, and collected."

"Because you wore me out," Lauren said. "I have never

been so thoroughly, and expertly, I might add, made love to in my life. I cannot let you ever leave my side. Ever."

"But how will we live?"

Lauren sat up. "In bliss." She threw off the bedspread, crawled off the bed, and stood, holding out her hand. "I want you to make love to me again."

Patrick laughed. "But there's nothing left to break."

"We didn't break anything," Lauren said. She frowned at a crooked picture. "We *almost* cracked that frame."

"The lamp," Patrick said.

"Okay, we broke the lamp."

Patrick took her hand and stood. "But there's nowhere new to do it."

Lauren looked at the door. "The hallway or the elevator?" She shook her head. "They have cameras in hallways and elevators." She turned toward the window. "Against the window." She led him to the window and fully opened the drapes. "I've never made love in the snow." She looked down at Patrick's penis. "I'm going to start calling that thing Old Faithful." She stroked it gently.

"The idea of making love to you in front of the world is very exciting," Patrick said. "But I don't want the world to see your booty."

"I do," Lauren said. She put her hands around his neck. "Pick me up."

He grabbed her under her thighs and lifted her. "The glass will be cold."

She positioned his penis against her clitoris. "You'll have to put it in. I've got to hold on tight to you, right?"

"Right," Patrick said. He moved his penis up and down against her clitoris until Lauren arched her back against the window. "You seem to like me doing that."

"Yes," Lauren whispered.

"What does it feel like?" Patrick asked.

"Like a heavy, hard, hot tongue licking me," Lauren said. "Like someone else is licking me while I'm with you."

"Someone else?" Patrick whispered, moving his penis more rapidly.

"Yes," Lauren said. "Like someone else is with us and warming me up."

"Your turn to narrate," Patrick whispered.

"I don't know if I can," Lauren wheezed. "But I'll try. Okay, um, while Patrick held her against the window, Terry licked Lauren's clitoris until Lauren could take no more."

"Terry?" Patrick said. "Who's Terry?"

"My roommate during freshman year at Howard," Lauren said. "She was gorgeous."

"Did you ever . . ."

Lauren smiled. "No."

"Describe her to me," Patrick said.

"Oh, man," Lauren said. "I'm close."

"Tell me about Terry," Patrick whispered. "What was gorgeous about her?" He entered Lauren but didn't thrust.

"I was so jealous of her," Lauren said. "She had perfect breasts."

"Describe them," Patrick said.

"They were C cups, perfectly round, with nipples that kind of pointed up," Lauren said. "Please go deeper."

Patrick thrust a little deeper. "What else about Terry was gorgeous?"

"Her booty," Lauren said, thrusting her hips against him. "She had a perfectly round booty, too. Apple Bottoms jeans were made just for her."

Patrick pulled out and rubbed his penis against her clitoris. "What's Terry doing now?"

"She's licking my clitoris," she panted.

"What are you doing to her?" Patrick asked.

"I'm gripping her head," Lauren said. "I want her to stop."

Patrick dipped his penis inside her then tapped it gently against her clitoris. "Why?"

"Because it's your turn," Lauren said.

"What will Terry do while we get busy?" Patrick whispered.

Lauren scratched at his neck. "Terry has left the room. It's only you and me now."

Patrick entered Lauren deeply and thrust her into the window. .

"Patrick," Lauren whispered. "I'm going to come so hard."

"So am I," Patrick said.

Patrick and Lauren nearly broke the window in room 2507 of the Millennium Hotel in downtown St. Louis, Missouri, while a blizzard raged outside.

And although Lauren went to bed with a seriously cold and sore booty, she buried her head in Patrick's chest, smiling into the darkness.

47

I will never be lonely again, Lauren thought after Patrick drifted to sleep under her.

I will also never be shy about sex again. This man . . . Wow. The things we did, the things he said, the things he made me say . . .

Okay, I said them of my own free will.

And . . . it . . . was . . . so . . . freaking . . . hot!

I liked Terry as a friend, and I really didn't have any fantasies about her, but why she came to mind, I don't know. I do know that if I ever want Patrick to become five feet long and hard as steel, all I have to do is mention Terry.

I would never let the real Terry in the same state *as my man.*

She leaned over and looked at the clock. *It's almost six a.m. We went at it for nearly* eight *hours. Who* does *that?*

She smiled.

Evidently, I do. We do.

She heard something hit their door.

Patrick didn't stir.

I wore him out, Lauren thought. *I wore out my coochie, too.* She winced. *I may have to get shock absorbers.*

She slipped out of bed and went to the door. She looked through the peephole, saw no one, unlocked the door, opened it, grabbed a newspaper, and shut the door gently. She took the paper to the bathroom, closed the door, and turned on the light.

At the bottom of the first page in a text box was a picture of her at the airport with the caption "Rendezvous in St. Louis."

Lauren sighed. *It* wasn't *a rendezvous . . . then.*

She turned to page twelve and saw five more pictures of herself, all of them from Tony's. "There's only one of me with Patrick," she whispered, "and you can barely see his face." She read the caption under the photo of her and Patrick evidently leaving Tony's: "Miss Short and an unidentified mystery date left Tony's without eating."

She turned off the light, went to one of her suitcases, and retrieved her laptop. She booted it up in the bathroom, signed on to the hotel's intranet, and went immediately to TMZ.com.

After three consecutive stories about celebrity "baby bumps" and one story detailing Charlie Sheen's latest brush with the law, Lauren saw herself staring into a camera while seated at Tony's.

"I look terrible," she whispered. "My hair was still wet." She read the article while shaking her head.

> *Lauren Short came in from the cold and the snow last night at Tony's Italian restaurant in St. Louis . . . because TMZ has learned, she had a secret rendezvous with an unidentified man, who stood her up.*
>
> *TMZ broke the story . . . last week about Chazz*

*"Action" Jackson ending their seven-year relation-
ship and three-year engagement.*

*There are reports that Short (38) left Tony's with-
out paying—and without a man. Again.*

Story developing . . .

Lauren closed her laptop. "Typical TMZ," she whispered. *They run with rumors until they turn into news, and
they never admit when they're wrong*—especially *when
they're dead wrong about everything, like they are now.*

She put the newspaper in the trash can, brushed her
teeth, returned her laptop to her suitcase, and climbed into
bed, snuggling up against Patrick's warm body.

She heard her stomach growl.

"Is there a cat in here?" Patrick asked.

"It's my stomach," Lauren said.

"We'll have to feed that cat, then," Patrick said. He
reached for the phone, but Lauren pulled his hand back.

"Not yet," Lauren said. "I can wait."

"As you wish," Patrick said. "Everything okay?"

Oh, just the usual lies in a newspaper and online, she
thought. *Nothing major.* "Yes. I had to brush my teeth."

"What time is it?" Patrick asked.

"A little after six," Lauren said. "Let's stay in bed all day."

Patrick yawned. "I wish we could. Or at least I wish *I*
could."

"What?" Lauren asked.

"I didn't want to ruin last night, but I have to get back to
Brooklyn," Patrick said. "My bus leaves in two hours."

No! "You're kidding," Lauren said. "Really?"

Patrick nodded. "Sorry."

"But it's still snowing," Lauren said. "And the bus
would be going through that mess. Nothing will be moving
out there today."

Patrick stretched his arms over his head and yawned again. "The bus got me here, and it will get me back home eventually."

Lauren pinned him to the bed. "But that's crazy."

"I have to get back to work so I can make more money to take you on another date," Patrick said. He pulled a check from under the pillow. "This should cover your plane ticket." He held it out, and Lauren snatched it.

"When did you write this?" Lauren asked.

"While you were in the bathroom reading the newspaper and going online," Patrick said. "Are we news?"

He knows? "Yes, but it's all a bunch of lies. How did you know what I was doing?"

"You talk to yourself," Patrick said. "I didn't catch everything, but I understood. And you didn't look terrible at any time at Tony's."

"There are no pictures of your proposal," Lauren said. "I should have run a search on YouTube. There should be some film." She looked at the check. "What do I need this for, anyway?" She tore it in half. "We're going to be married. You don't owe me anything. We are going to have one bank account."

Patrick blinked. "Are you sure about that?"

"Yes," Lauren said. "Why wouldn't I be?"

"I just thought . . ." He sighed. "Don't you want a prenuptial agreement?"

"No," Lauren said.

"I thought all celebrities had prenuptial agreements," Patrick said.

"Are you saying that celebrities can't marry for love?" Lauren asked.

"I didn't say that," Patrick said. "I'm just saying that you earned a lot of money which doesn't belong to me because I didn't earn it. I wouldn't feel right about spending any of it."

"I don't have a lot of money, Patrick," Lauren said. "I have maybe half a million in the bank, and now *you* have half a million in the bank."

Patrick shook his head. "No, I have . . . Well, *now* I have about twenty-two hundred dollars."

I just tore up a check for two thousand! "You were down to your last two hundred dollars?"

"Actually, my last fifty bucks until payday," Patrick said. "It's a hundred fifty for the bus ticket."

"You're nearly . . ." *This man nearly went broke for me.* "You were about to spend all you had on me."

"I'd spend everything I have to see your eyes shining like they're shining now," Patrick said.

"They're not shining," Lauren said. "They're filling up with tears." *No one has* ever *sacrificed himself for me before!*

"Don't cry," Patrick said. "I get paid next week. I'll survive." He hugged her. "I just wish I didn't have to leave you today."

"You're not leaving me," Lauren said. "I won't let you go. We'll get us some plane tickets to New York for *tomorrow,* not today. We are spending another erotic night in St. Louis, and we are going to make love in front of that window during the daylight this time."

"Which sounds wonderful," Patrick said, "but I doubt anything is going to be flying out of St. Louis today, maybe not even tomorrow."

"So I'll ride the bus," Lauren said. *I have never said this phrase in my entire life.*

"Lauren, please don't," Patrick said. "I want you to come with me, but you can stay a few days and then get a flight to New York when the weather clears."

"And miss thirty hours with you on a crowded bus? Not a chance."

"That's crazy," Patrick said. He tried to get up.

Lauren pressed down on his shoulders. "Oh, so it's not crazy for *you* to ride thirty hours on a bus, but it's crazy for *me* to ride thirty hours on a bus?"

"Right," Patrick said. He gently removed her hands and sat up, pulling her into his lap. "You are Lauren Short. Lauren Short travels in style. Lauren Short does not ride on a bus."

"I *used* to travel in style," Lauren said. "I don't have to anymore."

"But I want you to," Patrick said. "And it will give me time to prepare my apartment for your arrival."

"Don't you want me to travel with you?" Lauren asked.

"Of course I do," Patrick said. "And one day I'll be able to afford to travel in style with you."

Lauren leaped out of bed and began collecting her clothing. "I am going with you. You cannot stop me. It isn't crazy. It's love." She pointed at him. "Where you go, I will go from this day forward. Agreed?"

Patrick started to answer.

"Agreed," Lauren said. "We have less than two hours now, so you better get in that shower right now."

Patrick rolled out of bed and walked toward her. "Only if you join me."

Lauren shook her head. "We're not doing any *joining* until we get to Brooklyn, man. I have to give my coochie a rest."

He held out his hand. "I don't want you out of my sight either. Agreed? Agreed."

Lauren laughed as she took his hand. "You listen to everything I say."

"I certainly do," he said.

They entered the bathroom.

"I'm going to marry you when we get to Brooklyn," Lauren said, running the hot water. "You know that, right?"

"But we've only had one date," Patrick said.

"The world's greatest first date," Lauren said. "We can tell our children and our grandchildren we had one date and got married." She started the shower and stepped into the tub.

Patrick joined her and soaped up a washcloth. "You want children?"

"Yes, I want children," Lauren said. "At least two."

Patrick began washing her back. "But . . ."

"But what?" *A wash and a massage every morning? This is priceless!*

"I just thought . . ."

"Thought what?" *Oh yeah, right there. Dig into that muscle. Yes.*

"Your . . . figure." He turned her around and began soaping her breasts. "If you had two children, your body . . ."

"Will blow up like a balloon. I know," Lauren said. "What's your point?" *And be gentle with the washcloth there. . . . Oh yeah. He knows how tender it is. Yes. Slowly . . . lightly . . .*

"Your career, Lauren," Patrick said.

"I'm not worried about any of that now." *I couldn't possibly have another orgasm, could I? From a washcloth oozing with soap?*

Patrick put the washcloth in her hand. "We'd have to get a bigger place. I have a really small apartment."

Lauren put the washcloth back in Patrick's hand. "You missed a spot."

"Were you getting excited?" he whispered.

"You know I was," Lauren said.

Patrick used his finger instead. "I have a tiny apartment, Lauren."

Oh, geez. He knows the right speed, too! "So you'll be easy to find. I won't have to chase you far. Are your walls thick?"

"Solid brick," Patrick said. He massaged both breasts with his other hand.

He's magic. He can make both my breasts happy with only one of his hands! "You're going to make me scream so loud tonight." *And in about five seconds, too!*

"Actually *tomorrow* night," Patrick said. "It's a long bus ride."

"Oh yeah." She reached down and stroked his penis. "What I said earlier, about not wanting to join you?"

"Yes?"

"I changed my mind."

Patrick smiled. "I thought you might. . . ."

Half an hour of furious lovemaking later, barely dressed, with their hair going in every direction, Lauren and Patrick stepped off the elevator. . . .

Into a swarm of photographers.

Oh . . . no, Lauren thought.

"Miss Short, Miss Short!"

"Where are you going, Miss Short?"

"Who's this, Miss Short?"

"What have you two been doing all night?"

"Is this the man who stood you up at Tony's?"

"Is that a new hairstyle, Lauren?"

"Does Chazz know what you're doing?"

"What will Chazz think about all this?"

Flashbulbs blinded her temporarily. *This is why so many celebrities wear sunglasses indoors. Otherwise, we'd go blind.*

She let go of Patrick's hand and kept moving. "We are going to Brooklyn."

Phil Thomas blocked their path and thrust a voice

recorder dangerously close to Lauren's nose. "The airport still isn't open, Miss Short. All flights have all been canceled. How can you escape?"

"I'm not escaping, Phil," Lauren said, "and there *are* other ways to travel."

Lauren stepped around Phil and allowed Patrick to use her suitcases to plow ahead through the boisterous crowd of photographers, none of whom stayed in Patrick's path for very long.

"What other ways?" Phil yelled behind her.

Patrick used the suitcases to bang through the entrance doors, and they were momentarily alone on the sidewalk.

Lauren frowned at the mounds of drifted snow in the street. "Patrick?"

"Yes, Lauren?"

"We're not going to get a cab today, are we?" she asked.

"Nope."

Photographers spilled out of the hotel.

"Miss Short! Miss Short!"

"Where are you going?"

"Is this your bodyguard?"

"Does Chazz know about this guy?"

"Why are you going to Brooklyn?"

Lauren sighed. "How far is it to the bus station?" she whispered.

"About a mile," Patrick said.

"How are we doing for time?" Lauren asked.

"If we hustle," Patrick said, "we'll make it."

Lauren looked at Patrick, who had his duffel bag and her smallest bag looped around his neck, her medium suitcase under his right arm, and the handle of her large suitcase in his right hand. "I can carry one or two of those."

"I'm good," Patrick said. He smiled. "I need a good

workout after all the sleep I got." He winked and held out his free hand.

Lauren took it. "Let's go for a walk, shall we?"

"Let's," Patrick said, and they waded out into the snow.

"Miss Short! Miss Short!"

"Where are you going?"

"Brooklyn is in the other direction, Lauren!"

"Where'd you get those boots, Miss Short?"

They left photographers scrambling behind them and crossed Fourth Street through heavy snow and nonexistent traffic.

"Do you think they'll follow us?" Patrick asked.

"They'll probably try," Lauren said.

They hiked down Clark Avenue, past Busch Stadium and the police station, and then cut through Triangle Park to the bus terminal as photographers in four-wheel-drive SUVs tried to catch up with them on the side streets.

When they arrived at the Greyhound ticket counter, Lauren looked down at her jeans. *I'm soaked almost to my hips! Lovely weather in St. Louis this time of year. I wonder how St. Louis will look when winter actually begins.*

"Two tickets to Brooklyn on the next bus going east," Patrick said.

"Are you two together?" the woman asked.

Obviously! "Yes," Lauren said.

The woman smiled. "Hey, you're Lauren Short."

All day and all night. Hmm. Last night with Patrick, I was someone else entirely at times. "Please tell me you have two seats beside each other."

"We do," the woman said. "On the *next* bus. That bus won't leave until noon."

And we'll be surrounded by media monsters until then, Lauren thought. *That won't work.*

"Do you have two seats available for *that* bus?" Patrick pointed at a bus idling outside.

"Yes," the woman said. "One in front, one in back. They're the last two."

"We'll take them," Patrick said. He paid the woman in cash.

"But we won't be able to sit together," Lauren whispered.

Patrick smiled. "I think we will."

He collected their tickets, took Lauren's hand, and moved quickly toward the bus. After dropping off her luggage and his duffel bag to be loaded onto the bus, he let Lauren precede him inside. He pointed at an empty seat beside a heavyset man wearing a puffy ski jacket and pulled Lauren to him.

"Hi," Patrick said. "We have just gotten engaged, but our seats are far apart. Would it be possible for you to take a different seat so we can sit together?"

The man looked up at Patrick. "You want me to move?" The man looked at Lauren. "Hey, you're that actress. What's your name? Lauren something?"

"Lauren Short," Lauren said. "It's nice to meet you."

The man looked at Patrick. "You're engaged to her?"

Patrick nodded. "As of last night."

"Uh-huh," the man said. "Well, I might move my seat if I could get an autograph first."

Lauren signed the back of her ticket. She handed it to the man.

The man smiled and stood. "Thank you."

Lauren said, "No. Thank you. You're very kind."

"I'm on only until Indianapolis," the man said, handing Lauren his ticket. "Where are you two going?"

"Brooklyn," Patrick said.

The man moved into the aisle. "The Big Apple's getting pounded right now. Good luck getting there."

As the man moved to the back, Lauren sat in the window seat, and Patrick took the seat beside her.

"Piece of cake," Patrick said. He put his lips to her ear. "Do you think he would have moved if you weren't the famous Lauren Short?"

"No," Lauren said. "I do have some value."

"You're priceless," Patrick said, kissing her cheek.

Lauren looked at her ring. "So is this ring." She picked up his hand and kissed it, intertwining her fingers with his. "I have to get you one just like it."

The bus pulled out onto Fifteenth Street, photographers capturing the moment.

"Wow," Lauren said. "They're taking pictures of a Greyhound bus."

"They must be snow blind," Patrick said.

"Promise to hold my hand," Lauren said. "I rode my mama's bus, but not for very long."

"I can't hold your hand the entire time," Patrick whispered. "My hand might . . . travel."

"Where?" Lauren whispered.

"To your leg," Patrick whispered.

Not now. My leg is sopping wet from the snow. "Anywhere else?"

"I suppose you could help my hand travel wherever you wanted it to go," Patrick whispered.

"I'll probably sit on your hand all the way there," Lauren whispered.

"I don't think you've ever been shy about sex," Patrick whispered.

"I was," Lauren said, "but you bring out the hoochie in me." She sighed contentedly. "And that is not a bad thing at all."

Patrick smiled. "Have I said, 'I love you,' today?"

"No," Lauren said.

"I love you," Patrick said. He kissed her lips. "Sorry I had to drag you through the snow."

"I love you, too, and I wish we were back at the hotel," she whispered. She looked at the bus's windshield wipers as they streaked the glass. "We'd be in front of that window right now. . . ."

"What would we be doing?" Patrick whispered.

"Having an incredible adventure," Lauren whispered. She squeezed his hand. "But this is an adventure, too, and I'm glad I'm sharing it with you. What's our first stop?"

"Indianapolis in six hours," Patrick said. "In this weather, maybe longer."

I am so hungry! "Could we get something to eat when we get there?"

"I know a place," Patrick said, "where we can eat until we burst."

I hope to God my jeans dry by the time we get there, Lauren thought. *If they're wet when I burst, I might drown some people.*

48

During the eighty-minute layover in Indianapolis, Lauren and Patrick inhaled a dozen sliders, two large chili cheese fries, an order of ranch-flavored chicken rings, and two large Barq's root beers at a White Castle less than a block from the bus terminal. They returned to the bus through a scattering of flurries and a troop of Indianapolis photographers and reporters while eating fudge-dipped brownies on a stick.

"Why are you so hungry, Lauren?"

"Were those free-range chickens you ate? Do you know? Do you care?"

"Lauren, aren't you worried about your figure?"

"Did Chazz allow you to eat like this?"

"Should you be eating so much when there are so many starving children in the world?"

"What would Michelle Obama say about your lunch?"

Michelle Obama? Patrick wondered. *Why would the president's wife even care?*

They slept until they reached Columbus, Ohio, three hours later. While the other passengers disembarked there to stretch their legs, Patrick and Lauren stayed on the bus, snuggling as best as they could while photographers lurked in the terminal.

"I want to get married soon," Lauren said.

I'm afraid to ask this. "How soon is soon?"

"Tomorrow."

I knew she'd say that. "How about after Christmas?"

Lauren pouted. "That's four weeks away."

"That will give us time to get to know each other better, right?"

Lauren sighed. "I know all I need to know about you. You're kind, giving, forgiving, and romantic. You're everything I want in a man and more. You make me feel sexy, and I know our bodies were meant to be connected repeatedly."

"So we're sexually compatible, huh?" Patrick asked.

"Oh yes," she said. "We are emotionally, mentally, and sexually compatible—in that order. If I could, I'd marry you right now. But I need to get you a proper ring first." She smiled at her ring. "I love this ring. I am never taking it off."

"If we had a wedding at St. Agnes," Patrick said, "do you think your mama would attend?"

"Is St. Agnes a Catholic Church?" Lauren asked.

"Yes."

"She won't attend," Lauren said. "She's strictly a full gospel Baptist. What about your family?"

"I have none to speak of or to," Patrick said. "Your mama really wouldn't come to her own daughter's wedding?"

"The almost breast is still a stopper for her," Lauren said. "Even after fourteen years."

"Oh." He let his hand drift to her stomach. "It's still a stopper for me, too."

"Careful," Lauren said. "I ate a lot of grease."

Patrick rubbed her stomach. "Maybe you're still hungry."

Lauren closed her eyes. "I'm more sleepy than hungry," she whispered. "Somebody kept me up all night."

"You kept *me* up all night," Patrick said.

"I did," she said, yawning slightly. "My head's not too heavy on your shoulder, is it?"

"No." He stroked her hair. "Sweet dreams, Lauren."

"Kiss me," she said.

He kissed her.

"Now, don't wake me until we get to Brooklyn. . . ."

Lauren slept through stops in Zanesville, Ohio, and Wheeling, West Virginia, and hardly stirred as they pulled into Pittsburgh. Passengers occasionally snapped pictures of them with their cell phones, but they left them alone for the most part.

And that's a blessing, Patrick thought. *She is really worn out. I wish the media circling the bus and shouting ridiculous questions were as kind as these people have been.* He ducked as one photographer leaped up beside their window and took several rapid-fire pictures. *I don't know how she can sleep through all this. I also don't know how she can want to marry me so quickly. I know I'm ready, but I'm not really ready. I want her to be happy, but will she be happy with what I have to offer once we get to Brooklyn?*

While they waited out the two-hour layover in Pittsburgh, Patrick laid Lauren's black coat over her chest and legs. A moment later, he felt her hand crawling across his thigh and into his pocket, her fingers tapping at the tip of his penis.

I will never get any sleep as long as I'm with this woman.

He moved his hand into her lap and found her jeans already unzipped. He found her clitoris with his middle finger and made slow circles.

Lauren opened one eye. "I'll try not to scream."

He felt himself growing. "I wish I had a hole in my pocket."

"There will be one soon," Lauren whispered. "My nails are sharp."

Patrick sat back as she ripped a hole in his pocket. "I'm glad you have small hands," he whispered.

Lauren gripped his penis tightly and began to pant. "You're so big," she whispered. "You're gonna make me come. . . ."

Patrick felt Lauren's left hand press down on his.

Lauren's mouth opened wide. "Oh, damn. Oh, damn. Oh, damn . . ."

I may never sleep again.
No sleep till Brooklyn.
Or in Brooklyn either.
I will be the world's happiest insomniac.

49

As the bus caught up to the back edge of the storm and the snow thickened west of Philadelphia, Lauren woke while Patrick snored softly beside her. She turned on her phone, ignored a dozen messages from Todd, and checked the time—4:45 a.m.

She'll be awake. Pamela Jane Jimmerson is always up before the sun.

Lauren called her mother.

"Hello?"

Okay. Talk fast. "Mama, I'm engaged to Patrick Alan Esposito, and we are getting married very soon," she said quickly.

Lauren didn't hear a click.

"I just wanted you to know," Lauren said.

She still didn't hear a click.

"Are you still there?" Lauren asked.

"Yes," Pamela said.

It's a miracle! She spoke! "I hoped you'd be awake," Lauren said.

"I wasn't," Pamela said. "It's Saturday. I don't normally work on Saturday, remember?"

"Oh yeah," Lauren said. *I have lost an entire day on this bus.* "Sorry."

"I saw a picture of Patrick online," Pamela said. "He was kind of blurry."

"Since when do you go online?" Lauren asked.

"I've been going online for a long time," Pamela said. "Now, who is he? Is he another actor?"

"No, Mama," Lauren said. "He's a workingman. He's sitting right beside me."

"Where's he from?" Pamela asked.

"Brooklyn," Lauren said.

Patrick opened his eyes and raised his eyebrows.

"My mama," Lauren mouthed.

"How'd you meet him?" Pamela asked.

"We met online," Lauren said.

"Really?" Pamela said.

"It's not like that," Lauren said.

"It's not like what?" Pamela said. "All I said was, 'Really.'"

She thinks it's like that. "Patrick wrote an extremely kind letter to me after I broke it off with Chazz—"

"To hear Chazz tell it," Pamela interrupted, "he broke it off with you."

My mama watches TV now, too? "I did the breaking. I broke a window, too."

"You did?" Pamela said. "By accident?"

"I shattered it," Lauren said, "and it wasn't an accident."

"You were just showing your tail," Pamela said.

Not as much as Chazz showed me that night. "I was angry."

"You were still showing your tail," Pamela said. "Now, what's this Patrick Espo . . ."

"Esposito," Lauren said. "Patrick Alan Esposito."

"What's he do?" Pamela asked.

"He's a handyman," Lauren said. "He does plumbing, electrical, maintenance—you name it. Like Daddy did."

"Do you love him?" Pamela asked.

"Yes," Lauren said. "Very much."

"You loved Chazz, too, right?" Pamela asked.

"I thought I did," Lauren said. "I know now that I didn't. I've never felt anything like I'm feeling right now with Patrick. Oh, and I'm wearing the most beautiful ring he gave me."

"Chazz gave you a ring, too," Pamela said.

"It didn't mean anything, Mama," Lauren said. "This ring is for real."

"Is he good to you?" Pamela asked.

"Yes, Mama," Lauren said. "Patrick has been nothing but good to me and for me. Better than I deserve."

"You aren't hooking up with him on the rebound, are you?" Pamela asked.

"No, Mama," Lauren said.

"That's what they're saying on the television," Pamela said.

"Ignore whatever they're saying about me on TV, Mama," Lauren said. "You know most of it isn't true."

"How would I know?" Pamela said.

Lauren sighed. *She's itching for an argument, and I don't want to have one.* "Patrick is the kind of man I should have been looking for all along."

"What's all that noise?" Pamela asked. "I can barely hear you sometimes."

"We're on a bus, and we're . . ." She turned to Patrick. "Where are we?"

Patrick peered through the thickening snow. "We're coming up on Philadelphia, I think."

"*You're* on a bus," Pamela said.

"Yes, a Greyhound bus," Lauren said. "Flights from St. Louis were all canceled, so we took a bus. It's a long story."

"Was that his voice?" Pamela asked.

"Yes," Lauren said.

"He sounds Italian," Pamela said. "I thought he would be, as blurry as he was."

"He said one sentence, Mama," Lauren said.

"And he sounded Italian," Pamela said. "Is he?"

"Yes," Lauren said.

"Uh-huh," Pamela said. "Now, are you really serious about quitting acting?"

"Yes, Mama," Lauren said. "I'm in love, and I will have no time for acting."

"Patrick doesn't want you to do it anymore, does he?" Pamela asked.

"It's my decision, Mama," Lauren said. "I'm through."

"Uh-huh," Pamela said. "So you're on a Greyhound bus in Pennsylvania with your Italian fiancé."

"Right," Lauren said.

"I need to speak to him," Pamela said.

"Why?" Lauren asked.

"I need to make sure you're telling me the truth," Pamela said.

"I am," Lauren said.

"I don't believe it," Pamela said. "My daughter on a Greyhound bus? That's crazy. Put him on."

50

Lauren handed the phone to Patrick. "My mama wants to speak to you."

Patrick covered the phone with his hand. "What do I say?"

"Just talk to her," Lauren said.

Patrick put the phone to his ear. "Hello, Mrs. Short."

"It's Mrs. Jimmerson," her mother said, "and please call me Pamela."

"Okay," Patrick said.

"And Lauren's real name is Lauren Jimmerson," Pamela said. "She didn't tell you that, did she?"

"No, ma'am," Patrick said.

"I didn't think she would," Pamela said. "Hardly anyone knows or remembers—or cares. Has Lauren told you anything about me?"

"Just that you two haven't been speaking for a long time," Patrick said.

"Did she tell you why?" Pamela asked.

"Her breast," Patrick said. *Why did I say that? You don't say the word* breast *to your future mother-in-law in your first conversation with her!*

"Excuse me?" Pamela said.

"That scene in *I Got This*," he said quickly. "That movie she made after *Feel the Love*. Where her, um . . ." *Don't say it!* "Where she was a little overexposed."

"I knew what you meant when you said 'breast,'" Pamela said. "I just can't believe you said it."

"Neither can I, Mrs. Jimmerson," Patrick said. "I mean, neither can I, Pamela."

Pamela laughed. "It's okay, Patrick, and that breast of hers was the reason. That was the worst movie ever made. I almost had to change churches because of that movie."

What do you say to that? Patrick thought. *When you don't know what to say to your future mother-in-law, it's always best to stay quiet.*

"Are you really a handyman?" Pamela asked.

"Yes," Patrick said.

"Do you work long hours?" Pamela asked.

"Yes," Patrick said. "Up to sixteen hours most days."

"All right," Pamela said. "Lauren found herself a real man for a change. That last one was gay and trying not to show it. I never would have had any grandbabies. Are you going to give me grandbabies?"

We're not even married yet! "Yes, ma'am. She wants at least two."

"Where are you two going to live?" Pamela asked.

"I guess in Boerum Hill," Patrick said. "It's just south of downtown Brooklyn."

"You mean to tell me that my daughter will no longer be living in LA?" Pamela asked.

"I guess not."

"You guess not? Put Lauren back on."

Patrick handed the phone to Lauren. "She wants to talk to you now."

Lauren took the phone and listened for a few moments. "We haven't decided on that yet. . . . He did? I guess that's where we'll be living then." She handed back the phone. "Your turn."

"You should have told your intended spouse where you planned to set up house before you told her mama," Pamela said. "You two have a lot of things to discuss."

"Yes, ma'am."

"Do you have a spare bedroom for your babies?" Pamela asked.

I don't have a spare room, much less a spare bedroom! "No."

"Good," Pamela said. "Keep your babies close to you at all times. So, when and where is the wedding?"

I can't answer that yet! "Um, well . . ."

Pamela laughed loudly. "You two haven't even planned *that* yet? And you're going to give me grandbabies?"

"We were only engaged yesterday," Patrick said.

"What church do you attend?" Pamela asked.

"St. Agnes," Patrick said.

"Sounds Catholic," Pamela said. "Put Lauren back on."

Patrick handed the phone to Lauren. "You're up."

Lauren listened for a full minute. "Yes, Mama . . . I don't know that, Mama. You ask him." She handed Patrick the phone without comment.

"Are you going to raise my grandbabies to be Catholic?" Pamela asked.

"I don't know," Patrick said.

"You two don't know much of anything, do you?" Pamela asked.

"I guess not," Patrick said. "But I do know that I love your daughter more than life itself."

"You're not after her money?" Pamela asked.

"No," Patrick said. "I paid for the entire first date. I tried to pay for her plane ticket, but once we became engaged, she tore up the check."

"Is that so?" Pamela said.

"Yes," Patrick said. "I mentioned a prenuptial agreement, but she wouldn't hear of it."

"*Uh-huh,*" Pamela said. "What do you know about that?"

Don't answer, Patrick thought. *That was a rhetorical question.*

"Patrick, I don't know you," Pamela said, "but I do know my daughter. After that mess with Chazz, she is ready to get married to someone, and she'll want to be married very soon."

Patrick glanced at Lauren. "I know."

"I never figured she'd have a courthouse wedding, but I suppose it's inevitable," Pamela said.

"Do you think you could you come up for the ceremony, wherever we have it?" Patrick asked.

"I drive a bus Monday through Friday," Pamela said. "I can't afford to take weekdays off, and they often call me in on weekends."

"This is the first time I've missed work in fifteen years," Patrick said.

"Are you going to make a habit of it?" Pamela asked.

"No, ma'am."

"Good," Pamela said. "What's Lauren going to do all day while you're at work?"

So many questions! "I really don't know."

"She should get a real job," Pamela said. "A job that makes her really work."

"But she's an actress," Patrick said.

"She told me that she's going to quit," Pamela said.

"I don't think she meant it," Patrick said. "I really don't."

"Don't you two ever talk to each other? Put Lauren back on."

Patrick handed Lauren the phone.

Lauren glumly took it. "I was going to tell him. Okay, okay." She covered the phone. "Patrick, I am really thinking of retiring from acting." She uncovered the phone. "I told him. . . . Ask him yourself." She handed Patrick the phone.

"Are you going to let her quit acting?" Pamela asked.

I am so confused! "If that's what she wants to do."

"Do you want her to quit?" Pamela asked.

"No, ma'am," Patrick said. "I think it's what she was born to do."

"At least you're honest," Pamela said. "There's crazy money in acting, too much if you ask me. Getting paid for lying and being someone else. That's all acting is. Could you get her a job in Brooklyn?"

"I don't know," Patrick said.

"I know she has no real job skills," Pamela said, "but it wouldn't hurt to take her with you when you work. She doesn't know what work is. Her daddy was a handyman, too, and he took her around a couple times, but then he gave up. She was always making faces in people's mirrors. Maybe you can teach her some kind of trade."

"I don't know if I could do that," Patrick said.

"You're making her live in Brooklyn, right?" Pamela asked.

"I doubt I could make her do anything," Patrick said.

Lauren grabbed his arm. "Hey, now."

"You've already been making her do things," Pamela said. "She's riding on a bus. She hated riding the bus, even the one I drove. It was beneath her. Except for the Catholic thing, I think I'm going to like you. Are you a good Catholic?"

"I go whenever I can," Patrick said.

"At least you're spiritual," Pamela said. "Put Lauren back on."

Lauren snatched the phone this time. "What have you been saying to him? Oh, I will ask him. Okay, sure . . . soon, right. Bye." She turned off her phone and put it in her lap. She took his hand. "She wants to meet you as soon as we can get to D.C."

"She wants to meet Catholic, don't know anything me," Patrick said. "You're really thinking of retiring?"

Lauren nodded.

"You don't have to."

"I think I do," Lauren said. "I mean, how can I continue any kind of career when I'm going to spend my every waking moment with you?" She looked down at her phone. "I wonder . . ." She picked up her phone and pressed several buttons.

"What are you doing?" Patrick asked.

"I'm Googling myself," Lauren said. "Oh, my goodness! Look." She turned the phone toward him. "We've gone viral." She tapped the screen. "This is a video of you proposing to me."

Patrick watched himself drop to one knee. *I look like a beast! I can't believe this woman accepted my proposal!*

"You're a natural," Lauren said.

"I wasn't acting," Patrick said.

"And that's what makes you a natural," Lauren said. "And now you're famous."

"I don't want to be famous, Lauren."

I just want to be left alone and happy.

51

Well, what do you know? Lauren thought. *My mama is talking to me again. It might mean that she's taking me seriously. Well, she's taking me and Patrick seriously.* She smiled at Patrick. *I liked how he talked to her. He showed so much respect for a woman who was playing twenty questions with him. I knew she would. She used to do that with all my old boyfriends, not that there were many. Patrick passed with flying colors.*

"Why are you smiling?" Patrick asked.

I made my mama happy, and you're the reason. "I like to smile." She picked up her phone and deleted messages from Todd without listening to them. "My agent wants to talk to me for some reason."

"So call him," Patrick said.

"Why?" Lauren asked.

"Aren't you curious?" Patrick asked.

"No," Lauren said.

"Not even a little?" Patrick asked.

Hmm. I guess I am. Lauren called Todd.

"Lauren, baby, what the *hell* are you doing?" Todd asked.

"I'm riding on a bus," Lauren said. "What are you doing?"

"I'm going crazy!" Todd yelled. "My phone won't stop ringing."

"Isn't that a good thing?" Lauren asked.

"It's a *great* thing!" Todd yelled again. "That online video of yours started it all. I don't know who he is, but wow! The whole world wants a piece of you now. But I have to know something first. You're not having a nervous breakdown, are you?"

Lauren laughed. "No, Todd, I'm in love, and I'm engaged."

"So it's not a fling?" Todd asked.

"No," Lauren said. "This is serious."

"Hmm," Todd said. "It would have been better if this was only a fling."

"How do you figure?" Lauren asked.

"A fling shows you're over Chazz," Todd said, "but an engagement so soon might give people the idea that you've lost your mind. Some may even think you're throwing away your career over this guy."

"I did that seven years ago, didn't I?" Lauren asked.

"That was different," Todd said.

"How was it different?" Lauren asked.

"Yes, you stopped acting, but you were with one of the biggest names in the business," Todd said. "You were only waiting in the wings for him to let you fly."

"I was waiting to *get* wings," Lauren said. "And now I'm flying, Todd. Don't bring me down."

"Lauren, you're not thinking clearly," Todd said.

"I haven't had clearer thoughts in my life," Lauren said. She took Patrick's hand.

"He could be only after your money," Todd said.

"He isn't," Lauren said.

"How do you know?" Todd asked.

"I know," Lauren said. "He won't let me pay for anything."

"Well, what should I tell all these people calling me?" Todd asked. "I have at least a *dozen* bona fide offers right here in front of me."

"Tell them that I'm happy," Lauren said. "And then tell them that I'm not interested. Good-bye, Todd." She turned off her phone. "Todd's angry."

"Why?" Patrick asked.

"Because he can be," Lauren said. "He thinks I'm throwing my career away." She squeezed his hand. "I'm not because I don't have a career to throw away. It's gone. It's *been* gone. And now I'm happy for a change."

"I don't want you to give up acting because of me," Patrick said.

"I'm not," Lauren said. "I had my time, and now I want to have the time of my life with you." She looked out the window. "How much farther?"

"In miles or hours?" Patrick asked.

"Lie to me," Lauren said.

"I can't," Patrick said. "We've still got maybe six hours to go. This bus is running late."

Lauren rested her head on his shoulder. "Wake me when we get to Brooklyn."

"We have to change buses at Penn Station in Manhattan," Patrick said. "And there's an hour wait for the bus to Brooklyn after that."

"Why?" Lauren whined.

"I don't know," Patrick said. "I don't make the schedules."

"How far is it from Penn Station to your apartment?" Lauren asked.

"About five miles," Patrick said. "But in this weather, it's about half an hour by subway and an hour by bus. If we wait for the bus, we'll be dropped off three blocks from my apartment."

"Let's take the subway when we get there," Lauren said.

"If it's still running," Patrick said. "During Nemo, the A and Two trains had problems. We'll just have to see when we get there."

"I just want to get home," Lauren said.

Patrick smiled. "I like how you said that."

"I meant for you to like it," Lauren said. "Wake me when we get to Penn Station."

Seven hours later, after being buffeted by gale-force winds in New Jersey and sitting for a solid hour before getting through the Lincoln Tunnel, the bus crept into Penn Station.

Lauren woke to passengers cheering.

"We're here?" she whispered.

Patrick nodded. "And only five hours late," he said. "You just survived *thirty-three* hours on a bus."

After gathering his duffel bag and Lauren's luggage, they headed for the A train through a massive throng of people, many of them shouting photographers.

"Why are you here, Lauren?"

"Are you really engaged, or is this some publicity stunt?"

"Did you come here to eat, Lauren? Have you gained some weight?"

"Are you having an affair with your bodyguard?"

"Ignore them," Lauren whispered, and she held on to Patrick's elbow as he guided her through the crowd, flashes going off all around them. "I'm glad you know where you're going." *I have not missed this hustle and bustle one bit.*

"I really don't," Patrick said. "I don't hang out up here that often."

"It's only five miles away from where you live, right?" Lauren asked.

"Trust me," Patrick said. "Five miles can put you into a completely different world in New York City."

Lauren gripped his elbow more tightly. "Don't lose me."

"I won't." Patrick took out his MetroCard and swiped it once at a turnstile. "You go first," he said.

Lauren struggled through the turnstile.

He swiped his MetroCard again and bulled his way through the turnstile using Lauren's luggage.

That is some impressive luggage, Lauren thought. *I should do a commercial for them. They survive snow, paparazzi, and subway turnstiles with ease.*

"I'm surprised I had anything left on that card," he said. "This way."

Lauren warily eyed the photographers, most of whom stayed behind the turnstiles. She latched on to Patrick's bicep this time. *His elbow has to have gouges in it.* "What if you didn't have anything on that card?"

"I'd have to stand in line to load it up again," Patrick said, "and we might have missed the next train. I got lucky."

Patrick staked out a spot on the platform with her luggage, and Lauren huddled under his arm. When the A train squealed in and stopped, they waited until the car had nearly emptied before walking on. While Patrick stood among the suitcases, Lauren sat.

Okay, she thought. *What are the rules of the subway? I used to know them.* She looked at Patrick, who was staring at her luggage. *Oh yeah. Don't make eye contact. Stare at the floor. Don't make small talk. Just ride, keep quiet, and—*

"It's Lauren Short!"

And try not to let anyone know who you are.

Lauren looked in the direction of the voice and saw an elderly Hispanic man waving at her. She nodded.

"I see you on YouTube," he said loudly as the doors closed. "Very romantic. You are lucky man."

Patrick nodded, rolling his eyes at Lauren. "I am lucky man," he whispered.

"I'm lucky, too," she whispered.

Fortunately, the riders of the A train adhered to protocol and left them alone for the remainder of their journey to the Hoyt-Schermerhorn Streets Station.

"You might recognize this station," Patrick said. "Michael Jackson filmed the *Bad* video in here."

Lauren didn't see anything especially noteworthy as they left the station and climbed the stairs to the street, where mounds of blowing snow—and an army of paparazzi in down jackets, shooting pictures as if their cameras were machine guns—greeted them.

"There she is!"

"Lauren! This way!"

"Lauren, over here!"

"What took you so long?"

"Do you regret taking the bus?"

"What happened to your hair?"

"Why are you eating so much?"

"Does Chazz know you're here?"

Patrick turned to Lauren. "What do we do?"

"We walk," Lauren said.

"I am getting sick of their questions," Patrick whispered.

"Answer them or don't answer them," Lauren said. "It's up to you. Just don't whisper. The paparazzi can't hear very well. They love to misquote people. And whatever you do, don't do a Lily Allen."

"Who's Lily Allen, and what did she do?" Patrick asked.

"Lily Allen is the girl who sang 'Smile,'" Lauren said.

"Okay," Patrick said. "And?"

"You've never heard of Lily Allen?" Lauren asked.

"No," Patrick said. "What'd she do?"

"She punched out a photographer in London and got arrested," Lauren said.

"I won't do that," Patrick said. "I just don't want to say anything that might embarrass you."

"After all you've said and typed to me, man," Lauren said, "I don't think you could ever embarrass me."

Patrick shouldered his way through the first row of photographers, Lauren gripping his hand.

"Where are you headed, Lauren?" a photographer asked.

"State Street," Patrick said.

The photographer ignored him. "Where are you going, Lauren?"

"Like he said," Lauren said. "State Street."

Another photographer jumped in front of them, snapping away. "What's on State Street?"

"My apartment," Patrick said.

The photographer stepped in front of Lauren. "What's on State Street, Lauren?"

"He just told you," Lauren said. "My fiancé's apartment. Are you deaf?"

As snowflakes clung to her coat and windblown snow hit her cheeks, Lauren watched as other photographers raced ahead of them and kicked up snow.

"Did Chazz freeze your bank account?" someone yelled.

What? Lauren stopped, pulling Patrick close. "Who asked that?"

A man with a notepad stepped forward. "I did. Is it true?"

"Why would you ask such a question?" Lauren asked.

"Well, we heard you had to take a bus from St. Louis," the man said.

"All flights were canceled out of St. Louis because of the snow," Lauren said. "You do see the snow, don't you?"

The man only blinked.

Idiot. "We wanted to get home, so we took the bus," Lauren said. "It was the only safe way to get here."

"So Chazz didn't freeze your money," the man said.

"No," Lauren said.

"Why didn't you wait a few days to fly in?" the man asked.

"I have to work," Patrick said. "Do you mind?"

The man stepped aside.

They continued up Schermerhorn and took a left on Hoyt.

Another reporter, this one wearing a ridiculous yellow rain slicker, cut in front of them. "Why do you have to work, buddy? She's Lauren Short."

Patrick guided Lauren around him.

"You won't ever have to work again, buddy," the man said behind them. "She's your sugar mama."

Patrick stopped and turned around. "I am not your buddy, she will be my *wife,* and work is what I do."

That was a great answer, Lauren thought. *I liked how the veins in Patrick's neck bulged out. This man has fire, and I will need all his fire to warm me up when we get to his—I mean,* our—*apartment.*

"Sorry," Patrick whispered to Lauren.

"Don't be," Lauren said. "How much farther?"

"A couple blocks," Patrick said.

They continued down Hoyt and turned east onto State Street.

"Why were you in St. Louis?" another reporter asked.

Lauren smiled. "We were on our first date."

"Why'd you go to St. Louis for your first date?" yet another reporter asked.

"So we could avoid talking to people like you," Patrick said.

He beat me to it! "And to get engaged," Lauren said. She flashed her ring, and a snowflake nearly drowned it.

"But, Lauren, you got engaged after only one date!" a reporter shouted.

Lauren didn't turn to face the reporter. "It was the best date in the history of all dates. It was the perfect date."

"Where'd he get the ring?" a voice asked.

"*He* is walking right beside me," Lauren said.

"Where'd you get the ring?" asked a reporter with a high-pitched voice. "What's it made out of? How many carats?"

Patrick shook his head. "It's platinum, zero point four carats, it's an antique, and I got it at Gem Pawnbrokers, the one off Flatbush."

Really? Lauren thought. *Wow. I have a one-of-a-kind ring then. It's as unique as the man who bought it.*

"Sure thing, buddy," the annoying reporter said. "What have we seen you in?"

"Coveralls," Patrick said.

Patrick is good at this! Lauren thought. *I can't wait to see him in coveralls. I really can't wait to see him out of them.*

"What movies, wise guy?" the annoying reporter asked.

Patrick slowed to a stop. He faced the cameras. "I'm not an actor or a wise guy. I work for a living."

"Doing what?" a reporter asked.

"I do buildings maintenance," Patrick said.

"He's a handyman!" a photographer shouted.

Patrick nodded. "Right. I work for a living."

A female reporter scurried up to Lauren. "How did you two meet?"

"We met online," Lauren said. "A little over a week ago."

The reporter smiled. "A week? So this is a whirlwind romance."

Lauren looked at the snow swirling above their heads. "You could say that. It's a whirling snowstorm romance. A blizzard romance."

The reporter put her entire face in front of Lauren's. "Does Chazz know?"

This woman could have another career as a flight attendant. "Why would I care what Chazz knows or doesn't know? If he wants to know, he can watch Patrick proposing to me on YouTube."

"Isn't this relationship kind of sudden?" she asked.

"This relationship was twenty years in the making," Patrick said.

The reporters and photographers seemed to freeze.

My man is good at shutting people up! Lauren thought. *I should let him speak for me. I think I will.*

The annoying reporter stepped closer to Patrick. "So you were seeing Lauren behind Chazz Jackson's back?"

Patrick stared him down. "We've known each other seven days. Do the math."

He keeps beating me to it! Lauren thought. *I love Brooklyn men. They're so direct.*

"But you just said something about twenty years!" the annoying reporter screeched.

"I have had a crush on Lauren for twenty years," Patrick said. "I only recently fell in love with her."

"Lauren," the female reporter said, "what do you think Chazz will think about all this?"

"Chazz thinks?" Lauren laughed. "That's news to me."

The annoying reporter rolled his eyes and flipped through his notepad. "So, Lauren, did you quit *Gray Areas* because of this guy?"

How'd that news get out there already? Oh, it doesn't matter now. "This guy has a name," Lauren said, "and it's Patrick Alan Esposito, and no, I didn't quit because of Patrick. I quit because I didn't want to be on the show." She kissed Patrick's cheek, and the cameras clicked rapidly. "I took a much better offer."

"What are you working on next?" the female reporter asked.

A baby! "Getting married."

"No," she said. "I meant, what projects will you be working on next?"

"I won't," Lauren said. "I can think of no greater role than that of a wife and mother." *And I will be acting up a storm with Patrick in a few moments. Why aren't we there yet?*

"When are you getting married?" several reporters shouted.

"Soon," Lauren said.

Patrick motioned to a set of brown stairs leading into a brick apartment building. "We're here."

Finally! Lauren gripped the stair rail, and Patrick followed behind. Once inside the building, Lauren hugged Patrick fiercely.

"You were fantastic," she said. "You handled them perfectly."

"I almost cursed out that goofy guy with the stupid voice," Patrick said.

"He was a jerk." She opened the door and stuck out her head. She pointed at the skinny, annoying reporter. "You, yes, you. Come here."

The reporter slipped up the stairs. "So, when exactly are you getting married, Lauren?" He readied his pen.

"I already told you," Lauren said. "I just wanted you to know that you're a jerk, and you can quote me on that. Make sure you spell your own name correctly." She shut the door and laughed. She looked up another set of stairs. "How much of a climb?"

"We're on the second floor," Patrick said. "Now please understand. I haven't cleaned it up. I didn't expect you to follow me all the way to Brooklyn."

They started up the stairs.

"So I surprised you, huh?" Lauren said.

"You constantly surprise me," Patrick said. "I'm worried you'll think less of me when you see how I live."

"I can only think more of you."

Patrick stopped in front of 2B. "Be careful when you step inside." He opened the door. "The back wall appears in a hurry. You kind of have to step in and make a quick left turn."

He's kidding, right?

Lauren stepped inside.

He wasn't kidding.

She made a sharp left, walked through a skinny hallway, and entered a room with a couch, a coffee table, and a TV. From where she stood, she could see a bigger kitchen than the one in LA, a small bedroom through some glass doors, and a very nice bathroom.

And it's so clean!

Mainly because it's empty.

The first thing we need to do is get some light in here. We'll need some lamps. And some throw rugs. And some throw blankets. And something on these bare walls. His apartment is like a blank canvas, and I am going to add some color.

"It's about what I expected," Lauren said. "I like your bathroom. It has *two* sinks." She took off her coat. "It's cozy."

"It's tiny," Patrick said, setting down her luggage in the kitchen.

"It's your home," Lauren said. "And now it's my home." She hugged him and held him tightly.

And with a little work, it will be our *home.*

52

She's just being nice, Patrick thought. *She can't like this place. Even I don't like this place that much.*

He led her into the bedroom, lifted the window shade a few inches, crouched, and looked out. *And they're still out there? Why?* He saw film cameras, lights, and several news trucks, one truck blocking most of the sidewalk. "It looks as if all the networks are here. Don't they see this blizzard around them?"

Lauren sat on the edge of the bed, pulling her shirt out of her pants. "Should we give them a show? I like performing in front of windows for some reason." She laughed, then frowned. "No. I just started talking to my mama again. If the world saw us in the window, she wouldn't talk to me ever again."

Patrick pulled down the shade. "Is it always going to be this way?"

"They'll get cold and bored and go home soon," Lauren said.

Patrick sat beside her. "I meant, will they harass us whenever we go out?"

She rubbed his leg. "They might, and if they do, I know you'll take care of me like you already have. It is so much easier to deal with those idiots if you have help. We make a good team."

Patrick moved her onto his lap, then wrapped her legs around him. "If they weren't there, would you want to perform in front of the window?"

"You know I would," she whispered. "When we were in the window in St. Louis, I had my all-time best orgasm. Just the thought of us doing it for millions of people to see makes me hot." She started unbuttoning her shirt. "I'm getting hot just thinking about it."

"We need a shower," Patrick said.

"Yes, we do."

Patrick frowned. "It's a stand-up shower, no tub. It will be a tight squeeze for us."

Lauren's hands traveled to Patrick's crotch. "There definitely won't be enough room in there for both of us because of this thing."

"Do you mind showering alone?" Patrick asked.

"No," Lauren said. "I may use up all your hot water, though."

"Go ahead and try," Patrick said. "I installed a hundred-gallon Bradford White hot water heater in this building a year ago, and I've never gotten a single complaint."

"I assume a Bradford White means something," Lauren said.

"It's the best water heater you can buy," Patrick said. "Salthead only gave me a thousand toward a new one for this building. I made up the difference."

"Do the other tenants know you did this?" Lauren asked.

"No," Patrick said. "And I didn't do it for them. I take some seriously long hot showers at the end of the day." He winced. "Because I need to."

"Will you watch me take my shower?" Lauren asked.

"I will watch you do anything."

Patrick had to wipe steam away from the shower door every few seconds so he could see Lauren soaping up her body. He listened to her moans, sighs, and panting for several minutes until he could stand it no longer. He took off his clothes, opened the door, edged inside, and closed the door.

"I knew you couldn't stay away from me for very long," Lauren whispered, dripping her soapy washcloth across his chest. She pulled his erect penis down and ground on it between her legs. "Are these glass walls sturdy?"

Patrick nodded. *I hope so.*

"Lift me up."

He lifted her until she could grip the metal strips at the top of the glass walls.

"Stay still," she whispered. "Let me do the work."

Lauren lifted and lowered herself while Patrick soaped the rest of her. He watched his penis appear and disappear inside her. He felt the smoothness of her legs and pubis, watched the undulation of her stomach, heard her sighs increasing until she let out a delicious moan.

"Damn, man, why aren't you coming?"

"If I do," Patrick said, "I'll thrust you out of this shower and into the apartment upstairs."

Lauren lowered herself fully onto his penis, grasping him around the neck. "I've got all of you inside me." She smiled. "You feel that?"

Patrick nodded.

"I'm giving you a hand job without using my hands,"

Lauren said, stretching her neck away from him. "Are you going to come when I come?"

Patrick nodded, using his thumbs to rub on her clitoris.

"That's good. That's good. Oh *yes!*"

Patrick came when she shouted, nearly slipping and pitching her into the tile wall. "We need a bigger shower."

Lauren bit her lip and nodded. "We need a tub built for two."

"I'll get right on that."

"Yes."

After drying off and applying half a bottle of lotion, Lauren walked naked into the bedroom.

I am so glad I only have one window, Patrick thought. *She can walk around here like that all the time.*

Lauren peeked through the shade. "Are they crazy? You'd think the blizzard would be more important news." She sat on the windowsill, dangling her legs. "I want to get loud with you, and I don't care if they hear us."

This woman is trouble, Patrick thought. *I am beginning to love trouble.*

She spread her legs slightly. "We're going to do a love scene. A *bad* love scene."

Patrick moved in front of her. "How bad?"

"Really bad. I'll start." She licked her lips. "Bring your man meat over here."

"Oh, *that* kind of bad." He stroked his penis. "You gonna straighten it for me?"

Lauren laughed. "I said bad, not porno. We're going for an R rating."

"Oh, sorry," Patrick said. "Um, you come here, woman. Give me some good lovin'."

Lauren smiled. "Better." She widened her legs more and put her thumb in her mouth. "You got what I need?"

That's a sexy pose. "I got what you need."

She took her thumb out of her mouth and rubbed her right nipple. "You got it goin' on?"

That's an even sexier pose. "I got it goin' on."

She squeezed both breasts. "You gonna do me all night long?"

"I'm gonna do it to you until the cows come home," Patrick said.

Lauren stood. "Are there any cows in Brooklyn?"

Patrick shook his head.

Lauren put her hands on his face, then slid them down his body. "So they aren't ever going to come home, and that means . . . you gonna do me till sunrise." She squeezed his penis.

"I'm gonna do you till I have to go to work," Patrick whispered.

Lauren stroked him. "You gonna work me."

"Yeah," Patrick said. "I'm gonna work that thang."

Lauren let go, slid off the windowsill, and fell onto the bed. "That *thang?* Really?"

"I don't watch many movies like this," Patrick said.

"You were doing fine," Lauren said. She held out her arms. "Come make love to me."

Patrick dropped to his knees and kissed her thighs. "With or without dialogue."

"Just whisper. . . ."

Patrick kissed her clitoris. "Give me some good lovin'. . . ."

Lauren closed her eyes. "Don't give me your man meat till you're through down there. . . ."

As wet as she is, it won't be long. . . .

53

Lauren woke in complete darkness to a buzzing sound. She turned from Patrick's chest and looked at the windowsill where a cell phone vibrated in its charger.

"Patrick, your phone," she whispered.

Patrick stirred. The buzzing stopped. Patrick kissed the back of her neck and slipped out of the bed. Lauren saw only his shape as he picked up the phone, pressed a few buttons, and listened. For a long time.

"Who's calling at this hour?" Lauren asked, rolling over onto a warmer spot.

"Tenants," Patrick said.

"But it's Sunday," Lauren said. "And it's dark!"

Patrick sighed. "I rarely get a full weekend off."

Lauren buried her head in the pillow. "But it's Sunday." She felt Patrick sit on the edge of the bed.

"And I've been gone for four days. Luckily, these aren't real emergencies."

She heard him close his phone.

"I'd be crazy to leave you now."

"Yes, you would," Lauren said, and she pulled him under the covers. She ground her pubis into his thighs. "You got pretty crazy last night."

Patrick took her hands and placed them on his chest. "You bring out the crazy in me."

"I like crazy you inside of me," Lauren said, thrusting harder against him. "I can see why you like doing this to me."

He rolled over to face her. "You wore out my thrusters."

She rubbed her nose on his. "Do you think we made a baby?"

"We should have made quintuplets," Patrick said.

"Let's make sure," Lauren said. She climbed over his body, got out of bed, and went to the window. "I don't see anyone." She lifted the shade completely. "They're gone." She leaned onto the window, her nipples growing as she rubbed them on the icy glass. "Do me here." She closed her eyes.

She heard him get out of bed. "Are you sure?" he asked.

"Yes," Lauren said. She reached back and pulled her cheeks apart. "Do me hard."

She felt Patrick's penis move into her slowly until it filled her. She felt his large hands pulling on her hips. She felt ecstasy as he pumped himself into her, the window rattling and her breasts flattening on the glass as he did. She opened her eyes and saw a man walking his dog in the snow.

"Patrick?" she wheezed.

"Yes?"

"We have an audience."

Patrick froze.

"Don't stop," Lauren whispered, letting go of her cheeks and pulling him deeper. "It's only a man walking his dog. I don't think he can see us. Don't stop. Please. I'm so close."

She felt him grow even bigger, felt his sweat dripping onto her back, felt her legs weaken, felt the sting of his hands slapping her booty repeatedly, and when she came, she howled.

The dog lifted its head.

The man turned.

Lauren yanked down the shade. "That was close!"

Patrick seemed to throw his entire body inside her, and as he came, he lifted her off the floor and moved her to the bed, furiously pumping her while she braced herself against the wall.

As Patrick pulled out of her, Lauren collapsed onto the bed. "I am so out of shape," she said.

Patrick fell beside her. "I wish I had more windows."

Lauren smiled in the darkness. "I wish I had more stamina." She found one of his hands and put it on her chest. "I'm nearly hyperventilating, man." She slowed her breathing. "I have to know something."

"Just ask."

"*Can* you come before I do?" Lauren asked.

"I'm sure I can," Patrick said. "It's much more meaningful to me to come with you or just after you do."

"Meaningful," he says. This isn't just sex to him. Or to me. "The dog heard me howling."

"I doubt my neighbors did," Patrick said. "There are no early risers in this building. They're mostly older people." He pulled the covers over them. "I need to tell you something."

"Okay."

"When I came just then, I had the worst cramps in the bottoms of my feet," Patrick said.

"Oh, I hate those," Lauren said.

"But as soon as I came, the cramps went away," Patrick

said. "When I cramp up while I'm working, they don't normally go away until I take off my boots and stretch out my toes." He kissed her neck. "What does that mean?"

"I don't know," Lauren said. "Do you relax immediately after you come?"

"Yes," Patrick said. "Well, almost immediately."

"Do you get cramps in your feet often?" she asked.

"During the summer, yes," Patrick said. "And now I know the cure."

"I hope you get cramps often then," Lauren said. The glow of the sun began to light up the window shade. "Is this what a sunrise looks like?"

"Yes," Patrick said.

"I don't like it," Lauren said. "We need to catch up on our sleep."

"I agree," Patrick said.

She turned to face him. "I want to establish a rule. The first person who wakes up has to wake up the other person using only their tongue."

"I like this rule very much," Patrick whispered.

"I hope you fall asleep first so you can wake up first," Lauren whispered.

"So do I. . . ."

Six hours later, at a few minutes before one, Lauren left Patrick snoring softly and went to the kitchen. She drank several glasses of water, ate two slices of American cheese on some saltines she found in the cupboard, and brushed her teeth.

She returned to the bed. *Do I wake him? I just made the rule. But he looks so tired. I'll let him sleep. . . .*

Lauren dreamed she was being serviced sexually by several men, each man's tongue working a different part of her body. Two men worked on her breasts, another licked

her booty, and one man with dark eyes was greedily tasting
her—

"Damn!" Lauren shouted as she came and awoke at the
same time.

Patrick's head popped out from beneath the covers.
"Were you really asleep?"

"Yes," Lauren said, kissing him greedily. "I was dreaming, and the orgasm woke me up."

"Cool," Patrick said. "What were you dreaming about?"

I can't tell him three other men were licking on me, Lauren thought.

"You don't have to tell me," Patrick said. "It was good,
though, right?"

Lauren nodded. "Not as good as the real thing." She
guided him inside her. "Please be gentle. I am so sore."

"I'll try to be gentle," Patrick said.

Lauren put her hands over her head and watched Patrick
move in and out of her with a slow, easy rhythm. "All right,
I'll tell you," she whispered. "I was in bed with four men
working on me."

"That was some dream."

"You're not mad?" Lauren asked.

Patrick shook his head. "I have never had a woman tell
me any of her dreams. This is so instructive. Do you have
dreams like these often?"

Lauren shook her head. "No. You're making me dream."
That's what he's doing. He's making me dream again. "Do
you have dreams like that?"

"About men licking me? No." Patrick smiled and continued to pump her.

"I am so glad about that," Lauren said. "What is the
most erotic dream you've ever had?"

Patrick squinted. "Do you really want to know? It happened a long time ago."

"I want to know," Lauren said.

Patrick stopped pumping. "I had just seen *Feel the Love*. That night, I had an incredible dream involving you and—"

"Me?" Lauren interrupted. "I'm flattered. And who else?"

"I'd rather not say," Patrick said.

She rocked him until she was on top of him. "Who else?"

"Nia Long and Sally Richardson," Patrick said.

At least he has great taste. Those two women are gorgeous. "And what were we doing to you?"

"Oh, only you were doing something to me," Patrick said. "You were on top of me, and the other two were . . ."

Lauren started to grind. "What were they doing?"

"It's kind of funny, actually," Patrick said. "They were giving us directions. Put your hand here, bend your leg this way, lean back. They even told us what to say."

"Really?"

"Yeah." Patrick raised his eyebrows. "It was . . . hot."

"They were both naked, weren't they?" Lauren asked.

"No," Patrick said. "They were fully dressed in lab coats, and they were checking off things on a clipboard."

"Right," Lauren said. "Fully dressed."

"Well, they weren't wearing anything underneath," Patrick said.

"See-through lab coats, huh?"

"Kind of," Patrick said. "You didn't even seem to notice them."

Lauren flattened herself on him, grinding faster. "But you did."

"Yes, but in the end," Patrick whispered, "I only saw you. But I woke up before I could finish." He sat up and pressed down on Lauren's hips. "I am finishing that dream right now. . . ."

Patrick finished his dream.

I am finished, Lauren thought. *No more, no more . . . until tomorrow.*

"Nia Long and Sally Richardson, huh?" Lauren said hours later after yet another nap.

"Yes," Patrick said.

"Do you still have fantasies about them?" Lauren asked.

"No," Patrick said.

"What did you like about them?" Lauren asked.

"I liked their smiles," Patrick said.

Lauren pinched his arm. "Is that all?"

"Yes," Patrick said. "They had and they still have incredible smiles. Not as nice as yours, of course."

"Those two women are hot, Patrick," Lauren said. "And all you looked at was their smiles?"

"Yes," Patrick said.

"I'm sure you looked at other parts," Lauren said.

"No, just their smiles," Patrick said. "I always equate a nice smile with a nice person, and I hear they're both very nice people."

"They are," Lauren said. "I've met them both, and they are genuinely wonderful people first and outstanding actresses second. You have good taste in your dreams."

"And in real life, too," Patrick said. "I'd like to taste you again."

Lauren dropped her head back onto the pillow. "You have completely worn me out. Aren't you worn out?"

"A little," Patrick said.

"Liar," Lauren said.

"Feel me," Patrick whispered.

Lauren's hands moved down his body and found an erect penis. "No way. But why?"

"I'm in bed with my dream girl," Patrick said. "You'll just have to get used to it."

"I am really, really sore, Patrick," Lauren said. "And we both need our sleep."

"I know," Patrick said. "I just wanted you to know that I'm aroused by you whenever you're near me."

She kissed him passionately. "That's one of the nicest compliments I've ever gotten. Thank you." She stroked him gently. "When will it go away?"

"I'll probably wake up with it," Patrick said. "I'll try not to poke you while you sleep."

"Do I really excite you that much?"

"Yes." He pulled her hands up to his chest. "Sweet dreams."

"Have I told you I love you today?" Lauren asked.

"No," Patrick said.

"I love you, Patrick," Lauren said.

"I love you, too, Lauren," Patrick said. "Now sleep and dream of me. . . ."

Buzzing woke Lauren again the next morning.

It's Monday, she thought, *and it's still dark. Is darkness thicker in Brooklyn or what?* She felt the bed beside her and didn't find a chiseled, hot body. "Patrick?"

"Over here," Patrick said. He used the glow of his cell phone to illuminate his face. "Good morning."

"What are you doing?"

"I have to go to work," he said. He waved the phone over his body.

He's already dressed in coveralls! How didn't I wake up?

"I have to take care of some actual emergencies," he said. "Would you like to go with me?"

No. "You'll come back for lunch, right?"

"I probably won't be anywhere near here at lunchtime," Patrick said.

I don't want to be alone! "What would I have to do?"

"Only what you wanted to do," Patrick said. "But you are very welcome to stay here and keep warm. It's in the mid-twenties and windy outside, and the snow is at least a foot deep with snowdrifts pushing two feet. I will do my best to hurry back to you."

I left mid-seventies only a few days ago. "Will you teach me how to be a handywoman?"

"I could, I guess," Patrick said. "But it's going to be a long, cold day. Please stay here and rest."

I can't let this man out of my sight. "Will I get to hold your tools?"

"Yes." Patrick sighed. "I, um, I have to go get them first."

"Where are they?" Lauren asked.

"At Gem Pawnbrokers," Patrick said. "I used them as collateral for your ring."

He did what? "Turn on the light."

Patrick turned on the overhead light.

"You did what?" she asked.

Patrick looked at the floor. "I left my tools at the pawnshop as collateral for your ring. I'm not sure when they open or even if they'll open today because of the snow. I'm hoping they'll be open by nine."

Lauren looked at her ring. "You pawned your tools . . . for this ring."

"Sort of," Patrick said.

Lauren wrapped the covers around her and scooted to the edge of the bed. "You gambled your livelihood . . . for *me?* What if I didn't accept your proposal?"

"I'd be returning the ring today and trying to get some of my money back," Patrick said. "And my tools." Patrick smiled. "I know, it was a crazy thing to do."

Lauren's eyes filled with tears. "It wasn't crazy. It was love. You'd do anything for me."

"I would."

Lauren stood up, let the covers fall off her shoulders, and buried her face in his chest. "I love you so much."

"And I love you." He lifted her chin. "Aren't you cold?"

Lauren nodded. "I need a shower."

"You can get back into bed," Patrick said. "I promise to work quickly today."

Lauren shook her head. "I'm going with you. Did you already take a shower?"

Patrick nodded. "But you don't have to go."

"Why didn't you wake me?" She went into the kitchen, opened a suitcase, and took out a pair of panties and a bra.

"You were sleeping so peacefully," Patrick said. "And really, I want you to stay here."

"From now on, we shower together," Lauren said. "That's rule number two."

"An excellent rule."

Lauren went into the bathroom. "Hey," she said. "You broke rule number one."

"I tried," Patrick said, "but you were completely unconscious, and my tongue got tired."

No way! She stuck her head outside the bathroom. "You were down there, and I didn't respond?"

"No," Patrick said. "Well, you made little cooing sounds."

I must be more exhausted than I thought. "Well, thanks for trying. And find me something to wear."

After a shower, Lauren found a set of brown coveralls, one-piece red long johns, a Brooklyn Dodgers hat, a pair of red wool socks, and a pair of white tube socks lying on the bathroom sink.

She put on her panties and bra and stepped into the

long johns. *I look like a baggy brown Santa.* She slipped on the two pairs of socks and had to jump several times before the legs of the coveralls rode up her shins. After adjusting the straps and rolling up the cuffs, she stuffed her hair up under the hat.

"Ready?" Patrick said. He threw her a black down vest and a pair of brown leather work gloves.

"How do I look?" Lauren asked.

"You look . . ."

"I'm going for cute here," Lauren said. She turned to the side and stuck out her booty. There was no change in the view because of the baggy coveralls.

"You're still too sexy," Patrick said.

Lauren pouted.

"And cute," Patrick said. "Definitely cute."

She put on the vest and slapped the gloves on her thigh. "I am ready."

Patrick handed her a Pop-Tart. "I hope you like brown sugar cinnamon."

"Is this our daily breakfast?" she asked before biting the Pop-Tart nearly in half.

"We'll get coffee on the way," Patrick said. "You know, you don't have to go."

"Yes I do," Lauren said.

"Are you sure?"

"Positive," Lauren said. "Let's go to work." She put on her gloves and took his hand. "Let's go get the tools that got me my ring."

54

"There she is!"

"Wait a minute. Is that really her?"

"Lauren? Is that really you?"

"She's trying to get past us in a disguise!"

Lauren waved at about a dozen paparazzi from the top of the outside stairs. The paparazzi rushed to the bottom of the stairs and took pictures.

Thousands of them.

Patrick looked at Lauren.

Lauren shrugged and smiled.

Patrick growled.

Lauren kissed him.

Patrick smiled and led Lauren through the crowd.

"Where are you going?" someone asked.

"To work," Patrick said. "Something you should try to do."

A man scampered beside them as they walked down State Street. "This *is* our job."

"You harass people for a living," Patrick said. "That's not a job. It's a crime."

"I report on celebrities for a living," the man said.

"I'm not a celebrity," Patrick said.

"But she is," the man said.

Patrick quickened their pace as they went around the block to an Atlas ATM on Schermerhorn. He took out two hundred dollars.

Two paparazzi caught up to them. "What's the money for?" one of them asked.

Patrick sighed, shook his head, and led Lauren up the block to the Little Sweet Café at the corner of Hoyt and State. They entered the café, and as they made their way to the counter, they passed classic Boos butcher-block tables. The man behind the counter smiled while a pale young woman with turquoise-streaked hair struggled to write the day's menu on a chalkboard.

"I'm glad you're open, Freddy," Patrick said.

"I'm glad you're here, Patrick," Freddy said. He smiled broadly. "And you brought Lauren Short. I heard you were in the neighborhood. Welcome."

"Hi," Lauren said.

"Wow," the woman said. She dropped her chalk. "Wow!" she shouted.

"Zina," Freddy said. "Finish the sign."

Zina looked out the window. "Paparazzi! That is *so* cool." She spun around to Lauren. "I mean, cool to me. Probably not that cool to you. What are you wearing?"

Lauren put her hand on her hip and posed. "Like it? It's handywoman chic. All former actresses are wearing coveralls these days."

"I like it," Zina said. "I have to get me some of those. What size are they?"

"Size huge," Lauren said.

Patrick smiled at Freddy. "Two espressos and two hot chocolates."

Lauren pointed at the glass case. "And some of those cookies."

Patrick nodded. "And some of those cookies."

Zina stuck her head outside briefly, shut the door behind her, and giggled. "I wasn't going to come in today, but I'm glad I did."

Freddy handed Lauren her espresso and the cookies. "Let me know if it needs more sugar."

Lauren sipped it. "Just right."

"You'll love the hot chocolate," Zina said. "It tastes like hot Hershey's syrup."

Lauren sipped the hot chocolate. "This is *good*," she said. She bit off part of an oatmeal-raisin cookie. "Oh yes. Sugar, I've missed you." She fed Patrick the rest of the cookie. "We must come here every morning. No more Pop-Tarts."

"*Dude*," Zina said. "Pop-Tarts? Really? You know Freddy's crepes and cookies are legendary."

"Please," Lauren said. "Pretty please?"

"We'll see you tomorrow, Freddy," Patrick said.

"And the next day." Lauren gathered up the remaining cookies and put them in the paper bag Zina had handed her. Then she placed the bag in the middle pocket of her coveralls. "These cookies are fantastic."

It looks as if we'll be eating breakfast here from now on, Patrick thought as he paid. *I hope Freddy gives frequent-eater discounts.*

Lauren walked outside, munching on another cookie and sipping her hot chocolate as camera shutters whirred. "You all have to try the hot chocolate and some of these cookies."

The photographers took several hundred rapid-fire shots of Lauren eating a cookie.

Unreal, Patrick thought. *This city is nearly shut down*

*from a blizzard, and they're taking pictures of a woman
eating a cookie in Boerum Hill.*

"I'm not kidding," Lauren said. "Go try them. We'll
wait for you." She fed a cookie to Patrick.

No photographer snapped a picture.

"You don't know what you're missing," Lauren said.
"And I promise we'll wait right here."

Most of the photographers went into the small café, returning minutes later with cups of coffee and hot chocolate.

"They waited," one photographer said.

"I told you we would," Lauren said. She linked her arm
with Patrick's. "Come on."

"Where are you going?" asked one of the photographers.

"Where are we going next?" asked another.

"You'll see," Lauren said. "Enjoy the walk."

They doubled back on Hoyt and trudged down Shermerhorn to Gem Pawnbrokers, its roll-down security gate
down and coated with graffiti. Patrick and Lauren waited
beside a stop sign as snowplows crept by on Flatbush.

"He wasn't kidding," one photographer said. "He
bought her ring *here.* What a loser!"

Patrick stared him down. "How can I be a loser when I
won Lauren's heart and she's going to marry me?"

"Dude," the photographer said, "you bought her engagement ring at a pawnshop."

"As have millions of men throughout history," Patrick
said. "Are all of them losers, too?"

The photographer shook his head. "It's not done, man.
Not for a woman like Lauren Short."

Lauren finished another cookie. "Why are you here? Is
this news? We're standing in front of a pawnshop waiting
for it to open on a Monday morning."

"*You're* news, Lauren," someone said.

"How am I news?" Lauren asked.

The photographers looked at each other until one said, "You're a star."

"I *was* a star," Lauren said. "I'm much happier now, thank you."

"Did he make you wear that outfit?" someone asked.

"No," Lauren said. "These are my work clothes."

One of the security gates rose.

"I think they're opening," a photographer said.

Lauren took Patrick's hand. "You think?" She laughed.

Patrick moved toward the main door and turned. "Look around you. This city is at a standstill. Some people might not have any power. The streets are a mess. People are struggling to open up their businesses. Go do something useful for a change."

"Like what?" a photographer asked.

"Shovel some snow," Patrick said. "Help someone. Do anything but follow us around."

Patrick held the door for Lauren, and a photographer tried to follow behind her. Patrick stuck out his arm. "Are you serious?" he asked. "I wasn't holding the door for you."

The man took his picture. "I thought you were a gentleman."

"I'm only a gentleman to my lady," Patrick said, and he entered the pawnshop, the photographer edging around him and snapping pictures.

Vicky was again behind the counter, and when she looked up, her jaw dropped. "My God, it's Lauren Short."

"Hello," Lauren said, peering into the jewelry case.

Vicky blinked rapidly. "Um, hello. I'm one of your biggest fans."

"Thank you," Lauren said.

Patrick handed her five hundred dollars. "I think this squares us for the ring and the tax, if there is any."

Vicky took the money and gave Patrick his change. She squinted at the photographer. "Get the hell out!"

"I'm browsing," the photographer said.

Vicky moved swiftly around the counter and towered over the man. "I don't like to repeat myself. You're harassing my customers. Get the hell out."

The photographer snapped Vicky's picture and backed out of the shop.

"Sorry about that," Vicky said softly. "Um, Patrick, right?"

Patrick nodded.

"You weren't kidding about . . . ," Vicky said, cutting her eyes toward Lauren.

"No," Patrick said. "We're in kind of a hurry, Vicky. We have to get to work."

"We?" Vicky said.

"*Oui,*" Lauren said.

"Oh, um, sure," Vicky said. "One sec. I'll get your tools."

While Vicky went to the back, Lauren pointed at a platinum wedding band. "I like that one."

"It's nice," Patrick said.

Vicky carried the tools to the counter. "You're *both* going to work?"

"Yes," Lauren said. "Today is my first day on the job. Patrick is going to teach me the tricks of the trade."

Vicky shook her head. "Really?"

Lauren smiled. "Every handyman needs a handy-woman. That sounds like a song."

"I, um, I sold your ring to him," Vicky said.

"It's perfect," Lauren said. "Thank you, Vicky. And thanks also for kicking that prick out of here."

Vicky blinked.

"I'm a real person, Vicky," Lauren said. "I even wear coveralls sometimes."

"You look good in them," Vicky said. "Of course, you'd look good in anything."

"No I wouldn't," Lauren said. "But I do hope to start a new fashion trend." She looked up at Patrick. "Are we ready?"

"Yes," Patrick said.

"Good-bye, Vicky," Lauren said. "I'll be back soon to buy Patrick's ring."

Vicky smiled. "Okay."

Once outside, Patrick moved swiftly through the photographers with Lauren holding his elbow. They started down Third Avenue.

"Are those your tools?" a photographer asked.

"No," Patrick said. "I just robbed the place."

"Smart-ass," someone said.

A mousy photographer with a peach fuzz mustache jumped out ahead of them. "Why were your tools there?"

"I used them as collateral for a loan," Patrick said. "A loan to get Lauren's ring."

The mousy photographer laughed. "You pawned your tools for her engagement ring?"

Lauren sighed. "Isn't it romantic?"

A photographer behind them scowled. "This has to be a scam. I'll bet they're making a movie together, like *Cinderella* in reverse. First they wait for us back at that café, and now this."

Lauren tugged on Patrick's arm. "I need to say something."

"Go ahead," Patrick said. He repositioned his tool bag on his shoulder. "Let him have it."

"This is not a stunt," Lauren said. "We are not making a

movie together. Patrick pawned his tools to get a loan to buy me this exquisite ring." She waved it in front of the photographers. "He sacrificed for me. That is love, pure and simple."

"Lauren, do you expect us to believe that you are marrying a guy who has to pawn a bunch of used tools to buy you a used ring?" one asked.

"Yes," Lauren said. "That's what love is."

"That ain't love," the mousy photographer said. "That's tacky."

Patrick wheeled on him, his tool bag nearly striking the man in the face. "I think everything you do and say is tacky."

Lauren hugged Patrick from behind. "It does no good to explain love to them. They'll never understand it. They don't understand anything pure or simple, though they should, as purely simple as they are."

"True," Patrick said. He held out his hand. "Care to go walking with a simple man?"

She took his hand and squeezed it. "What a simply wonderful idea."

They continued down Third Avenue.

"Where are you going now?" someone asked.

"To work," Patrick said.

"*Both* of you?"

"Yes," Patrick said.

"And you're dragging Lauren Short along?"

"I am going of my own free will," Lauren said. "I'm going to learn another trade."

Patrick turned onto Baltic, Lauren at his side, and pointed at the apartment towers ahead. "That's where I grew up."

"You grew up there?" a photographer asked. "In the Gowanus Houses?"

"Yes," Patrick said.

They continued up Baltic.

"Buddy, you haven't gone very far in life, have you?" someone asked.

Patrick squeezed Lauren's hand more tightly. "I guarantee they won't follow us through the Houses," he whispered. He looked back. "I didn't have to go far. I just had to get out." He smiled. "If you want, I can introduce you to some of my friends in there. I'm sure they're all dying to have their pictures taken."

As soon as they crossed Bond Street, the photographers vanished.

"Where'd they go?" Lauren asked.

"I'm sure they'll catch up to us on the other side," Patrick said, relaxing his grip.

"Is it that bad here?" Lauren asked.

"It can be," Patrick said, "but it's no worse than any other neighborhood in Brooklyn. There are good people, and there are bad people, and they're all trying to survive."

They passed children of all colors building snowmen in the middle of the street, the staccato of Spanish mixing with the patois of the Caribbean.

The photographers were waiting for them in front of the Pululo Grocery & Deli at Baltic and Hoyt.

"Did you see any of your friends, buddy?" a photographer asked.

"No," Patrick said. "Most of my friends are dead or in jail."

Patrick stopped in front of a redbrick apartment building next to Wonderland Kids Spa. "Ready?"

Lauren nodded. "Ready." She turned to the photographers. "Will you be here when we're through? I *do* hope so. I have *so* enjoyed our little walk."

Patrick led her down some snowy stairs to Mrs. Gildersleeve in 1B.

Mrs. Gildersleeve opened the door. "Patrick. *There* you are. It's about—"

"Hello," Lauren said.

Mrs. Gildersleeve's eyes popped.

All this hassle today has been worth it just to see her expression, Patrick thought.

"You're . . ." Mrs. Gildersleeve blinked at Patrick.

"Lauren Short," Lauren said. "Hi."

"May we come in?" Patrick asked.

"Oh, yes, of course," Mrs. Gildersleeve said. She stood back and let Lauren inside, Patrick following behind. She closed the door. "You're really Lauren Short."

"Yes," Lauren said.

Mrs. Gildersleeve fell back against the door. "I don't believe it."

Patrick set down his tool bag. "Your message said you had a leak."

"Um, yes, under the kitchen sink," Mrs. Gildersleeve said. "It's more than a drip this time. It leaked out onto the floor." She hurried around them to the kitchen.

"You have an amazing effect on people," Patrick whispered.

"I think it's you," Lauren whispered.

While Patrick had his head and half of his upper torso under Mrs. Gildersleeve's sink, Mrs. Gildersleeve offered Lauren some coffee.

"I'm okay," Lauren said. "I already had some espresso and hot chocolate."

Patrick popped his head out. "You do have a leak. It's fixable, though."

Mrs. Gildersleeve sipped from a mug, her hands shaking slightly. "When Patrick told me, um, that you were his friend, naturally, I was skeptical."

"Why?" Lauren asked.

"Well, he's . . ." She looked down at Patrick. "No offense, Patrick, but you're a maintenance man and she's a movie star."

"I *was* a movie star," Lauren said. "I'm starting a new life with Patrick now."

Patrick pointed at the tool bag. "Lauren, could you hand me the biggest wrench you can find in there?"

Lauren unzipped the bag and handed him a wrench as long as her arm. "Is this it?"

Patrick nodded. "You're one for one." He twisted slightly and returned to the pipe under the sink. "Make sure you talk loudly, okay? I don't want to miss anything." He began tightening both coupling nuts.

"We will," Lauren said.

"How did you two meet?" Mrs. Gildersleeve asked.

"We met online," Lauren said. "He wrote me a sweet e-mail after my breakup. That e-mail lifted my spirits, and I wrote back. And then Patrick wouldn't stop writing to me. He's been mercilessly stalking me from three thousand miles away."

Patrick laughed. "Why didn't you get a restraining order, then?"

"Because I can't be restrained around you," Lauren said. "I can't. I've been stalking him just as mercilessly. Hey. *You* took Patrick's picture. Right here in this kitchen. I recognize the blue ducks."

"Yes," Mrs. Gildersleeve said. "I did."

"Did he tell you about St. Louis?" Lauren asked.

"Yes," Mrs. Gildersleeve said. "And I thought he was pulling my leg."

"Patrick doesn't lie." She nudged his leg with her foot. "Do you?"

"No," Patrick said. "I haven't learned how. I'm not an actor."

Lauren nudged his leg again. "What are you trying to say?"

"I'm not saying a thing," Patrick said.

He tightened the jamb nut and felt the bottom of the trap, flecks of rust falling onto his forehead. *She needs a new trap.* He slid out. "All fixed. For now. Next time we come, I'll have to replace your trap." He stood and handed the wrench to Lauren.

Lauren hugged it to her chest. "For me? I don't know what to say. Thank you. You really like me, don't you?"

"I love you," Patrick said.

"He gave me a wrench," Lauren said. "I wonder how many men give wrenches to their wenches." She placed it in the tool bag and zipped it up. "It was nice to meet you."

"It was . . ." Mrs. Gildersleeve smiled weakly. "It was nice to meet you, too, Lauren."

Lauren moved to the door, Patrick followed, and in moments they were up the stairs and in front of only three photographers.

"Lauren, what did you just do?" one of them asked.

Lauren bit her lip, fluttered her eyes, and put the back of one gloved hand on her forehead. "Oh, it was brutal," she said sadly. "I don't know if I can accurately tell you the sheer horror I've just witnessed."

Patrick heard cameras going into overdrive. He also tried not to laugh.

"I handed a . . ." She sniffled. "I handed a wrench to my man. It was *so* heavy. I thought my arm would snap in two." She dried an imaginary tear. "And he . . ." She grabbed Patrick by his coverall straps. "This strapping, strong man took that wrench. . . ." She whimpered. "He took that wrench, and he stopped a *leak*. I wish you had been there. It was so . . . inspiring." She bowed and threw in a curtsy. "The end." She laughed. "And we're coming back soon to replace her trap." She squinted at Patrick. "What's a trap?"

"The curvy part of the drain at the bottom," Patrick said.

"Ah," Lauren said. "The curvy part of the drain at the bottom." She shook her head at the reporters. "We're working. That's all. There's no show here."

"Where are you going now?" a photographer asked.

Lauren smiled at Patrick. "Where to?"

"Over to Bergen," Patrick said. "They have no hot water. The pilot light probably blew out during the blizzard."

"It sounds *so* dangerous," Lauren said.

"It isn't," Patrick said. *And she has to know that.* "I'll let you relight it."

"I love playing with fire," Lauren said, and she hugged him.

Two of the photographers faded away. The lone photographer shook his head. "I don't believe it. You're really becoming a handywoman." He checked his watch. "I gotta go."

Lauren smiled. "Good luck with your pictures."

"I won't need luck," the man said as he moved away. "These pictures are golden."

For the rest of the morning, with no paparazzi harassing them, Patrick and Lauren made the rounds, relighting three water heaters and a furnace. They were strolling toward Patrick's apartment—after savoring a meal of smothered chicken, candied yams, and string beans at the Soul Spot on Atlantic—when Patrick's phone rang.

"A pigeon just flew through my kitchen window!" Mr. Hyer screamed. "There's glass everywhere!"

"Is the pigeon still alive?" Patrick asked.

"Oh yes, it's roosting on my refrigerator and whistling 'The Star-Spangled Banner,'" Mr. Hyer said. "Of *course* it's dead! There are feathers and bird guts everywhere!"

"I'll be right there, Mr. Hyer," Patrick said.

"What do I do until then?" Mr. Hyer shouted. "I'm freezing my ass off!"

"Try to hang something over the window," Patrick said. "A bath towel will do."

"Why?" Mr. Hyer shouted.

"So no other pigeons join their friend and you can block the cold air." He closed his phone. "Back to Baltic."

"A pigeon flew through a window," Lauren said. "Why would a pigeon fly through a window?"

"It was probably confused from the storm," Patrick said. "Or it just wanted to make Mr. Hyer's day more exciting, I don't know."

Upon arriving at the apartment building on Baltic, Patrick went first to the basement to cut up some cardboard boxes with a box cutter and collect six three-foot-long two-by-fours.

"You've done this before," Lauren said.

"Pigeons are little missiles," Patrick said. "They bounce off most of the newer windows but not these old ones."

He and Lauren walked up to 3B. Patrick picked through his tool bag and laid out duct tape, a whisk broom, a dust-pan, a heavy-duty stapler, a power screwdriver, a box of wood screws, and a heavy-duty garbage bag in the hallway.

"Mr. Hyer doesn't like me to take the tool bag into his apartment," Patrick said. "He says it makes too much noise, which is strange, because he can barely hear." He put every-thing into the pockets of his coveralls. He looked at the door. "I'm assuming there's glass everywhere in that kitchen. Be careful. You whisk up the glass, and I'll do the repair." He paused before knocking. "One more thing. Mr. Hyer might remember me, and he might not. He's about ninety. I would stand behind me until it's safe." He knocked loudly, and Lauren jumped. "Sorry."

A series of locks moved and clicked until a hunched-over, balding man ripped open the door and snarled, "It took you long enough, um . . ."

"Patrick."

"I knew that," Mr. Hyer said, stepping aside.

Patrick moved inside, Lauren gripping his back pocket, and then he carefully and quietly removed everything from his pockets and laid it on the kitchen table. "Mr. Hyer, this is Lauren."

Mr. Hyer slumped into a bright orange wooden chair beside the kitchen table and held a light blue cardigan sweater tightly to his chest. "Who's she?"

"Lauren is my assistant today," Patrick said.

"Hello," Lauren said.

"We'll have you fixed up in no time, Mr. Hyer," Patrick said.

Patrick took the garbage bag and covered the pigeon before working the bird into the bottom of the bag. He stepped carefully around hundreds of pieces of glass to the window itself. "Be careful, Lauren."

"I will." She began whisking pieces of glass into the dustpan and dumping the glass into the garbage bag.

"It just flew into the window like a cannonball!" Mr. Hyer yelled. "Glass everywhere! I thought I was under attack! It was Pork Chop Hill all over again!"

Patrick removed large shards of glass from the left window frame. Then he opened the right window and stepped through to the fire escape and began measuring, writing down the window's dimensions on a little notepad he took out of his middle pocket. "Lauren, Mr. Hyer served in

Korea. He earned a Bronze Star, a Silver Star, and a Purple Heart."

Lauren smiled at Mr. Hyer. "I'm honored to know you, Mr. Hyer."

Mr. Hyer squinted at Lauren. "Who's she?"

"My assistant, Lauren," Patrick said. He returned inside and cut four pieces of cardboard based on his measurements.

"Oh," Mr. Hyer said. "*Your* assistant. *I* need an assistant. I'm an old man. I could freeze to death before anyone notices, and now you have *both* windows open!"

"I would notice, Mr. Hyer," Patrick said.

"What would you do with my body?" Mr. Hyer asked.

"I'd donate it to science, Mr. Hyer," Patrick said.

"You *would*," Mr. Hyer said. "I hate pigeons. Flying rats . . . grenades with wings . . ."

Patrick stapled two pieces of cardboard to the outside window frame, then sealed them with duct tape. After power driving screws into the two-by-fours, he screwed them tightly into the frame a few inches apart. He stepped through the other window and shut it. "I have to get the glass cut to fit, Mr. Hyer."

"Why can't I have all new windows?" Mr. Hyer asked. "Windows from *this* century."

"You know why," Patrick said.

"Damn neighbors." Mr. Hyer looked at Lauren. "They want to keep the building authentic. Can you believe that? They actually like drafty, warped, *authentic* windows."

Patrick stapled the other two pieces of cardboard to the inside frame and sealed them with duct tape. After screwing in the other three boards, he shut the window and latched it. "That should do it."

"Oh, that looks like shit," Mr. Hyer said.

Patrick moved his hand around the edges. "I can't feel any cold air, though."

"It still looks like shit," Mr. Hyer said. "How long do I have to look at it?"

"If I can get the glass cut tomorrow morning," Patrick said, "I can have you fixed up by lunchtime. Is that okay?"

"It's okay," Mr. Hyer said. "It's not as if I'm expecting any guests." He blinked at Lauren. "Who's this?"

"This is Lauren," Patrick said. "She's my assistant."

Lauren whisked the last bits of glass into the dustpan. "Hello, Mr. Hyer."

Mr. Hyer looked her up and down. "She looks too young to be working at any job."

"Thank you," Lauren said.

"You any good with plumbing, honey?" Mr. Hyer asked. "This one hasn't got a clue. My toilet backs up every other day."

"He's an expert with my plumbing," Lauren said.

"Huh?" Mr. Hyer said.

Patrick laughed as he collected his tools. "We're done, Mr. Hyer. Anything else we need to check on for you?"

"No," Mr. Hyer scowled.

"I'll call you before I come to replace your window," Patrick said.

"Yeah, yeah, yeah," Mr. Hyer said.

"It was nice to meet you, Mr. Hyer," Lauren said.

Mr. Hyer rose and pointed at Lauren. "You stay in school, young lady. You don't want to do a job like this forever."

"Good-bye, Mr. Hyer," Patrick said.

Outside 3B, Lauren whispered, "Stay in school?"

"Mr. Hyer was a guidance counselor about thirty years ago," Patrick said, zipping up the tool bag and putting it over his shoulder. "He usually tells me to stay in school, too. Today he forgot. You must have distracted him."

After disposing of the glass in a snow-filled Dumpster, they walked a few blocks without an entourage to Bergen Street and Mrs. Moczydlowska's apartment.

"Anything I should know here?" Lauren asked.

"I don't know if I can adequately prepare you for Mrs. Moczydlowska," Patrick said. "Be prepared for anything and everything."

Mrs. Moczydlowska was eerily silent as Patrick and Lauren looked for rats. After twenty minutes, Patrick and Lauren met in the kitchen.

Lauren shrugged.

"No sign of them," Patrick said. "No droppings anywhere."

"I still hear them," Mrs. Moczydlowska said.

"Not as much as before, though, right?" Patrick asked.

Mrs. Moczydlowska shook her head. "No. They are quieter."

Patrick noticed the closed oven. *She listened to me.* "They're getting bored. They'll move away shortly. Any other issues?"

"No," Mrs. Moczydlowska said. "You go now." She walked them to the door. "Good-bye."

Patrick paused outside Mrs. Moczydlowska's closed door. "Something's wrong," he said.

"What?" Lauren asked.

Patrick shrugged. "That is by far the shortest time I have ever been in her apartment."

"She didn't even seem to notice me," Lauren said.

Oh, she noticed, Patrick thought. *And that's probably the problem.* "Well, we're done for the day."

They started down the hallway to the stairs.

Patrick heard a door open.

"Patrick!" Mrs. Moczydlowska yelled.

Patrick sighed. "Do you mind waiting for me?"

Lauren sat on the top step. "I don't mind."

Patrick returned to Mrs. Moczydlowska's door. "Yes?"

Mrs. Moczydlowska fumbled with her hands. "Are you going to marry this person?"

"Yes," Patrick said. "I am going to marry Lauren."

"Will you be moving away with her to California?" she asked.

"No," Patrick said. "We're living here, in Boerum Hill."

Mrs. Moczydlowska narrowed her eyes. "But why?"

"This is my home," Patrick said. "This will be our home."

"But she is . . ."

"Beautiful, I know." Patrick smiled.

"No," she said sternly. "I mean she is famous."

"Okay," Patrick said. "She's famous. We're still living here."

"But I am confused," she said. "Famous people live in big houses in California. She has a big house in California."

"That house belongs to her ex," Patrick said.

"But I saw her house on the television today," she said.

"That was Chazz Jackson's house," Patrick said.

Mrs. Moczydlowska sighed. "He was saying mean things about her. He said that she betrayed him. That she cannot have the best, so she settles for the worst. And he called you a boy toy."

"Really?" *I've never been called that.*

"What is this boy toy?" she asked.

"A new, younger man," Patrick said.

"But you are older than she is, yes?" she asked.

"Yes," Patrick said. "By two years."

Mrs. Moczydlowska looked down the hallway to Lauren. "She is . . . She looks so young."

"I'll tell her you said that," Patrick said. "She'll be glad to hear it."

"Do you love her?" she asked.

"Very much."

"I can see that," she said. "You were not so much looking for rats as you were looking at her."

"She's quite beautiful to look at," Patrick said.

Mrs. Moczydlowska stepped back into her apartment. "You will answer if I call tomorrow."

"Of course," Patrick said. "I'm not quitting this job. You're stuck with me."

"You say this *now*," she said.

"I say this now, and I'll say it tomorrow," Patrick said. "I am not quitting and moving to California."

"Will she come with you every time?" she asked.

"She might."

Mrs. Moczydlowska shook her head. "I do not like this arrangement one bit. I may call your boss."

"*Will* you call my boss?" Patrick asked.

Mrs. Moczydlowska looked up briefly. "No. I will try to get used to the idea. Good-bye." She shut the door.

Patrick returned to Lauren and pulled her to her feet. "Let's go home."

They started down the stairs.

"What was that about?" Lauren asked.

"She's not happy with the new arrangement," Patrick said.

"Oh," Lauren said.

"She says she will try to get used to it," Patrick said.

"She kind of dotes on you, you know," Lauren said.

"Yep," Patrick said. "I've never been completely sure, but I think I remind her of her husband."

"I saw his picture," Lauren said. "You don't look anything like him. Do you know what happened to him?"

"No," Patrick said. "Maybe he was a handyman, too."

They moved outside, into the snow.

"There aren't any rats in her apartment, are there?"

"I doubt it," Patrick said. "There's never anything really wrong. She just likes my company."

"So do I." She put her arm around his waist.

"She thinks you're young," Patrick said.

"I am when I'm with you," Lauren said. "So, are we really done for the day?"

Patrick nodded.

"How'd I do?" Lauren asked.

They turned up Hoyt. "I think Salthead would hire you as a buildings maintenance apprentice. The pay isn't that great, no more than ten bucks an hour, but there are some excellent benefits."

Lauren smiled. "Such as?"

"Me."

"Oh, get me an application immediately," Lauren said. "I *must* have this job."

"No application necessary," Patrick said. "You're hired."

They turned onto State Street.

"Can you honestly see yourself living like this?" Patrick asked.

"Honestly, no," Lauren said. "I'm exhausted, and I didn't really do much of the work. I can see myself with you, though. I can even see myself doing *this* with you. Most days. Not Sundays, okay? There's something wrong about working on Sundays."

"Okay," Patrick said. "I'll try to have everything perfect every Saturday." He saw passing people do double takes, but no one stopped them or harassed them.

"I know you don't want to hear this," Lauren said, "but I have plenty of money, you know. Neither of us would ever have to work again."

"Half a million doesn't go as far as it used to, especially in this city," Patrick said. "Rent for a larger apartment alone will cost you up to sixty grand or more per year."

"I have more than half a million, Patrick," Lauren said. "I have half a million in the *bank*. I have also made many wise investments. I have plenty of stock, too. All I have to do is cash it in."

"I want to support you."

"I know you do, and I respect that so much," Lauren said. "You don't know how much. I'm just saying that you don't have to. We could live anywhere, do anything, and go anywhere."

"That's money you earned."

"That's money I want to share," Lauren said. "With you and only you."

"Couldn't we call it an emergency fund or something? You know, to be used only in case of emergency."

"I guess we could. . . ."

She doesn't like the idea. "We haven't had any emergencies yet, right? We have a roof over our heads, we're wearing some really chic clothing, and we get plenty of exercise. What more do we need?"

They arrived at the apartment and removed their boots at the door.

"Well, we need some more light in our apartment," Lauren said. "And some rugs. The floor is too cold. And a one-way window, you know. We can see out, and they can't see in. And some art for the walls. Some color! Lots of color! We could even re-cover that couch."

"But it's brown," Patrick said. "Your favorite color."

"I have other colors on this body," Lauren said, removing the straps from the coveralls and letting them fall to the floor.

"Really? Where? I didn't see them."

Lauren extricated herself from her long johns. "You want to see all the colors of my body?"

"Oh yes."

She removed her bra. "Then you'll need to put in more lights."

"I have a flashlight," Patrick said. "It has a very powerful beam."

Lauren removed her panties. "That'll do . . . for now." She raced to the bed and hid under the covers.

Patrick found his flashlight.

This could get very interesting. "Miss Short?"

"Yes?"

"What are you doing under those covers?"

Lauren giggled.

"I hope you're not doing anything naughty," Patrick said.

Lauren giggled again.

He could see the outline of her hand working furiously under the covers. "Are you . . ."

"Am I what?" Lauren asked.

"Are you masturbating, Miss Short?" Patrick asked, moving onto the bed.

"No," Lauren whispered.

This I have to see.

Patrick worked his head under the covers and turned on the flashlight. *Oh, I didn't expect to see a freckle* there. *I think I shall kiss it for being in such a unique and tender spot. I wonder if she'd like me to suck on her fingers while she does that. . . . Oh yes, she does. I hope the flashlight batteries last. I have a lot more exploring to do.*

55

For the rest of that week, Lauren and Patrick worked long days and played long into the night.

They replaced Mr. Hyer's window while he slept, undisturbed, on his couch. Patrick checked his pulse just in case.

They unclogged several Dutch drains. They drank espresso and hot chocolate at the Little Sweet Café. They also ate too many sweets because Freddy "paid" them with free cookies for allowing him to post their picture on the wall behind the counter.

Meanwhile, the media went to work. Lauren read a story aloud while Patrick rubbed her feet.

From the *New York Post*:

> **LAUREN, WE HARDLY KNEW YOU:**
> **FALLEN ANGEL DATING WISEGUY?**
>
> We don't know Lauren Short at all.
> Lauren Short, Chazz Jackson's fresh ex,

has been slumming around Brooklyn with
"handyman" Paulie Esposito, who report-
edly threatened several reporters outside the
pawnshop where he allegedly bought Lauren
her supposedly platinum engagement ring. . . .

"You didn't threaten them," Lauren said.

"Yeah, I did," Patrick said. "I questioned their integrity."

"They don't have any integrity to question," she said,
turning on the TV. "I think your eyes threatened them. You
have dangerous eyes."

After watching several stories about stars in and out of
rehab and traffic court, they looked on as a reporter on *Access Hollywood* gushed, *"Don't* adjust your set. You are actually seeing actress Lauren Short in coveralls. Lauren has
gone from former mega movie star and Chazz Jackson's
leading lady to Brooklyn handywoman overnight. Cinderella has lost her dress, her glass slipper, *and* her Prince
Charming and has gone back to the cinders. . . ."

"You look good," Patrick said. "I never thought I'd say
that about anyone in coveralls."

"Thank you." Lauren smiled. "And *you're* my Prince
Charming."

"I like it when you lose your slippers," he said, working
her heels. "You have very sexy feet."

Lauren switched over to *Entertainment Tonight.* After a
puff piece on random actors successfully "saving" a beached
dolphin at *low* tide in Malibu, they watched a choppy review
of their recent run-ins with the paparazzi.

"The fallout from Lauren Short's breakup with Chazz
Jackson continues," the host said. "Lauren has reduced
herself to being a plumber's helper. She has given up glitz
and glamor for pipe cutters, slip-nut wrenches, and toilet
seals. . . ."

"I like helping you with your plumbing," Lauren said. "You keep springing leaks." *And I'm about to spring a leak if he keeps rubbing and squeezing my toes!*

"It's because you put my plumbing under so much pressure," Patrick said.

"I like releasing your pressure," Lauren said.

"I like making you leak, too."

Their story continued on *ET* as a fat, badly dressed, effeminate reporter walked along Hollywood Boulevard. "Oh, it's a *scandal*," he said. "The princess has kissed a *frog,* and the *frog* is still a *frog!* Our poor little Lauren has gone from rags to riches to rags again. But we suppose that once you've had Chazz Jackson, there's nowhere else to go but down. Oh, how the once gorgeous have fallen!"

"I like your tongue, too," Lauren said. "It's so long and thick."

"You have a cute little tongue," Patrick said.

Lauren sat up. "There's Chazz." She turned up the volume.

"She lost her king," Chazz said, "so now she has a pauper. I'm sure she'll tire of her boy toy soon, especially when he can't pay the rent or buy her toilet paper. He bought her ring at a pawnshop! The ring I gave Lauren cost more than what he'll earn in a million lifetimes."

"I didn't think he knew that word," Lauren said.

"Rent?" Patrick said.

"Funny," Lauren said. "And his math is off."

"Not by much," Patrick said. "Where's the ring?"

"In the Pacific Ocean."

"Nice," Patrick said, working his fingers up to her calves. "I knew you had a good arm."

"Oh, there's my agent," Lauren said.

"I knew Lauren was under a lot of stress," Todd said, "but throwing her career away like this on a whim, and over a man she barely knows! I never thought it could happen! I'm still working on her behalf, but it's difficult to do when she doesn't answer her phone! Lauren, turn on your phone!"

"Todd has lost most of his hair," Lauren said. "I'm probably the reason."

"He yells too much," Patrick said. "Why haven't you turned on your phone?"

"I don't want to," Lauren said. "I wish Todd would accept my decision to retire. He's mad that I'm costing him money."

"What percentage of your earnings did he take?" Patrick asked.

"Ten percent," Lauren said.

"Hey, that's my raise," Patrick said.

"You're getting a raise?" Lauren asked.

"Yes, ma'am," Patrick said. "We'll be able to afford one more roll of toilet paper this month."

"Oh, goody."

As they snuggled on the couch, Patrick's phone rang.

"Hello?" Patrick listened for a few seconds before covering the phone. "It's some guy named Sam Gabriel from *Us Weekly*."

"Oh, put him on speaker," Lauren said.

Patrick hit the SPEAKER button and set the phone on the arm of the couch. "How did you get this number?"

"I know some people," Sam said.

"You mean you *paid* someone to give up the number," Lauren said.

"Oh, hello, Lauren. It's Sam Gabriel. I did a story on you ages ago. Just after *I Got This*."

"And you did your best to turn me into a tramp with that story," Lauren said. "I remember. What do you want now?"

"I'd like to interview Patrick," Sam said. "I want his take on this affair."

"It's not an affair," Patrick said.

"I am engaged to be married, Sam," Lauren said. "This is not an affair."

"Oh, right, sure," Sam said. "So would you rather do the interview over the phone or come in to the city? Or I can come there. I'm flexible."

"I'm not interested," Patrick said.

"We'll pay you ten thousand dollars," Sam said.

Wow! Lauren thought. *Are we that juicy of a story?*

"Still not interested." Patrick reached for the phone.

"Twenty-five thousand, then," Sam said. "I can't go any higher, and no one else will pay you this much."

Patrick snatched up the phone. "Good-bye." He turned off the phone. "I didn't think they paid people for interviews."

"They don't usually," Lauren said.

"Is it because I'm an ordinary guy?" Patrick asked.

"Maybe," Lauren said. "I don't mean to be difficult, but you just passed up twenty-five thousand bucks, man. That's a lot of cookies and espresso."

"It's our business, not the world's," Patrick said. "If we decide one day to let the world know about us, *we* will tell it."

Later they watched the late-night talk shows and shook their heads at the monologues.

"Lauren Short couldn't have the prettiest man in the world, so she settled for this." The host showed a picture of Patrick swinging his tool bag past a photographer's face.

"Do I really look like that?" Patrick asked.

"They Photoshopped that one to make you look more sinister," Lauren said.

Patrick shook his head. "No, I think I was angry for real in that one."

Lauren shivered. "I hope I never make you angry."

"You can't," Patrick said.

The host continued. "I hear they're going to be doing a remake of *Beauty and the Beast,* and *he* won't need makeup. They're also going to do a new version of *The Hunchback of Notre Dame.* He'll be the hunchback, and she'll be the belle. Get it. She's the b-e-l-l-e. . . ."

Lauren turned off the TV. "I am so sorry about all this."

"I'm not," Patrick said.

"It has to bother you somehow," Lauren said.

"It doesn't."

It has to. No one, not even a longtime celebrity, can take this kind of abuse for very long. "Not even a little bit?"

"No," Patrick said.

"They're saying you're a wiseguy, Patrick," Lauren said. "That's character assassination."

"I'm surprised the real wiseguys aren't going on TV to dispute it," Patrick said. "They are some proud men, and some of those wiseguys are good guys helping their communities."

"I'm just so sorry it's happening to you," Lauren said.

"Don't be," Patrick said. "I know the truth. You know the truth. That's all that matters."

"This constant barrage can change a person," Lauren said. "It's like water dripping on a rock. Eventually, the rock breaks."

"I don't know how to be anyone but myself," Patrick said. "I've had forty years of practice."

"But some of what they're saying is outright slander," Lauren said. "They can't even get your name right."

"The truth always comes out," Patrick said. "Besides, no matter what they say, they can't take away what I have."

"And what do you have?" Lauren asked.

"You," Patrick said. "I got the girl."

"Say that again, and emphasize *girl*."

"I got the *girrrl*."

That is so sexy. "I like to be called a girl. How old did I look today?"

"Eighteen," Patrick said. "Barely legal. When do your parents expect you home? I'm sure you have homework. I need to see some ID."

She hugged him to her. "You are so good for me." She slid off the couch and held out her hand. "Come on." She led him to the bedroom and took off her coveralls. "I need your advice."

"I doubt I'll give you good advice," Patrick said. "When you're getting naked, I can't think straight."

Lauren shook her booty. "Should I put my clothes back on?"

"Oh no, of course not," Patrick said. "I like not thinking straight."

Lauren kicked the coveralls behind her. "Here's what I need to know. Should I bust out Chazz for the 'man' he isn't?"

Patrick removed his coveralls. "What good would it do?"

Lauren shimmied out of her long johns. "It would take the focus off us. Maybe permanently."

"Wouldn't the media say something like, 'She was engaged to a bisexual man and didn't know it'?" Patrick pulled his T-shirt over his head.

"Yeah," Lauren said, undoing her bra under her T-shirt. "They'd call me clueless, and they'd be right. I was."

"He's an actor," Patrick said, pulling back the covers. "He was acting."

Lauren removed her socks. "I just want to see him squirm a little, you know?"

"Like I'm squirming now," Patrick said, sliding under the covers and removing his underwear. He tossed it across the room.

Lauren stood on the bed, toying with her underwear. "I

like to make you squirm." She slipped out of her underwear and took off her T-shirt.

"And after you make Chucky squirm, what then?"

"I don't know," Lauren said, squatting in front of him. "I'd like to see a hundred microphones shoved into *his* smug face."

Patrick stroked Lauren's thighs. "And then?"

Lauren stretched her right leg forward, resting her heel on Patrick's shoulder. "And then I'd like to hear these people rake him over the coals with their questions and comments. I'd like to see *Entertainment Tonight* and these late-night hosts do jokes about him."

Patrick kissed her right ankle. "And then?"

She stretched her left leg forward, resting it on the headboard. "And then . . ." Lauren sighed, found his bulge under the covers, and began stroking him. "And then . . . I don't know what."

"Will it change anything?" Patrick asked.

He gets so hard so fast! "No. It won't change a thing. You've talked me out of it."

"Out of what?" Patrick said.

Lauren squeezed his penis. "I was about to go out there and shame him."

Patrick turned to look at the window. "They're out there? Again?"

Lauren nodded. "I know they're out there waiting to get reaction quotes. That's what they do to keep a story going. They want my reactions to all this negativity they've started. What do you think about what so-and-so is saying about you? That sort of thing. It's so juvenile, as if the media is still in middle school. It's their way of keeping sadness and despair in the news, and sadness and despair sell. People don't want to watch good news on TV. They want to see sorrow, pain, and accusations."

Patrick sat up and wrapped her legs around his waist. "If you went out there like this, there would be no sadness, despair, sorrow, or pain."

"Oh, I plan to put a hurting on you first." She maneuvered his penis inside her. "Oh, this is *much* better. I'm still going out there once we're through." *In a few seconds! Wow!*

"To do what?" Patrick asked. "Oh, that's nice. I like your booty when it bounces on my legs like that."

"I will keep bouncing," Lauren said. "When you make me come in about ten seconds, I'm going to go out there to tell them the good news."

"What good news?" He thumbed her clitoris furiously. *Oh, damn! I can't believe I have orgasms this quickly!* "Damn! That wasn't even ten seconds."

"Is that a bad thing?" Patrick asked, thrusting upward.

"No!" Lauren cried, her spasms increasing. "I just don't want you to think I'm a freak."

Patrick pressed hard on Lauren's hips, grinding her as he came, his mouth greedily sucking on her nipples. "I'm surprised I'm able to do this after a hard day."

"You're going to have a hard night, too," Lauren said. She fell off him. "Let's get dressed and go talk to them."

"No cuddling?" Patrick asked.

"Later," Lauren said.

"What do I say?" Patrick asked.

"Go with the flow," Lauren said. "You're good at improv."

Outside on the steps, in the cold, and wearing only coveralls, boots, and a blanket, Lauren addressed the photographers, who gleefully snapped countless pictures while Patrick stood behind her in coveralls, boots, and a heavy brown coat.

"I'd like to make a statement," Lauren said.

"Lauren, what do you think about what Chazz said about you?"

"What do you think of your negative press?"

"What do you think of your star meter? It tanked today."

"Is it true you can't pay the rent?"

"Are you about to go on welfare?"

"Do you like being called a fallen angel?"

"Are you out of toilet paper?"

Really? Oh, my God! "One, I don't care what any of you think. I never have, and I never will, mainly because I don't think any of you actually think. Two, *you* are responsible for the negative press, not me. If you didn't start it, there wouldn't be any of it. Three, the star meter is and has always been a joke. Four, I do not care what Chazz says. Five, we are doing quite—"

"Is it true that you don't have any toilet paper?" a reporter interrupted.

Lauren zeroed in on him. "What do you think? No. Don't answer that. I'll only hear silence." She counted to three. "You hear that silence?" She counted to five. "Now, where was I?"

"Five," Patrick said.

"Thank you," Lauren said. "Five, Patrick and I are doing quite well. We are not slumming in Brooklyn. We are living quite happily together, and I love going to work with him. Six, I am not, nor have I ever been, an angel, so calling me 'fallen' or otherwise is foolishness. Seven, we will be married tomorrow."

"Tomorrow?" Patrick whispered.

Lauren turned to him. "You have any plans?"

"No," Patrick said. "Tomorrow is good." He kissed her.

"What about Chazz?"

"Aren't you worried what Chazz will say?"

"You barely know the guy! Isn't this all too soon?"

"If you want to know what Chazz thinks," Lauren said, "ask him."

"Aren't you worried he'll be angry?"

"No," Lauren said.

"What about your fans?"

What fans? No. I can't say that. I still have a few. "Last and certainly not least, I'd like to thank my fans for still being my fans, even after all these years. I won some awards and had some fame a long time ago, but nothing I've ever won and no amount of fame can compare to the love I feel for this man. And I hope my fans find love like this one day, too." She pulled Patrick's hands in front of her. "Patrick is extraordinary to me in every respect. *Every* . . . respect. Now, if you'll excuse me, I need to rest. I'm getting married in the morning."

"Lauren, aren't you worried that marrying this man will doom your career?"

Lauren laughed. "I doomed my career when I started *dating* Chazz Jackson. My career *ended* the day I became *engaged* to Chazz Jackson. Don't get it twisted. Patrick is giving me a second chance at happiness, and I intend to take full advantage of it."

"But don't you think this is all too soon after your breakup?"

Lauren smiled. "No. You can never have happiness or true love soon enough." She turned and pushed Patrick toward the door.

"Are you currently taking any medication?"

"Do you have to get married, and if you do, is it Chazz's baby?"

Are they serious? Lauren wheeled around. "Let me put it this way. I have a better chance of winning the lottery a million times in a row than having Chazz Jackson's baby."

"What's that supposed to mean?"

Lauren smiled. "Ask him."

Lauren entered the apartment building and shut the door.

"Lauren! Lauren!"

"What are your boots made out of?"

"Yeah, aren't you worried that PETA will protest your choice of boots?"

Lauren almost returned to the reporters. *My boots? PETA? Are they serious? Who cares!*

Safely inside the apartment, Lauren disrobed hurriedly and jumped into bed.

Patrick stood beside the bed. "Are you okay?"

"I've never been better," Lauren said. "What will we need to get married?"

They looked up the information online and found that they needed birth certificates and picture IDs.

"Good thing I brought all my records with me," Lauren said.

"Do you always think ahead like that?" Patrick asked.

"Not usually," Lauren said.

Patrick rubbed her thighs. "You know, it's bad luck to see the bride on the day of the wedding."

"Do you believe that?" Lauren asked.

"No," Patrick said.

"Good," Lauren said. "I would like an early wedding gift. I want a burrito."

Patrick looked toward the window. "I'll have to go out there again, and I don't want to go out there again."

Lauren pouted. "Please? I'm hungry."

"I'll do anything for you," Patrick said.

"I like your willingness to serve, Patrick," Lauren said. "It's very sexy."

"Right," Patrick said. "Microwaved there or cooked in the oven here?"

"Microwaved, of course," Lauren said. "It's so much softer and juicier that way."

56

Patrick left the apartment building, plowed through the swarm of photographers without speaking, and walked across the street to Downtown Gourmet Deli.

"Where are you going?"

"Are you leaving Lauren all alone?"

"Did you two have a fight?"

"You don't really want to marry her, do you? Think of the consequences!"

"Is she crying?"

"Why are you doing this to Lauren?"

"How does it feel to ruin Lauren's career?"

"How does it feel to be less than half the man Chazz Jackson is?"

Patrick entered the deli, chose two large beef burritos, and put them in the microwave. While he waited for them to cook, he picked up a two-liter of Coke as a dozen reporters entered the deli behind him.

"Is that your dinner?"

"Is this the best you can do for her?"

"What kind of man serves a star microwaved burritos?"

"Is Coke Lauren's favorite soda?"

"Where did you get *your* boots?"

"Yeah, what animal was senselessly slaughtered so you could have them?"

These people are insane, Patrick thought. *They're absolutely senseless. Most of the photographers use leather carrying cases.*

When the burritos were done, Patrick took them to the counter and rolled his eyes at Danny, the late-night cashier. "You ever have one of those days, Danny?"

Danny nodded. "Oh yeah. Nothing like you got going on, though."

"Be glad." Patrick paid and received his change. "Every day is starting to be one of those days."

Danny leaned forward. "I hear you, man. But at least business has picked up around here."

Patrick turned and saw reporters snatching sodas and snacks. "I'm glad someone's benefiting from this." He looked at the newspaper rack and saw a headline in the *Globe:*

LAUREN SHORT DESTITUTE! FORCED OUT OF MANSION AND SHOPPING AT GOODWILL!

The reporter waiting behind him put his pork rinds and Sprite on the counter. "So, buddy, how does it feel to ruin someone's life?"

Patrick collected the burritos and the two-liter. "You tell me. You're the experts." He stared the man down. "Well, tell me."

The man blinked.

"That's what I thought," Patrick said. "Lauren is right. You don't have a single rational thought in your head." He pointed to his left. "Bellevue Hospital has a few openings for you guys." He nodded at Danny. "See you, Danny."

"Any time, Patrick," Danny said.

As he crossed the street to the apartment building, photographers crisscrossed the sidewalk, taking his picture.

"Did you buy toilet paper, too?"

"Where is Lauren's Kleenex?"

"Do you always shop there?"

"What crime family are you part of?"

"What do you have against Pepsi products?"

"Is it true you only have your GED?"

This is madness, Patrick thought. *They will now have a complete photo essay of a man buying two burritos and a two-liter of Coke.*

Once inside the apartment, Patrick presented a burrito on a plate to Lauren. "I hope it's still hot."

Lauren held it up. "It is. I saw them follow you into that store. What'd they ask you?"

"Among other things," Patrick said, letting his coveralls drop to the floor, "where I bought my boots."

"Oh no," Lauren said. "PETA's going to get you." She took a huge bite, cheese sauce dripping onto the plate. "This is pretty good."

Patrick slid in beside her with his burrito. "Hey, slow down. This is the first, second, and third course. We have soda for dessert."

Lauren rubbed her shoulder on his. "You're my dessert. I want to eat fast and get busy again." She wrapped her lips around the burrito and took another large bite. "You like how I eat this burrito?" she asked as she chewed.

Patrick nodded.

"Do you like how I eat your burrito?" she asked.

"Yes," Patrick said. "Do you like how I . . ." He cleared his throat. "I was going to say something about a taco."

Lauren laughed. "That's nasty! But go ahead and say it."

"Are you happy about how I eat your taco?" Patrick asked.

"Yes," Lauren said. "Your tongue is very saucy."

"Because you're spicy down there," Patrick said.

Lauren finished her burrito two bites later. "I want another burrito." She felt under the covers for Patrick's penis. "Oh, here's one. It feels so hot and juicy." Her head disappeared under the covers.

"Mmm," Patrick said. "I feel the need to eat a taco." He pulled Lauren's booty to his face. "I am still so hungry. . . ."

Several hours later Patrick's phone buzzed them awake. He listened to the messages.

"Everything okay?" Lauren whispered.

Patrick closed his phone. "No emergencies so far."

Lauren laid her head on Patrick's chest. "To work first or to the courthouse?"

"It won't be open yet," Patrick said.

"So we'll rest a bit more. . . ."

Blaring car and truck horns woke Patrick three hours later. He checked the clock on his phone. *I have slept in after sunrise for the first time in . . . I can't remember a first time.* He smiled at Lauren. *And you're the reason. I know I'm going to get used to this.* He rubbed Lauren's bare shoulder.

"It's time to go get married," he whispered.

"That's the nicest thing anyone has ever said to me at any time of any day," Lauren whispered. "What should I wear?"

"We may be working afterward," Patrick said. "So . . ."

She smiled. "I'll be the first bride ever to wear coveralls."

After they both showered and dressed for work in long johns, coveralls, boots, black knit hats, and gloves, Patrick picked up his tool bag, Lauren grabbed two brown sugar–cinnamon Pop-Tarts from the toaster, and they walked outside into a thick crowd of rowdy reporters.

"Lauren, Lauren!"

"Why did you sleep in?"

"Are you really getting married to this guy today?"

"She's not getting married today. Look what she's wearing!"

"Are you working today? I thought you said you were getting married today!"

"I *am* getting married today," Lauren said. "And this guy has a name. It's—"

"What about your career?" a reporter interrupted.

Patrick growled. *I will not tolerate this rudeness any longer.* "Stop interrupting her."

The reporter ignored him. "What about your legacy, Lauren? Aren't you worried about what your die-hard fans will think?"

"I'm not worried about anything like that," Lauren said. "In fact, I'm too happy to—"

"Then why are you wasting your talents with someone like this?" the reporter interrupted.

Patrick stepped in front of the reporter. "I told you not to interrupt her. You've interrupted her twice. Apologize."

"It's my job to ask questions, buddy," the reporter said.

"And to *listen* to the answers," Patrick said.

"I listen," the reporter said.

"No, you don't," Patrick said. "You're too busy thinking up your next question."

"It's my job," the reporter said.

"So it's your job to be rude," Patrick said. "Do they pay you more the ruder you are?"

"Now *you're* interrupting her," the reporter said.

"You must be paid more than anyone else here," Patrick said. "Apologize."

"I don't have to apologize for doing my job," the reporter said.

Patrick stared him down. "Apologize for being rude to the lady, and she *is* a lady."

Camera shutters whirred as the reporter's face turned red. Some photographers even swung away from Lauren and focused on the reporter.

Lauren smiled and munched on her Pop-Tart.

"Now," Patrick said.

"Um, I'm sorry, Lauren," the reporter said.

Patrick stepped beside Lauren. "Now, listen to her all the way through before you ask your next question. All of you."

"Thank you, Patrick," Lauren said. "My future husband's name is *Patrick* Alan Esposito, not Paulie. Get it right this time. Do I need to spell it for you? Go ahead. Write it down." She waited until they had. "You asked about my legacy. Look, I made a few movies. That's all. I'm not going to be in any history books, and I'm definitely not going to win any lifetime achievement awards."

The rude reporter looked at Patrick. "May I ask another question now?"

Patrick smiled at Lauren. "Are you through with your answer?"

Lauren finished her Pop-Tart and took half of Patrick's. "Yes."

"Go ahead," Patrick said.

"But you're giving up your calling," the reporter said. "What you were born to do."

"And what is your question?" Lauren asked.

The man squinted and looked around. "I did ask a question."

Lauren shook her head. "You made a statement. And this is your job?"

The man turned even redder. "Why are you giving up your calling?"

"That's better," Lauren said. "My calling?" Lauren laughed. "Look, I am happy with this man. I've never been happier. I am doing what I really want to do for the first time in a long time. You'd love for me to come out here sniveling and sad and begging for toilet paper. I spent seven years being sad, and that is over. I do not need to be in movies or on TV to have a career or a legacy, and who's to say that my calling hasn't changed? Maybe my calling is to be a wife and mother. Maybe I was born *not* to act anymore." She turned to Patrick. "We're working on a family, aren't we?"

Geez, Lauren, Patrick thought. *Why don't you simply tell them we're having sex? That's what they're going to write about anyway.* Patrick looked down. "Yes, we are."

Lauren rolled her eyes. "Don't be so shy about it."

Patrick smiled and looked up. "Yes, we are working on a family." He laughed. "As often as we can."

Lauren laughed. "That's better." She turned to the reporters. "A family is a lasting legacy, isn't it? Now, if you'll excuse us, we're on our way—"

Patrick's phone rang.

Lauren sighed. "I think we're on our way to a service call."

"My toilet is overflowing again!" Mr. Hyer screamed into the phone. "It's a shit waterfall!"

And on our wedding day, Patrick thought. "Mr. Hyer, we're on our way." He closed his phone.

"We're obviously on our way to save Mr. Hyer," Lauren said. "Another pigeon?"

"He says his toilet is an overflowing waterfall of, um, goo," Patrick said.

"He didn't say 'goo,' did he?" Lauren asked.

Patrick shook his head.

"Does that mean those lines are backed up again?" Lauren asked.

Patrick nodded.

Lauren snatched the rest of Patrick's Pop-Tart and ate it. "Weren't we just there yesterday?"

Patrick nodded. "This is the third time in the last month."

"They need to change their diet," Lauren said.

Several reporters laughed.

"Well," Lauren said, "they do."

"They're not getting married today," a reporter said, backing away. "No one goes to work on their wedding day."

"We do," Lauren said.

"They're just trying to throw us off," another reporter said, putting his camera away.

"The stench might," Lauren said.

They walked down Hoyt to Baltic followed by no reporters or photographers, descended into the dark basement, and worked several hours in the stink.

"Oh, that's seriously bad," Lauren said, holding her gloves in front of her face. "My eyes and nose are bleeding."

"Welcome to my glamorous life," Patrick said as the snake chewed on.

"How can you stand it?" Lauren asked.

"I know this is going to sound gross," Patrick said.

"Don't say it then," Lauren said.

"But it works," Patrick said. "I breathe in as deeply as I

can as soon as I get into something like this. I practically huff it."

"That's nasty," Lauren said.

"Yes, but eventually my brain gets used to the smell, and I don't smell it anymore." He smiled. "I don't smell it at all now."

"I do," Lauren said. "I'll breathe through my gloves, thank you. We need to put some Lysol in that bag."

When the drain finally cleared, they walked outside, expecting to see paparazzi.

There were no paparazzi.

"They must have smelled us coming," Patrick said.

"I know I reek," Lauren said.

Patrick sniffed her neck. "You still smell like you."

She gripped his arm. "Patrick, I don't have your ring yet. We can't get married properly until I get you a ring. Let's go back to that pawnshop. I saw one I liked the other day. I think I've earned . . . at ten bucks an hour, times two weeks . . . didn't work Sundays . . . six times sixteen times ten . . . I made about a thousand bucks. Pay up."

"That's more than I paid for your ring," Patrick said.

"So?"

"You're not mad?"

"Why would I be mad?" Lauren asked. "You picked out that ring for *me*. Chazz had some jeweler design one for me. Chazz didn't pick it out. Do you think a pawnshop takes credit?"

"You're really not mad?" Patrick asked.

"No." She hugged him. "It isn't the ring. It's what it represents. It's who it represents. You're thrifty, old-fashioned, and shiny like the ring."

"Well, two out of three," Patrick said.

"So, do you think that pawnshop takes credit?" Lauren asked.

"Let's find out."

They walked unimpeded by anything but snow and snowplows from Baltic to Gem Pawnbrokers, entered the pawnshop, and waved Vicky over to the jewelry case.

"I saw a ring in here the other day that was huge enough for Patrick's thick fingers," Lauren said. "I think it was platinum."

Vicky pulled out a ring. "This one?"

Lauren nodded.

"What's that smell?" Vicky asked.

Lauren slid the ring onto Patrick's left ring finger. "You smell a septic backup over on Baltic. We snaked that mess until it gave up the fight. We're working with the occupants of the dwelling to lower their fiber intake." She laughed as she turned to Patrick. "Is it too tight?"

"Yeah," Patrick said. "It's cutting off the circulation."

"I'm keeping you out of circulation," Lauren said.

"I can size it for you," Vicky said.

Patrick worked the ring off and handed it to Vicky. "Could you do it now?"

"We're getting married today," Lauren said. "Do you take credit?"

Vicky blinked. "Um, sure." She took the ring to the back, sized it, and brought it back.

Patrick slipped it on. "Much better."

Lauren handed her a MasterCard, and Vicky completed the transaction.

"Where are you getting married?" Vicky asked.

"We haven't decided," Patrick said. He looked outside. *Where is a good wedding spot that won't draw too much attention in Brooklyn?*

"I wish I could be there," Vicky said.

"Do you have any suggestions for my special day?" Lauren asked.

"Change your clothes," Vicky said.

"Don't knock coveralls, Vicky," Lauren said. "They are extremely comfortable. And they come off *so* easily."

Once outside, Patrick took Lauren's hand. "She'll tell the world what you said and what you bought."

"I hope she does," Lauren said. "We need more headlines."

"No, we don't," Patrick said.

"How about FALLEN STAR BUYS WEDDING RING AT PAWN-SHOP?" Lauren suggested.

"Or BOY TOY LETS STAR BUY WEDDING RING AT PAWN-SHOP," Patrick said.

"I like this one," Lauren said. "DESTITUTE FORMER AC-TRESS PAWNS LAST ROLL OF TOILET PAPER FOR RING."

"Boy toy grateful," Patrick said.

"Boy toy very cute," Lauren said.

They walked up Shermerhorn to Court Street and then headed over to the New York City Marriage Bureau housed in the Brooklyn Municipal Building on Joralemon Street, Patrick with his tool bag, Lauren's hand in his. As they approached the Brooklyn Municipal Building, they saw a swarm of reporters and photographers on the sidewalk out front kicking up snow around massive gray pillars.

"They found us," Patrick said.

"They were waiting for us," Lauren said. "Ready?"

"To get married, yes," Patrick said. "To deal with them, no."

"I want to be more dramatic this time," Lauren said. "Is that okay with you?"

"Can you be any other way?" Patrick asked.

"What are you trying to say?" Lauren smiled and squeezed his hand. "This might actually be fun. Follow my lead. Feel free to improvise."

A burly reporter stepped into their path. "Are you really getting married, Lauren?"

"Yes," Lauren said. "I told you I was. Weren't you listening? Don't you people ever listen? What is the point of talking to you at all if you don't listen to what I say?"

"You're getting married dressed like that?" the reporter asked.

"Yes," Lauren said. "What's your point?"

"No point," the reporter said. "Just wondering, um, why."

"It is so good to wonder, isn't it?" Lauren asked. "And it's a wonderful day."

Another reporter blocked the entrance. "Think about what you're doing!"

"You better think about what *you're* doing," Lauren said. "You're blocking a public entrance. I think you can be arrested for that."

The reporter stepped aside as cameras whirred.

"Lauren, Lauren, do you *have* to get married?" a reporter shouted.

"Yes, I do," Lauren said, her lips forming a pout. "And I need to tell you all why."

Here we go, Patrick thought. *Here comes some drama. I hope I don't laugh.*

The reporters quieted down considerably.

"Give me some room here," Lauren said. "This is going to be one of my longer answers."

It was so quiet, Patrick could hear his stomach growl. *I shouldn't have let her eat both Pop-Tarts. I have to assert myself more around her, especially with breakfast foods.*

"Ladies and gentlemen," Lauren said. "I have some *very* serious news."

She is really milking this, Patrick thought. *Those digital cameras have to be out of memory by now.*

"I have to get married because . . ." She sighed and covered her face with her hands. She dropped her hands, and her lower lip began to quiver. "I have to get married because . . . because I'm in love." She laughed loudly, and the first row of photographers leaned away from her. "The end." She looked up at Patrick. "How was that?" she whispered.

"I liked it," Patrick whispered. "The lip quivering thing was most effective."

"Yeah?" She bit her lower lip. "How's this?"

"Very sexy," Patrick whispered.

"There has to be more to it than that," a reporter said. "You don't marry a nobody for no real reason."

"Love is the *best* reason," Lauren said. "And Patrick isn't a nobody, and he never will be a nobody. He is everything I could ever even hope to want."

"What do you think of all this?" a reporter asked Patrick.

"Does it really matter to you what I think?" Patrick asked.

The reporter rolled his eyes. "Oh yes," he said. "It matters a *lot* what you think."

Patrick stared him down. *They all want me to go off. These people are waiting for me to cause an incident. This is how they make the news. This is how they get paid ridiculous sums of money. They want to push me over the edge, but I'm not going to give them the satisfaction.* "I think . . . that we're going to go inside and get a marriage license." He held the door for Lauren, and they entered the building.

In the city clerk's office on the second floor, they met

Jarrell, who babbled at them when he wasn't taking their picture with his phone.

"I am *so* glad I waited to go on break," Jarrell said. "You two kept me waiting so long! I knew you were coming today. What took you so long?" He handed them the certificate of marriage form. "Please write as neatly as you can."

"So you can take a picture of it, huh?" Lauren said.

"You know it," Jarrell said. "A man has to make *some* extra money around here, right? They'll never pay me enough for what I do here."

Patrick watched as Lauren filled out her side of the form, listing her full name, her birth name, and her surname after marriage. *Lauren Elizabeth Esposito?*

"Are you sure?" he whispered.

"I am taking you *and* your name," Lauren said. "I don't need a stage name when the world's a stage and you're the only one I want to play with."

Next to "usual occupation," Lauren wrote, "Handy-woman," and next to "type of industry or business," she wrote, "Buildings maintenance."

"Are you sure about that?" Patrick whispered.

"Yes," Lauren said. "And now I am no longer *legally* an actress. It's official." She filled out her parents' information and handed him the form. "Your turn."

He filled out the form and left his father's name and information blank. Instead of "handyman," he wrote, "Buildings maintenance supervisor."

After they showed Jarrell their birth certificates and IDs and paid a forty-dollar fee, Jarrell signed the form.

"Can we go get married now?" Lauren asked.

"You have to wait twenty-four hours, honey," Jarrell said.

"There's a waiting period?" Lauren asked. "I didn't know there was a waiting period. That's so strange."

"Tell me about it," Jarrell said. "Once you have the license to possess a handgun in this state, there's no specific waiting period for purchasing a handgun, and yet you have to wait twenty-four hours to get married."

"That makes no sense!" Lauren cried. "Patrick, what are we going to do?"

She won't want to wait, Patrick thought. *It's not in her nature.*

"We can say our vows anytime we want, can't we?" Lauren said. "It's a free country. We could say them right here if we wanted to."

Jarrell whipped out his phone. "Oh, *please* do." He hit several buttons. "Talk fast. I don't have a lot of memory on this phone. I knew I should have upgraded last month. Can you do your vows in fifteen seconds?"

"We're not saying them here," Patrick whispered.

"We can say our vows today and have someone official sign it later, right?" Lauren asked Jarrell.

"Sure," Jarrell said. "Let me know when you're starting."

"We're not starting," Patrick said. "Father Giovanni can sign it next week." He looked from Jarrell to Lauren. "Let's find a nice park."

Lauren smiled. "Isn't there one across the street? It looked nice."

"Yes, Columbus Park is okay, but it's so small." *We could go to Adam Yauch Park, named after the "No Sleep till Brooklyn" Beastie Boy, but it's a couple miles away—and we can't make Lauren wait. We need to be married close by in Boerum Hill. Boerum Park. That's where we'll go.* "I have a better idea."

"Okay," Lauren said then fluttered her eyes at Jarrell. "We're getting married in a park."

"Which one?" Jarrell asked.

"A nearby one," Patrick said.

"Oh, that's helpful," Jarrell said. "Could you give me a hint?"

"I could," Patrick said. He shrugged. "Boerum Park."

Jarrell grimaced. "You're kidding."

"It's where I'm from," Patrick said.

Lauren hugged Patrick. "It's a beautiful day to be married in a park."

"That's no park, honey," Jarrell said. "It's a vacant lot."

"It's a playground," Patrick said.

"A playground!" Lauren smiled. "A playground sounds *perfect*."

57

"Lauren! Lauren!"

"Are you *really* getting married today?"

"Where are you going now?"

"To our wedding in Boerum Park," Lauren said as she and Patrick edged through the crowd of reporters and photographers.

"Isn't that near the Gowanus Houses?" a reporter asked. Patrick nodded.

Lauren gripped his hand tightly. *We might even get some privacy there.* "Good choice."

"Why aren't you getting married in a church?"

"Hey, buddy, you look Catholic. Are you Catholic? He's Italian. He has to be Catholic."

"Where's the bridal party? Are they waiting for you?"

"Who's going to be your maid of honor, Lauren?"

"Yeah, who's going to be the best man? Aren't all your friends dead or in jail?"

The media, once again, have no clue, Lauren thought.

News crews in vans crept alongside the throng of photographers surrounding them as they walked down Court Street to Warren Street. When they arrived at Boerum Park, they found it packed with children who were having a massive snowball fight, nearly as much snow in the air as there was on the ground.

We're getting married in a snowball fight, Lauren thought. *This is great!*

She packed a snowball and fired it toward the photographers. Within moments, the children around them started pelting the reporters with snowballs.

Lauren pulled one little boy aside. "What's your name?"

"Darius," the boy said.

"Darius, I need you and your friends to protect us from those evil people over there," Lauren said, pointing at the photographers. "They are trying to ruin our lives. Do you think you could do that?"

Darius nodded. "Sure. But why?"

"We're getting married here in a few minutes," Lauren said.

Darius's eyes popped. "You're getting married . . . *here?*"

"Yep," Lauren said. "Make lots of snowballs, and if any of them get too close to us during our wedding, you nail them."

"And we won't get in trouble?" Darius asked.

"Nope," Lauren said. "You'll also get on TV."

"Weird," Darius said.

Patrick towered over Darius. "But fun." He knelt and whispered into Darius's ear.

Darius smiled broadly. "You got it."

Lauren pulled Patrick aside. "What are they going to do?"

"We need a wedding party," Patrick whispered. "Only this one will be an armed and dangerous wedding party."

While Patrick and Lauren stood in the middle of a snow-covered basketball court, Darius organized about a dozen children who made mounds of snowballs in a rough circle around them. As soon as the children were in place, they held up snowballs, turned, and faced the photographers, who jockeyed for position behind a black metal fence.

Several of the children held a snowball in each hand.

While the kids pelted any photographer stupid enough to come near the basketball court, and cameras rolled and other photographers snapped away from a somewhat safe distance behind the fence, Patrick set his tool bag down and took Lauren's hands in his.

"Here we are."

"Yes," Lauren said. "Here we are. Center court in a playground." She looked around. "This is a happening church."

"Ladies first," Patrick said.

I don't know whether to laugh, cry, or scream! Lauren thought. *This is insane! Oh, his hands are so sweaty. Wait. My hands are sweaty. Our hands are sweaty. He's as nervous as I am. I guess that's a good sign.*

"Are you at a loss for words?" Patrick asked.

Yes! "In a wedding, the man goes first."

"I never want to be first in our marriage," Patrick said.

"Are you starting your vows?" Lauren asked.

"No," Patrick said.

"Oh," Lauren said. "I thought you were. Use that line. I like it."

"Lauren, I never want to be first in our marriage," Patrick said.

"Neither do I," Lauren said.

"I am content to be last," Patrick said.

"So am I," Lauren said. "And that way our *love* will last."

"Nice turn of phrase," Patrick said.

"I do have some skills," Lauren said. "Keep going."

"Lauren, I want you to be the first person I see in the

morning and the last person I see every night for the rest of my life," Patrick said.

"So do I," Lauren said. *Oh, this scene is going nowhere. All I'm doing is agreeing with him.* "Let's not do vows. Why don't we have a conversation instead of making vows?"

"Isn't that what we've been having from the very beginning?" Patrick asked.

"Well, yes," Lauren said.

"So we've been making our vows all along, huh?"

She hugged him. "You say the most amazing things." She stepped back and smiled. "I love you so much."

"I love you, too," Patrick said.

"I love everything about you, but I really love your hands," Lauren said. "They're strong, and they're steady. My feet have never felt better."

"I love your eyes," Patrick said. "I can never get tired of looking into your eyes."

"My hands are getting stronger, aren't they?" Lauren asked.

"True, but your eyes are the strongest part of you," Patrick said. "They have the strength to hold me all night long."

He's good at this. "I like your voice, too. It's deep and strong and *so* sexy."

"I love it when you whisper," Patrick whispered.

Lauren shivered. "Not in front of the children," she whispered. "And I can't wait to have children."

"Neither can I," Patrick said.

"You're very good in bed," Lauren whispered.

Patrick looked at the kids surrounding them. "Thank you," he whispered, "but you're the reason. You bring out the best in me."

"At least three times a day, okay?" Lauren laughed. "I want to kiss you and start our honeymoon right now."

Patrick wiggled his left hand. "I need a ring first. You're already wearing yours."

"And I will never remove it." Lauren pulled Patrick's ring from a coveralls pocket and slid it onto his finger. "Now can we start our honeymoon?"

Patrick lifted her high in the air before bringing her face close to his. He kissed her tenderly. "Our honeymoon has officially begun."

This man, this moment, this scene, Lauren thought. *This is love.* "I now know what real love is."

"What is it?"

"Love is feeling absolutely weightless and helpless in someone else's arms and not being afraid," Lauren said. "And as long as one of us has *his* feet on the ground, I know it will last."

"What about your feet?" Patrick asked.

"Oh, I'm sure I'll put them down every now and then." She kissed him again. "Hello, Mr. Esposito."

"Hello, Mrs. Esposito."

As Patrick returned Lauren gently to the ground and picked up his tool bag, the children showered them with snow. He took Lauren's hand, and they walked out of the park and then directly through the throng of reporters and photographers as more snow rained down.

"What did you say to each other?"

"What were your vows?"

"Do you know those kids?"

"Did you plan all this?"

"Weren't there any churches that would marry you?"

"Is this for real?"

"What's his ring made of?"

"Do you think the mayor could do more to remove snow from this part of Brooklyn?"

"Couldn't you afford a *real* wedding?"

Patrick stopped on the snowy sidewalk, turned, and faced the reporters and photographers. "What you just witnessed was and is real."

"We couldn't hear your vows," a reporter said. "What'd you say?"

"You weren't supposed to hear them," Patrick said.

"What did you say?"

"Come on, have a heart, buddy!"

Patrick sighed. "It was a personal conversation, one that will continue for the rest of our lives. You wouldn't understand any of it anyway."

"Tell us what you said!" a reporter shouted.

What foolishness! Lauren thought. "It is none of your business, so hush."

The reporter hushed, but only for a moment. He moved away from the crowd and approached Darius. "Hey, kid. Yeah, you. Did you hear what they said to each other? I'll give you a dollar if you tell me. . . ."

A buck? Lauren thought. *Is he crazy? He'll need at least twenty bucks each for those kids.*

"Where are you two going on your honeymoon?" a photographer asked.

Lauren smiled at Patrick. "Yes. Where are we going? And please don't say St. Louis."

"I thought St. Louis worked out rather nicely," Patrick said.

Lauren blushed. "Well, yes, it did, but . . ."

"How about . . . D.C.?" Patrick said.

Lauren smiled. "That'd be perfect!" Lauren faced the reporters and photographers. "We are going to Washington, D.C."

"D.C.? What's in D.C.?" a reporter asked.

"The White House, the Capitol Building, the Smithsonian . . ." Lauren rolled her eyes.

"No. Why go to D.C. for your honeymoon?" the reporter asked. "It's not very romantic."

"We're going to D.C. to see my mama," Lauren said. She turned to Patrick. "I want to take the bus again."

"We *could* take the train," Patrick said. "It'll be quicker."

"You're not taking her someplace exotic and warm?" a photographer asked.

"*I* keep her warm," Patrick said.

Patrick's phone buzzed. He swung it to his ear and listened for a moment. "Be right there."

"Baltic again?" Lauren asked.

"Bergen," Patrick said. "Mrs. Moczydlowska."

"You're going on a service call? Now?" The reporter shook his head. "You just got married!"

"So it's a working marriage," Lauren said. "I think more marriages would last if more spouses worked together, don't you?"

"You are so very wise," Patrick said.

"You're rubbing off on me," Lauren said.

During the two-block walk to Bergen, Patrick called Lauren "Mrs. Lauren Elizabeth Jimmerson Esposito," and Lauren called him "Paulie." They answered none of the dozens of questions flying around them, most of them concerning the composition and cost of Patrick's ring.

Mrs. Moczydlowska opened her door as they came up the stairs. "Hurry," she said, motioning with a chubby hand.

They hurried.

"It is the leak under the kitchen sink again," Mrs. Moczydlowska said.

Patrick took a wrench from his tool bag, opened the cabinet under the sink, and went to work.

"How are you today, Mrs. Moczydlowska?" Lauren asked. *I hope I said her name right.*

"I am fine," Mrs. Moczydlowska said. She pointed at a wrapped gift on the kitchen table, a simple white envelope on top. "A wedding gift for you and Patrick."

"That is so nice of you," Lauren said. "How did you know?"

Mrs. Moczydlowska pointed at a dusty thirteen-inch TV on the counter. "I saw it on the TV. It interrupted my news, so I watched."

Our wedding was live *on the news?* Lauren thought. *There is no other news today in a city hit by a blizzard? Is all that snow invisible to news stations in New York City?*

"How'd it look?" Lauren asked.

"Snowy," Mrs. Moczydlowska said. She nodded at the gift. "Open it."

Lauren opened the envelope and found three twenty-dollar bills. "You didn't have to do this."

Mrs. Moczydlowska beamed. "Of course I have to. It is a tradition. I want to give you flowers, but they charge too much and they die so quickly, and I do not go out as I used to."

Lauren opened the gift and held out a brown, gray, and white wool blanket. "This blanket is so beautiful. Is it wool?" *And yet it's so soft!*

"It is Polish wool blanket I got in Zakopane when I was much younger," Mrs. Moczydlowska said. She turned away. "I know you will get better gifts."

"These are our *only* gifts," Lauren said, "and even if we do get more gifts, none will be more special than these. Thank you."

"It is nothing," Mrs. Moczydlowska said.

"It is everything." Lauren hugged her.

"It is really nothing," Mrs. Moczydlowska said.

"This will look fantastic on our couch," Lauren said. "And I can definitely use it. Patrick keeps the heat low at our apartment."

"It is what he wants me to do here, too," Mrs. Moczydlowska said. "He would have us freeze to death."

"That's not true," Patrick said from under the sink.

"You have too much hot blood," Mrs. Moczydlowska said.

"I'll agree with you there," Lauren said.

"I hope I am not interrupting your honeymoon to Washington," Mrs. Moczydlowska said, smiling. "I have never been there. I watch your wedding. So beautiful. I was married in winter. Much colder in Poland but so beautiful." She looked into the other room. "My husband could not wait until spring." She sighed. "A winter marriage is a good marriage. There is an old saying. 'When snows fall fast, marry and true love will last.'"

"Is that a Polish saying?" Lauren asked.

"No," Mrs. Moczydlowska said. "I read it in a book. The saying is from a place called Kentucky. I have never been there either."

Patrick slid out from under the sink. "All fixed. Just a little leak." He hugged Mrs. Moczydlowska. "Thank you for the gifts. We'll see you when we get back."

"When?" Mrs. Moczydlowska asked.

"The day after tomorrow," Patrick said.

"Hmm," Mrs. Moczydlowska said. "That is okay. But if you two are gone any longer, I will worry."

"Don't worry," Patrick said.

"It is my job to worry," Mrs. Moczydlowska said. "I am good at it."

"Yes, you are," Patrick said. "I will see you in two days."

Mrs. Moczydlowska smiled at Lauren. "I will be waiting to see *both* of you in two days."

On the way back to their apartment, Patrick smiled and stared a long time at Lauren.

"What?" Lauren said.

"Nothing," Patrick said.

"There's something," Lauren said.

"Just that I think she's beginning to like you already," Patrick said. "She said 'both.' You're becoming her daughter or something."

"Which reminds me," Lauren said. "We can't go on our honeymoon if the accommodations aren't ready." She took out her phone and called her mother. "Mama, we're coming to visit you tonight."

"Why?" Pamela asked.

"We just got married," Lauren said.

"And you're coming *here* for your honeymoon?" Pamela asked.

"Our honeymoon will never end," Lauren said. "We're just starting it with you."

"Not in *my* house," Pamela said. "When will you get here?"

Lauren looked at Patrick. "When will we arrive?"

"Sometime after midnight, I guess," Patrick said.

"Sometime after midnight," Lauren said.

Pamela sighed. "You'll have to knock loudly."

"We will," Lauren said. "See you soon."

"Bye," Pamela said.

Lauren closed her phone. "She didn't sound too happy."

"This is kind of a shock to her, isn't it?" Patrick asked.

"I guess," Lauren said. "But she knows me. She knows I can't wait. She'll get over it." *I hope.* She squeezed his hand. "Can we maybe do something shocking when we get home?"

"You read my mind," Patrick whispered.

"You're so easy to read," Lauren said.

"It must be what love is, huh?" Patrick asked. "We can read each other easily."

"You think you can read me, Mr. Esposito?" Lauren asked.

"Yes, Mrs. Esposito," Patrick said. "You're an open book."

"Okay," Lauren said, "what am I thinking right now?"

Patrick laughed. "I can't say it out loud."

"Sure you can," Lauren said.

"Okay," Patrick said. He put his lips to her ear. "You want to christen the apartment."

How did he know that? "Well . . ."

"I'm right, aren't I?" Patrick asked.

"Technically, yes," Lauren said.

"Only technically?" Patrick asked.

Lauren shook her head. "You nailed it. I'm already getting excited. Let's hurry!"

After Patrick carried Lauren across the threshold, Lauren checked the Amtrak schedule, and Patrick called in "sick" to work for the next two days, Patrick and Lauren christened every room in the apartment.

It didn't take long in the small apartment.

They tried the kitchen counter and found it a little too high for Patrick to stay inside her. The bathroom counter was a little too low, and Lauren's booty kept sliding into one of the sinks. The couch made a terrible racket, and the hardwood floor under the faux wood linoleum moaned.

"We need to oil this thing," Lauren said as she panted. "We need to oil the entire apartment."

"There's an interesting thought," Patrick said, carrying her to the front door.

Lauren kept trying to open the door while Patrick attempted to thrust her up to the ceiling, and the shade in the bedroom became a yo-yo with Lauren yanking it open and Patrick pulling it closed.

"It's broad daylight, Mrs. Esposito," Patrick said.

"I *know,* Mr. Esposito," Lauren said. "My booty needs some sun. Yours, too."

Exhausted, they showered together, dressed, and emptied Patrick's tool bag before packing two days' worth of clothing inside it.

"*Now* we can go see my mama," Lauren said.

"We didn't try the coffee table," Patrick said.

"When we get back," Lauren said. She looked at the coffee table. "Will that little table hold us?"

"It's solid oak," Patrick said.

She smiled. "I love good wood."

58

Wearing jeans, sweaters, heavy coats, and boots, Patrick and Lauren took the subway to Penn Station to catch the Amtrak train. Few people took notice of them on the subway or while they stood in line to pay for their train tickets.

Maybe we're finally becoming ordinary and anonymous, Patrick thought. *It's nice not to have people staring and taking pictures of us for a change.*

"I'm paying," Lauren said.

"I got this," Patrick said. *I think I do,* he thought. *It's only one seventy for both of us round-trip.* He dug into his pocket and came up with one hundred ten dollars. "It seems I'm a bit short."

Lauren smiled. "Well, she's *my* mama, after all." She dug out her MasterCard.

"And you're *my* bride," Patrick said. "I am supposed to pay for the honeymoon. Let me find an ATM."

"Come on," said the man behind them. "You're holding up the line."

Patrick glared at the man. "Do you mind? We're having our first married argument."

Lauren nodded. "We are, aren't we?"

"Come on, come on," the man said. "I can't miss this train."

Lauren looked at the man. "Neither can we, all right? We're on our honeymoon, so do you mind?"

The man turned away.

Lauren looked up at Patrick and sighed. "So, what's it going to be, Mr. Esposito? Are you going to get out of line to find an ATM and make us miss this train, or are you going to let me pay?"

"You can pay this time," Patrick said.

"I *have* to pay this time," Lauren said. "Someone wasn't prepared to pay."

"Because you . . ." He stepped closer and whispered, "Because you banged my brains out."

Lauren smiled. "I did, didn't I?"

"I will pay you back," Patrick said.

Lauren paid. "I'll expect some extra special favors as payment."

Oh, how I love this woman. "I can do that."

Once on the train, they wandered to the Café Car and ordered Tuscan Italian panini sandwiches, a cheese and cracker tray, four slices of Sara Lee pound cake, and two Starbucks Frappuccinos, spreading them out on a free table and sitting side-by-side.

"This is our wedding reception," Lauren whispered. "We are saving a mint on our wedding, aren't we?"

"I guess," Patrick said.

"We may be one of the few couples to spend less than five hundred bucks on our wedding and honeymoon," Lauren said.

"I wish I could do more for you," Patrick said.

"I am content," Lauren said. "And this day has been a *lot* of fun. I'll be talking about this day for the rest of my life."

As they started to feast, Lauren took out her phone and surfed to ET.com. "We're on! Look!"

Patrick looked at the tiny screen and saw a picture of himself holding Lauren high in the air at Boerum Park. *Wow,* he thought. *Lauren is short. No, maybe it's the camera angle.*

The *Entertainment Tonight* host smiled and said, "Actress Lauren Short and her handyman, Patrick, exchanged their vows during a nasty snowball fight in a vacant lot in Brooklyn today. . . ."

"It was a *park,* not a vacant lot," Lauren said. "And if the photographers hadn't tried to get closer, there wouldn't have been a nasty snowball fight. And we're technically not married until Father Giovanni signs the form. And I'm not an actress anymore, and you're *much* more than a handyman. *ET* didn't get *any* part of this story right."

"You look so cute," Patrick said. "I'll bet young ladies all around the country will be wearing coveralls in no time."

"They sure are comfortable," Lauren said. "Oh, here comes the kiss."

"That was a great kiss," Patrick said.

"The best kiss I have ever had," Lauren said. "Look how high in the air I am."

"When asked for a comment on this shocking new development," the host continued, "Lauren's former fiancé, mega star Chazz Jackson, said that any marriage that began in a vacant lot could never last."

"They'll be divorced before Christmas," Chazz said. "They may even be filing for divorce as we speak. Lauren is too used to the finer things in life because of me to settle for a man who has the worst beard I've ever seen. Lauren is only doing this to get back at me. She'll be asking me for a New Year's Eve date. I guarantee it. You'll see."

"Ha!" Lauren shouted. "You'll be out with *all* the Chippendales on New Year's Eve, you jerk!" She grimaced and looked around. "I didn't mean to be so loud," she whispered.

"It's okay," Patrick said. "You were talking in all caps. It's a perfectly understandable response to jerks on TV."

"The frostbitten couple," the *ET* host smirked, "is currently on their way to their honeymoon in . . . Washington, D.C.? Really? They're going to our nation's capital for their honeymoon? Are we sure about this? Who goes to D.C. in December? Even Congress runs away from D.C. in December. And they're riding the train? This is a joke, right? This isn't a joke. Lauren Short is now Lauren Esposito, and she is *not* riding in a carriage with a prince. . . ."

Lauren shook her head. "Such foolishness. But she *is* right. I'm *not* riding with a prince. I'm riding with a king."

"And that makes you my queen," Patrick said. He kissed her and tasted pound cake. "Your lips are sweet and intoxicating."

"You're going to be drunk for the rest of your life," Lauren said.

After finishing their meal, they sat quietly watching New Jersey fly by until a heavily bundled black woman approached and sat opposite them.

"I hope you don't mind," she said, setting her purse on the table. "I hate to eat alone."

Well, sit yourself down, why don't you? Lauren thought. "It's okay. Hi. I'm—"

"I know who you are," the woman interrupted. "I'm Delia Jones."

"Nice to meet you, Delia," Lauren said.

Delia pulled a Baggie from her purse, took out a quarter of a sandwich, and began munching away. "Are you two really on your honeymoon?"

"Yes," Lauren said, sniffing the air. "Is that chicken salad?"

"It is," Delia said. "Made it myself."

"I can't remember the last time I had homemade chicken salad," Lauren said. "It smells so good."

Delia handed her half of her sandwich. "Tell me what you think."

Lauren finished the half in three bites. "Delicious."

"I watched your wedding," Delia said, "what I could see of it with all those snowballs flying around. A snowball hit the camera right in the lens. Those kids had good aim."

"Yes, they did," Lauren said. "So . . . what did you think of the wedding?"

"It was different," Delia said. "You had to be cold."

"Patrick kept me warm," Lauren said.

"You're going to D.C. to see your mama, right?" Delia asked.

"Yes," Lauren said. "I'm going to introduce my new husband to her."

"Your mama hasn't met him yet?" Delia asked.

"No," Lauren said. "She has only spoken to him on the phone so far."

"Why didn't she come up for the wedding?" Delia asked.

"Mama had to work today," Lauren said. "She drives a D.C. Metrobus."

"You're her only child, right?" Delia asked.

Delia is well informed. "Yes."

"And yet your own mama missed your wedding," Delia said. "You two have a falling-out?"

Lauren nodded. "I haven't seen her in fourteen years."

"Fourteen years?" Delia said. "That's a seriously long time not to see your mama. Why so long?"

"Well," Lauren said, "I did this movie a while back. . . ."

Not long after Lauren finished her story, Delia disembarked in Trenton. Before long Philadelphia, Wilmington, and Baltimore were behind them, and then the train arrived at Union Station in Washington, D.C.

Photographers greeted them and impeded their movement as they tried to step off the train.

"Lauren, where are you headed?"

"Is this what you really wanted for your honeymoon?"

"What do you think of the situations in North Korea and the Middle East?"

"Are those boots waterproof?"

"Did you *pay* those kids to throw snowballs at those reporters?"

"When's the last time you were in D.C.?"

"Do you think coveralls will one day replace the traditional wedding gown?"

"Is it true you're suffering from frostbite and hypothermia?"

Are any of them serious? Lauren held Patrick's hand. "We are going to my mama's house in Congress Heights."

The photographers murmured to each other.

"Are you all going to follow us?" Lauren asked. "It's only a couple miles away. There might not be much room on the street to park, but you're welcome tag along."

"Congress Heights?" a reporter said. "At this time of night?"

"Yes," Lauren said. "That's where I grew up, and that's where my mama lives."

All but one female photographer backed away.

"Your loss," Lauren said. She smiled at the lone photographer. "You're going to have an exclusive, aren't you?"

"Oh, I'm not going," the photographer said. "I was just waiting for an answer to my question."

"Which was?" Lauren asked.

"Where did you get those boots?" she asked.

Lauren laughed. "Are you kidding? That's the only question you want answered?"

The photographer nodded. "I like them."

"Oh, my goodness," Lauren said. "I got them at New York Speed on Melrose in LA."

"Expensive, huh?" the photographer asked, snapping several pictures of Lauren's boots.

"I didn't pay more than fifty bucks for them," Lauren said.

"Really?" The photographer smiled. "Do they sell them online?"

I don't know! "I'm sure they do."

"Thanks," the photographer said, and she hurried away.

Maybe to order some shoes? Lauren thought. *What utter, complete foolishness!*

She and Patrick finally stepped off the train and headed through the famous main hall in Union Station to the taxi stand out front. As he held open a door for Lauren, Patrick turned to look behind him and saw no photographers.

"We're alone," Patrick said.

"I thought we might be," Lauren said.

"We have to go to D.C. to be alone," Patrick said. "Crazy."

When they got into a taxi, Lauren said, "Five thirty-two Lebaum Street, Congress Heights, please."

The driver looked back at her. "Really?"

"Really," Lauren said. "It's less than six miles from here, right?"

"Yeah," the driver said. "But Congress Heights at one thirty in the morning? Are you sure?"

"I'm sure," Lauren said. "You're taking me home for the first time in fourteen years, and my mama is waiting up for us."

The driver squinted at his GPS screen. "All right." He pulled the taxi away from the curb. "You're that actress, right?"

Lauren nodded and then shook her head. "I *was* an actress. Not anymore."

"At least you had the good sense to escape Congress Heights," the driver said.

"I heard it was getting better there," Lauren said.

"Yeah, well," the driver said, "anything would be an improvement. Unemployment is still around twenty-five percent, and there still isn't a decent place to sit down and eat, unless you like IHOP."

"There's nothing wrong with IHOP," Lauren said. "How's crime these days?"

"It's quieter," the driver said. "Still higher than anywhere else in the city."

"I hear that Homeland Security is relocating to St. Elizabeths," Lauren said. "That's really close to my mama."

"Homeland Security wouldn't have anything to do with what happens on the streets," the driver said. "There was a shooting on Alabama Avenue just last night."

"We'll avoid Alabama Avenue," Lauren whispered.

After passing the Library of Congress and crossing the 11th Street Bridge, they took Martin Luther King, Jr. Avenue to Lebaum.

When the taxi stopped in front of a small colonial, Lauren gripped Patrick's hand tightly. "We're here. It still looks the same."

Patrick paid the driver with two twenties. "Thanks," he said.

"The fare is only twenty," the driver said, "and I already included the tip."

Patrick shrugged. "She wouldn't let me pay for the train tickets, so I have some extra cash. Take your wife to IHOP."

"Right," the driver said. "But I'll take her to the one in *Columbia* Heights. Take it easy."

As soon as they were out of the taxi, Lauren opened a chain-link gate and started up a concrete walkway that split a flat yard, the grass yellow but thick.

"The house originally had three bedrooms and one bath," Lauren said, "but Daddy added a full bath, a half bath, and another bedroom." She dragged Patrick up concrete stairs to the porch. "How do I look?"

"Perfect, as usual," Patrick said.

"I'm nervous," Lauren said.

"Why?" Patrick asked.

"My mama was my first audience," Lauren said, "and she's still my toughest critic." She knocked loudly. "I hope she's in a good mood."

"And if she isn't?" Patrick asked.

Lauren sighed. "Then, well, she isn't, and there's nothing anyone can do about it."

Pamela Jimmerson opened the door a minute later and looked past them. "Where are the reporters?"

"Back at Union Station," Lauren said.

"Good," Pamela said. "Come on in."

As Patrick entered the house, he glanced at Pamela. She was shorter, darker, and sturdier than Lauren was, flyaway gray hairs waving above her cornrows. She wore a pair of jeans, a Howard sweatshirt, and some brown slippers.

"Hello," Patrick said.

Pamela nodded.

Lauren reached out to hug Pamela. "It's good to see you, Mama."

Pamela rolled her eyes and gave her a quick hug. "How was your trip?"

"Quiet, for the most part," Lauren said.

"I don't believe that," Pamela said. "Nothing is quiet if you're involved."

She has that right, Patrick thought.

They trailed Pamela through a narrow hallway and past a sitting room where a short sofa faced a flat-screen TV on a stand.

"You bought a TV, Mama," Lauren said.

"Obviously," Pamela said.

Patrick appraised the house, noting the Berber carpet, the crystal doorknobs, and a ceramic tile kitchen floor. *There's not much I could do here because Lauren's father has beaten me to it. Her daddy was a craftsman, not a handyman.*

Pamela led them upstairs and paused in front of the first door. "I have to get up at four." She sighed. "Which is in about two hours since *some* people don't know how to visit at a decent hour."

"Don't you want to see the wedding?" Lauren asked. "I can show it to you on my phone."

"I already watched it on *Entertainment Tonight,*" Pamela said. "You looked . . ."

"Nice," Lauren said quickly. "I looked nice, right?"

"That's not what I was going to say," Pamela said.

"I know," Lauren said. "Well, how *did* I look?"

"Well, if you know, you tell me what I was thinking." Pamela folded her arms against her chest.

"You thought I looked . . . stunning," Lauren said.

"I was stunned, all right," Pamela said. "Coveralls? Really? And baggy ones at that. You weren't wearing them. They were wearing you. At least you didn't wear white."

"Mama," Lauren said, her eyes dropping.

"You couldn't wear white, right?" Pamela said. "What color was that? Tan? First tan bride I've ever seen."

Lauren sighed and opened the door. "When do you get off tomorrow?"

"You should know my schedule by now," Pamela said. "It hasn't changed in twenty-three years."

"Can't you get off early?" Lauren asked. "We want to treat you to dinner."

"I can meet you at Popeyes around five," Pamela said.

"Not Popeyes," Lauren said.

"I happen to like Popeyes," Pamela said. "I always know what I'm getting at Popeyes. The menu may change here and there, but it's mostly the same day after day after day. No surprises at Popeyes. Unlike *this*."

Lauren nodded. "This is a good surprise, isn't it?"

"There are no good surprises at two in the morning, Lauren," Pamela said. She looked up at Patrick. "You *are* going to say more than hello, aren't you? Feel free to join the conversation."

"I'm just minding my manners, Pamela," Patrick said.

"Minding your tongue is more like it," Pamela said. "I don't blame you a bit. Good night." She turned, walked down the hallway to the next door on the right, opened it, stepped inside, and shut it behind her.

Lauren turned on a light inside their room. "Except for the TV, not much has changed since I lived here." She bit her lip. "Especially in here. Wow, Mama. You had fourteen years to clean it out. Why didn't you?"

"Because it's *your* room," Pamela said through the wall. "If *you* want it clean, *you* have to clean it."

There are some seriously thin walls in this house, Patrick thought. *It's as if Pamela is inside the room with us.*

"But it's *your* house," Lauren said.

"This was never my house," Pamela said. "This is your

daddy's house. And I didn't have a thing to do with that room, Patrick. That was all Lauren's doing."

I have gone back in time to the nineteen nineties, Patrick thought.

Posters of the Fugees, Boyz II Men, Bone Thugs-N-Harmony, Monica, Puff Daddy, Tupac, Sir Mix-A-Lot, Will Smith, and Run-DMC completely covered the wall next to her bed. Posters for *Men in Black, The Color Purple, Pretty Woman,* and *The Matrix* crowded the ceiling.

Lauren sat on the edge of the bed. "I had the biggest crushes on Richard Gere and Keanu Reeves back then."

Patrick put the tool bag on top of a simple white desk. "Interesting," he whispered.

"You don't have to whisper," Lauren said. "She can hear you. You heard that, Mama?"

"Yes," Pamela said. "But I *don't* want to hear it. I want to sleep."

Lauren rolled her eyes. "My mama hasn't changed much either. Except for the gray hair. When did you stop dyeing it?"

"I do dye it," Pamela said. "I've just been a little too busy working. You know what work is, right? Something you do every day and need a good night's sleep to do well?"

"It doesn't take that long to dye your hair, Mama," Lauren said. "And anyway, gray looks good on you."

"No, it doesn't," Pamela said, "and I am *not* going to talk to you through the wall all night, so hush."

"We used to talk through this wall all the time," Lauren said.

"Look," Pamela said, "I am getting up to work in two hours. I do not want to kill anyone tomorrow or in the next five minutes."

"Good night, Mama," Lauren said.

"Good night, Lauren," Pamela said. "And no fornicating in there."

Lauren's mouth dropped open. *"Mama!"*

"It's not going to happen," Pamela said. "It's too late for any of that. You probably already got some today anyway. Isn't that right, Patrick?"

I'm glad that wall is there so she can't see me blush. "Yes, ma'am."

"Y'all go to sleep," Pamela said. "I want to hear some serious snoring, okay?"

"Yes, Mama," Lauren said.

After disrobing and snuggling for a few minutes in Lauren's double bed, Patrick felt Lauren's hand moving down his stomach.

He grabbed her wrist.

"You can't stop me," Lauren whispered.

Patrick shook his head. "Please don't," he whispered.

"I can't help myself," Lauren whispered.

"If I have to come in there," Pamela said through the wall.

Lauren's hand vanished. She put her lips to Patrick's right ear. "After she leaves in the morning then."

"What if I call in sick?" Pamela asked.

Lauren turned to the wall. "Will you?"

"No," Pamela said.

"She'll be gone by five," Lauren said. "I can wait until then."

"Such disrespect," Pamela said.

Lauren sat up. "Okay, Mama. We'll fornicate when we get back to Brooklyn."

"That's better," Pamela said. "Good night. For the *last* time."

Lauren slipped out of bed, went to her desk, and pulled

out a piece of paper and a pencil. She wrote hurriedly and handed the paper to Patrick.

> *I will tease you all day tomorrow. And remember our rule.*

"Here?" he mouthed.

Lauren nodded, writing, "Rest your tongue."

Patrick shook his head. He took the pencil and wrote, "You told your mama you wouldn't."

Lauren smiled. "Mama won't be here to know," she mouthed.

"What are you two plotting in there?" Pamela asked.

Lauren returned to bed. "Mama, please. We're trying to get some sleep. We've had a long day."

"Uh-huh," Pamela said. "I hear paper crinkling. Are you two passing notes?"

Paper-thin walls, Patrick thought. *So thin you can hear paper crinkling.*

"You don't want us whispering," Lauren said.

"Plotting, always plotting," Pamela said. "*Please* go to sleep."

"I'm trying," Lauren said, "but you keep talking to me."

"Oh, hush," Pamela said. "Kiss him and go to sleep."

Lauren kissed Patrick's cheek. "Good night," she whispered, and in a few minutes, she was purring.

Patrick looked up and focused on the movie posters above him. *Here I am, snuggling with a very pretty woman, and I'm caught in some sort of Pamela-Lauren matrix, with Pamela maybe six inches away from us behind that wall.* He closed his eyes. *I hope I can out-sleep Lauren.* He sighed softly. *It won't matter. She's an actress. She can fake being asleep better than I can.*

I had better rest my tongue.

59

Lauren waited as long as she could with her eyes closed, but Patrick didn't wake up by eleven a.m. She slipped out of bed, checked her mama's room and found it empty, brushed her teeth, returned to bed, sneaked under the covers, and found that Patrick was already erect.

She threw back the covers and stared at his face. *He's still asleep, and yet he's hard as a rock! Who's he dreaming about? Forget that rule!*

She shook him violently. "Wake up!"

Patrick opened his eyes. "Is it time to get up?"

"You're already up," Lauren said. "Literally."

Patrick looked down. "Oh." He yawned. "I told you that sometimes happens."

"Who were you dreaming about?" Lauren asked.

"I wasn't dreaming," Patrick said. He pointed at his fading erection. "I wake up that way whenever it gets cold. You stole most of the covers last night." He swung his legs to the edge of the bed. "Where's the bathroom?"

Lauren shook her head. "Not so fast." She straddled him. "I have to have you."

"And I have to pee," Patrick said.

She looked down at his deflated penis. "Where did it go?"

"It's cold in here," Patrick said. "And I *really* have to pee. That Frappuccino I drank on the train is screaming to get out."

"When you get back, then."

Patrick shook his head. "I intend to respect your mama's wishes." He cradled her face with his hands. "I cannot afford to have your mama angry at me. Ever."

"She was only cranky because she was tired," Lauren said.

"Really?" Patrick asked.

"She's kind of cranky a lot," Lauren said.

"I have to keep making good impressions," Patrick said. "And I can't make good impressions if I go against her wishes."

"How will she know?" Lauren asked.

"She'll ask me, and I'll tell her," Patrick said. "I won't lie to you, and I won't lie to her."

Lauren poked out her lower lip. "But I want you to make rapid impressions inside me right now."

"I promise that I will make countless impressions inside of you when we get back home." Patrick held on to Lauren's thighs and stood.

"Countless?" Lauren said.

"Countless." He turned and set her on the bed. "Now, where's the bathroom?"

After showering together and dressing in jeans, boots, and sweaters, Lauren and Patrick walked half a mile to Martin Luther King, Jr. Avenue and entered the MLK Deli, where they ordered bacon, egg, and cheese wraps and coffee for a late brunch. No one looked their way or spoke to them as they waited in line.

This is strange, Lauren thought. *Surely someone here should recognize me.*

After she paid, the cashier smiled, winked, and said, "Welcome back, Lauren."

Hmm, Lauren thought. *Maybe they are all just being polite.* "It's good to be back."

They ate their wraps as they walked up Martin Luther King, Jr. Avenue and looked through the barred windows at City Beats, the shoe store next to African Queen Braids.

"I used to get a crab platter from Aabee Seafood and just walk up and down this street eating fresh crab and talking to people," Lauren said. "Now everyone has bars on their windows and stays inside." She looked across the street. "The Pizza Place is gone? Man, this street has changed. Jamaicans made great pizza for a decent price over there."

They finished their brunch and continued to Styles Unlimited, a hair salon.

I know someone in here will know me. Lauren thought. *They have to.*

As soon as she entered the salon, a slim black woman with blond hair, black pants, black shoes, and a black top ran up to her. "I heard you were coming!" she shouted. "Let me see that ring!"

Lauren looked on the wall next to the entrance and saw her ancient head shot, dust coating the glass. *This is more like it, though they need to dust off that thing.* "Hi, Trula." She showed Trula her ring.

Trula looked up at Patrick. "Hey."

Patrick nodded.

"What do I call you now, Lauren?" Trula asked.

"You *know* me, Trula," Lauren said. "Just call me Lauren."

Trula looked up at Patrick again. "Not Mrs. Esposito?"

Patrick shrugged.

"Just Lauren," Lauren said. She sat in the first chair. "So, what's been going on?"

Trula moved behind Lauren. "You got a lot of time?"

"I know I haven't been here in years, Trula," Lauren said. "Just give me a condensed version."

"I wasn't talking about that," Trula said. She roughly finger combed Lauren's hair. "I'm talking about *this*. You want us to do something about *this*, don't you?"

"What's wrong with my hair?" Lauren asked.

The taller, plumper black woman who was fixing a little girl's braids in the next chair looked over at Lauren. "Just everything." She smiled. "Hey, Lauren."

"Hey, Wanda," Lauren said. "You're still here, too?"

Wanda shrugged. "Where else am I gonna go?" She chuckled. "And your hair does need help. Aren't there any salons in Brooklyn?"

"I don't need a salon," Lauren said. "I've gone natural. It's supposed to look a little wild."

Wanda chuckled. "You can still do *something* with it. Damn."

Lauren laughed. "Okay, Wanda." She smiled at Patrick. "Is it okay if I get my hair done? We have plenty of time before we meet Mama for dinner."

"It's okay," Patrick said.

"These ladies aren't cheap," Lauren said.

"Just easy," Trula said. "I mean, *Wanda's* easy. I require some dinner and some dessert first."

"Hush," Wanda said.

"Oh, where are my manners?" Lauren smiled at Patrick. "Ladies, this is my husband, Patrick. Patrick, that's Wanda, who did my hair for many years, and this is Trula, who I went to school with."

"A hundred years ago," Trula said. "We *know* who he is, Lauren. He's on the TV all the time."

"I didn't think he was some random guy you picked up on the street," Wanda said.

"At least not on this street," Trula said. "He definitely isn't from around here." She squinted at him. "You're from New York, and you don't speak?"

"Hello," Patrick said.

"He speaks," Wanda said.

Oh, how I have missed this place! Lauren thought. *This place speaks "home" to my soul. It doesn't matter who you are when you walk in here because you're family—and you're also fair game for anything anyone says about you.*

Lauren squinted at Patrick. "You need a haircut."

"Send him next door to Pro Cut," Trula said. "They aren't busy right now."

"I don't want him out of my sight," Lauren said. "One of you can cut him, can't you?"

Wanda turned her chair around, and the little girl smiled at herself in the mirror. "I can cut him," Wanda said.

The little girl slid off the chair, handed Wanda a one-dollar bill, collected a backpack, and left the salon.

"Can you believe that child?" Wanda said. "Every single day she comes in and tells me, 'I need some maintenance.' She can't be older than five. I didn't know that word when I was five."

"She's smart, though," Trula said. "A dollar a day for maintenance is a lot less than redoing her whole head every two weeks."

Wanda removed the booster seat from her chair. "Have a seat, Patrick."

Patrick sat.

Wanda wrapped a cape around him and tied it loosely at his neck. "You got some thick hair. I could probably dread it."

"Over my dead body," Lauren said.

"Yeah," Wanda said, forcefully turning Patrick's head back and forth. "You really can't run your fingers through dreaded hair. And some white men look so foolish in dreads."

"I'll say," Trula said.

Wanda fluffed Patrick's hair with one hand. "You want a shave, too?"

"No," Lauren said. "I like his beard."

Wanda rolled her eyes. "At least let me even it up. It doesn't grow the same all over. That okay with you?"

"Sure," Patrick said.

Wanda shook her head. "I was *talking* to Lauren."

"Oh," Patrick said.

"No offense, Patrick," Wanda said, "but even though it's on your face, it's *her* hair. You understand?"

"I think so," Patrick said.

Wanda laughed. "It doesn't matter what you think about your hair from now on. You know that, right?"

"I'll try to remember that," Patrick said.

"Just don't take too much off," Lauren said. "It's cold in Brooklyn, and Patrick is my blanket."

"It's cold here, too," Wanda said. "Glad that snow missed us." Wanda began combing through Patrick's hair.

"Patrick," Trula said, fluttering a cape around Lauren, "you ain't the first white man Wanda's had in that chair."

"Trula, why you acting up for company?" Wanda asked.

"His name was Albert, and we weren't open at the time," Trula said. "Wanda was, though."

"I hope you disinfected your chair afterward," Lauren said.

"That was a long time ago," Wanda said. "Least I've had someone in the past ten years, Trula."

"Oh, hush," Trula said. She began gently brushing Lauren's hair. "I'm still waiting for Mr. Right."

"Ain't no Mr. Right gonna come through that door," Wanda said. "The best you'll ever get is Mr. Right Once in a While."

"I told you to hush," Trula said. She faced Lauren and put her hands on the arms of the chair. "So Chazz is gay."

Nice transition. Lauren nodded. "I'd like to think he's more bisexual than gay, but . . ."

"Bisexual, gay, it don't matter," Trula said. "The man is confused. You're lucky to be rid of him. Did he give you any signs?"

"Yes," Lauren said, "but I missed them all."

"He is an actor, after all," Trula said. She leaned close to Lauren's ear. "Your man is fine, girl."

"I know."

"Does he have a brother?" Trula whispered.

"Nope," Lauren said.

"A cousin?" Trula whispered.

"I don't know," Lauren said.

"Find out," Trula said.

"Patrick," Lauren said, "do you have any cousins?"

"Not that I know of," Patrick said.

"Figures," Trula said, frowning. She pulled the brush across the left side of Lauren's head.

"Ow," Lauren said.

"You got a nest up here, girl," Trula said. "We might find a few eggs, too. Well, would you look at that? My first cell phone. It still has that long-ass antenna, too. I wondered where I had lost it. And look—the battery's still good. Not like cell phone batteries today."

"It's not *that* bad," Lauren said.

"Yeah, it is," Trula said. She left the brush clinging to the side of Lauren's head. "It's trying to eat my brush now."

"Right," Lauren said.

"Girl, it's amazing I can get this brush through any part

of your head, all that work you've been doing," Trula said. "Work is bad for your hair."

"No it isn't," Lauren said. "And I intend to keep doing it."

"Invest in some wigs, then," Trula said. "You know, for when you go out."

"I'd rather stay in with Patrick," Lauren said.

"He must be pretty good," Trula whispered.

"He is," Lauren whispered.

"How good?" Trula whispered.

"Good good," Lauren said. "The best."

Trula sighed. "Figures." She worked the brush free. "When'd you figure out Chazz was gay?"

"Honestly, I didn't know until I caught him with his pants down," Lauren said.

"Eww," Wanda said. "Were they down around his ankles?"

Lauren nodded.

"Why don't men just take their pants all the way off?" Wanda asked. "Leaving them on makes them waddle like penguins." She smiled at Patrick. "You take them all the way off, don't you?"

Patrick nodded.

"I am so glad she found you," Wanda said.

"I'm glad, too," Patrick said.

Wanda began tidying and edging up Patrick's beard. "I don't know how you can stand all those reporters, Patrick. I know I would be cussing them out."

"I feel like doing it sometimes," Patrick said.

Trula looked toward the front window. "I don't see any reporters out there now."

"They know better than to come to Congress Heights," Wanda said. "Y'all might actually have a stress-free day, and you had to come to the hood to get it."

"It's a shame you have to go away from your home to get some peace," Trula said.

"It'll calm down now that we're married," Lauren said. "There's not much drama in marriage, at least not to them. We're officially boring now."

"Until you have a baby," Trula said. "You two are having children, right?"

"Yes," Lauren said.

"Well, when you do," Trula said, "*please* don't do any baby bump pictures. If you do, I will lose all respect for you."

"I won't," Lauren said.

"And don't wear any of those tight-ass dresses when you're pregnant," Trula said. "All them actresses trying to make pregnancy sexy. It ain't. I know."

"Yeah?" Lauren said. "You have kids?"

"Two," Trula said. "Latanna and Latasia. I have twin girls."

"Oh, show me pictures," Lauren said.

"You only gotta show her one," Wanda said.

"Hush," Trula said, turning the chair toward the mirror where a series of pictures was taped along the edges. "There they are."

"Oh, they are so precious," Lauren said. "How old are they?"

"Twelve, and driving me insane," Trula said.

Do I ask about the daddy? Lauren thought. *Better not.* "They're gorgeous."

"And that's the problem," Trula said. "These boys won't leave them alone."

Wanda faced Patrick as she evened up his sideburns. "You think the reporters will ever leave you two alone, Patrick?"

"I don't know," Patrick said. "I hope so."

Wanda turned Patrick around. "I decided not to cut much of your hair for Lauren's sake since you're her blanket and all."

"It's so *cold* in Brooklyn," Trula said. "I need my man blanket."

"Well, I do," Lauren said.

"How's it look?" Wanda asked.

"It looks good," Patrick said.

"It *is* cold in Brooklyn, Trula," Lauren said. "And windy, too."

"So you won't want your neck exposed, huh?" Trula asked.

"No," Lauren said.

"Then why do you put your hair up under your hat?" Trula asked.

"To keep things like cell phones with long-ass antennas from falling into it," Lauren said.

"Uh-huh," Trula said. She pulled up a clump of Lauren's hair. "I could do a nice sloppy updo."

"Sloppy?" Lauren said.

"It will still look a little wild," Trula said, "but you won't have any hair around your neck, though. Or I could do a Grecian updo with some braids in front. I could even let the braids fly free."

"I'd look like Medusa," Lauren said.

"Yeah," Trula said. "You'd look scarier than your mama does."

"My mama isn't that scary looking," Lauren said.

"Yeah, she is," Trula said. "But if I give you a Grecian, you'd have no hair around your neck. I *could* give you a frohawk. Tight on the sides, piled up in the middle and down the back of your head. The back of your neck will be warm at least."

"Do I have enough hair for that?" Lauren asked.

"Once I detangle it in about three days, yeah," Trula said.

Two hours later Lauren smiled at her reflection. *This will give Patrick more of my neck to kiss. Hmm. I need some long, dangling earrings now to make my neck look shorter.*

She left the chair and posed in front of Patrick, who had read nearly every issue of *Hype Hair* and *Jet* in the shop while he waited. "How do I look?"

"Great," Patrick said.

"She looks better than great, Patrick," Trula said.

"I'd rather not say exactly how she looks," Patrick said.

Lauren moved closer, rubbing her knees on his. "Tell me."

"Can I whisper it?" Patrick asked.

Lauren shook her head. "They're practically family. Go ahead."

"You look very sexy," Patrick said. He reached out and stroked the side of her head. "But . . ."

"But what?" Lauren asked.

"I don't see that lasting for very long," Patrick said.

Lauren smiled. "Why?"

Patrick sighed. "Because . . ." He sighed again. "Because I will probably ruin it when I pull on it."

"I knew he was a hair puller the second I saw his hands," Trula said. "Damn. I need me another man quick."

"You got to get you some longer hair first," Wanda said.

"That's what extensions are for, girl," Trula said.

After posing for a new picture for their wall, Lauren attempted to pay.

"No," Trula said. "It's on the house."

"At least let me tip you two," Lauren said.

"Let her tip us, Trula," Wanda said. "I've only made a whole dollar from a five-year-old today."

"Oh, all right," Trula said.

Lauren used her debit card to "tip" Trula and Wanda two hundred dollars.

"Can you afford this?" Trula whispered.

"Yes," Lauren said. "We just won't have any toilet paper for a few weeks."

Trula's eyes popped. "Really?"

"No," Lauren said. "We're fine no matter what the media says. Thank you both for the conversation."

"You're welcome," Wanda said. "Don't be a stranger, now."

"I was until I got here." *I may even come back tomorrow before we leave for some "maintenance," and it should only cost me a dollar.*

Lauren and Patrick drifted up the street to Malcolm X Avenue and Popeyes, where they found an empty booth near an entrance. Lauren checked the time on her phone.

"Mama should already be here. Are you nervous?"

"No," Patrick said. "Just hungry."

"Do you really like my hair this way?" Lauren asked.

He took her hands and squeezed them. "You could be bald and you'd still be the sexiest woman on earth."

"You didn't answer my question," Lauren said.

"I thought I did," Patrick said.

"Well, you did," Lauren said. "But . . ."

"I like it," Patrick said.

"Only like?" Lauren asked.

"Lauren, as long as the rest of you is attached to your hair," Patrick said, "I will *love* whatever you do with your hair as long as I can play with it."

"That's better," Lauren said. "Oh, there's Mama." She waved to Pamela.

Pamela shrugged and went directly to the counter.

"Mama must be hungry," Lauren said. "Come on."

As they stood in line behind Pamela, Pamela turned and stared at Lauren's hair. "Oh, *now* you get your hair done."

"You like it?" Lauren asked.

"It looks better than it did," Pamela said. "Is that all you did all day?"

"No," Lauren said. "We went to the MLK Deli and walked around, too."

"Ooh, you gave Patrick the grand tour, huh?" Pamela asked.

"I wanted to go to the Pizza Place," Lauren said.

"I miss that place, too." Pamela sighed. "It's so hard to keep a business running with all the robberies on that street. City Beats gets it the worst."

After they ordered spicy Bonafide Chicken combos with red beans and rice, they moved to a booth and sat.

"You two and that wedding of yours are all over the news," Pamela said. "People told me there's something on every channel, even BET."

"All that will die down," Lauren said. "You'll see."

"I hope it doesn't," Pamela said. "This is the first good news people have had to watch on TV in a long time. Your wedding is a story people can smile about."

"It's good to be good news, isn't it, Patrick?" Lauren asked.

Patrick nodded, chowing down on a drumstick.

"Slow down now," Pamela said. "Popeyes is good, but it ain't that good."

Patrick chewed more slowly.

"You two obviously married for love and for love alone," Pamela said. "That's rare. You're giving people hope that maybe they can find true love, too. That's good news."

"Well, Mama," Lauren said, "there's an attraction, too."

"You fell in love *before* you saw each other, right?" Pamela asked.

"Well, I saw him before I met him, because he sent me a picture," Lauren said. "He was wearing coveralls. And then we used Skype, and—"

"Spare me the details," Pamela interrupted. "I'm just saying that you fell in love with him before you *really* met him, and I'm saying that's a good thing."

"And I'm saying that there's an attraction, too," Lauren said.

Pamela stared at Lauren. "Why can't you just agree with me? We're saying the same thing."

"It's more fun to disagree," Lauren said.

Pamela nodded at Patrick. "Is he always this quiet?"

"No," Lauren said. "He's just hungry."

"Is Congress Heights any different than Brooklyn?" Pamela asked.

"Not really," Patrick said, wiping his lips with a napkin. "It's a little less crowded, I guess."

Pamela looked around the dining room. "You don't look uncomfortable, you being the only white man in here."

"I hadn't noticed," Patrick said.

"Either you're a liar or you're too busy getting your grub on," Pamela said.

"He doesn't lie, Mama," Lauren said.

"Or you're unaware of your surroundings," Pamela said.

"Or his surroundings don't matter to him," Lauren said.

"Let him answer, girl," Pamela said. "Does being the only white man in here matter to you, Patrick?"

"No," Patrick said.

Pamela smiled. "I like how you try to set those reporters straight."

"It doesn't do much good," Patrick said.

"Well, keep it up," Pamela said. "One day they might actually listen to you. When do you two have to be back?"

"Tomorrow," Patrick said.

"Some honeymoon." Pamela said. "But it's about the length of mine. Lauren's father was a hardworking man." She reached out and grabbed Lauren's wrist, turning her hand over. "They're getting rougher."

"I use lotion," Lauren said.

"It means you're working hard," Pamela said. "It does the soul good to work hard. That other 'job' of hers wasn't work, Patrick."

"It most certainly was," Lauren said.

"Looking pretty and speaking lines someone else wrote, not thinking for yourself—that's not work," Pamela said. "Solving problems, getting dirty, going home with a backache that requires a massage—*that's* work. I'm so glad you're making my daughter respectable for a change, Patrick. I'm proud of her. I can talk to folks about her job now."

"You weren't proud of me before?" Lauren asked.

"Your first movie, yes," Pamela said. "Your character had morals. I had no trouble facing folks. That next one, though . . . That girl was a mess. She was a hoochie."

"She was not!" Lauren shouted.

"Hoochie, through and through," Pamela said. "And don't you be showing your tail in here."

"Well, don't be calling me a hoochie then," Lauren said.

Pamela rolled her eyes. "I gotta go. I need my rest." She collected her plate and stood.

"Wait a minute, Mama," Lauren said. "You can't start an argument and leave."

"Sure I can," Pamela said. "I'm done eating. I have to work in the morning, and you have to catch the train, so let's go."

"But I'm not through arguing with you," Lauren said.

"We can continue this on the way home," Pamela said.

The second the Popeyes door closed behind them, Lauren asked, "So after *Feel the Love,* you weren't proud of me at all?"

"No," Pamela said.

"But it was what I was paid to do," Lauren said.

"You could have turned it down," Pamela said.

"I needed to get paid, Mama," Lauren said. "I had bills."

"I'm sure something else would have opened up, something wholesome," Pamela said. "You had talent."

"I *have* talent," Lauren said.

"My point is this," Pamela said. "Once you did that movie, the rest of your roles were all hoochies, too."

"They weren't all hoochies," Lauren said. "Not all the time."

"Yeah, they were," Pamela said. "You were snapping your fingers, throwing out your hips, whining, sucking your teeth, showing your cleavage, and using improper English all the time. You were a straight hoochie."

"That didn't make *me* a hoochie," Lauren said.

"You could have fooled me," Pamela said. "But think about it. Those hoochie roles helped you hook up with Chazz. He wasn't interested in you right after *Feel the Love,* was he? No. He only wanted you after you played all those hoochies. That one movie ruined your life, and you didn't even know it."

They had reached the house. Pamela opened the gate, walked up the walkway and the stairs, and unlocked the front door.

"Mama," Lauren said, following Pamela inside, "how would you know? You told me you didn't watch any of my movies after *I Got This* came out."

Pamela shut the door and pointed to the sofa in front of the TV. "Take a load off, Patrick," she said. "This might take a minute."

Patrick sat on the sofa, and Pamela slid in beside him.

"I watched every last one of your movies, Lauren," Pamela said.

Lauren paced behind the sofa. "You did? I didn't think . . ." *She cared.*

"What? That I wouldn't watch your movies? It was the only time I got to see you, Lauren." She nudged Patrick's leg with hers. "She hardly ever called me, Patrick. Can you believe that? Her own mama. She went Hollywood on me, and she couldn't even lift a phone."

"I *did* call you," Lauren said. "*All* the time. But you wouldn't speak to me."

Pamela sighed. "What have I always told you?"

"You've *always* told me a *lot* of things," Lauren said.

"Hear that attitude, Patrick?" Pamela asked. "Get used to it. It's in her DNA. From her daddy's side, not mine."

"I'm not getting an attitude," Lauren said, "and when I do, it's all because of you, not Daddy."

"What I told you was if you can't say something nice, don't say anything at all," Pamela said. "You called, I had nothing nice to say, so I stayed silent."

"So . . . you've started talking to me because . . ." *She has something nice to say!* "You have something nice to say."

"Right," Pamela said. "You're finally settling down and being the daughter your daddy and I raised. You found a real man, and you now have a real job." She turned to Patrick. "Did y'all have sex on your first date in St. Louis?"

"Mama!" Lauren shouted.

"I'm not asking you," Pamela said. "I'm asking Patrick. Well, did you?"

Patrick looked at the floor. "Yes, ma'am, we did."

Pamela laughed. "He *is* honest. Too honest. Patrick,

you're supposed to lie when someone's mama asks you that question."

"You already knew we did," Patrick said.

"I figured you did," Pamela said. "When are you having babies?"

"Soon," Lauren said.

"I'm asking *him,*" Pamela said. "He has to pay for them."

"I have plenty of money, Mama," Lauren said.

"Ignore her, Patrick," Pamela said. "When?"

"Soon," Patrick said.

"Can you afford them *and* her?" Pamela asked.

Patrick looked briefly at Lauren. "Yes and no. I am getting a ten percent raise."

"What do you mean by 'Yes and no,' Patrick?" Lauren asked.

"I think I can afford the children," Patrick said.

"Oh, that's not fair," Lauren said. "I'm not that high maintenance."

"Yes, you are," Pamela said. "So, Patrick, is work steady?"

"Yes," Patrick said. "Those buildings and their tenants need constant attention."

"That's good." Pamela yawned. "I gotta be up early. When's your train?"

"Seven," Patrick said.

"I'll be gone before you get up," Pamela said. "Lock up, okay? I don't have much, but it's paid for." She stood, arched her back, and yawned again. "Patrick, you snore like a freight train."

"Oh, I'm sorry," Patrick said.

"Don't be sorry," Pamela said. "It reminded me of Lauren's daddy. I slept like a baby for almost two hours. Keep it up." She faced Lauren. "You still purr like a kitten."

She was listening, Lauren thought. *My mama listened to me sleep.*

"I have a wedding gift for you two," Pamela said, "but it's not quite ready. I hope you understand. You didn't give me any time to prepare it, you know."

"I know," Lauren said. "Mama, thanks for . . . everything."

"I'll accept that," Pamela said. "And no note passing later tonight, okay?"

"Okay," Lauren said.

Pamela approached Lauren, gave her a quick hug, and went down the hallway.

"So, what do you think of my mama?" Lauren asked.

"She's probably listening," Patrick whispered.

"You listening, Mama?" Lauren asked.

"Yes," Pamela said. "Speak up, Patrick."

"Go ahead," Lauren said.

"Your mama is the nicest person I have ever met and will probably ever meet in my entire life," Patrick said. "I can see where you got your beauty, charm, and grace."

"Hear that, Mama?" Lauren said.

"Yes, and it is the truth," Pamela said. "Good night."

Lauren sat in Patrick's lap. "I think she likes you."

"I'm glad she does," Patrick whispered.

Pamela returned. "What's that supposed to mean, Patrick?"

"I'd never want to be on your bad side, Pamela," Patrick said.

"And that is also the truth," Pamela said. "Good night." She disappeared down the hallway.

"Good night, Mama," Lauren said. She kissed Patrick's forehead. "You done good, Mr. Esposito."

"I did?" Patrick said. "I didn't say much."

"That's what you done good," Lauren said. "My daddy didn't ever say much around Mama either."

Patrick pulled her closer. "So I remind you of your daddy?"

"A little," Lauren said. "You have the same quiet strength about you."

"I'm not always quiet," Patrick said.

"I know," Lauren said. She pulled up her shirt. "I need your strength now. Massage my back, please."

Patrick's hot hands kneaded her lower back. "This might make you shout."

Lauren nodded. "I want to. You know I do."

Patrick kept massaging. "You'll just have to show some restraint."

"That feels so good," Lauren said. She rested her head on his shoulder. "Do you think you could make love to me silently?"

"Nope," Patrick said. "Never."

"I hope I have another nasty dream tonight then," Lauren said.

"You do?" Patrick said. "Why?"

"Because I am so horny right now," Lauren said.

"What do you want to dream about?" Patrick whispered.

"Please don't get me started," Lauren whispered. "I won't be able to sleep."

"Tell me," Patrick whispered.

"I'm already getting wet, Patrick," Lauren whispered. "I want to grind on you so badly."

"Go ahead," Patrick whispered. "Grind away."

She looked into his eyes. "You want me to dry hump you on my mama's couch?"

"It will be another first for me," Patrick whispered. "Tell me what you want to dream about."

Lauren moved until she was straddling one of Patrick's legs and started to grind. "You're . . . licking me, and your tongue is so hot, while your fingers are . . ." She leaned back and closed her eyes. "They're inside me, and . . . oh, damn." She stopped grinding, but her body continued to shake. "What is *wrong* with me?"

"You're coming?" Patrick whispered.

"Yes," Lauren said. "And all I did was hump your leg." She felt his crotch. "Are you close?"

He nodded.

She gripped his penis through his jeans. "I want this so bad."

"I'm glad," Patrick whispered. "Finish your dream."

She squeezed and rubbed his crotch. "And then you put this deep inside me, and it fills me completely, and I put my feet on your shoulders. . . ."

Patrick's body jerked. "Wow," he whispered.

"Wow?" Lauren said. She smiled. "Wow? You come while sitting on my mama's couch, and all you can say is, 'Wow'?"

"We need to get back to Brooklyn," Patrick said.

"Yes," Lauren said. "We do, but it's such a long train ride. Why don't we see if we can get a room in the sleeper car?"

"Yes," Patrick said. "Let's get one of those, but we're not going to sleep at all."

Lauren shook her head. "Nope." She smiled. "I hope it has a big window."

"So do I," Patrick said.

"And then people in three states can see us making love at a hundred miles per hour," Lauren whispered.

"I want to get on that train right now," Patrick whispered.

"So do I," Lauren whispered. She stared into his eyes. "I love that you love making love to me."

"And I love that *you* love that *I* love making love to you," Patrick said.

Lauren blinked. "You should write romantic comedies with lines like those."

"Are you having a good honeymoon, Mrs. Esposito?" Patrick asked.

Lauren curled up in his arms. "I am, Mr. Esposito. And this was only the first day. I want a lifetime honeymoon."

"So do I."

60

After a claustrophobic lovemaking marathon on Amtrak and a long shower and nap when they returned to the apartment, Lauren and Patrick dressed in jeans, sweatshirts, boots, and heavy coats for the walk to St. Agnes.

As they slipped and slid on barely shoveled sidewalks, Patrick said, "We're getting married for real today." *Sort of. All Father Giovanni has to do is sign the marriage certificate.*

"Are you nervous?" Lauren asked.

"No," Patrick said, squeezing her hand. "I'm just sad we won't have an audience. I know my mama will be there in spirit, though. She loved St. Agnes."

They walked into St. Agnes and across tile floors under simple chandeliers to the short railing in front. A colorful painting of Christ on the back wall was illuminated by dozens of flickering candles throughout the sanctuary.

"It's beautiful," Lauren whispered. She looked around. "It's not what I expected."

"What did you expect?" Patrick asked.

"I don't know," Lauren said. "More ornamentation, I guess."

"I like this church because it's simple," Patrick said. He nodded at the wooden benches behind them. "Those benches are not very comfortable, but then again, you're not supposed to be comfortable in the presence of God."

"Patrick Esposito!"

Patrick turned and saw Father Giovanni coming toward them from the back of the church. Except for the white clerical collar peeking out of a St. John's University sweatshirt, there was nothing about him to suggest he was a priest.

"That's him?" Lauren whispered.

"That's Father Giovanni," Patrick whispered.

"He's wearing blue jeans," Lauren whispered.

"He's a workingman, too," Patrick said, and he turned Lauren to greet Father Giovanni.

Father Giovanni clasped Lauren's free hand in both of his. "This must be the bride," he said. "Welcome, Lauren." He then clasped Patrick's hand. "Welcome back, Patrick."

Patrick pulled out the marriage certificate. "We need you to sign this so we can make our marriage official."

Father Giovanni took the certificate and smiled. "I saw your wedding. Snow instead of rice or birdseed. A much easier cleanup. I suppose it's a little too late to give you my 'Are you sure you want to get married?' speech."

Patrick nodded. "It is."

"You obviously love each other," Father Giovanni said. "Anyone watching you two on television would know that you two are deeply in love."

"We are," Lauren said.

Father Giovanni stared at the certificate. "I could sign this form and send you on your way, but Patrick's mama would torment me for eternity if I didn't do this properly.

Let's do this right." He guided them to a white table crowded with golden candlesticks and an oversize Bible under the painting of Christ.

"Turn and face each other," Father Giovanni said.

Patrick gripped Lauren's hands. "Are you ready?"

Lauren nodded. "I've been ready."

"Patrick and Lauren," Father Giovanni said, "have you come here freely and without reservation to give yourselves to each other in marriage?"

"Yes," Patrick said.

"Yes," Lauren said.

"Will you honor each other as man and wife for the rest of your lives?" Father Giovanni asked.

"Yes," Patrick said.

"Oh yes," Lauren said.

"Will you accept children lovingly from God and bring them up according to the law of Christ and His church?" Father Giovanni asked.

"Yes," Patrick said.

"He said children," Lauren said, smiling. "Yes."

"Patrick, do you take Lauren to be your wife? Do you promise to be true to her in good times and in bad, in sickness and in health, to love her and honor her all the days of your life?"

"I do," Patrick said.

"Lauren, do you take Patrick to be your husband—"

"Yes," Lauren said.

"Let me finish, Lauren," Father Giovanni said.

"She's a little impatient, Father," Patrick said.

"I can see that." He laughed. "Lauren, do you promise to be true to him in good times and in bad, in sickness and in health, to love him and honor him all the days of your life?"

"I do." Tears trickled out of her eyes. "I really, really do."

"What God has joined, men must not divide," Father Giovanni said. "And neither should reporters, photographers, exes, and *Entertainment Tonight*. You're married."

"That's it?" Lauren asked.

"I could give you two a sermon," Father Giovanni said. "A nice long one. Something from the Old Testament."

Lauren shook her head. "No, that's okay. Kiss me quick, Patrick."

Patrick kissed her quickly.

Father Giovanni signed the form. "And now it's official. I hope to see you two in mass soon."

"We'll be there as often as we can," Patrick said. "Thank you."

"Wait," Lauren said. "Aren't you supposed to announce who we are now?"

"Oh, sure," Father Giovanni said. "I now present to you Mr. and Mrs. Patrick and Lauren Esposito."

The trio looked into the empty sanctuary.

"I could hum a recessional while you leave," Father Giovanni said.

"That's okay," Lauren said.

"It would be no trouble," Father Giovanni said.

"Okay," Lauren said. "You can hum something."

"Beethoven's 'Ode to Joy' is a favorite recessional of mine," Father Giovanni said. "Unless you'd like some Stevie Wonder. I will, of course, have to *sing* that one."

"Which one?" Lauren asked.

Father Giovanni cleared his throat, smiled, and sang, "Ooh, baby, here I am, signed, sealed, delivered, I'm yours."

Lauren laughed. "That's perfect! Keep singing."

While Father Giovanni of St. Agnes belted out "Signed, Sealed, Delivered I'm Yours" before an empty sanctuary, Patrick lit a candle for his mother, and Lauren lit a candle for her father.

They danced through the snow most of the way home, and they danced together daily and nightly through mid-December, because the weather, the sewer drains, the media, and the pigeons cooperated.

They also "dated" each other all over Brooklyn, ate well, and ignored any paparazzi as best they could. They went to Lucali on Henry Street in Carroll Gardens for calzone. They ate heaping plates of meatballs, artichokes, and smoked pancetta at Barboncino in Crown Heights. They watched Johnny Depp in *Black Mass* at Cobble Hill Cinemas on Court Street. They drifted hand in hand through Clover's Fine Art Gallery and Russell Mehlman Art on Atlantic Avenue and sat in the cheap seats for a Net-Knicks game at Barclays Center. They took photos with and signed autographs for real people, and their public displays of affection and nearly ever kiss got heavy play online and in the *Post*.

Over the course of a few weeks, Lauren transformed the apartment into an inviting space full of light. They found several industrial floor lamps and a two-headed table lamp at cityFoundry on Atlantic. Patrick built a custom shelving unit for the TV and two side tables, which flanked the couch. After adding two tan slipper chairs, they found moving through the apartment to be a "sideways only" proposition. Lauren hung multicolored paintings on handmade paper by Brooklyn artist Karin Batten and a framed collage called *New Growth* by Rhia Hurt. A trip to GRDN on Hoyt produced towering snake plants and flowing golden pothos vines resting in stone pots under a Rex Water Heater clock.

"Now all we need is a new tub," Lauren said as they sat on the couch in the main room.

"I'm beginning to like that shower," Patrick said. "I like the coziness."

"So do I," Lauren said, digging her toes into the blanket.

"Oh, man!" she cried. "There's something that I keep forgetting to do!"

"What?" Patrick asked.

"Promise you won't be mad," Lauren said.

"I won't be mad," Patrick said.

"Well, I'm living here, but I still have an apartment in LA," Lauren said. "My lease is up at the end of the month, and the end of the month is almost here. I need to get out of that lease now." She hit a series of buttons on her phone and set it on one of the side tables.

"Kingdom West Property Management," a man said. "This is Ricardo Campagna. How may I help you?"

"This is Lauren Esposito, and I am vacating my lease at the end of this month," Lauren said.

"Lauren . . . oh!" Ricardo shouted. "Lauren Short! You will not be back?"

"No," Lauren said. "I'm sure you know that I live in Brooklyn now, so I'd like you to start showing my apartment."

"I already have been," Ricardo said.

He's probably giving paid tours, Patrick thought.

"Oh, that's good," Lauren said. "You can keep anything in the apartment. I won't need any of it."

"You're kidding," Ricardo said.

"I'm not kidding," Lauren said.

"Even the dresses?" Ricardo asked.

"Even the dresses," Lauren said. "I don't wear dresses like those anymore."

Ricardo's voice became a whisper. "May I have them?"

Lauren laughed. "Are you a size eight?"

"Almost," Ricardo said.

Patrick stifled a laugh. *I thought I had heard everything. Wow.*

"You can have them, Ricardo," Lauren said. "I only wore them once or twice."

"I will cherish them forever," Ricardo gushed. "Thank you so much."

"Have you done anything with my car?" Lauren asked.

"I had to have it taken away," Ricardo said. "The seagulls were not kind. It cleaned up very nicely, though."

"You washed it," Lauren said.

"Oh yes," Ricardo said. "It looks brand new now."

"But if you took it away . . ."

"Oh, I can see why you would be confused," Ricardo said. "I found your keys and took it away to wash it. It is such a lovely shade of green. It matches my eyes."

Lauren's mouth widened. "Ricardo, have you been driving my car?"

"Only for a few weeks," Ricardo said. "It gets terrible gas mileage, but I look very good in it."

He's been driving her car! Now, I have heard everything.

"Ricardo," Lauren said, "do you want the car, too?"

"You would give me your dresses *and* your car?" Ricardo cooed. "Oh, that would be wonderful!"

Lauren rolled her eyes. "I think the title—"

"I am looking at the title now," Ricardo interrupted. "You have to sign it."

Patrick laughed loudly, mouthing, "Wow!"

"Is there someone else there?" Ricardo asked. "Is that Patrick?"

"Yes," Lauren said.

"Hello, Patrick," Ricardo said.

"Hey," Patrick said. *I don't want to talk to this guy!*

"Ricardo," Lauren said, "please send the title to me, and I'll sign it over to you." She gave him the address.

"This is like a dream come true," Ricardo said. "Thank you, thank you, thank you!"

"And you can mail my damage deposit to me with the title," Lauren said.

"Oh, I can't do that," Ricardo said.

"Why not?" Lauren asked.

"You left your air-conditioning unit on, and it leaked all over the carpet," Ricardo said.

"There is no carpet under that air conditioner," Lauren said. "I only had carpet in my bedroom."

"It was a very bad leak," Ricardo said. "And the cleaning cost of the car was substantial as well."

"The damage deposit was five hundred bucks," Lauren said. "It cost that much to clean my car and replace a carpet?"

"I think so," Ricardo said.

"But I am *giving* you my dresses and my car," Lauren said.

"And I shall cherish them forever," Ricardo said. "I will mail the title to you today."

Lauren looked at the ceiling. "Fine, Ricardo. I'll look for it in the mail."

"Good-bye, Lauren," Ricardo said, and then he hung up.

Lauren clicked off her phone. "That was very strange."

Patrick shook his head. "I now have a better definition of the word *gall*. Wow. I'll bet there's nothing wrong with the carpet."

"Probably, but it doesn't matter anymore," Lauren said. "I have everything I need right here."

"Are you sure about all this?" Patrick asked. "Your car? Your dresses?"

"They're only clothes," Lauren said. "And I'll save a mint on car insurance."

"I'm just wondering what you'll wear here," Patrick said.

"What I've been wearing," Lauren said. "Jeans and a hoodie."

"But . . ." Patrick sighed. "I don't know. I thought you'd want something nicer to wear when we go out."

"We *could* do a little shopping," Lauren said. "For you, too." She smiled. "I think we need to play a little dress up." She nodded. "You and I are going to make our own style."

61

A week before Christmas, they shopped, and Lauren's MasterCard sizzled up and down Atlantic Avenue and Smith Street.

They bought stylish yet understated outfits at the Brooklyn Circus, Steven Alan, Brooklyn Industries, Free People, Lucky Brand, Article&, Epaulet, and LF Stores. They also bought new boots at DSW.

Patrick wished he had several more pairs of arms for all the bags.

At the Melting Pot, the owner looked at the mounds of clothes on the checkout counter. "Can we use you two in our advertising?" the owner asked. "We can pay you, say, five hundred. Each."

Lauren looked at Patrick. "What do you think?"

Patrick had lost track of the total bill four stores ago. "What do *you* think?"

"I'd rather have the clothes," Lauren said.

The owner blinked. "You don't want to be paid?"

"These clothes will pay me," Lauren said. "And I promise to wear them often, when I'm not working, of course."

"Um, sure," the owner said. "I'll draw up a contract."

Lauren shook her head. "There's no need for a contract. If you give me these wonderful clothes, I will wear them whether I'm in an advertisement or not."

"I'll get my camera, then," the owner said, and she disappeared into the back of the store.

Lauren smiled at Patrick. "Do you have time for a photo shoot?"

"I guess," Patrick said.

"I'm sensing resistance," Lauren said.

"I'm no model," Patrick said.

"Sure you are," Lauren said.

"What do I do?" Patrick asked.

"Not much," Lauren said. "The focus, I'm sure, will be on me, of course. You just stand near me, looking sexy."

Patrick laughed. "I can try to do that."

Within days, pictures of the two of them posing in various outfits out on Atlantic Avenue appeared in shop windows and on signs, walls, and telephone poles throughout Boerum Hill and beyond.

"I hope this mean we're done shopping for Christmas," Patrick said. "I was going to get you some clothes anyway."

"You were?" Lauren asked. "Really?"

"No, not really," Patrick said. "I was going to get you some gift certificates. You wouldn't want me picking out your clothes. So, are we done shopping for Christmas?"

"I'm done shopping," Lauren said. "They should be arriving any day now."

"They?" Patrick asked.

"Your presents," Lauren said. "While you've been sleeping, I've been shopping on the Internet."

Patrick blinked. "I'm way behind, then."

"Yes, you are," Lauren said.

"How many presents did you get me?" Patrick asked.

"Only three," Lauren said.

Patrick smiled. "Then I will get you three."

Because he had no credit card, Patrick couldn't use the Internet to shop, and so he sneaked away to local shops and stores while Lauren napped. Hiding Lauren's gifts, however, was next to impossible. There was simply no room anywhere in the apartment since the closet was filled to bursting with their new clothes and Lauren's gifts to him filled most of the space under the bed.

He wrapped them as soon as he entered the apartment and stored them in the unused dishwasher.

I have finally found a use for the dishwasher.

On December 23, Patrick rearranged the main room so that it could accommodate a seven-foot spruce and wedged the tree into a corner vacated by one of the plants. He and Lauren decorated it with Styrofoam peanuts from the boxes containing her gifts to him.

The two of them squinted at the tree.

"Next year," Lauren said, "we'll use real ornaments."

"Agreed," Patrick said.

On Christmas Eve a massive box arrived from Pamela. Inside was a pink tool bag, LJE stitched on the side, filled with an assortment of tools.

"My daddy's tools," Lauren said. "This is so cool." She attempted to lift the bag out of the box, but she could barely budge it. "I hope I won't need everything in here."

Patrick picked through the tools and removed a circular saw, two orbital sanders, ten pounds of clamps, and a twenty-eight-piece socket and wrench set. "Now try."

Lauren lifted the bag with ease. "Now we're bookends."

I have never seen a pink tool bag, Patrick thought. *It won't be pink for long.*

On Christmas morning, while a ham and candied yams

were cooking in the oven and a pot of green beans was simmering on the stove, Patrick presented Lauren with an antique Art Deco platinum necklace, bracelet, and earrings, all of which matched her ring somewhat.

"You're kitting me out," Lauren said. "These are great. Did you get these at Gem?"

Patrick nodded.

"Okay, it's your turn," Lauren said.

"I'm not done." He handed her another present.

"But you just gave me three things," Lauren said.

"I gave you jewelry," Patrick said. "That's *one* thing."

Lauren smiled. "I like how you think." She opened the second present and found purple, formfitting two-piece long johns.

"Why purple?" Lauren asked.

"You're royalty," Patrick said.

Lauren kissed him. "They're kind of kinky. Do they glow in the dark?"

"We'll have to find out." Patrick handed her a small, thin present. "This one was the hardest to find."

She opened the present and found a single wooden clothespin, a series of musical notes burned into the wood. She held it up. "I've never gotten a clothespin before."

"It's for when the smell gets too bad for you," Patrick said. "And those notes are the first few notes of our wedding song."

"It's certainly one of a kind," Lauren said. "Thank you. I can hum the song while I try not to breathe."

Patrick sighed. "I was going to get you some steel-toed boots, but they're not very romantic, and we already bought some new ones. I wish I could have gotten you more."

"You picked out every present especially for me," Lauren said. "These are more than enough." She clipped the clothespin to her nose. "You know, this might actually work. I can't smell the tree." She clipped the clothespin to her shirt. "And now it's your turn."

He first opened a Blu-ray copy of *I Got This*.

"It just came out," Lauren said.

"May I watch it now?" Patrick asked.

"Why watch it when you can see the real almost breast?" Lauren asked. "We'll look at it later."

A dozen pairs of boxer briefs in a rainbow of colors spilled out of the next wrapped box. "Why so many?" he asked.

"I plan to borrow them often," Lauren said. "Open your last one."

Patrick opened a small box and found a platinum cross on a chain. "What did this cost?"

"I will never tell you," Lauren said. "But you're worth every single penny. Put it on."

He fastened the chain around his neck. "This is . . . this is really nice."

"I expect it to be bouncing off my booty in a few minutes, man," Lauren said.

Patrick's phone rang. *It never fails,* he thought.

Lauren sighed. "I'll get my tool bag ready."

Patrick flipped open his phone. "This is Patrick."

"Merry Christmas, Patrick," Mrs. Moczydlowska said.

"Is everything all right, Mrs. Moczydlowska?" Patrick asked.

"I am fine," Mrs. Moczydlowska said. "The apartment is fine. I just call to wish you and Lauren a Merry Christmas."

Patrick waved his free hand at Lauren. "Well, Merry Christmas to you, too, Mrs. Moczydlowska. We'll see you later this week, okay?"

"Okay," she said. "Give my best to Lauren."

"I will. Bye." He snapped his phone closed. "No emergency. She just wanted to wish us a Merry Christmas."

"That's so nice," Lauren said. She unclipped the clothespin from her shirt, lifted her shirt, and maneuvered it to her right breast. When she let the clothespin clamp down on her nipple, her eyes widened and her mouth opened. "Ow." She brought the clothespin out from under her shirt. "This wasn't made for nipples. I like your fingers better."

Someone knocked on the door.

"Are we expecting someone?" Lauren asked.

Patrick shook his head. *This is by far the busiest Christmas I have ever had.*

"It might be a reporter," Lauren said.

"I'll get rid of whoever it is," Patrick said.

"I'll be waiting in the bedroom," Lauren said. "With the clothespin attached somewhere."

Patrick went to the door and looked through the peephole at a tall, broad-shouldered man with silvery hair, brown eyes, and some major five o'clock shadow on his face. He wore a long black coat, charcoal dress pants, and shiny black wing tips. *He doesn't look like a reporter, and he doesn't look like a door-to-door salesman either.*

Patrick left the chain on the door and opened it a few inches. "What can I do for you?"

The man smiled. "Merry Christmas."

And the man is definitely Italian. "Merry Christmas," Patrick said.

"You are Patrick Alan Esposito, yes?" the man asked.

And he's definitely from Brooklyn. "Yes."

The man patted his chest. "I am Patrizio Alanzo Biancardi."

"From Biancardi's meats?" Patrick asked.

"Yes," Mr. Biancardi said. "How did you know?"

Geez, he is *a salesman.* "Lucky guess."

The man moved closer to the door. "You do not recognize me."

"No, I don't," Patrick said. "Should I?"

"It is like looking into a mirror, Patrizio." He stepped back from the door. "Can you see me better now?"

Patrick's hands lost feeling. *Is this . . .* "My name is Patrick."

"I blame Caterina for that," Mr. Biancardi said. "You were supposed to be Patrizio, but Patrick is just as good. May I come in?"

And he knows my mama's real name. She went through life as Cathy to everyone but me. "Who are you again?"

"I am Patrizio Alanzo Biancardi," Mr. Biancardi said. "I came today because I cannot think of a better time to visit with my son than on Christmas. You are taller in person, by the way. The television makes you look shorter."

Patrick closed the door, undid the chain, and fully opened the door. "What's going on?"

Mr. Biancardi sighed. "You were named after me. I am Patrizio Alanzo. You are Patrick Alan."

"I was named after my *Irish* father," Patrick said.

Mr. Biancardi laughed. "Caterina told you that? You are no more Irish than I will ever be. You are full-blooded Sicilian. My family is from Palermo. Your mama's family is from Carini. She told you this, yes?"

She did. "Yes. I mean, about Carini. She didn't mention Palermo—or you."

"You still do not believe me." He nodded. "It is quite a story. I would have trouble believing it, too. But I can prove it all to you."

"How?" Patrick asked.

"Your mama's name was Caterina Donatella Esposito," Mr. Biancardi said. "She was five-foot-two, with long black hair and the darkest brown eyes. They were almost black they were so brown. One of her eyebrows was bushier than the other one. It always made her look evil, but she wasn't evil at all."

It did. "All this proves is that you knew her."

"I knew her very well," Mr. Biancardi said. "Caterina thought Frankie Valli was a better singer than Sinatra was. I did my best to change her mind, but she would not change her mind. 'My Eyes Adored You' was her favorite song. Caterina smoked Winston Lights and drank Gordon's gin exclusively. If there was no Gordon's, she only drank water. Her *penne all'arrabbiata* was spicy enough to cure colds in anyone within ten blocks. She used too many red chili peppers and too much garlic."

That's . . . that's all true.

"I met your mama at Farrell's, near Prospect Park, in nineteen seventy-three," Mr. Biancardi said.

"My mama never went to Farrell's," Patrick said.

"She did before you were born," Mr. Biancardi said. "Not many women did back then. It was not the nicest bar for women, but your mama was tough. That is what I loved about her. The men would throw out the lines, and your mama would throw them right back. Most men stopped throwing lines. I took one look at her in all those mirrors they have at Farrell's, and I said to myself, 'She is the one for me.' "

"Patrick," Lauren called from the bedroom, "who is it?"

Mr. Biancardi smiled. "Ah, your new wife. She is cooking ham and . . . yams, I think. It smells so good."

"It's a Mr. Biancardi," Patrick called out.

"Who?" Lauren said.

"I can explain everything," Mr. Biancardi said. "Please give me the chance."

Lauren came and stood beside Patrick. "Hello."

"Merry Christmas," Mr. Biancardi said. "May I call you Lauren?"

"Yes," Lauren said. "Merry Christmas to you, too."

Mr. Biancardi smiled broadly. "I am Patrizio Alanzo Biancardi. I am Patrick's papa."

Lauren grabbed Patrick's arm. "Really?"

"I'm not so sure," Patrick said. "He says he is."

"Well, let's find out for sure." Lauren smiled. "Please come in."

"Thank you." Mr. Biancardi moved past Patrick and into the apartment. "You are so much more beautiful in person, Lauren."

Lauren pushed a few pieces of wrapping paper off the couch and sat. "Thank you. Won't you sit down, Mr. Biancardi?"

Mr. Biancardi sat. "This is nice. So many plants. So much light. So much color." He chuckled at the tree. "An interesting tree."

Patrick shut the door, shoved his hands into his pockets, and moved slowly toward the couch.

"How did you find us?" Lauren asked.

"Oh, it was easy," Mr. Biancardi said. "I look at you two on the television, and I recognize State Street. State Street hasn't changed in fifty years. I only have to ask across the street at the store for which apartment, and here I am."

"Forty years late," Patrick said.

"Patrick, please," Lauren said.

"It is okay, Lauren," Mr. Biancardi said. "I have a lot of explaining to do. Believe me, Patrizio, I would have married your mama and been there to raise you as your papa, but there were some . . . complications. About the time you were born, I was indisposed at a facility of the state."

My papa is a felon. Great. Just great. "You were in prison."

"I prefer to think of it as an extended vacation away from the world, but yes, I was in prison," Mr. Biancardi said. "But now I am new to the world again. I came here today to see my son and my new daughter-in-law in the hopes that I will one day be able to hold my *nipoti,* my grandchildren."

Patrick turned and rested his back on the wall. "After forty years you just . . . show up. All this time, and today of all days you show up. No cards, no phone calls, nothing for forty years."

"Patrizio, some things happened long ago that kept me away," Mr. Biancardi said.

"My name is Patrick," Patrick said.

"I told her not to name you after me, and she listened to me," Mr. Biancardi said. "She did not always listen to me. She was very stubborn, his mama."

"Patrick takes after her," Lauren said. "Right now, as a matter of fact. Come sit down, Patrick."

Patrick remained still. "Why are you here now?"

"I do not expect you to accept me as anything but a man who has inconvenienced you on Christmas," Mr. Biancardi said. "But I *am* your papa. That is the truth. You have done very well without me. You seem happy, and that makes me happy. There is so much color and light in here, Lauren. It is beautiful."

"You said things kept you away," Patrick said. "What things?"

Mr. Biancardi looked at his hands. "I killed a man."

Patrick closed his eyes. *And not just any felon. A murderer. No wonder Mama never spoke of him.*

"I admitted my guilt, so there was no trial," Mr. Biancardi said. "I have spent most of my life away from the world."

"A convicted murderer," Patrick said. *Some merry Christmas this is.*

"Patrizio, I killed a man who was a threat to your mother and to you," Mr. Biancardi said. "He was also a problem for some other people, whom I wish to remain nameless. For doing this thing, you and your mama were left alone and compensated."

Patrick pushed off the wall. "How were we compensated?"

"Your mama never had to work, did she?" Mr. Biancardi asked.

"She received welfare checks," Patrick said.

"And some other checks *for* your welfare," Mr. Biancardi said. "She was taken care of."

"In the Gowanus Houses," Patrick said. "Oh, we were certainly taken care of, all right."

"They were a safe place for you and her," Mr. Biancardi said. "A place to disappear. The man I killed was well connected. The seventies were a difficult time in New York. 'Don Carlo' Gambino, 'Big Paul' Castellano, John Gotti, 'Tony Ducks' Corallo. You have heard of them? It was a time of transition."

Patrick blinked. "You killed a *made* man."

Mr. Biancardi nodded. "And in doing so, I insured that you would be born."

Patrick moved closer to the couch. "How was this guy a threat to my mama?"

"He thought she was pregnant with his child," Mr. Biancardi said. "He was married. She was not from the right family. He was from Catania, and she was from Carini." He shook his head. "It mattered then. Not so much now. The world has changed."

"How do you know that the man you killed wasn't my father?" Patrick asked.

"Your mama and I did the math." Mr. Biancardi smiled. "She was very good at math. She had been with this man before she met me, but she became pregnant after she stopped seeing him and she met me. We even told this man he could not be the father, but he would not listen to us."

"Who was this guy you killed?" Patrick asked.

"I would rather not say his name," Mr. Biancardi said. "This man had been defying Mr. Gambino and Mr. Castellano by distributing narcotics in New York for many years. 'Deal and die,' Don Carlo used to say. This man selling drugs was bad for business. Hence, the man had to be removed. I was chosen to do this thing because of my *faida,* my feud with him over your mama, and in return for this service, you and your mama were allowed to live free and clear, provided I go away for a while and keep my peace. I have kept my peace, and now I am free."

"The resemblance is unmistakable," Lauren said.

"I know it is," Mr. Biancardi said, looking at Patrick. "You have my hands, my nose, and my receding hairline."

"And your squint," Lauren said.

"Yes," Mr. Biancardi said. "You also have your mama's smile, lips, and eyes."

Patrick drifted to the Christmas tree. "And you chose to unload all this on me on Christmas."

"I know the timing is bad," Mr. Biancardi said, "but when is the timing good for this kind of thing? I have paid my debt to society. I was sentenced to forty years, and I served every second of forty years. That does not happen very often."

"So why are you here?" Patrick asked. "Do you need money?"

Mr. Biancardi laughed. "He is so much like his mama! She was not a trusting woman, Lauren. It took a long time for her to trust me. Patrizio, Patrick, I have plenty of money at my disposal. You do not do a favor like this and not receive compensation. Even forty years later, they have not forgotten me. Whatever you may think of them, they are honorable men. They are men of their word, and they keep their word. And I have not forgotten you."

"Right," Patrick said. "It took you forty years to *remember* me."

"Where are you staying, Mr. Biancardi?" Lauren asked.

"At a halfway house," Mr. Biancardi said. "They let me come here today, even though I'm not supposed to leave the Bronx."

"At least *they* have the Christmas spirit," Lauren said. "Is it a nice place?"

"It is better than prison," Mr. Biancardi said. "It is a block from Arthur Avenue and the best restaurants in the city. I will be on parole for a time, of course, and I start my job tomorrow, cutting meat at Biancardi's, the family business. I used to cut meat there many years ago. If you come to Biancardi's, Lauren, I will, as they say, hook you up."

"We will definitely visit," Lauren said. "Won't we, Patrick?"

"Um, yeah." *I can't wait to visit my papa, the butcher who became a murderer.*

"And any time you visit, you will get the family discount," Mr. Biancardi said.

"I'm not part of your family," Patrick said.

"But you are," Mr. Biancardi said. "You are a Biancardi. Anyone who sees you there will say the same. You are shining and brave. That is what 'Biancardi' means."

"I'm keeping my real last name," Patrick said.

"As you should," Mr. Biancardi said. "You know, I have kept up with you over the years, Patrick."

"How?" Patrick asked.

"I talked to your mama on the phone at seven o'clock every night," Mr. Biancardi said.

That's . . . true. Mama always took the phone into the other room. "She spoke Italian."

"She did this to protect you," Mr. Biancardi said. "Did she teach you Italian?"

"Not much," Patrick said.

"She listened to me again!" Mr. Biancardi clapped his hands. "Twice in one lifetime. But she told you your papa was Irish. I have nothing against the Irish. They were friendly to me in prison. But I will have to talk to Caterina about that when I get to heaven."

"Heaven?" Patrick said. "Really?"

"I am a changed man," Mr. Biancardi said. "I never missed mass in prison. I prayed for you and your mama all the time, and it seems my prayers have been answered. You have a good wife and a good life."

"It hasn't always been good," Patrick said. "I grew up in the Gowanus Houses, remember?"

"Living there with your mama made you tougher," Mr. Biancardi said. "I was not there to toughen you up, yes? Now not even a New York reporter can shake you. And I also paid for your schooling, so to speak."

"That's a lie," Patrick said. "Mama paid for my schooling."

"No," Mr. Biancardi said. "I made sure there was extra in the checks when you were going to school. I also made arrangements for your mama's cancer treatments and her funeral and burial. I am sorry the treatments did not save her."

I thought Medicaid paid for that! "How could you afford all that?"

"I did a favor for important men," Mr. Biancardi said. "I kept my silence for forty years, even after those important men died or went to prison. Their successors have looked out for me, and I have looked out for you and your mama. She did not tell you about me even on her deathbed, did she? Such a stubborn woman."

"I wish she *had* told me all this," Patrick said.

"And what if she had?" Mr. Biancardi asked. "What would you have done? Would you have lived a different life?"

"I might have," Patrick said.

"Patrizio, I loved your mama very much," Mr. Biancardi said. "I did not want to go to prison and be away from her. That was so hard for me. But the hardest part was not being able to help raise you. I did what I could to take care of her and you, and one way was to keep all this quiet. You are the son of a murderer, but you grew up without this knowledge. Your friends did not know. Your teachers did not know. Your employers did not know. That made your life easier. You did not have the stigma."

"I will now," Patrick said. "The media will find out."

"So they find out," Mr. Biancardi said. "But understand this thing. You would not be here now if I had not killed a man. If that makes me only a murderer to you, so be it. You are here because I am a murderer. I would do it again. I would do anything to protect my family. I believe that you would also do anything to protect your family."

"Does Patrizio have other family?" Lauren asked.

Don't call me that name, Lauren.

"Oh yes," Mr. Biancardi said. "And they are all waiting to meet him. Call Biancardi's anytime, Patrizio, and you will speak to a cousin or an uncle or an aunt. I have six brothers and sisters. You have no half brothers or sisters. You are my only child. And this reminds me." He pulled out a thick white envelope from his jacket. "I do not know you well enough to buy a specific gift for you. I hope this will suffice." He turned and held out the envelope to Patrick.

And now he wants me to accept some blood money. "I don't want it."

"I earned this money, Patrizio, as a plumber in prison,"

Mr. Biancardi said. "You would think they would put me in the kitchen, but they made me into a plumber. Forty cents an hour, six hours a day, five days a week, fifty-two weeks a year, for forty years. I earned every cent of this money."

"I still don't want it," Patrick said.

"It is almost twenty-five thousand dollars, and I want you to have it." Mr. Biancardi stretched out his arm.

"I don't need it," Patrick said.

Mr. Biancardi's eyes softened as he returned the envelope to his jacket. "I can see that you are proud. Your mama is once again to blame." He smiled. "You told that reporter, 'I work for a living.' I was so proud of you. I am proud of you. Most men would have taken this money without a question. You did not even ask how much it was. But tell me, Patrick, will you stop me from spoiling my grandchildren?"

"No, he won't," Lauren said.

"Good," Mr. Biancardi said. "I will start a college fund for them with this money."

"Thank you," Lauren said. "That is so generous. Isn't that generous, Patrick?"

Patrick nodded slightly.

Mr. Biancardi stood. "I am sorry I interrupted your first Christmas together." He moved toward the door, offering his hand to Patrick.

Patrick stared at the hand.

Mr. Biancardi nodded and dropped his hand to his side. "I am sorry this did not go as well as I had hoped."

Patrick looked at Lauren.

"Talk to him," she mouthed. "He's your father."

Patrick nodded. "You were a plumber, huh?"

"Yes," Mr. Biancardi said. "In forty years I replaced around five hundred toilets and unclogged several thousand pipes. The prison was not modern. Much like this neighborhood."

Patrick stared at Mr. Biancardi's hands. His knuckles were gnarled and his palms rough and calloused. "But this neighborhood is not a prison."

"That is true," Mr. Biancardi said. "Very true. Thank you for letting me into your home. I was afraid you would throw me out into the street. I was as fierce as you are many years ago, but now I have grown soft." He turned to Lauren. "You have married a fine man. I wish I had helped to raise him." He looked briefly into Patrick's eyes. "I truly wish that."

Patrick opened the door.

Mr. Biancardi walked out.

Patrick closed the door.

"He seems like a very nice man, Patrick," Lauren said. "Why were you so cold to him?"

"I don't know. I just . . ." He sighed. "He killed someone, Lauren."

"I'm glad he did," Lauren said. "You wouldn't be here for me to love if he didn't."

"We don't know that," Patrick said.

"He did a heroic thing," Lauren said. "Your mama was in danger."

"We don't know that for sure, either," Patrick said. "My mama never acted as if she was in danger in her life."

"He protected her well then," Lauren said. She slid off the couch and embraced Patrick. "Just like you're protecting me."

"But why him?" Patrick asked. "Why'd they have to pick my father to kill that guy?"

"You *did* miss him growing up," Lauren said.

"Yeah." He nodded. "I did."

"You have him now," Lauren said. "And we have plenty of food. He could stay for Christmas dinner." She led him to the window in the bedroom. "He's about to cross the street. Invite him to dinner." She opened the window. "Mr. Biancardi!"

"I'll do it," Patrick said.

"Well, go on," Lauren said.

What do I call him? "Patrizio!"

Mr. Biancardi turned. "Yes?"

"Would you like to eat Christmas dinner with us?" Patrick asked.

Mr. Biancardi smiled. "I would like that very much."

"Come on up," Patrick said. He closed the window.

"Our first houseguest," Lauren said. She hugged him. "Patrizio. That is so sexy. Patrizio Alanzo Esposito. That's a whole lot of 'oh,' and that's what you'll get from me later tonight."

Mr. Biancardi knocked on the door.

Patrick went to the door and opened it. "You don't have to knock."

"But this is not my house," Mr. Biancardi said.

"In ways even I may never understand," Patrick said, "you helped build this house." He felt tears forming in his eyes. "You're my papa." *A man of honor, a man who is shining and brave, a man who sacrificed forty years of his life for my mama and me.* "I will never understand the courage it took to take another man's life, but you will always be welcome here."

Mr. Biancardi wiped away his own tears. "Thank you."

Patrick held out his hand, and Mr. Biancardi took it. "Thank you for having big hands."

"Thank you for having your mama's heart," Mr. Biancardi said.

Patrick motioned him inside. "I hope you're hungry. I'm sure we've made too much."

Mr. Biancardi stopped and turned. "Can she cook?" he whispered.

"I heard that," Lauren said from the kitchen.

Patrick smiled. "Yes, she can cook."

"You have pasta in the house?" Mr. Biancardi asked.

"There's some linguine in the pantry," Lauren said.

"She has excellent hearing," Mr. Biancardi said. "I feel I must add to the meal, Lauren. But will you allow me to cook in your kitchen? Patrizio's mama would not allow it."

"Of course I will let you cook," Lauren said.

Patrick helped him out of his coat.

"I will be a good *nonno* to your children," Mr. Biancardi said. "I promise."

"And I will try to be a good son," Patrick said.

"You already are," Mr. Biancardi told him.

Lauren put a box of linguine on the counter. "What else will you need, Papa? I can call you Papa, right? Even if your son won't say it."

"You can call me Papa anytime you want," Mr. Biancardi said, rolling up his sleeves. "While you boil the linguine, I will make the sauce. I will need bacon, fresh spinach, minced garlic, milk, cream cheese, butter, salt, nutmeg, and pepper."

Lauren blinked at him. "All that?"

"All that," Mr. Biancardi said.

"I'll tell you what we *do* have," Lauren said. "We have bacon, milk, butter, garlic salt, regular salt, and pepper. We only have some provolone."

"Hmm," Mr. Biancardi said. "We will have to improvise, then."

"I could go out and get what's missing," Patrick said. "If anything's open."

"No, no," Mr. Biancardi said. "I must teach you to make the sauce."

"Please teach him something," Lauren said. "All he can cook are Pop-Tarts."

Mr. Biancardi gripped both of Patrick's shoulders. "We have a lot of work to do."

Patrick nodded. *We sure do.* "I do make a great Philly steak and cheese, though."

"Did you use rib-eye beef?" Mr. Biancardi asked.

"No," Patrick said.

"He uses the frozen stuff," Lauren said.

"Sacrilege!" Mr. Biancardi cried. "Oh, you have much to learn, much to learn, Patrizio. Don't overcook that linguine, Lauren. I need it al dente. You must get a bigger kitchen soon, Patrizio, so we do not step on each other's toes. Now, where is that bacon?"

Lauren pulled a pack from the refrigerator.

"Oh, it is too thin," Mr. Biancardi said. "I will have to double it up. You come to Biancardi's, and I will slice you the thickest, best-tasting bacon on earth. . . ."

Patrick backed out of the kitchen. He looked at the gifts strewn here and there around the couch and smiled at the Styrofoam peanuts on the tree. He adjusted several of the lamps to shine more light into the kitchen. He pulled out the cross and kissed it.

"Where's my son?" Mr. Biancardi cried. "He should be in here learning."

"Be there in a minute," Patrick said. *I'll be there in a minute. Papa.*

I need to soak all this in first.

It's not every day that I get to see my wife—and my papa—preparing a feast for me.

62

The true story of Patrizio Alanzo Biancardi hit the front page of the *Post* the day after Christmas, and the rest of the media dutifully blew it completely out of proportion. Even *The View* couldn't resist weighing in, with guest co-host Brooke Shields starting the conversation while Lauren and Patrick ate a rare soup and sandwich lunch at their apartment.

"Let's talk about Lauren Short and Patrick Esposito," Brooke said.

"You mean *Patrizio* Esposito and Lauren *Esposito,*" Whoopi Goldberg said. "She took *his* name, remember?"

"I think it's sweet," Sherri Shepherd said.

"Why?" Kathy Griffin asked. "He's the son of a Mafia hit man. She's related by marriage to a wiseguy."

"Patrick's father is not a wiseguy, Kathy," Sherri said.

"He sure looks like one to me," Kathy said. "Did you see his picture?"

Sherri sighed. "You can't blame Patrick for what happened before he was born."

"Maybe," Kathy said, "but I still don't see what's so sweet about their relationship."

"Lauren married for love," Sherri said. "Not for money or fame or eye candy or publicity or power or appearances or any of the other stupid reasons celebrities get married these days. It has to be love. They always look so happy in photos."

"Well, Patrick is quite a beast," Brooke said, "and he never smiles."

"Because he's a Brooklyn guy, a real man, a handyman," Whoopi said. "He's got no time to smile."

"Well," Kathy said, "you know he'll be faithful to Lauren. She'll never have to worry about him straying."

"You can't say the same about Chazz," Brooke said. "What's he been through? Five or six new women since Lauren?"

"Chazz didn't know or appreciate what he had," Sherri said.

"That Patrizio has to have it going on," Whoopi said. "Lauren hasn't stopped smiling since she moved to Brooklyn. I can always tell where she is on a cloudy day. I see this beam of light all the way from Newark."

"It won't last," Kathy said. "Love on the rebound never lasts."

"Unless it's with a basketball player," Whoopi said. "Patrizio's tall enough. I'll bet he's very good around the rim. . . ."

When the segment went to commercial, Patrick asked, "Am I good around the rim?"

"Oh, you're very good around the rim," Lauren said. "I like it when you dunk, too."

"I like dunking you," Patrick said.

"I like to be dunked," Lauren said. She sighed. "I just wish this would all blow over. It was so quiet for a few weeks, and now this. I can't stand to have people second-guess our marriage or our families. What business is it of theirs to critique what we have?"

"None," Patrick said. "I wish they'd be kinder to Papa."

"You called him Papa," Lauren said.

"So I'm practicing," Patrick said. "I know he can handle the scrutiny, but it's so hard to read about it. They're making him sound like a serial killer when all he did was take out one bad guy."

Lauren pointed at the television. "At least *The View* didn't go there. I could never be on that show. Talking about dirt all day doesn't sound like fun." She sighed. "But it's how networks pay their bills because they know people will tune in to hear all the dirt."

"Getting paid to gossip," Patrick said. "What a racket." He kissed Lauren's neck.

"What are you doing, man?" Lauren asked.

"Trying to create a racket," Patrick said.

"I want to play some basketball for some reason," Lauren said.

"I may hang around your rim for a long time," Patrick said.

"You won't have to wait long," Lauren said.

"And then we'll have a dunking contest," Patrick said. "Which I will win."

"You better," Lauren said. She reached for one of his coveralls straps. "I like it when you slam me."

"You make it so easy to score," Patrick said.

Lauren's phone rang. She checked the caller ID. *Todd. Why aren't I surprised?* She answered the call. "Hi, Todd. I'm putting you on speakerphone. Say hello to Patrick."

"Hello, Patrick," Todd said. "Or do you prefer Patrizio? Patrizio is getting better play on Twitter."

"Whatever, Todd," Lauren said. "What do you want?"

"Are you two sitting down?" Todd asked.

"We're about to have a dunking contest, Todd," Lauren said. "Talk fast."

"I can call back," Todd said.

"Go ahead," Lauren said. "We need to do a little stretching first anyway."

"You two have been nominated for a People's Choice Award," Todd said, "for Favorite Viral Video Star."

"There is no such category," Lauren said.

"There is," Todd said. "They brought it back this year because there are so many good candidates. I think you two have a *great* shot at winning this year."

"We have a couple videos out there," Lauren said. "Which one?"

"Some fan of yours recently made a video of all your clips and called it 'True Love,' " Todd said. "It chronicles your romance from your engagement in St. Louis to your wedding in Brooklyn. Al Green's 'Let's Stay Together' plays in the background, and it is very slick."

"Our romance has made us popular, Patrick," Lauren said. "Isn't that great?"

"That's ridiculous," Patrick said.

"It is?" Lauren asked.

"I meant . . ." Patrick sighed. "*Not* our romance. *We're* not ridiculous. The idea that we'd be nominated is ridiculous."

"That video has over ten *million* hits," Todd said. "That's not ridiculous at all."

Ten million! Wow! "That's amazing," Lauren said.

"I called you two today because the show is in LA in a few weeks," Todd said. "I wanted to give you enough lead time since I know how you two like to travel on buses."

"Very funny, Todd," Lauren said, turning to Patrick. "Do you want to go?"

"Not really," Patrick said. "But if you want to go, I'll go. I know you miss it."

"Miss what?" Lauren asked.

"The glitz and the glamour you gave up for me," Patrick said.

"Are you kidding?" Lauren said. "I look fantastic in coveralls."

"Yes, you do," Patrick said. "But don't you miss some aspects of that life?"

"No," Lauren said. "I may even wear my purple long johns, my coveralls, and my new boots to the ceremony. It could be fun, but it will be even more fun if you go with me. I absolutely despise awards shows. I mean, you make *one* movie, and then you go to see if you won something at a half dozen different awards shows. It's so much overkill."

"Hello?" Todd said. "Have you forgotten you're talking to me?"

"Actually, Todd, we have," Lauren said.

"*Please* don't wear coveralls, Lauren," Todd said.

"Who's going to stop me?" Lauren asked. "Has Chazz been nominated again for Favorite Action Movie Star?"

"Yes," Todd said. "For the eighth year in a row."

Now I really want to go. "Wouldn't it be fun to be in the same room with Chazz, Patrick?"

Patrick nodded. "You know, I'd like to meet Chucky. I have a few things I'd like to say to him."

"So do I," Lauren said. "We will definitely be there. Thanks for calling, Todd."

"There's one more thing," Todd said. "I've seen some of your clothing ads, and they look great. I don't know what they're paying you, but I know you two could make a *lot* more money than you're currently making if you went national or even international. I've gotten phone calls from Banana Republic, Benetton, and even Speedo."

"Speedo?" Lauren said.

"They think you two would look great in swimsuit ads," Todd said.

"They can't be serious," Patrick said. "I would look ridiculous wearing a banana hammock."

"No, you wouldn't," Lauren said. *Speedo's sales would skyrocket!*

"Six figures minimum, Lauren," Todd said. "What are you making now?"

"We're making nothing," Lauren said.

"What?" Todd cried.

"We get to keep the clothes as payment," Lauren said, "and they're very cool clothes."

"But you're Lauren Short," Todd said. "You could be making much more!"

"I am Lauren Esposito, a Boerum Hill, Brooklyn girl," Lauren said, "and I prefer to work for clothes."

"Lauren, think of the future," Todd said. "You could use this awards show to restart your career, and a few national ad campaigns would blow you up bigger than you were before. I've even heard some whispers about you and Patrizio making some coin as an on-screen couple."

"Really?" Lauren gasped. "Do you have anything concrete?"

"No, but I'm getting feelers," Todd said. "Not as the leading couple, of course, but as the *other* couple."

Figures. "Hey, Patrick. We're becoming a semi-'it' couple without even trying."

"What is the 'other' couple?" Patrick asked.

"The 'other' couple is the foil for the dysfunctional main couple," Lauren said. "We put them back together after they fall apart. We could finally be an ordinary couple—in a movie. What do you think?"

"You already know what I think," Patrick said. "Do you want to go back to acting?"

"Not really," Lauren said. "I guess that's a thanks, but no thanks, Todd. Bye."

"But, Lauren," Todd said, "you have a *major* opportunity here to—"

Lauren turned off her phone. "We're going to LA."

"So you can confront Chucky," Patrick said.

"So *we* can confront Chucky," Lauren said. "And I also want to see what you look like in a suit. You didn't wear one for my wedding."

"You just want to show off your boy toy," Patrick said.

She moved over to him and sat in his lap. "No. I want to show off my husband, my one true love, my man. I want you at that show with me so you can put all those fake men to shame."

"I'll need a suit," Patrick said. "And I have no idea where to go to get one."

"Call Papa," Lauren said. "Your daddy knows how to dress. He'll know the best place to go."

Patrick called Biancardi's. "I need to speak to Patrizio, please."

"Put him on speaker," Lauren said. "I love the sound of his voice."

Patrick turned on the speaker, and a moment later his father answered. "Patrizio? Is everything okay?"

"Yes, Papa," Patrick said. "I need to know where to get a good suit."

"The *best* suit," Lauren said.

"No, not the best suit," Patrick said. "A *good* suit. One I can afford."

"What is the occasion?" Mr. Biancardi asked.

"We've been nominated for a People's Choice Award," Lauren said, "and we'll be going out to LA in a few weeks."

"To walk the red carpet," Mr. Biancardi said. "I see. In that case, you must go to Barneys on Madison Avenue in Manhattan. They will take care of both of you, I assure you."

"Will it be expensive?" Patrick asked.

"A good suit should be expensive," Mr. Biancardi said.

"How much are we talking?" Patrick asked.

"Oh, five thousand should do it," Mr. Biancardi said. "Do you need some money?"

"We're okay," Patrick said.

"I still know a few people there," Mr. Biancardi said. "Let me make a call."

"It's okay, Papa," Patrick said. "We'll manage."

"One call," Mr. Biancardi said, "and they will treat you like a king."

"I don't want to be a king, Papa," Patrick said. "I just want a suit."

"You will have both," Mr. Biancardi said. "Ciao!"

Barney's, a half-hour ride on the 4 train away, was more an art gallery than a clothing store, with nine floors of clothing from nearly every clothier Lauren had ever heard of.

This is heaven, Lauren thought. *They have put heaven on Madison Avenue. I may never leave this store.*

Precisely five seconds after they stepped inside the street-level doors, a sharply dressed man approached them.

"My name is Paul." He shook Patrick's hand. "You are here for a suit." He nodded at Lauren. "And you are here for an evening gown for the People's Choice Awards in Los Angeles."

"Did my father call you?" Patrick asked.

"Yes," Paul said. "The Biancardi family is one of our oldest customers, and your father wishes for you to get to the royal treatment today."

"I only need a suit," Patrick said.

"And you will get a suit," Paul said. "Follow me."

After getting measured by two tailors in a spacious dressing area, Patrick stood in only a T-shirt and boxers in front of Lauren.

"You know," Lauren said, "if this wasn't a formal affair, I'd let you wear that in LA."

Paul returned with an Andrea Campagna wool, two-piece, navy chalk-striped suit. When Patrick put it on, it fit like a glove.

My husband will be the hottest man there, Lauren thought. *Look at how that jacket fits his shoulders! My God, I have married a flawless man.*

"Mrs. Esposito," Paul said, "is this acceptable?"

Lauren nodded.

Paul took a long navy Rake coat from a hanger. "It is supposed to be chilly in LA. This is cashmere." He helped Patrick into the coat. "How does it feel, Mr. Esposito?"

"Expensive," Patrick said.

"You look fantastic," Lauren said. *In another life, Patrick could easily have been a movie star, and I would have been the fan writing to him.*

Patrick lifted his arm and looked at the tag. "I'm wearing a five-thousand-dollar coat, Lauren. And the suit cost five thousand, too."

"We'll take it," Lauren said. "All of it."

"It's way too much," Patrick said.

"You *need* a suit, Patrick," Lauren said. "Agreed? Agreed."

Paul turned to Lauren. "And now for you, Mrs. Esposito. We have something exclusive for you."

On the third floor, a small army of designers circled Lauren until she was wearing a pleated silk tulle J. Mendel gown in dove gray. Sleeveless and V-necked, with a plunging V back, it left little to the imagination.

I will freeze if I wear only this, Lauren thought. *It barely feels as if I'm wearing it.*

A shoe specialist paired the dress with crystal-covered round-toe pumps with four-inch heels in meridian blue.

I have never been so tall, Lauren thought. *Not that anyone will be able to see these exquisite pumps under this long gown.* She looked at her transformation in a mirror. *These shoes and this dress have taken ten pounds off my body.*

"How do I look?" Lauren asked.

"Like Cinderella," Patrick said.

"I feel like Cinderella," Lauren said. "But, Paul, I'm going to be cold."

Paul handed her a Denis Colomb cashmere shahtoosh shawl in Altai blue. "This will keep you warm." He held out a piece of paper. "If you will sign this, we will have your garments delivered to your home the day before the show."

Free delivery, too? Lauren signed the paper. "How would you like payment?"

"Everything has been taken care of," Paul said.

"Really?" Lauren said. "Everything?"

Paul nodded.

"Really?"

Paul nodded again.

"Patrick's papa paid," Lauren said.

Paul smiled.

"That beautiful old man," Lauren said.

Once she was back in her changing room, Lauren called Biancardi's, and Patrick's father answered. "Papa, you outdid yourself. The dress is gorgeous, and Patrick's suit is amazing. Thank you so much."

"It is nothing," Mr. Biancardi said. "How did Patrizio look?"

"Like you," Lauren said. "Only taller and broader."

"So he looked handsome," Mr. Biancardi said. "I am glad."

"It cost so much," Lauren said.

"It is my wedding gift to you," Mr. Biancardi said, "and if Patrizio has a problem with it, you send him straight to me, and I will straighten him out."

"I'll make sure he doesn't have a problem with it," Lauren said. "That suit and that coat were made for him."

Back at the apartment, Lauren moved all the new lights into the kitchen.

"What are you planning, Cinderella?" Patrick asked.

"You clean up nicely, Prince Charming," Lauren said, "but I'm much more attracted to you when you're dressed down or undressed." She set her phone on the floor. "We're going to make a movie."

"That explains all the lights," Patrick said. "Is there a script?"

"No," Lauren said.

"What about costuming?" Patrick asked.

"We are both going to wear coveralls and nothing else," Lauren said.

"Sounds drafty," Patrick said. "What's my motivation?"

Lauren laughed. "You're taking all this too seriously."

"Come on, Lauren," Patrick said. "This is a fantasy come true. This is my first scene in a movie with you. I don't want to mess it up."

"You won't," Lauren said. "Your motivation is to make me come loudly."

"I can do that," Patrick said.

"I am going to fix something under the sink," Lauren said, "and I want you to assist me. Go to wardrobe now."

Patrick quickly disrobed and put on his coveralls while Lauren did the same. "Is this going to be a bad love scene or a porno this time?"

Lauren loosened the straps on her coveralls so more of her breasts would show. "Oh, definitely porno this time." She knelt in front of the kitchen cabinet and adjusted the film settings on her phone. "This will have to be a quick scene. I only have five minutes of memory at most, so talk and perform fast." She turned on her phone and put her hand behind her. "Hand me your tool, Mr. Handyman."

She heard an unzipping sound and felt the full weight of Patrick's penis in her hand.

"Is this the right tool?" Patrick asked.

"Oh yes," Lauren said, stroking him. "It might be too large to fix my hole, though." She let go of his penis and unzipped herself. "I just need some lubrication." She slipped her hand through the opening and began fingering herself rapidly. "I am getting so hot. You need to cool me off."

Patrick unbuttoned her straps and pulled her coveralls down to her ankles. "Will a wet tongue cool you off?"

"Oh yes."

Lauren felt Patrick's hot tongue licking her from the back of her neck down to her clitoris. Lauren took the clothespin from a pocket and waved it behind her. "Clip this to a nipple."

"Are you sure?" Patrick asked.

"No," Lauren said in a small voice.

"Maybe you should do it," Patrick said.

Lauren turned the clothespin sideways and clipped it to her right nipple, exquisite pain shooting through her entire breast. She grimaced for the camera. "Put your tool inside me now." She felt his penis filling her completely. "Now pull my hair."

Patrick pulled gently on her hair.

"Harder," Lauren said.

Patrick yanked hard on Lauren's hair.

I should have no worry lines on my forehead now. "Turn me over."

Patrick lifted her off the floor and spun her around, pulling her feet up to his ears.

Lauren picked up her phone and aimed it at her breasts, the clothespin bouncing as Patrick resumed pumping.

"Doesn't that hurt?" Patrick asked.

Lauren unclipped the clothespin and clamped it vertically to her left nipple. "Yes. Very. I like you doing me on the floor, Mr. Handyman."

He began pumping furiously. "You're going to have tile print on your booty."

"Oh, God, I hope so." She wedged the phone between her chin and collarbone. "Give me that tool, Mr. Handyman!"

Patrick laughed. "I'm plugging up all your leaks!"

Lauren closed her eyes. "Plug away," she whispered. "Don't stop until a 'damn' bursts out of my mouth. . . ."

Oh, damn. Here I come. . . .

63

During the second week of January, on the afternoon of the People's Choice Awards show, Patrick and Lauren flew out of JFK without a single member of the media noticing.

"They're all in LA sucking up to the real celebrities," Lauren said as they boarded the plane without incident or flash through the separate coach entrance.

Fellow coach passengers and the crew, however, noticed and applauded as they took their seats.

"Why are they clapping?" Patrick whispered.

"Well, it might be because we're dressed to the nines as Cinderella and Prince Charming," Lauren said. She carefully centered the gown on her knees. "I told you it would be easier to go dressed, and look at the response from our fans."

"Your gown might get wrinkled," Patrick said.

"It's pleated," Lauren said. "No one will notice."

After posing for several pictures and signing a few autographs, they watched *Access Hollywood* on Lauren's phone while the plane sat at the gate because of some malfunction. The first story brought Cinderella and Prince Charming crashing back to earth.

Laura Saltman, the "Dish of Salt," asked Chazz, "How broken up are you over Lauren's sudden marriage to a Brooklyn handyman? And be honest, Chazz."

"Not much, Laura," Chazz said. "Really. Lauren *Short*— and I refuse to say her married name, because she won't have it for long—Lauren *Short* never treated me like a man. Lauren always came up short." He grinned. "I tried to teach her how to keep a man satisfied, but she wasn't a very good student, if you know what I mean."

Lauren gripped the phone so tightly the case cracked. Patrick gently removed the phone from her hand.

"But you were together for seven years, Chazz," Laura continued. "You should have taught her *something*."

"Evidently," Chazz said, "some people are just unteachable."

Patrick wisely turned off the phone.

"*Unteachable* is not a word, you jerk!" Lauren hissed. "Oh, this is the last straw! Telling the world I didn't satisfy *him!* Oh, I can't wait to tell the world the truth!" Lauren rose up in her seat and saw that many passengers were staring at her. "Oh, sorry about that." *Go back to what you were doing while I burst a blood vessel in my brain!*

"I'll take care of it," Patrick whispered.

"I should do it," Lauren whispered.

"Your mama would agree with me," Patrick whispered.

"Let's find out." She turned on her phone. After dialing the number, she sat back and tried to breathe normally.

She did not succeed.

"Mama, did you hear what Chazz is saying about me now?" Lauren asked. "Did you watch *Access Hollywood* tonight?"

"I never watch that show," Pamela said. "What's he saying now?"

"Basically that I never learned how to satisfy him sexually," Lauren whispered.

"Why are you whispering?" Pamela asked.

"I'm on a crowded airplane, Mama," Lauren whispered. "What do you think I should do?"

"Nothing," Pamela said. "His lies will catch up to him soon enough."

"Mama, millions of people believe those lies," Lauren said.

"Then those millions of people will feel especially foolish when the truth comes out," Pamela said. "Chazz has always been an overgrown child. Don't act like a child in response."

"So you want me to do nothing?" Lauren asked.

"Yes," Pamela said. "And in your case, the more nothing the better. Stay calm and don't start anything tonight. I will be watching."

"Bye, Mama." She hung up. *Thanks for nothing, which is what she wants me to do.* "She was no help. We need to call Papa."

"Why?" Patrick asked.

"He'll know what to do," Lauren said. She dialed Biancardi's. "Let me speak to Patrizio."

Patrick held out his hand. "I'll speak to him."

Lauren sighed and put the phone in his hand. "Make sure you tell him everything."

"I will." He put the phone to his ear. "Papa . . . ? Yes, I'm on the plane. . . . No, we're still on the ground . . . Have you heard what Chazz—" Patrick covered the mouthpiece. "He's heard. He's cursing in Italian now." He uncovered the mouthpiece. "No, don't get on an airplane, Papa. . . . You're not allowed to leave the Bronx. . . . What would *you* do if you were standing in front of him?" Patrick widened his eyes. "Um, isn't that illegal? I know you know some guys, Papa, but—" He shook his head. "I know Lauren's honor is at stake. That's why I called you. What would you do that doesn't involve 'some guys' and a Louisville Slugger?"

That's what I'm talking about, Lauren thought.

"He might need them to walk, Papa," Patrick said. "I'll think of something. Make sure everyone at Biancardi's watches, okay? All right. See you soon." He ended the call. "That went about like I expected it to."

"He wants to take a baseball bat to Chazz's kneecaps, doesn't he?" Lauren asked.

"Worse," Patrick said. "He wants to cut both of Chucky's Achilles tendons."

Yes! "Well, I don't intend to be civil when we get there," Lauren said. "Chazz cannot slander me without penalty." She put her lips on Patrick's ear and whispered, "I am an astonishing lover."

"You are," Patrick said. "But I got this."

"You don't know him like I do," Lauren said. "It's only going to get worse. The next time he talks about me, he'll turn me into a lesbian."

"I've known people like him," Patrick said. "When they're backed into a corner, they wilt. He's a coward."

Lauren looked at her fingers. "I wish I had longer nails."

"I'll take care of it," Patrick said. "Relax. Enjoy the ride."

"What ride?" Lauren asked. "We're not moving!"

"Patience," Patrick said.

"What are you going to do?" Lauren asked.

"You'll see," Patrick said. "I got this."

"Tell me," Lauren whispered.

"Trust me," Patrick said. He squeezed her hand. "I've

been waiting for the right moment, and tonight is the right moment."

"What are you going to say to him?" Lauren asked.

"You'll see," Patrick said. "Now please relax. We're on a date to LA, and we're dressed like royalty. We should be enjoying ourselves, right?"

Lauren nodded. "If you give me a sneak preview of what you're going to say, I might settle down more quickly."

"I know," Patrick said.

"Don't you want me to settle down?" Lauren asked.

"Yes," Patrick said.

"Then tell me something," Lauren said.

"Okay," Patrick said. "I am going to . . ."

"What?"

Patrick kissed her forehead. "I'm going to keep you in suspense. Please trust me."

"I guess I don't have any other choice," Lauren said.

After cuddling for most of a five-hour flight, when they arrived at LAX and left the terminal, they chose a bright pink Yellow Cab SUV to be their carriage.

The driver did a double take when they climbed into the backseat. "Lauren Short?"

Lauren didn't correct him. "The Nokia Theatre, please."

"Um, that's a no-drive zone tonight," the driver said. "It'll be limousine city."

"We know," Lauren said. "But think of the publicity you'll get. A bright pink cab alone in that sea of black-and-white limousines."

"I don't know if the cops will even let me get near the place," the driver said.

"Well, if they won't," Lauren said, "we don't mind walking. We're already running late, and the show starts in ninety minutes. Get us as close as you can as fast as you can."

The driver sped away and avoided the freeways, taking a

zigzag route that eventually put them on South Figueroa where he crept through heavy traffic as far as West Twelfth Street in the shadow of Staples Center.

"It's blocked off from here," the driver said, pointing at the wooden barricades ahead. "There's no way I can get closer."

A police officer waved them toward West Twelfth.

Lauren rolled down her window. "Excuse me," she said sweetly, "we have to get to the Nokia Theatre."

The officer walked over. "Not a chance tonight, not from here." He squinted at her. "Lauren Short?"

"Hello," Lauren said.

The officer peered into the cab. "Why aren't you in a limo?"

"I can make a more unique entrance in this vehicle, don't you think?" she asked.

"You'll sure stand out." He clicked on his microphone. "One pink cab coming through."

Two officers removed one of the barricades.

"Thank you so much," Lauren said. "Come on. Let's go!"

The driver eventually merged between a black limousine and a white limousine then stopped abruptly at the curb as a swarm of photographers began snapping away.

Patrick paid the driver double the fare. "We need to get back to the airport right after the show. Can we call you to come pick us up?"

The driver shrugged. "They might not let me in again, so I'll just find a space here and wait for you."

"Thank you," Lauren said.

Patrick opened his door, stepped out, and stretched his hand inside. "Are you ready, Cinderella?"

Lauren gripped his hand tightly and stepped out of the cab. "Why, yes, kind prince."

They sauntered down the red carpet through a blitzkrieg of flashbulbs as reporters peppered them with questions.

"Lauren, is it true you're getting a divorce?"

"Patrick, how does it feel to have the worst beard in show business?"

"Lauren, have you called Chazz for your New Year's date yet?"

"Couldn't you afford a limo?"

"Lauren, is it true that you don't know how to satisfy a man?"

"Patrick, does Lauren satisfy you?"

Lauren raised her eyebrows at Patrick.

"Not yet," Patrick said.

They posed for official photos in front of a People's Choice Awards sign, CBS logos in abundance.

"I thought I was getting used to all this," Patrick said, "but I'm not. I have led an anonymous existence for so long that it is crazy that people are even noticing me."

Lauren smiled broadly as the flashes continued. "You look fantastic."

"Thank you," Patrick said, "but I still feel out of place. These people aren't *looking* at me. They're *staring* at me."

"Because you're so handsome," Lauren said.

"They gaze in awe at you," Patrick said. "They gawk at me. I feel like an animal at the zoo, and they're just waiting for me to entertain them, even though I don't know any tricks."

"Yes, you do," Lauren whispered, biting her lip.

"Well, I know a few tricks," Patrick said.

Their official pictures finished, they moved along the red carpet through a gauntlet of reporters on either side. *This is like a cattle drive,* Lauren thought. *Only the cattle here wear ten-thousand-dollar dresses and suits.*

"What do you think about what Chazz said, Patrick?"

"Chazz called you out, Patrick. What are you going to do?"

"Are you shaving off your beard soon?"

"How could you afford that dress and that suit, Patrick?"

"Did Mafia money pay for your outfits?"

"How long have you had sexual difficulties, Lauren?"

Lauren turned sharply to Patrick. "I have to say something!" she whispered tersely.

"Not yet," Patrick said.

"But you can set them straight about my abilities," Lauren whispered.

"That's none of their business," Patrick said. "I'd much rather go to the source of the problem, and he's inside. I work better one-on-one."

"Yes, you do, but . . ."

He dipped her nearly to the ground and kissed her deeply. "Trust me."

That was a great kiss. Whoo. "Are you trying to shut me up?"

"Yes," Patrick said.

Lauren saw a massive black man in a tux outside the entrance. "Before we go in, we have to answer André's questions. It's a tradition. He's *Entertainment Tonight*'s regular red carpet reporter, and he is usually kind to me."

They approached André, Lauren smiling brightly. "It's been a long time," she said.

André didn't smile. "Lauren, what can you say to our viewers concerning the recent controversy about your abrupt breakup and hasty marriage?"

That isn't the worst question he could have asked, but still. "What controversy? I fell in love with Patrick, and I am extremely happy. There's nothing controversial about true love."

"Even if most people don't agree with your choice of man?" André asked.

That was low. She smiled her most dazzling smile. "Oh, but, André, have you asked most people this question?"

André took a breath. "Well, no."

"Then how do you know that most people don't agree with my choice?" Lauren asked.

André took another breath. "*Some* people disagree."

Though I could, I can't afford to make him look too bad. He has a lot of followers. "André, many women want a man who's handy, while others want a man who's all man. People are just jealous that I . . . have . . . both." She kissed Patrick's cheek. "It was good to see you again." She took Patrick's hand and led him briskly inside the entrance door. "Do you mind if I gawk at you tonight?" she whispered.

"No," Patrick said.

"Kiss me again," Lauren said. "And dip me so low that my hair hits the carpet."

Patrick did as he was told.

The flashes were blinding.

Patrick leaned in and whispered, "Doesn't your face ever hurt from smiling so much? Mine is killing me."

"I will massage your face later," Lauren whispered. "In a very special way."

Patrick blinked and nodded. "We haven't done that yet. We need to try it on the plane."

Lauren put her arms around Patrick. "I love traveling with you. Our itineraries are so free form."

After an usher escorted them to their aisle seats in the second-to-last row, they sat and looked up at the stage where two huge screens flanked a gaudy, glowing purple representation of the People's Choice Award.

"They put the real stars up front," Lauren said.

"I'm feeling better already," Patrick said.

A nearby flash drew their attention to the aisle.

It's Sam Gabriel from Us Weekly *and a tall, hairy pho-*

tographer in a tux and high-tops. How charming. "Hello, Sam."

"Hello, Lauren," Sam said. "Happy to be here?"

"Yes," Lauren said, taking and holding Patrick's hand.

"Anything I should know about?" Sam asked. "You know, something interesting that might happen tonight?"

"No," Lauren said sweetly. "What do you think will happen?"

"Well," Sam said, "after all that's happened, I just thought *something* was going to happen tonight. Is it true that *family* money paid for your dress?"

"That's none of your business, Sam," Lauren said.

Sam looked down front. "Oh, there's Chazz. You heard what he said on *Access Hollywood,* right?"

"I did," Lauren said.

"Do you care to comment?" Sam asked.

"No," Lauren said.

"Aren't you going to confront him?" Sam asked.

I want to, but I have to trust my man. "No."

"You're not?" Sam laughed. "But tonight is a golden opportunity to confront him."

"Tonight is a golden opportunity to enjoy the show," Lauren said. "I won't be confronting him, Sam."

Patrick will.

Sam shook his head and drifted with his photographer down the aisle.

Patrick put his lips close to her ear. "I thought Chucky would be bigger."

And I was almost the bride of Chucky. "It's all about camera angles. He's only five-eight. He's a little shorter than Jason Statham. Oh, look at the frown on his date's face. I'll bet she *knows.* I'll bet she's horny and can't do anything about it."

Sam returned to Lauren's side. "I think Chazz and his date are coming up the aisle."

He's headed this way. Is he crazy? She turned to Patrick and whispered, "I feel like taking off my earrings and throwing some hands."

"I got this," Patrick whispered.

"Can I, please?" Lauren whispered. "Only one or two punches. I promise only to maim him."

"Not in that gown," Patrick whispered.

"I could take it off," Lauren whispered.

"Later," Patrick whispered.

"You say the nicest things."

She looked at Chazz and his date, Chari, a blond, leggy Victoria's Secret model, as they waved and joked with people on their way up the aisle. *Wow. Chazz is such a small man. Why did I ever waste seven years of my life with him? Wearing that string tie, that V-shaped goatee, and those dark glasses, he's trying to look like a younger Mickey Rourke and failing badly.*

Lauren took a deep breath and exhaled slowly. *Let's get this beat down started.*

Chazz stopped beside Lauren, and several photographers formed a semicircle around him while Sam posted himself a few feet away. "Hello, Lauren Short."

"Hello, Charles Ransome," Lauren said.

"Why, Lauren, you look so much older," Chazz said. "And tired. Is marriage to Patty all that bad? My, how you've aged since I broke up with you and you settled for him. Have you filed for divorce yet?"

Lauren looked sideways at Patrick.

Patrick shook his head slightly.

Lauren smiled for the cameras. "You know that's not true, Charles. *I* broke up with you. Have you fixed that window yet?"

Chazz's eyes widened slightly. "She was distraught over my dumping her, and she tried to kill herself by jumping into the ocean from my picture window. I suppose she thought it was a romantic gesture."

Lauren cut her eyes to Patrick.

Patrick shook his head.

Come on, man! The suspense is killing me! "I did no such thing. You replaced that window with tinted or one-way glass, didn't you? You wouldn't want the world to see what I saw that night."

Chazz's eyes narrowed slightly. "I should have sent you a bill, but I didn't want to wait a few centuries for your descendants to pay me back because you're only a handy-woman now."

Lauren smiled up at Chari. "*You* know what I'm talking about, don't you, Chari? His unusual nocturnal proclivities."

Chari blinked.

She has no clue. I need to break it down for her. "I feel so bad for you." Lauren leaned her head out into the aisle and whispered, "Just make sure Chazz uses a condom, or you might have to take an HIV test."

Chari's eyes popped. "What?"

She doesn't know! Wow.

Lauren saw Sam scribbling furiously on a notepad.

Well, at least that little nugget is out now.

Chazz tugged on Chari's arm. "It was *not* nice talking to you, as usual. Let's go."

They're getting away! Lauren reached out quickly and latched on to Chari's free hand. "I wasn't masculine enough for Charles."

Chazz pulled Chari toward him. "Always a pleasure, Lauren. Enjoy your retirement. Oh, wait. You can't retire, can you? You'll have to work on pipes and sinks and toilets until the day you die."

Lauren released Chari's hand. "Better a plumber who works on pipes than a sexually confused man who works on other men's pipes." She turned fully to Patrick and mouthed, "Now?"

Patrick only smiled.

Well, do something, Patrick! You say you got this—so get this!

Chazz stepped closer. "You're insane." He turned to Sam. "She's insane. Obviously. Look who she's with. The son of a Mafia hit man who buys used rings at pawnshops and had to take a pink cab to this show."

"Now?" Lauren mouthed to Patrick.

Patrick nodded, stood, and stepped carefully past Lauren's feet to the aisle.

Finally! Go get him!

Patrick towered over Chazz but said nothing as more photographers moved in and people around them pulled out cell phones to begin filming.

Ah, Lauren thought. *He wanted to build up more of an audience. I always knew he was a ham at heart.*

"Ah, the handyman," Chazz said.

Patrick smiled, crossed his arms, and stared down at him. Chazz let go of Chari's hand and moved up the aisle past Patrick before turning and facing him.

So you can appear taller, Lauren thought. *They see how really short you are, you jerk!*

"Do you speak?" Chazz asked. "Do you know how to speak? Can you *afford* to speak?"

Patrick laughed so loudly, several photographers stumbled backward. He turned to Lauren. "You were right, Lauren. Chucky is short." He returned his focus to Chazz.

"On a lot of things. Including class, humanity, and common sense."

Chazz coughed, his eyes flitting back and forth.

Patrick moved closer. "I want you to apologize to Lauren."

"For what?" Chazz asked loudly. "I have nothing to apologize for. She should be apologizing to me."

Patrick let his arms fall to his sides. "You tell lies, Chucky, but I won't hold those against you because you lie for a living. However, I do need you to apologize to Lauren for having to take an HIV test because of you."

Chazz's eyes darted around him. "I don't know what you're talking about." He turned away from Patrick and looked at Sam. "He's crazy. His father is a murderer, and his mother was a whore. That kind of combination has to make you crazy. No wonder Lauren ended up with him."

No jury would convict you if you killed him right now, Patrick. At least break his jaw. Please? One right cross, and his face will always lean left. Lauren saw veins bulging in Patrick's neck. *Oh, it's on now!*

"You're wrong, as usual, Chucky," Patrick said. "It hasn't made me crazy. It has made me more powerful than you'll ever be. My mother was not a whore. I am her only child, she raised me by herself, and she is a saint. My father killed a man so I could be born. I am his only child. He is a saint. They were the best parents I could have ever had. Now, apologize for nearly giving Lauren a death sentence."

Chazz stepped to his left. "Get out of my way."

Patrick stepped with him. "No. We're going to end this now. Either you apologize to my wife, Chucky, or the world will know what kind of man you aren't."

Beads of sweat formed quickly on Chazz's forehead. "What?"

"Apologize to my wife, or everyone watching will know exactly what you are," Patrick said.

"Is that a threat?" Chazz asked, his voice becoming hoarse.

"This is beginning to sound like one of your lame movies," Patrick said. "I don't threaten. I promise, and I always keep my promises."

As much as I want him to kick Chazz's ass, this verbal beat down is much better, and Sam Gabriel is writing down every word while those photographers record everything.

"No one will believe you," Chazz said.

"Unlike you, Chucky, I never lie, and the media knows this." Patrick nodded at Sam. "Have I ever lied to anyone in the media?"

Sam and several photographers shook their heads.

Chazz looked down. "You don't have the balls."

Patrick smiled. "You don't want to test me, little man. You don't have a stunt double nearby to fight for you."

Lauren laughed loudly, and so did several other people including Sam, who quickly wrote it down.

"If you touch me, I will have you arrested," Chazz said.

"Why any human being, male or female, would ever want to touch you, I have no idea," Patrick said.

Lauren laughed even louder. *That's* my *man! Yes!*

"Get out of my way!" Chazz cried, putting his hands in front of him.

Patrick blocked him easily. "I don't know much about show business, Chucky, but I know this is a live television show. Strange things often happen on live television shows, Chucky. People have been known to interrupt acceptance speeches and go off. People have been known to ramble on and on and on while the rest of the world watches, amazed. And the next day those videos are everywhere. I'm sure you'll win another award tonight, Chucky, though I don't know why, and that's when I'll read them this." Patrick pulled out a folded piece of white paper.

He wrote it down! Oh, my goodness!

Patrick held the paper in front of him. "I'm sure they'll translate my words into every language on earth. Instantaneously. Some of my words will even become headlines. Something like . . . HANDYMAN HAMMERS GUTLESS HOLLYWOOD STAR or HANDYMAN NAILS MOVIE "HERO" WITH THE TRUTH or simply IS THIS THE END FOR CHUCKY? Those headlines have nice rings to them, don't they?"

"You won't," Chazz said softly.

"I am a man of my word," Patrick said. "I am the son of a man who kept his word for forty years. I have been rehearsing this speech for days, and Lauren has been helping me memorize it."

Oh, my God! Patrick is telling a lie! His first lie! And Chazz will believe it because he has no conception of the truth!

"You are going to apologize to Lauren *now,*" Patrick said, "and you had better mean it, or I *will* interrupt you later."

Chazz squatted down next to Lauren. "Lauren, I'm sorry," he whispered.

"Tell her why you're sorry," Patrick said.

"I'm sorry you had . . ." He leaned in closer. "I'm sorry you had to take an HIV test."

"Tell her what you could have done to her," Patrick said.

"But I'm careful," Chazz said. "I've been careful."

Patrick started to unfold the paper. "Ladies and gentlemen, I'd like to set the record straight here tonight. Chucky, here, is not the man you think he is."

"All right, all right." Chazz sighed deeply. "I could have killed you, Lauren, and I'm sorry," he whispered.

"Do you accept his apology?" Patrick asked.

Not really. He's not exactly apologizing of his own free will. "I guess I'll have to."

Chazz stood and looked at Patrick. "Are we done here?"

Patrick put the paper in his jacket pocket. "Almost. I don't want to hear you say another thing about Lauren or me. Ever."

"And you'll . . . keep things quiet," Chazz whispered.

"I will," Patrick said. "And that's a promise."

Chazz eyed Sam. "We'll, um, we'll talk."

Sam nodded.

Patrick stepped aside, and Chazz pushed his way through photographers, their cameras whirring on overdrive. The photographers didn't even glance back at Lauren and Patrick, leaving them completely alone.

We're finally not the story! I hope they hound him as relentlessly as they did us. "Thank you, Patrick." She kissed him tenderly.

Patrick sat. "Anytime."

Chari stood swaying in the aisle next to Lauren. "Is he really . . . gay?"

Lauren nodded. "He's heavily into man love, yes."

"Oh, *hell* no!" Chari cried. Several polysyllabic curses later, she turned to leave the theater.

"Wait," Lauren said.

Chari stopped.

"Come here," Lauren said.

Chari approached slowly.

"How'd you get here?" Lauren asked.

"A limo," Chari said. "Why?"

"I'll bet it's parked outside," Lauren said. "Do you have a key to his house?"

"Lauren," Patrick said.

"I got this," Lauren said. "Do you have a key?"

"Yes," Chari said. "But I don't have it with me."

What a ditz! I'll just have to talk her through this. "I'll bet that limo could take you to get that key."

"Okay," Chari said.

Come on, lightbulb, turn on in her head. "So *you* go get the key, and then you go to his house."

"I don't want to go back there," Chari said.

"That window broke *really* easily," Lauren said.

"Lauren," Patrick said.

"I'm just saying that window broke really easily, Patrick," Lauren said. "There's absolutely no harm in saying that a huge picture window overlooking the Pacific Ocean shattered into a million pieces with a well-placed fist and a well-thrown elbow."

"Oh, I see what you're saying!" Chari cried. She smiled. "I think I'll break them all. God, I hope it rains." She touched Lauren's arm. "Thanks, um, for the warning."

"It's not too late, is it?" Lauren asked.

"Are you kidding?" Chari asked. "I was only with him to get my start in the movies. Later." She stalked up the aisle and out of the theater followed by a small herd of photographers.

Lauren picked up Patrick's arm and put it around her shoulders. "Chazz's house is going to be so airy tonight. I never liked that house. I like our cozy apartment much better." She smiled. "You kept me in far too much suspense, Mr. Esposito."

"I was waiting for the right moment," Patrick said.

"I was about to get up and punch him in the goatee," Lauren said.

"I know," Patrick said. "You wore him down, and I finished him off."

"We tag teamed him," Lauren said. "And you were

amazing. I especially liked when you said he didn't have a stunt double handy."

"Thank you," Patrick said. "I have my moments."

Lauren kissed his earlobe. "But you lied," she whispered. "Your first lie."

Patrick shook his head. "It wasn't the first. I lied to get the hotel room and the reservation at Tony's."

"What did you tell them?" Lauren asked.

"I said that you were traveling incognito and couldn't put the reservation in your name," Patrick said. "It's all I could think to do at the time."

"Well, don't make a habit of it," Lauren said. "What's really on the paper?"

He withdrew the paper from his jacket and handed it to her.

She opened it. "I signed this at Barneys."

"I know," Patrick said.

"Why do you have it?" Lauren asked.

"I talked to Paul while you were changing," Patrick said, "and I took it from him."

"Why?" Lauren asked.

"I'm not yet comfortable accepting gifts from my papa," Patrick said. "I need to explain to him that you and I don't need his help."

"But he told me that your suit and my gown are his wedding gifts to us, Patrick," Lauren said. "He gave us those gifts. You needed a suit, and I needed a gown. He provided for our needs."

"The total was close to twenty-five thousand dollars, Lauren," Patrick said. "The same amount he tried to give me Christmas Day."

"It has to be a coincidence, Patrick," Lauren said. "He bought us these things because he loves us. He wants to show us *his* love for us. He didn't have a chance to before. Please accept these gifts."

"It *is* a nice suit," Patrick said. "And I certainly don't have twenty-five grand handy. You think Barneys would let us return these?"

"No," Lauren said. "And you look flawless in that suit. You're the most handsome man here, and everyone has to know it. And with a few alterations, our daughter can wear *this* gown at her wedding. And if we have a son, he can wear that suit at *his* wedding. It's much fancier than a tux."

"You wouldn't wear that gown again?" Patrick asked.

"For what occasion?" Lauren asked. "I'm retired, remember?"

"So maybe I have a Cinderella fantasy," Patrick whispered.

"What if I turn into a pumpkin?" Lauren asked.

"I'll simply enjoy your pumpkin pie," Patrick whispered.

"So nasty," Lauren whispered.

Music swelled suddenly from nearly every speaker.

"Do they have to play it so loud?" Patrick asked.

"Yes," Lauren said. "Some of these stars are heavily medicated. Loud music keeps them conscious."

"Pinch me if I fall asleep," Patrick said.

"You won't," Lauren said. "The music only gets louder."

After an endless series of awards was given to an endless series of actors and musicians whom neither Lauren nor Patrick recognized—"We are so out of touch," Lauren whispered at one point—*Gray Areas* won for "Favorite New TV Comedy."

Oh, my God! There's the cast, crowded around the podium, Lauren thought. *Even Randy! And there's Annie Smith in her hat!*

"Are you sorry you quit that show?" Patrick whispered.

"Not one bit," Lauren said.

At the end of her acceptance speech, Annie said, "We have to thank Lauren Esposito for putting us on the right path and helping us write the pilot. Thank you, Lauren."

The spotlight swung wildly from the front of the theater to the back, illuminating Lauren and Patrick. Lauren smiled and waved. *I have led the strangest life. The show I ran away from wins an award with a "script" I wrote by fussing about the original script. Only in Hollywood.*

After another series of awards was given to people who were famous mainly for being famous—"Who votes for these awards?" Patrick asked—the smarmy host announced the nominees for "Favorite Viral Video" and showed a few short clips.

Backflip Fail Face Plant starred a cheerleader who flipped and landed squarely on her face. The spotlight found her wearing a halo brace a few rows in front of Patrick and Lauren.

Human Mannequins on Parade featured people dressed as mannequins who were frightening mall goers. Lauren couldn't tell the difference between the mannequins and the stars in the front row.

Nuns Attacking Purse Snatcher was black-and-white security footage of three nuns beating a purse snatcher into submission. Lauren thought one of the nuns used brass knuckles. Patrick thought another nun pulled a set of nunchakus from under her habit. Lauren thought this particular pun was the all-time worst.

The Love Kittens was the shortest clip, and it showed three cuddly kittens saying, "I wuv you, Mama" several times.

While the rest of the audience oohed and aahed at the kittens, Lauren turned to Patrick. "That can't be real."

True Love featured Patrick lifting Lauren into the air

and kissing her in Boerum Park while "Let's Stay To-gether" blasted from the speakers.

No one in the audience oohed or ahhed.

"And the winner is . . . *The Love Kittens!*"

It figures, Lauren thought. *We were beaten out by three kittens. Geez.* She looked at Patrick and laughed.

"Lip-synching kittens," Patrick said, shaking his head. "I guess cuteness beats pain, scaring people, true love, and angry nuns every time."

Much later, as Patrick was beginning to nod off, Chazz won the award for "Favorite Action Movie Star." While the rest of the audience gave Chazz a standing ovation, Lauren and Patrick sat holding hands.

"What people don't know," Lauren said.

"Sam Gabriel was practically stepping on my heels," Patrick said. "He had to have heard everything we said."

The applause swelled to a crescendo once Chazz made it to the podium.

"That doesn't mean it will make the news," Lauren said. "You heard what Chazz said to him, right? 'We'll talk' means the story won't run. Chazz's studio will pay Sam top dollar to keep that story from ever getting out."

Patrick stood. "Let's blow this joint. I don't want to hear anything he has to say. Do you?"

"Good idea," Lauren said. "Let's."

As they walked arm in arm up the aisle, Lauren noticed no eyes following them. *If we were in the front and we walked out like this, it might mean something.* She smiled up at Patrick. "I do think we're becoming anonymous, Mr. Esposito."

"Finally," Patrick said.

When they entered the lobby, Sam appeared but without his photographer. "Making an early exit?"

"Yes," Lauren said, wrapping the shahtoosh shawl around

her shoulders. "We had a lovely time, and now we're flying home."

"Is that really why you're leaving so early?" Sam asked.

"I guess I just can't stand being in the same room with a fake," Lauren said.

Sam flipped open his notepad. "Did you really have to take an HIV test?"

"Yes," Lauren said. "It was negative, thank God."

"Do you still have the test results?" Sam asked.

"No," Lauren said. "Why would I keep them?"

"It would have made great copy, you know, scanned in," Sam said.

"It wouldn't prove Chazz was the reason I had to take the test," Lauren said.

"It would make people wonder, though," Sam said. "You were with the guy for seven years. Who else could it have been to cause you to take that test?"

"That's in the past now," Lauren said.

"Could I trouble you for an interview about all this sometime?" Sam asked. "To set the record straight."

Lauren heard Chazz droning on and on. "The record will set itself straight one day. Besides, whether you publish the story or not, you're going to get paid, aren't you?"

"What do you mean?" Sam asked.

"You'll make big money if you run this story, but you'll make bigger money if they pay you *not* to run it," Lauren said. "Suppressing the truth in this town is always much more lucrative."

"I'd still like to interview you one day," Sam said. He handed her his card. "Call me anytime."

Patrick guided Lauren outside, and as soon as her heels hit the red carpet, she bent down and removed her pumps and then stretched out her cramped toes on the carpet. "This is *so* much better." She handed Sam's business card

496 *J.J. Murray*

to Patrick. "I am done. Roll the credits. The end. No more interviews. Please dispose of this for me."

"With pleasure," Patrick said. He crumpled it up and shot it into a trash can.

They continued down the red carpet toward the street, just another couple out walking on a chilly January night in Los Angeles.

"Speaking of pleasure," Lauren said, "I need to heal your face from all that smiling you did tonight, but I do not want to squeeze into the bathroom on that plane."

"It's okay," Patrick said. "You can heal me when we get home."

"I like that word," Lauren said. "Let's go home." She surveyed the sea of limousines and immediately found the pink Yellow Cab SUV. "Our carriage awaits."

"And I get to leave with Cinderella," Patrick said.

64

Their overnight flight from Los Angeles arrived at JFK at eight a.m.

No photographers, paparazzi, or reporters greeted them.

"The media only likes a winner," Lauren said.

"Or a whiner," Patrick said.

"That, too," Lauren said.

As Patrick and Lauren strolled through the bustling airport, heads turned here and there, and a few people pointed and smiled at the goddess and her escort, but no one swarmed them for pictures or autographs.

Has the spell been broken? Patrick thought. *Are we finally ordinary?*

Even their cabdriver didn't recognize them until they pulled to the curb in front of their apartment on State Street.

"Hey, aren't you the two on that *True Love* video?" he asked.

"Yes," Lauren said.

"That was my wife's favorite," he said. "You two should have won. Better luck next year, huh?"

"There's not going to be a next year, but thank you," Lauren said.

No media lurked on State Street either. They took the stairs to the second floor.

"How does it feel to be ordinary?" Patrick asked.

"I don't think we'll ever be ordinary," Lauren said.

Once inside the apartment, Lauren flopped onto the couch. "I've missed this place."

Patrick removed his coat. "We were only gone for twenty hours."

"I've missed it," Lauren said. She tossed the shawl toward the TV. "I'm comfortable here. I can be myself here. You're here. I like myself when I'm around you. I don't have to be anyone else."

Patrick removed his tie. "I like your self. If that makes any sense."

"It does," Lauren said.

Patrick sat next to her and kicked off his shoes. "I watched how your eyes lit up with all that attention. Whenever that spotlight hit you, you glowed."

"It was a bright light," Lauren said. "I had no other choice but to glow."

"You loved the attention, though," Patrick said.

"Okay, I'm a ham," Lauren said. "I admit it." She moved her legs up onto his thighs.

"I know you're going to miss it," Patrick said, massaging her feet.

"I'll miss the attention, but I won't miss the scrutiny," Lauren said. "As if my every word and gesture, and even my silence, means something significant. They used to ask me what I thought about things. Turmoil in the Middle East—your thoughts. Global warming—your thoughts.

The presidential election—your thoughts. Gun control—your thoughts. I'm barely an expert on being me, and they wanted my opinion on things I knew little about. That doesn't stop most celebrities from giving their opinions, though."

She sighed. "I'm tired of being under a microscope. If I burp, I don't want anyone to rumor me into being a drunk. If I stumble, I don't want anyone to rumor me into rehab. If I gain weight, I don't want anyone to call what's under my shirt a baby bump. If I make a face, I don't want anyone to think I'm crazy or in need of medication."

Patrick squeezed each toe. "But you've given up so much."

"I haven't given up anything," Lauren said. "I've gained the world."

"In a seven-hundred-square-foot apartment in Brooklyn," Patrick said.

"It's big enough," Lauren said. "We spend most of the time in the bedroom, anyway."

Patrick massaged her calves. "We should probably get a bigger bed."

"No," Lauren said. "I couldn't sleep if there was more space between us."

Patrick pulled her into his lap. "We should at least get an apartment with a bigger kitchen and more windows."

Lauren draped her arms around his neck. "You really like performing in front of a window."

"I like it because you like it." He kissed her nose.

"I do," Lauren said. She rested her head on his shoulder. "I really appreciate what you did for me. You stuck up for me. You stood up for me."

"I will always stand up for you," Patrick said.

"You take after your papa," Lauren said.

I guess I do. He took off his suit jacket and laid it on top of Mrs. Moczydlowska's blanket. "I was so uncomfortable in this suit. Wool and I do not agree."

"You looked so *hot* in it," Lauren said.

"I look ordinary in everything I wear," Patrick said.

"You'll never be ordinary, Patrick," Lauren said. "You're very sexy, the sexiest man I've ever known." She took his right hand in hers. "I like this kind of ordinary. I can count on this kind of ordinary. I like holding hands with the man I love because I know what his hands will be doing to me later. That's why I squeeze them so often. Have I told you I love you today?"

"You've shown me," Patrick said. "That's better than saying it."

"Oh, I have to say it, too," Lauren said. "I love you."

Patrick looked into her eyes. "You really love me, don't you?"

"I do," Lauren said. "They aren't just words. They're not lines from some script. I mean it every time I say it."

"It's definitely in your eyes," Patrick said.

"When you look at me that way, I get all shy, Mr. Esposito," Lauren said.

"Not a chance," Patrick said.

"True." She put his hand on her stomach. "Everything I say from now on will be completely off script. We can make our own scripts. We'll also do our own shows."

"I like those shows," Patrick said.

"I like giving you shows," Lauren said. "You're a very appreciative audience."

"And I get a front-row seat," Patrick said. "I like being the only person in your audience."

65

Patrick might not be my only audience for long, Lauren thought. *On the flight back I had a sudden craving for Alaskan salmon sprinkled with broken Zagnut bars. I tolerate salmon, but I cannot stand Zagnut bars because they get stuck in my teeth. I have to get to a drugstore to make sure. I should go now, but I'm not as impatient as I once was. Tomorrow. We'll have plenty of tomorrows. Tomorrow we'll find out if I'm going to be someone's mama.*

She stood and shimmied out of the gown then posed in front of him in only panties and a bra.

"Bravo!" Patrick cried. "Encore! More leg! I wish I had flowers to throw on the stage!"

Patrick's phone rang from inside his jacket.

"Are they kidding?" Lauren moaned. "We just got back!"

Patrick pulled the phone from a jacket pocket. "It might be Papa." He flipped the phone open. "Hello?" He squinted. "It's Todd." He handed the phone to Lauren.

"How'd you get this number, Todd?" Lauren asked.

"When my favorite actress won't answer her own phone," Todd said, "I have to find other ways."

"But you're interrupting my show," Lauren said.

"What show?" Todd asked.

"The one I'm giving my husband." She pulled a bra strap off her shoulder. "He's about to throw flowers onto the stage."

Patrick removed his pants and tossed them at her feet.

"He's just thrown a thousand-dollar pair of pants at me, so talk fast," Lauren said.

"Lauren," Todd said, "*Saturday Night Live* wants you!"

What? "Really? Why?"

"Erika James imploded after the last show and cursed everyone out," Todd said.

"Why?" Lauren asked.

"I don't know if you've been watching this season or not, but she flubs a lot of lines, even though they're written on the cards," Todd said. "They confronted her about this, and she went off. She trashed her dressing room and quit. They tried to get her back, but she vanished into thin air. I know that's redundant, as skinny as she is, but isn't that wonderful? Erika James is gone, and they want *you!*"

Erika James suddenly developed some range. I have a little more respect for her now.

"They need you *this* weekend, Lauren," Todd said. "Isn't that great? You're going to be a star again!"

This is happening too fast! "*This* weekend?" She watched Patrick remove his socks and shirt.

"You'll get to play 'the Loneliest Woman in the World'!" Todd cried. "You'll get to do live comedy. Isn't that fantastic? And when Chazz cohosts next month, wow! The ratings are going to go through the roof!"

She smiled as Patrick removed his T-shirt. *But I'm no*

longer lonely. I don't want to play that lonely role again, and if I'm carrying another little person in me, I won't have time to be lonely.

"And the amount of money they're offering is almost as much as what you made on your first two movies *combined*," Todd said. "This is your lucky day!"

I've already had my lucky day, and I'm looking at him. I love him because he's not part of that false Hollywood world. He's from the real world. Why would I ever go back to unreality? This little apartment, this man— She stifled a burp. *Wow. Now I want strawberry Pop-Tarts with mustard and chili sauce on them. I have to be pregnant. This place, this man, this baby, with her strange food cravings—these make up my world now. I like that word. Now. I need to let now happen more often and not worry so much about then.*

"Lauren? Are you still there?"

"Yes, Todd." *Barely.*

"You haven't missed any rehearsals, and they've got big plans for you, huge plans," Todd said. "You'll need to show up Tuesday morning and—"

"Tell them . . . ," Lauren interrupted. "Tell them that I'm flattered they would consider me, but I am officially retired now. Forever."

"You have to be joking!" Todd cried. "This is what you've always wanted!"

"I thought I did, but I don't." She took Patrick's hand and pulled him off the couch.

"Lauren, this is your last shot!" Todd cried. "If you turn this down, no one will ever want you again!"

I only need one person to want me from now on. Oh, and a child or two to need me. She led Patrick into the bedroom. "I know that, but I have to do this."

"What am I going to do with you?" Todd asked.

She pointed at the bed. "Nothing, Todd."

Patrick slid under the covers. A moment later he threw his boxers toward the closet.

"I won't need your services anymore," Lauren said. "Thank you for all you've done for me, but—"

"Lauren, listen to reason for the first time in your life!" Todd interrupted.

She removed her bra and panties, and as Patrick held up the covers, she slid in beside him. "I *am* listening to reason. What I have is golden. I won't give that up."

"But, Lauren!" Todd cried.

"Good-bye, Todd," Lauren said. "Please don't call me again." She snapped the phone closed and set it on the nightstand.

"Everything okay?" Patrick asked, his hot right hand moving down her back.

"I have never been better," Lauren said.

"What did Todd want?" Patrick asked.

"He told me that *Saturday Night Live* has an opening," Lauren said.

Patrick's hand stopped moving. "And you just turned it down? I thought that's what you've always wanted."

Lauren rubbed her nose on his chest. "This is all I want. This is all I need." *And what I think is growing inside me is more than I'll ever need, and she won't stare into mirrors. She'll stare into her daddy's eyes, and she'll watch her daddy's hands. She's going with us while we work, and that child will know how to repair anything and everything. And if she just happens to want to be in the class play, I'll let her perform—but only once. Just to see. As tall as Patrick is, I hope she's tall and plays the tree.*

She let her hand wander around his stomach. "Do you mind if I spend the rest of my life earning your love?"

"Earning *my* love?" Patrick said. "We'll earn each other's love."

"That's going to be so much fun." She kissed his neck. "I have to know something, though. Why did you *really* pick St. Louis for our first date?"

Patrick sighed. "I thought it was halfway between here and LA, but I was off by about five hundred miles."

She moved on top of him, her knees tight against his hips. "Don't know much about geography, huh?"

"No," Patrick said. "I do know about biology, though." He lifted her booty slightly until he was inside her.

"Yes, you do." *Do I tell him now? No. I can wait. I'm finally learning patience. This "now" with only my husband is too special.* She started a slow grind. "Five hundred miles off. I thought you were good at measuring things."

Patrick massaged her breasts. "Well, you were rushing me on the phone—"

Lauren grabbed his hands tightly. "Me? Rush you? Never!" She laughed as she kissed his hands. "I think you picked St. Louis on purpose."

"It was a random moment," Patrick said. "Omaha just didn't sound as romantic as St. Louis did."

She dropped his hands and braced herself on his chest. "It wasn't a random moment, Patrick. You don't do random. You were trying to meet me halfway, weren't you?"

"I was trying," Patrick said. "I just wasn't succeeding."

Lauren sat up straighter and arched her back. "But meeting someone halfway defines true love, doesn't it?"

"It does," Patrick said.

"We met each other halfway." *We shared each other's worlds, and his world "won."* "Do you care to meet me halfway in this bed for the rest of the day?"

He sat up and wrapped his arms around her. "I'll need lots of rehearsal time. I'm not much of an actor."

"You're too honest to be an actor," Lauren said.

"That's a good thing, right?" He nibbled on her neck.

"It's a very good thing," Lauren said. "Do you think you could take a lifetime of directions from me?"

"I could," Patrick said, "but I might do some directing myself, too. I have plenty of ideas."

"Codirectors," Lauren said, resuming her grind. "That's usually a problem."

"Not when you're raising children," Patrick said.

Lauren bit her lip. *And we might be raising a child very soon. We'll have to get more Pop-Tarts soon. I know we have mustard and ketchup. Oh, salmon and Zagnut bars, too.* "Give me some directions."

"Put your hot body on mine," Patrick said, smiling. "Let me . . . *feel the love.*"

Lauren laughed. "Oh, *I got this.* I think I'm going to love this movie. Is there lots of sex?"

"Yes," Patrick said. "But mostly, there will be a lot of love."

"I think I can live with that," Lauren said.

For the rest of my once glamorous and now blessedly, blissfully contented, ordinary, and gloriously happy life.